Dear Ava

Wall Street Journal Bestselling Author

ILSA MADDEN-MILLS

Dear Ava

Wall Street Journal Bestselling Author
ILSA MADDEN-MILLS

Dear Ava
Copyright © 2020 by Ilsa Madden-Mills
Cover Design by Letitia Hasser, RBA Designs
Photographer: Corey Thomas
Model: Christian Hogue

Little Dove Publishing
ISBN: 9781660191413

First Edition Feb 2020

Table of Contents

Dedication

For every Ava in the world. Let your fire burn bright.

Theme song: "Skyscraper" by Demi Lovato

FROM THE AUTHOR

Recommended for ages 18 and over.

1

Junior year

My hair covers my face and I shove it away, my heart speeding up and pounding as my eyes flare open in the dark. The air is cold, an early winter nipping on the heels of fall.

Where am I?

Straining to recall, I distinctly remember the road that brought me to these trees, a narrow, rutted lane, can barely even call it a road, really just a path used by tractors, ATV vehicles, and cars with good front-wheel drive.

No matter the road you take, it doesn't matter if it's beautiful or ugly, hard or smooth, paved or pitted with ruts—it's your road to take. What matters is how it ends.

One of the nuns told me that once, but I can't recall why—wait, *God* my head hurts as if someone took a sledgehammer and whacked me.

Blinking, I swallow and focus, mentally willing the pain to stop.

Where am I?

A high keening sound breaks into the night, and I jerk, realizing it's me making that weird noise. Shivering at the eerie sound, I stop, sucking in air then hissing with the effort it takes as I attempt to sit up. I decide against it when agony reverberates through my lower body. There's a gnawing there—

Screw it. Just let me lie here.

I'm in tall grass, that I do know, and I breathe slowly, orienting myself as I stare up at the starry sky and look for answers. The moon is full and bright, illuminating the high pine trees towering over me, their branches rustling as the wind blows, like ghostly hands rubbing their fingers together. Watching the slow, creepy movement reminds me of a horrid Grimm fairytale where a young girl ventures out into the enchanted forest to pick flowers, only to be gobbled up by a monster.

I close my eyes.

Open them again.

This isn't an enchanted forest, but it's definitely the woods.

How did I get here?

Twisting my head, I see the embers of a low bonfire glowing several yards away in a mostly open meadow. Images dance in my head—me at the fire, laughing, dancing, drinking—

I inhale a sharp breath as another memory pierces, and I kick it down. *Just not ready.* My hands clench the dirt and damp leaves underneath me. My clothes are dirty. At least I didn't wear my red and white cheer outfit. No, I had time to change into a mini skirt and a new blue tank top with scalloped lace at the top, "the perfect match for my eyes," Piper had said even as she told me not to—what? What did she tell me not to do?

More pain spirals in my head, and I wince, swallowing convulsively to pull moisture into my dry mouth.

I focus on that meadow.

Before I was in the woods, there was a party there, the Friday night kegger after the football game. Yes. At one point, people and music and cars encircled this meadow. Guys still in jerseys, some in jeans and preppy shirts, pretty girls decked out in expensive clothes I can't afford, jewelry and shoes I'll never have...

It's empty now.

I lick dry, chapped lips when my stomach swirls. Bile curls in my gut. I'm not sure how my addled brain knows poison lies somewhere within me, but it does, and my body wants to eject it.

But it's so hard to move, and I'm exhausted and sore, and if I could just close my eyes and drift...

The wind blows again and an owl hoots. Something howls off in the distance, a dog or a coyote.

Definitely not a wolf, I remind myself. This is rural Tennessee, not Alaska.

My body twitches in disagreement. *Doesn't matter! Leave this awful place!*

But, I'm so tired and weak and maybe if I just go back to sleep and wake up again, this will all just be a bad dream—

Those ghostly fingers in the trees brush again and I snap to awareness, forcing my eyes to stay open.

I sit up and prop my back against the tree behind me. A collection of pictures tiptoe through my mind: Jolena and me getting ready for the party at her place and my nervousness at being surrounded by the opulence of her huge mansion, then us arriving at the field party in her black Range Rover. We chugged shots of Fireball before we got out to join everyone. She offered, her ruby lips smiling, and I took it anxiously, needing the bravery for my first kegger. These people weren't like me, didn't *really* know me, except as Chance's girl. They're the Sharks at Camden Prep, rich and popular and pretty much assholes except for Chance. They rule the school. They decide who comes to the parties. They decide if you're good enough.

My fingers press on my forehead. Knox Grayson, QB1 and the leader of the Sharks, was the first person I saw when we walked up to the fire, his arm curled around...Tawny? Yeah. With the golden brown hair like sunlight. She's not just pretty; she's beautiful, wrapped in wealth and superiority —*ah, crap, forget her.* She doesn't even know my name. It's an image of him, of Knox, that lingers...the long, ugly scar that runs down from his right temple, through the hollow of his cheek, slicing into his upper lip. The devil. Hades. I call him that in my head sometimes before I shove him out of my thoughts and lock him away tight. My subconscious has always known to flee when I pass him in the hall, to run like the hot winds of hell are at my back.

He watched me walk up with Jolena, an intimidating glint in his narrowed gaze.

What are you *doing here?* his face said with a curl of those twisted lips.

His little looks—oh, how can I call them little? They've

always been big looks, sweeping and brushing over me then dismissive, reducing me down to nothing but the air he breathes, the very dust motes that float around our hallowed school.

But...tonight—*God, it's still the same night, right?*—I forged ahead, swallowing my misgivings about him because Chance appeared in front of me. Beautiful, sweet Chance. My heart, which feels sluggish and weak, beats a tad quicker. He's a Shark, in that inner circle, but he *likes* me. He's been mine since this summer, little touches and slow kisses. We're building up to more, so much more. A leftover wisp of joy caresses me as I recall him twirling me around, kissing me on the cheek, and asking me to sing. After much prompting and cajoling and another shot of Fireball, I stood in the bed of someone's truck and belted out "Skyscraper" by Demi Lovato. Cheers rang out. Even Jolena smiled, and I don't even think she really likes me. I felt...elated.

Things get fuzzy after that.

Stumbling around inside my head, I wince at the images I see. Chance is there, but he isn't glad to see me anymore—which is weird because he invited me. He begged me to come. He made other promises too, but suddenly I see him right up in my face, jawline clenched, eyes blazing with anger.

What...what did I do to him?

Doesn't he know I've put him on a pedestal and thought he might be different? I didn't want to fall so fast. I don't love much. I don't. To allow love in makes one vulnerable and it—

Forget him.

What is *wrong* with my body?

A lone tear wets my face and I wipe it away fiercely, surprised by the emotion.

Stop it, Ava.

You're just in the woods, and God knows you've slept in worst places.

Still, another drop of moisture sneaks out, and I swallow down the lump of emotion in my throat.

This is just me being drunk. That's all.

Nothing terrible has happened. Nothing at all.

I...I drank too much. That's it.

I suck in air as more faces from the party zoom in and out of my head, their features vague, funhouse images playing out, a horrible fair ride gone wrong. I see Knox leaving with Tawny. I watch Chance with another girl and my heart cracks. I see Jolena whispering to the other girls on the squad while they stare daggers at me.

What did I do?

Faster and faster and faster the events tumble around until I feel sick and lean over and vomit.

When I was ten, I managed to escape Mama at a fair, which wasn't really an escape because she didn't care what I did as long as I eventually came back. She slipped inside one of those rusty trailers on the outskirts where the carnies lived. That night, she followed a man with thinning oily hair, a bushy beard, and a red bulbous nose. He pushed money into her hands and they wobbled off to disappear into that tiny metal house while I dashed for the rides, zeroing in on the Zipper. *Most Exhilarating Ride at the Fair* the blinking red lights said, but once the lady clamped that bar down and hurtled me into the sky, I screamed, my hands white-knuckled and clenched, certain the next spin into the heavens would be my last and I'd come crashing down, my guts flowing over twisted metal when the thing hit the earth.

But, I didn't cry. Not one time. Even when I went back to that trailer and snuck inside and Mama was on her knees in front of the man. His pants were at his ankles as her hands cupped his privates. Her eyes flashed at me then up at him, a sly look on her face. A long moment passed, seeming to stretch into eternity, then she motioned for me. *Come here, Ava. Try this.*

He zipped his pants and lurched toward me, and I flew out that door and ran and ran and ran. He chased me while I flew past the Zipper, past the corn dog stand, past the goldfish game, and right out the exit. I didn't see Mama for two days.

Focus, please Ava, time is passing and you're not right in the head and your body is wrong, just stop thinking about Mama and get yourself up and go go go go go go go go go go...

With a huge breath, I push myself up more. God, I hurt everywhere. I touch my face, checking for injuries, but there's no swelling or blood. My arms are fine, goose bumps rising in the chilly air. I rub down my chest, squinting in the darkness. My shirt is shoved up to my throat, exposing my plain white bra, issued to me by the nuns at Sisters of Charity. The cups have been maneuvered down, and I adjust it with careful, slow movements, putting my breasts back inside. I don't let myself think about how they came to be like that.

My legs are jelly but still there, and I huff out a laugh as if expecting fatal injuries. No Zipper death yet. Ha.

Wait... I let out a primal sound, as if my body knows, only it's taking my brain a minute to catch up. My skirt is bunched up around my hips, my pelvic area bare. No plain white underwear from the nuns. Dimly, I process the leaves and twigs from the woods digging into my bottom. My hands flail uselessly over my skin as if the scrap of material might magically appear.

Oh, Ava, oh Ava, you know what this is—how could you be this naïve...

Craning my neck, I lean forward and take in small, purple-looking bruises on my inner thighs. I touch myself, there, and groan at the pain from the swollen tissue. My heart picks up more, flying inside my chest. Blackness dances in front of my face.

"No, no, no..." I say then vomit off to the side, again. Finally, the alcohol is coming up.

More memories—*are they real?*—slam into my mind.

Me heading off to the line of trees. I had to pee. Was Jolena with me? No. I shake my head as an image of someone else pops up, male, looming over me, leading me away. He took my hand and told me he had something to tell me, and for some reason I followed him—

I touch my mouth.

He kissed me hard.

He yanked my hair and shoved me down to the ground.

Clarity and realization take over the cloudy memories, cutting like a sharp knife. I don't remember details, most of it totally blank, but a monster was with me in these woods.

I hear Piper's voice in my head. *Don't trust them, Ava. You might be a cheerleader today, but no one gets inside their group.*

But...I just wanted to be close enough to be with Chance.

I wanted to live in his world.

Where is he now?

My thoughts drift, and I don't know how long I sit in the grass, grappling with what happened one second then wailing again the next as the reality of it settles around me.

Clinging to a tree, I try to stand but slide back to the ground.

Long minutes pass, and I'm aware of the moon as it moves through the trees. Just a little more time and I can walk.

I can.

I have to.

Someone needs me out there. I brush my fingers over the cheap, gold-plated locket around my neck, touching the flimsy chain. He's small and tiny and if he doesn't have me and if I don't get up, what will happen then?

I can never desert him...

That thought gives me strength, just enough to crawl away from the trees and across the open meadow. Past that meadow is that old road, and beyond that is a real highway where I can flag someone down—

I hear the soft rumble of a vehicle as headlights flash in front of me, a car swinging into the field. A brief elation rises in me then crashes and burns.

What if it's *him*?

My anxiety ratchets up, panic beating at me, and my muscles burn as I attempt to crawl back the way I came.

Wait till morning. My head's not right, but I can wait it out.

I'm good at hiding.

Always have been.

The bright glow of the lights blinds me, and my head swings wildly around, looking for somewhere to go.

Run, run, run...

Shuffling sounds break the stillness, a car door slamming, a voice calling out.

Fear courses through me and I cover my face, ashamed to be so defenseless. Me. ME.

Broad shoulders stand over me, and he speaks, and I blink up. I can't see him with the beams of light from his car in my eyes. More talk from him. I can't respond. I retch instead.

He walks toward me. Bends down. Strong arms come down and sweep me up. Shifting around in his embrace, I try to fight, but it's nothing but a flinch, no struggle, no girl from the inner city who knows how to fight. I'm empty, my body unable to resist him putting me in his car, snapping the seat belt around me. He speaks, maybe my name, asking me questions, but I can't think straight. I can't do...anything.

He pulls away from the field, the car moving fast, so fast, and my head lolls to the side on the seat, staring at my captor.

Who is he?

Do I know him? I squint, catching a glint of chiseled jawline and furrowed brow. His head turns and his steely gaze locks with mine. I think I see anger, and just when I think I know him, just when it's on the tip of my tongue—there's nothing but darkness as I slip away and sink back into oblivion.

2

AVA

Ten months later

The sun beats down on me as I get out of my dark green, older-model Jeep Wrangler, Louise, and give her a little pat. There's a dent on the driver's side—came that way—and the paint is rusted at the edges of the hood and over the wheels. I worked three summers waiting tables at a dingy all-night diner in downtown Nashville to buy her, and it's my sole possession in the world. I paid for it with carefully scraped together money from every tip I got, and I got plenty because I was the best waitress there, pasting a broad, welcoming smile on my face for every truck driver, blue collar worker, and late-night drunk person. Sometimes if the waitstaff was full, I cleaned the kitchen, took out trash, or mopped the floor. Lou would text me any time one of his servers didn't show up or called in sick, and I'd drag myself up out of my bed at the group home and jog the two blocks to the diner, half-asleep but ready to put the time in for the dollars. I find a smile. Louise isn't pretty, but she's mine.

Parked next to me is a sleek black Porsche, and on the other side is a red Maserati. I sigh. Almost a year since I've been a student here, yet nothing has changed.

I sweep my eyes over the grounds ahead of me. Welcome to Camden Prep, otherwise known as my own personal hell, a prestigious private school in the middle of Sugarwood, Tennessee, which happens to be one of the richest small towns in the US, home to senators, country music stars, and professional athletes.

Bah. Whatever. I hate this place.

Slinging my backpack over my arm, I sprint through the parking lot, carefully evading the cars, recalling a freshman guy who accidentally scratched another car once, and one of the Shark's, no less. Later, they cornered him in the bathroom and made him lick their shoes. The best advice for anyone who isn't a Shark is to stay away from them. Don't look. Don't touch. Pretend they don't exist. Those guidelines got me through my freshman and sophomore years. Junior year—well, we won't even go there, but now that it's my last year, I'll be living by those rules again.

Tension and apprehension make my heart race more and more the closer I get to the double doors of that ivy-covered main entrance bookended by two castle-style gray turrets. The final bell for classes hasn't rung yet, and I have exactly five minutes to get to my locker and get to class. Arriving late was my plan because *a girl like me has to have a fucking plan.*

As I jog, I tug at my new school uniform, a mid-thigh red and gold plaid skirt, something the administration instituted to blur the lines between the haves and the have-nots. As if.

Everyone already knows who the rich kids are and who are the ones like me. Just look in the freaking parking lot. "I love you, Louise," I mutter. "All these jerks have is something their parents bought them."

I stop at the door, inhaling a deep breath. You'd expect a regular glass door for a school, but this isn't an ordinary place. The door here is made from heavy, beveled glass, the kind you see in old houses. Freshman year, I thought it was beautiful with the red dragon carefully etched into the upper section, but now—ha. Dread, thick and ugly, sucks at me, sliding over me like mud even though I gave myself a hundred pep talks on the twenty-minute drive in from the Sisters of Charity in downtown Nashville.

"Steel yourself," I whisper. "Beyond these doors lie hell-hounds and vampires." I smirk. If only they really were. I'd pull out a stake and end them like Buffy.

Sadly, they are only human, and I cannot stab them.

I pat down my newly dyed dark hair, shoulder-length with the front sides longer than the back, a far cry from my long blonde locks from last year. Cutting and dying my hair was therapy. I did it for me, to show these assholes I'm not going to be that nice little scholarship girl anymore. Screw that. I gather my mental strength, pulling from my past. I've sat in homeless shelters. I've watched Mama shoot needles in her arms, in between her toes, wherever she could to get that high. I've watched her suck down a bottle of vodka for breakfast.

These rich kids are toddlers compared to me.

So why am I shaking all over?

No fear, a small voice says.

I swing the doors open to a rush of cool air and brightly lit hallways. The outside may look as if you've been tossed back a few centuries, but the inside is plush and luxurious, decorated like a millionaire's mansion instead of a school.

Smells like money, I think as I stand for a second and take it all in. It's still gorgeous—can't deny that. Warm taupe walls. White wainscoting. Crown molding. Leather chairs. And that's just the entrance area. I walk in farther, my steps hesitant. Majestic portraits hang on the wall, former headmasters alongside framed photos of alumni, small smiling faces captured in senior photos. The guys have suits on, the girls in black dresses. By the end of this year, my picture will be encased in a collage and placed with *my* classmates. A small huff of laughter spills out of me, bordering on hysteria, and I push it back down.

Students milling around—girls in pleated skirts and white button-downs like mine, guys in khakis and white shirts with red and gold ties—swivel their heads to see who's coming in on the first day of classes.

Eyes flare.

Gasps are emitted.

Fighting nervousness, I inhale a cleansing breath, part of me already regretting this decision, urging me to turn around and run like hell, but I hang tough, fighting nausea. I swallow down my emotions, carefully shuffling them away, locking them up in a chest. I picture a chain and padlock on those memories from last year. I take that horror and toss it into a stormy ocean. There, junior year. Go and die.

With a cold expression on my face, one I've been practicing for a week, my eyes rove over the students, not lingering too long on faces.

That's right, Ava Harris, the snitch/bitch who went to the police after the party, is back.

And I'm not going anywhere.

All I need is this final year, and I might be able to swing a full ride at a state school or even get a scholarship to Vanderbilt. *Vanderbilt.* My body quivers in yearning. Me at a prestigious university. Me going to class with people who don't know me. Me having something that is mine. Me making my own road, and it's shiny and flat and so damn smooth...

My legs work before my brain does, and as I start down the hall, the crowd parts, more students seeing me and pausing, eyes widening.

The air around me practically bristles with tension.

If I were a wicked witch, I'd cackle right now.

My fists clench, barely hanging on to my resolve.

You're better than any of them.

But inside, my words of encouragement feel hollow.

Piper rushes up and throws her arms around me. "She's back! My main girl is back! OMG, I HAVE MISSED YOU SO MUCH!"

Seeing her exuberant, welcoming face is exactly what I needed. Pretty with long strawberry blonde hair pulled back with two butterfly clips, she's been my friend since we had a chorus class together freshman year. She can't carry a tune, but I love to sing. I had a solo at every single concert at Camden BTN. Before That Night.

Piper is still talking, rambling about what I've been doing this summer. Working, I tell her, and she tells me how she went out to Yellowstone with her parents on an awful month-long road trip with her two younger brothers in an RV. I nod and smile in all the right places, and she seems to think I'm okay. Good.

She shoves at her neon pink cat-eye glasses and smiles as she squeezes my hand. "I'm so glad to see you. Also, my parents are insisting you come to dinner soon. It's been a while."

Indeed.

"Are you, you know, okay?" she says.

Before I can answer, someone jostles into us, moving away quickly, but not before I hear *snitch* from his lips.

My purse falls down with the force of his shoulder.

And so it begins.

Helping me get my bag, she turns her head and snaps at the retreating back of the person who bumped into me. "Watch it!" Then, "Jockass!"

Rising up, I crane my neck to see who it was. Red hair, football player: Brandon Wilkes. I barely know him.

She blows at the bangs in her face, schooling her features back into a sweet expression even though her eyes are darting around at everyone as if daring them to say one word against me. "Anyway, I'm glad you came back. We haven't gotten to talk much, and that is your fault, which is fine. I gave you space like you asked."

She never did pull punches.

I haven't called her like I should have, but I needed distance from this place and everyone here. I tried in the beginning, but when she'd bring up school and the football games and her classes and everyday things about the day-to-day at Camden, I felt that pit of emptiness tugging at me, a dark hole of memories and people I didn't want to think about. Her life went on—*as it should have*—while I was stuck wallowing in the past.

"But you're here now." She smiles, but there's a wobbly quality to it.

"Yeah." I give her a wan smile, putting as much effort into it as I can. Her parents were the ones who took me to the hospital last year. Nice people. Hardworking. Not rich. She's a scholarship student like me and got into Camden because her math and science scores are insane. She lives here in Sugarwood while I commute from the group home. Before I turned sixteen, a nun brought me to school in an old yellow van.

She jumps when she hears her name over the intercom, talking fast as lightning. "Yikes! I need to run. My mom is here. Can you believe I forgot my laptop on the first day? I'm such a ditz! See you in class, 'kay? We have first period together, yes?" She gives me a quick hug. "You got this."

But, do I?

Truly, I want to run and get back in my car and leave this place behind forever, but then I think about my little brother Tyler. Goals...must stick to them.

Before I can get a word out—typical—she's gone and bouncing down the hall like Tigger from *Winnie the Pooh.*

I miss her immediately, feeling the heat of everyone's eyes on me.

It's funny how no one really noticed me during my freshman and sophomore year here. Nope. I was the girl who kept her head down and blended in as well as I could, trying to keep my upbringing off the radar...until the summer before junior year when I ran into Chance at a bookstore and he showed interest.

Then when school started, I got it in my head to be a cheerleader. Mostly, I told myself it would look good on my college applications, plus I assumed it would take less time than soccer or tennis—but the truth is I did it for *him*. I wanted Chance and Friday night football games and parties with the in crowd.

Just.

Stupid.

The lockers seem a million miles away as I push past all the onlookers, my hands clenched around the straps of my backpack. Whispers from the students rise and grow and spread like a wave in the ocean.

And of course...

The Grayson brothers are the first Sharks I see, holding court with several girls as they lean against the wall. Knox and Dane. Twins.

I flick my gaze in their direction, keeping my resting bitch face sharp and hard, taking in the two guys, their matching muscular builds, tall with broad shoulders. They may look almost identical, but they're like night and day. Knox is the cold one, never smiling, that scar slicing through his cheek and into his upper lip, disrupting the curve of his mouth and the perfection of his face. I swallow. Screw him.

I refuse to spend this year afraid.

His lips twitch as if he reads my mind, that slash on his mouth curling up in a twisted movement, and I glare at him.

You don't scare me, my face says.

He smirks.

Thick mahogany hair curls around his collar and his eyes are a piercing gray, like metal, sharp and intense, framed by a fringe of black lashes. His scrutiny doesn't miss much and makes me antsy—has since freshman year when I'd catch him looking at me, studying me as if I were a strange bug. When I'd get the guts to boldly look back—*Like what you see?* —he'd huff out a derisive laugh and keep walking. I'm beneath him. A speck. He as much as said so after our first game last year.

"What do you want?" he says with a sneer as I ease in the football locker room. Cold eyes flick over my cheer skirt then move up and land on the hollow of my throat. It's not cool enough at night for our sweater uniform so tonight my top is the red and white V-cut vest with CP embroidered on my chest.

"Where's Chance?"

He stiffens then huffs out a laugh and whips off his sweat-covered jersey along with the pads underneath.

His shoulders are broad and wide, his chest lightly dusted with sparse golden hair, tan from the sun, rippling with powerful muscles, leading down to a tapered and trim waist. He has a visible six-pack, and my gaze lingers briefly on a small tattoo on his hip, but I can't tell what it is. He isn't brawny or beefy-looking like one might expect from a guy blessed with his athletic prowess, but sculpted and molded and—

Dropping my gaze, I stare at the floor. I shouldn't be ogling him. Chance is my guy.

I hear male laughter from one of the rooms that branch off from the locker room, maybe the showers, and I deflate, guessing that's where Chance is.

Glancing up, I intend to ask him to tell Chance I came by to congratulate him on his two touchdowns, but my voice is frozen. Knox has unlaced his grass-stained pants and is shucking them off. His legs are heavily muscled and taut, unlike the leaner build of

Chance. His slick underwear is black and tight, cupping his hard ass, the outline of his crotch—

"Like what you see, charity case? You can look, but you can't touch."

Anger soars, replacing my embarrassment. I know I'm just the scholarship girl at Camden, but why does he have to constantly remind me?

"Don't worry about me touching anything. *I don't like ugly." The words tumble out before I can stop them. I meant his superior attitude, not his face, but I see the moment when he freezes and takes it the wrong way.*

He touches his face, tracing his scar while his jaw pops. "Get out. Only players allowed in here."

I pivot and go for the door, forcing myself not to run. "Asshole," I mutter.

His laughter follows me.

RUMOR IS he doesn't kiss girls on the lips, but no matter how bad that scar screws up his face, he's still the head Shark nonetheless.

Today, he's wearing a fitted white button-up, his tie loose as if he's already annoyed with it. He spends a lot of time in the gym, I imagine, working on that muscular body, maintaining that quarterback status. He holds my gaze for several seconds before dropping his and looking down at his phone.

I hear him laugh under his breath.

Some things never change.

Dane is a near replica except his face is Adonis perfect, his hair longer and shoulder-length, brushing his shoulders. He's the same height as Knox, about six three, but his jawline is more angular, thinner. And his eyes? Oh, boy. They're road maps, bloodshot as hell.

Yeah, they were both at the party.

Fear brushes across my spine and my body tenses. That night, someone (the person who picked me up) placed me on one of the couches on Piper's front porch. Then he rang the doorbell and left before Piper's mom came to the door. Sometimes, I wonder if that person might have been—

All thoughts stop, and my feet stumble when I see who's next to Knox: Chance. I get a good look at how he pales, his blue eyes flaring at me as he shoves his hand into his sandy-blond hair.

That's right, dickhead, here I am: Ava, version 2.0.

Gone is the girl he kissed like he meant it.

Familiar shame rises up inside me, and I battle it down. What happened was not my fault. Even though the drug test said I didn't have any drugs in my system (only alcohol), I refuse to believe it. Or maybe it was *just* the alcohol. I don't know, and it drives me insane.

I also had a rape kit performed—I cringe at that humiliating memory, the cold, impersonal room, the invasive questions. *Are you sexually active?* Yes, I'd had sex before. *How long has it been since your last consensual intercourse?* Six months. *Who was he?* A guy from Sisters of Charity who now lives in Texas. *How many partners have you had?* Just one, just one—until this. *What kinds of medications do you take?* None. Then they moved me to another room for an exam, where they inspected me from head to toe, swabbing every inch, from my mouth to my toenails. They took photos of the bruises on my inner thighs. They took my clothing and put it in a paper bag. They asked me details about what led up to the assault, wanting me to tell them step by step what happened, and even though the nurse was kind, so incredibly kind, I had to hide my face when I told her I couldn't remember who it was.

And in the end...

Nothing.

They determined I'd had sex, rough sex, but no semen or reliable DNA was found.

And Chance? His last text after I went to the police: **Stop lying about the party. You aren't the person I thought you were. You're just a slut.**

That nasty word slices into my heart, cutting deep. I'm *not* promiscuous. I didn't screw around at Camden; I was too busy working, studying, and taking care of my brother. Besides, it shouldn't freaking matter if I *had* screwed every guy here.

Drunkenness does not equal acquiescence.

I must be insane because I linger in front of the three of them and study the lines of Chance's face, his square chin, the dimples on either side of his mouth, the ones that deepen when he smiles.

There's a frown there now.

Yes, I mentally whisper, my mouth tightening. *I hope seeing me pisses you off. I'm not here for you, jock. I'm here for* me.

With that fake smile back in place, I move on. I'm almost to my locker, number 102, when two girls appear in front of me, blocking my path.

Geeze. At least I'm getting it ALL over with at once.

A long exhalation leaves my chest as I take in Jolena and Brooklyn, my former cheer pals. My lips twist. They were never *really* my friends. Not once have they called or texted me in the past ten months.

Jolena, the clear queen bee, is in red heels, her dark auburn hair twirled up in a high ponytail that accentuates her striking cheekbones and ruby lips.

"Well, well, well, if it isn't Ava Harris. I can't believe you have the nerve to show your face here. Please tell me you aren't going to try out for cheer." The words are said with a perfect fake smile.

I'm not surprised she approached me right off the bat. It's what I expected—anger and resentment. By going to the police, I ratted on the popular kids. To me the party was a meaningless side note compared to what happened at the end of it, but to some, I committed an act of treason. I'm the rat and snitches get stitches and all that jazz.

Plus, there's the video of me with football players, her boyfriend included.

Just another sick carnival ride.

THE YOUNG DETECTIVE taps a pen on the table. "Miss Harris, is it possible you consented to sex? Your behavior at the party was, well, indicative of..." His dry voice trails off, but I get his meaning. "I know most of these boys. Good parents. Great football players. It's okay if you had consensual sex with—"

"No!" I call out. "No, no, no..." My shoulders hunch and I want to crawl away.

"There's video of you dancing with Liam Barnes, Dane Grayson, Brandon Wilkes..." He lists several more, each name a slice of pain. "Let me show you."

He sticks a laptop in my face and hits play. I don't know who took it or who gave it to them. It's dark and grainy, but there's no mistaking my tank top and blonde hair. Or the guys. I'm in a circle dancing and laughing up at them, my hands on their shoulders, moving one to another. My eyes are shut. "Closer" by Nine Inch Nails blares.

"Turn it off," I whisper, holding my stomach. "Please."

"HELLO? ARE YOU LISTENING, MORON?" Jolena says. She's shorter than me, even in her high heels, and I tower over her, thankful at least for my five foot, eight inches. I've never met my sperm donor—some man who got my mom pregnant—but I figure I get my height from him since she's petite.

"Move out of my way," I say, keeping my voice low, struggling to keep it from cracking.

"Oh, it has claws. Make me." She takes a step closer until I can smell the cloying scent of her flowery perfume.

I battle my jumpy stomach. "Trust me, I've known meaner girls than you. Wanna try me?"

Her lips curl and she laughs, the sound tinkling out to several other students who've stopped to watch. She throws her gaze around, surveying them all, and some of them visibly shrink away. Others come closer, their faces almost fascinated, wondering what I'll do, what she'll do...

A delicate shrug comes from her. "Consider yourself warned. None of the cheerleaders want you back. We don't need sluts on our squad."

My gut reaction is to just dart away. It's what I would have done if I'd had an interaction with her in the past, because I just wanted to make things easy for myself here. Don't make waves. Graduate.

I hear her muttering behind me as I walk away, calling out a juicy name, but I tune it out, focusing on deep breathing.

My hands tremble as I fumble with the locker combination I received in the mail with my registration packet last week.

"You look different," are the words I hear from my left. My eyes dart to the guy who said them, taking in the clipped light brown hair on the sides, the top longer and swept back, the dark brown eyes. About six foot and muscular with a hint of mischief in his gaze, he flashes a grin. "You used to have light hair. The black is wicked cool. Saw you when you parked your car." His accent is obviously Bostonian, maybe Southie, with the R sound missing. *Pahked yah cah.*

He arches a brow, and the silver piercing there glints in the florescent lighting. "Name's Wyatt. I'm new since last January, but I heard all about you. I've seen your picture in the yearbook. We're locker neighbors." *Locka neigbahs.* Another grin as he leans in closer to me. "People are staring at you like crazy. You're like...a celebrity. Welcome back. I'm honored to be your neighbor." He places a hand over his heart.

Ha.

I didn't expect anyone to be nice, and I don't trust the feeling. I turn toward my locker, gripping the lock. The combination doesn't work, and he watches me try it a third time until it finally gives. I fling it open, blocking his face.

Wyatt shuts his locker and shuffles away in my peripheral vision. My eyes move down to a sealed envelope at the bottom of my locker. I frown. How did this get here? I check the outside and glance at the small vents where someone must have pushed it through.

For Ava is scrawled across the envelope, and chills ghost over my neck, imagining who would have left it. Plus, how did someone find out my locker number? I received all the information about registration details just a few days ago. I chew on my lips and stuff my lunchbox inside the space, tempted to just leave the letter there. I eye it and my hand shifts closer, my fingers an inch away when I stop. What if it contains anthrax? I roll my eyes at my own ridiculousness. I'm smart enough to know anthrax spores released into the air could harm not only me but several people, including the person who delivered the letter. Okay, fine, but I'm still not touching it. I'll grab some gloves from the science lab later and then toss it in the trash.

I'm putting my lock back on when I change my mind and fling the door open again, snatch up the letter, and tear at the flap. What if it's from Piper?

Dear Ava,

~~Your eyes are the color of the Caribbean Sea~~.

Shit. That's stupid.

What I really mean is...you look at me and I feel something REAL. And that never happens.

It's been ten months since you were here, but I can't forget you.

I've missed seeing you walk down the hall.
I've missed you cheering at my football games.
I've missed the smell of your hair.

And then everything fell apart that night.

*If you need **anything**, I want to be there for you. Text me. Please. 105-555-9201*

P.S. I'm a Shark, but I'd never hurt you.

P.P.S. I've tried to fight it with everything I have, but I want you. Still.

My heart pounds as I read the words, and I'm vaguely aware of a bell ringing and students streaming past me, heading to classes. I want to crumple the letter and set it on fire. I want to piss on it.

And that makes me laugh.

Who left this?

Of course, I don't believe it for a second. First of all, it's from one of the football players—a Shark—and they all despise me. It was *their* party, and they were the ones the police focused their investigation on.

They all said the same thing: Ava Harris was drinking when she came. No one gave her drugs or a drink. No one saw her go into the woods. No one assaulted her.

The late bell rings, startling me out of the past, and I stuff the letter into my backpack, slam my locker, and bolt for my first class.

3

Knox

I park my black Mercedes-Benz G-Class in a spot and turn the ignition off.

"Fucking hot new ride," Chance says from the back seat as he gets out, slinging his backpack over his arm. His pale blue eyes crinkle in the corners, still sporting a tan from his vacation in Maui this past week. "You always get the best toys, Knox." He huffs out a laugh, and I shrug, knowing there's no jealousy in the words. His family wealth is old money, passed down from generations of well-to-do lawyers and even a governor, but it doesn't rank up there with mine and Dane's—our dad's a real estate millionaire.

I step out of the car. "Nothing but the best for the Graysons." There's sarcasm in my tone. No one gets it but my twin.

My brother Dane gets out of the passenger side and pats the hood of the car. "Yeah, dear old Dad was feeling guilty for leaving us home most of the summer to work in New York. Nice way to appease us, don't you think?" His tone is deadpan, his face expressionless except for the lines of tension around his lips.

He's fine, I tell myself, my eyes following him as he walks around to join us.

Liam crawls out from the back seat. A six-four linebacker for our team, he's our star defensive player and on his way to a big college. ESPN has him ranked higher than anyone on the team, including me. He needed a ride this morning but told me his dad is dropping something off for him later—a new black Escalade.

With a wicked grin, he smiles as he straightens, stretches out his arms, and looks over at the school, taking in the stately structure, the turrets on each side, the ivy that grows from the bottom, draping the gray stones. "Are you getting chills like I am, boys? Senior year—it's ours." He cracks his knuckles and rubs his hands together. "And I'm going to bang every girl I want. More than you assholes. As my dad likes to say, boys will be boys." He laughs.

"Only you keep score," Chance says with an eye roll.

"So you and Jolena are off again?" comes from Dane. "Guess I'm not surprised. You two are a soap opera." He laughs, amusement wiping some of the tension away. He's like that, swinging from one emotion to the other.

Liam shrugs broad shoulders, running a hand through his side-swept, white-blond bangs—old-style Justin Bieber. "Too many girls in the world to be tied down to just one."

"You'll be back together before the day is over," Dane muses.

Chance chuckles. "Careful there, Liam. I do recall you getting a rash on your dick this summer from one of those college girls you picked up at the club we snuck into. Damn, she was hot—but an STD? That doctor's appointment had to be embarrassing."

Liam's face reddens. "It was curable, okay? Don't be telling people—it will kill my game."

I smirk. "I'm going to make it the morning announcement." I mimic tapping a microphone. "Welcome back, students. This is Knox Grayson, your quarterback for the Dragons. It's going to be a fine year at Camden Prep, but before we get started today, I'd like to touch on STDs—well, not actually *touch*, but you know what I mean. We'll be using Liam Barnes as our visual aid. Also, a riddle to brighten your day: What's worse than lobsters on your piano? Anyone?" I throw a glance around at the guys, smirking at Liam's red face, the color deepening. "It's crabs on your organ, of course. Just ask Liam."

Chance snickers, and Dane guffaws. "Good one, bro."

I shrug. "I have my moments."

"And Liam makes excellent material." Chance gives me a fist bump.

"Screw you, QB1," Liam mutters. "You just wait and see what happens on the field."

I arch a brow, feigning nonchalance at his little threat, but my hackles rise. Doesn't seem to take much these days, especially when it comes to mouthy football players. "It's just a joke."

Liam's face flattens. "Still not amused. I don't appreciate being the butt of your joke."

I laugh then, deep and long, satisfaction washing over me because I annoyed him. There's weird competitiveness between us. Maybe it's an offense-versus-defense kind of thing, but mostly it stems from me being in charge of the team, coupled with the fact that I had Jolena sophomore year before him. I tapped that fast and got out, and for all his blustering about not being serious with her, he doesn't want me near her.

Sex with her was just water to me—tasteless, meaningless, nothing but passing the time. I'm not even sure she really wanted *me*, but she made all the right noises and pretended, eager to be one of my girls under the bleachers. She didn't give a shit about who I was, but you can bet she told everyone she had the quarterback. Funny—I never tell anyone who I fuck, but people always know.

Liam rolls his shoulders. "You've been acting weird lately, Knox. Worried about winning a state championship already?" He gives me a once-over. "Don't worry, I'll win those games for us. You just throw some pretty passes and I'll do all the hard work."

"Fuck off," I say softly.

Then, I smile.

He gives me a double take then darts his eyes away. Distaste is evident on his face. Four years with this scar on my face and he still can't stomach it.

Dane grows still next to me and gives me side-eye, which I refuse to acknowledge. Liam is *his* best friend, and like the good twin he is, we're in sync; he knows when I want to use my fists.

"Come on, let's go in," Dane murmurs, his shoulder jostling mine.

"Mmmm, maybe Liam and I need to hash out some shit before we walk in," I say lightly.

Liam swings his head back to me, meeting my eyes and turning his unease into a careful smile. "Ah, man, forget it. It's gonna be a good year, alright? Our team's going to win that trophy this year. You and me, right, Knox? We're tight. We've been tight since freshman year."

It's me and Dane who are tight, asshole. Never you. "Yeah," I say.

The four of us step onto the long sidewalk that leads to the entrance. Liam opens the door, and I head in first, carefully searching the faces in the foyer then the hallway.

Nothing.

She isn't here yet.

Wait.

A blonde girl catches my eye down the hall, her face hidden and ducked. My steps falter, pausing as I trail behind the other three guys. I'm about to head toward her—

I touch my scar, rubbing it.

Nope. Nope.

Don't follow her, Knox. Let it go. Right.

A familiar dark green Jeep flashes in my peripheral as it whips into the lot and speeds past the sidewalk. I frown, my gut tensing up. *Ava.* So the blonde wasn't her. A tight feeling settles in my chest, and unease mingled with excitement washes over me as I watch her park and get out of her car. I bite my lower lip, my body tightening.

With what?

Tension? Fear? Lust?

Yeah, I'm a regular split personality.

Part of me never wants to see her face again, but the other side of me...well, that's the one I have to worry about.

~

LIAM RUSHES off to the headmaster's office to get his schedule figured out while Dane, Chance, and I linger close to the door, checking out the incoming freshmen and waiting for the friends we haven't seen over the summer.

But I know why I'm really standing here.

Dane leans his head against the wall and scrubs his face.

"What's up with you?" I ask, one eye on the door, watching.

He raises his head. "Nothing. Stop hovering." Gray eyes the same color as mine give me a look. His pupils are dilated.

My jaw grinds, but I keep my lips zipped. The more I ride him, the more belligerent he gets, and you can't argue with—

Shit.

There she is.

It's been months since she graced the hallowed halls of Camden with her long, lean legs and big aquamarine eyes.

A suffocating feeling grows in my chest.

She.

Is.

Here.

My thoughts jumble back to the past. I still remember the day she showed up freshman year, that look of hope on her face, full of optimism that Camden was going to be a new beginning for her. She made me look at her, and I hated it. Even now, I itch to peel the sensation right off my skin.

No feelings allowed in this body for her.

Not a single one.

"She's back," Dane says, straightening up from the wall, an enigmatic expression on his face. "Gotta give it to her—she's got balls."

"Mmmm," I say, studying her while she isn't looking.

Gone is the long blonde hair, replaced with jet black. She looks harder. Her mouth is frozen in a smirk with bright red, glittery lipstick on her full lips, accentuating the sensual curves there, the paleness of her skin. Small freckles dot over her nose, same as before, but it's the tense set of her jaw that tells you she's not the same. Her skirt is a hair too short by the school guidelines, the hem hitting about three inches above her knee instead of the required two. I wonder if scholarship students get the last pick when it comes to uniforms. I guess their clothes are free, like the textbooks. Do they give her just a couple of sets of each one? Two jackets, a few shirts and skirts? I can't even count the number of uniforms in my closet at home, so many khakis, perfectly starched white shirts, and a myriad of ties.

Her red blazer with the Camden dragon crest is draped over her arm, her white blouse snug around the fullness of her breasts. On her feet are ragged black Converse. My gaze lingers, taking in the tall white socks on her calves.

"Why are you staring at her like that?" Chance hisses at me, standing on my other side.

"Like what?"

Who is she deep down? To walk into this place, eyes lit with a vicious edge.

My hands curl.

She's so sweet.

So forbidden.

"Like you're fascinated or some shit." His voice is hushed.

"Mmmm," I murmur.

I can feel him still watching me watching her as he says, "Leave her be."

I narrow my eyes at her, not even listening to him, feeling

annoyed by the vulnerable hunch in her shoulders that grows, the one she keeps attempting to straighten as she walks closer to us.

I shrug, keeping the movement cool and light. "She's definitely a spark that just might ignite and catch fire."

"And burn us all down in the process," Dane mutters. "I agree with Chance—stop."

"Can't do it," I answer under my breath. I lick my lips, battling internally to drop my gaze from her, feeling baffled by it.

She came back, she came back, she really did it.

Chance's jaw pops as he watches her, grappling with control.

She seems rooted to her place in the hall, sweeping her eyes over us. Students jostle past her, giving her a wide berth.

Come on, little Ava.

Come closer to me, fierce girl.

One more step.

Let me touch you. On the arm. Your hand. Anything.

Please.

My fingers twitch.

"I can't believe she's back," Chance grunts and looks at me, keeping his voice low so she can't hear us. "Did you know?"

"Why would you think I'd know?" I say dryly.

"Because you always know shit. Your dad is on the board."

I laugh. Oh, if he only *knew* the information I have—all of it about defiant, charity case Ava. I have so many details about her life it makes my head spin, makes my cock hard—

Stay far, far away.

Chance's chest rises. "My father took my car away after

that party. I still don't have it—when I did nothing wrong. She was my date, and that was all it took for him to judge me and hold me responsible."

Yeah, but he left with Brooklyn.

Annoyance tugs at me. "Weren't you in love with her?"

He inhales sharply, but his voice is subdued. "No."

Liar.

I chuckle under my breath.

My gaze lingers on her heart-shaped face, watching as she stumbles, her feet pushing forward and stopping about four feet from us, staring at Chance. Hate flows from her, almost palpable. Hot. Electric.

He pales and his throat bobs, some of that anger leeching out of him and turning into...hmmm, fear? Nothing ruffles him these past months like someone bringing up Ava, and seeing her for the first time since that night—well, he looks as if he's seen a ghost.

He drops his eyes.

"You over her for real?" I stare at him hard.

"Fuck yeah."

Last year, he was totally lost in Ava. I saw it when he gave her puppy dog looks in class, and shit, even I heard angels singing when she gazed back at him. I saw it when he'd throw down his helmet after a game and dash over to pick her up and twirl her around. He talked about her constantly, how he thought she might be *the one*. He didn't brag about his sexual conquests with her. No, he kept that under wraps.

He and I have been best friends since our days at the elementary campus. When I showed up one day in middle school with my face in stitches, swollen and red, and he asked me what the hell happened, I told him it was nobody's business. He accepted it, made it his own personal crusade to tell everyone to *Back the fuck off and stop asking.* When he lost his mom sophomore year to cancer, I stayed by his side for weeks, playing mindless video games and talking about nothing to ease him. I know what death is, the grief it brings.

Chance's jaw grinds. "I never thought I'd see her again."

I stare down at my phone. "Yet here she is. Random factoid: did you know date rape drugs wear off pretty fast?"

Chance flinches. "Just stop, Knox. She wasn't assaulted. She lied."

"Mmmm," I murmur.

Dad easily obtained the police report for Dane and me after her interview and everyone else's at the party. I know about the bruises on her inner thighs. I know she doesn't remember much. And those police interviews with the players? A fucking joke, or at least I think so, though it was a tense few days with my dad's scrutiny squarely on us for the first time in a while. Dane was one of the guys dancing with her in the video, and then there was *my* predicament. Still, once our obligatory interview with the cops was over, Dad flew us to LA for a U2 concert as if nothing had happened.

Dane may have told me to stop staring, but even he has her in his sights, a low, wary look in his gaze.

She certainly draws the eye.

"Guess it doesn't matter," I say to Chance. "Nobody believes some scholarship girl." I study my nails.

His reply is lost when Brooklyn appears next to Chance, batting her lashes up at him as she curls her fingers around his upper arm. "Hey, baby," she murmurs, sending a scathing glance back at Ava. "You okay?"

He gives her a nod. "Of course. Why wouldn't I be?"

Brooklyn smiles at him and wanders off to slide in next to Jolena, and I watch them huddle together for a moment then approach Ava.

How will she handle it?

Will she stay at Camden when life gets tough?

Because it will.

It's going to be fucking bad for her—

Chance snaps his fingers in my face, and I realize I'd forgotten about him. His eyes have followed mine to the girls several feet away. "You're a dick. Stay away from her," he finally says.

I laugh.

We all know he doesn't mean Brooklyn.

"Both of you shut up. We're all dicks. We're Sharks," Dane says just as the bell rings.

Sharks. I don't know where the name came from, this "club" we're in, but it's been around for years. Our dad was one. Chance's too. We stick together. Mostly it's jocks from the various sports teams, born to the richest parents. We don't have a ceremony with hooded cloaks and candles and hazing. Either you're part of the inner circle or you're not.

We straighten, pick up our backpacks, and head down the hall, cutting through the less fortunate, making our way to class.

Yet...

I can't stop my eyes from lingering on Ava's back as she struggles with the combination on her lock. Her head is tilted down, the strange dark hair draped on either side, exposing the graceful arch of her neck taut with tension. The skin there is creamy and perfect.

She walked in here like she owns the place, but she doesn't.

I do.

Still...

The very air around her seems lit with an aura of expectancy.

Emotion, something unnamed, rare and beautiful, brushes down my spine.

I tense.

Rein it in.

4

AVA

I'm so freaking late, practically running when I dash into my History of Film class. The teacher, Mrs. White, is an older lady with gray curly hair and small wire-rimmed glasses. She's wearing a baggy dress with huge pockets on the sides and old sandals. Rather absentminded and a bit quirky, she has a rep as a fun teacher. She lifts her head when I come to a stop, my shoes squeaking on the slick tile. Everyone already has a seat, and it's clear from the seating chart on the whiteboard that she doesn't have my name down. Great. That's what last-minute registration gets me. It's going to be like this all day, me showing up and not being on the roll.

She stops talking, a surprised look on her face as she motions me forward. Everyone cranes their neck to get a look at me as I walk up to her desk, maneuvering through the small desk tables, each one seating two students. Dang, I'm going to have to actually sit next to someone. I send a prayer up that it's not one of the Sharks, hoping for just a regular student like me. I pass by Piper, whose eyes are wide. I grimace when I see she's been placed next to Dane. She sticks out her tongue at me and rolls her eyes so hard it actually looks painful, and I bite back a grin.

"Sorry I'm late, Mrs. White. It won't happen again."

"Snitch," a male voice coughs out, and her gaze goes behind me, searching the class for the person who did it.

"That's enough," she says firmly then glances at me. "It's fine, Ava. First day we give some leeway." She messes with some papers on her podium, shuffling them around, her finger going down a list. "I don't have you on my roll, and honestly this class is so popular with juniors and seniors, almost every seat is filled."

"I registered late. Sorry." I keep my spine straight. "Just put me in a chair in the back. I don't even need a table." Nervously, I tug at my skirt.

A deep male voice comes from my left. "I have an empty seat, Mrs. White. Liam dropped."

Her head rises, and I follow her gaze, my gut churning, recognizing that voice.

My eyes find Knox Grayson's. Again, there's no expression on his face, just that superior, disdainful smile.

Mrs. White's eyebrows hit the roof, and I guess she's just as surprised as I am that one of the Sharks has offered to let me sit with him.

Games.

Fucking games.

I tear my eyes off Knox's face.

"I'd prefer the seat in the back," I tell Mrs. White quietly, leaning in, but unfortunately my words must carry because someone in the front giggles, and I hear the silky voice of Jolena.

"Wow, a girl who doesn't want to be next to Knox—priceless." Her laughter tinkles.

The teacher puts her elbows on the podium and leans in until our faces are close and there's no chance anyone will hear. "I'm good with whatever you want. I can put you in the back, but honestly, it's only going to isolate you from everyone. I don't want that, and in the end, you may miss some things if you can't see the overhead. You could take the seat up front with Knox, and if you have any issues *at any time*, come to me and I'll take care of it." Her voice is soft, pity dripping like acid.

Pity. *Please.*

I want justice.

Not likely. They have money. They own this town.

Miss Harris, is it possible you consented to sex? Your behavior at the party was, well...

She spreads her hands. "It's up to you though, Ava. Whichever you want."

Sit in the back or sit next to the head Shark?

My throat tightens as I ponder my options, but I already know what I *need* to do: establish myself as fearless, just like inmates do when they walk into a prison.

Swallowing hard, I give her a tight nod, pivot, and walk to Knox's desk.

Someone lets out a gasp—Jolena.

Good. Take that. I am stronger than BTN.

Knox's eyes are narrowed as he sits back in his chair, never shifting his gaze as I slide into the seat next to his. He takes me in, cocking an eyebrow as if he's surprised.

He's a foot away from me, but I swear I can feel the heat from his body looming close. I scoot my chair a few inches farther from his, making a horrid scraping noise on the tile. He huffs out a laugh and slides his away from me until his chair is next to the wall, putting even more distance between us.

Good, it's like that then.

Never liked you from the get-go, even before that party, my face says as I shoot him a glare.

Same, his eyes say.

"Ava," he says in acknowledgment, his voice husky, laced with dark undertones. His tone reminds me of the night, steel wrapped in black velvet, hinting at secrets and barely leashed power. Since freshman year, I've avoided him, but it's not the scar, because things like that don't bother me. I've lived with kids with scars and burns on their faces, sometimes on their entire body. Luka had cigarette burns up and down both forearms.

"Mr. Cold and Evil. We meet again."

The last time I was this close to him was in Greek Myths junior year when he sat behind me, feet propped up on the bottom rail of my desk. It was the most tense I'd ever been in a class. He'd breathe and I'd hear him, the sound grating on my nerves. He'd lean forward and my hair would move as it he touched it. I'd pass papers back to him and our fingers would brush. When our eyes would meet, I'd drop mine, and he'd laugh. Once...

"HEY, CHARITY CASE, TURN AROUND."

Ugh! *I turn in my seat. "What?" My hands clench as I hold myself tight under his scrutiny. My heart thumps so loud I wonder if he can hear it. Ever since seeing him almost naked in the locker room, something is definitely weird between us.*

"Why did Hades fall for Persephone?"

"Read your textbook, Shark."

His voice is low, his eyes liquid metal. "I did. Seriously, I don't get it." His gaze lingers on my neck, staring at my locket. "Come on, answer me."

Oh, what the heck. If it will make him stop bothering me... "Hades was lonely in hell. It's a dark, isolated place. She symbolizes light and good. Opposites attract. Why can't a devil want an angel? They were in love. Happy."

"Opposites, huh?" He taps his pen on his desk, thinking, and glances at Chance a few rows over. "You and Chance—serious?"

Ah, so that's what this is. "Does it bother you that he's with me? You think I'm not good enough for your best friend. Chance is perfect. He isn't a devil."

His lids go to half-mast. "Like me."

I look at his scarred lip.

"Ah, low blow. You know just how to cut me, charity case."

"Ava is my fucking name," I hiss then flip back around. Asshole!

KNOX LAUGHS UNDER HIS BREATH, and I come back to the present.

"Didn't know you'd given me a nickname. Guess this means you've been thinking about me." He pauses. "I kind of like Cold and Evil. Fits me. Truthfully, I'd prefer Hot as Fuck, but you do you."

I glance at his face, taking in the long patrician nose, the sculpted cheekbones, the way his dark hair lays around his face. He's rolled up the sleeves of his button-down, the muscles of his forearms tightly roped and defined. His upper arms are bulky, his shirt tight against them.

I tear my eyes off him and stare down at my laptop, shuffling around to get my things arranged. I slam down my notebook and pen.

For some weird reason, I have perfect clarity on seeing him with Tawny, his hand tucked into the back pocket of her jeans as they walked away from the bonfire and got into his car.

Yet...

It feels as if something big happened *before* they left, an elusive memory that dances just out of reach and is up in smoke before I can grab hold and pin it down. It's been like that for months, bits and pieces all jumbled together.

"We're going to be working on a movie project for the next few weeks, so where you're sitting today is your permanent seat for a while," says Mrs. White as she begins her lecture.

"Great," I mutter.

Knox gives me a dark look. "My sentiments exactly."

She continues. "We're going to focus on movies at least twenty years old. Some perhaps you've heard of. Some are iconic, some suck, and I can't wait to get your thoughts on the issues they cover, which you'll put in a five-thousand-word essay."

Groans come from the students.

"What kind of movies, Mrs. White? My dad doesn't let me watch sexy films, so I hope they're all G-rated." It's Dane, his voice lazy as he sits next to Piper.

A few people snigger until Mrs. White gives them a

pointed glare. "I'll make sure you get *Charlotte's Web*, Dane. Too bad, really, especially with so many good movies on the list, like *The Godfather*, for one. Guess I'll assign that one to someone else."

He deflates. "Please don't give me *Charlotte's Web*. The spider dies and all that crap. I hate it when people die in movies."

"Too late," she says, already writing his and Piper's names on the board.

I chance another glance over at their table, and Piper does a gagging motion at me as she points to him. I grin. Dang, I've missed her.

The teacher goes down the list of pairs, assigning movie titles. *Field of Dreams* goes to Chance and his partner, Brooklyn, and from the way she's tracing her fingers over his hand on the desk, she's evidently happy to be next to him.

I flip back around and face the front, my hands clenched in my lap.

"Not over him?" Knox drawls. "He's dating her, you know. Might be serious. He claims it is. Never seen him be so *nice* to a girl. Do you still love him?"

I slide my eyes to him.

His facial expression never changes. Cold. "Not that he's a bad guy, but you and him don't go together." He pauses as if a light bulb just clicked on. "Huh. Maybe it was all about security when it came to him. Nice, clean-cut, boy next door. Is that what you saw in him?"

The. Nerve.

He doesn't know *me*.

I cared about Chance.

I study my nails.

"I do that too—look at my nails. It says *I know what I know and you don't know shit.*"

I blow out a breath.

"Nothing to say? I guess that means you're still carrying the torch. Silly girl. How can you want him when he left you high and dry?"

Anger flares to the surface at the memories he brings up. "Zip your lips, Cold and Evil, or I'll punch you in the face."

His head leans in close, too close. "I believe you, which is funny, because I took you for the quiet type, but I think I always knew you were something else underneath..." He laughs and leans away from me, but not before the air around him shifts and I catch his cologne. He smells like the ocean, salt and sunshine and coconuts, and my chest swells.

I turn my head and stare at him, facing off with those gray eyes. "What kind of cologne is that? Eau de fish?"

He looks at his nails.

"It reeks."

It's freaking divine.

He whistles and stares at the ceiling. Rakes a hand through his hair.

"And if your girlfriends aren't telling you the truth about your stupid cologne, they're pussies."

I swear I see his mouth twitch.

"Maybe cats would like it. *Meow.*" I claw at him, and he breaks with a smirk.

"It's actually something my mom picked up in Paris. She bought it for me every Christmas. Guess I have enough to last a lifetime."

"Ah, Paris. Nice. Beautiful place—Eiffel Tower, cheese, wine, fancy accents, poodles. I shop there all the time."

"Really?" An eyebrow pops. "I wouldn't have known from the state of your shoes. When's the last time you had a new pair?"

I give him a fake smile. "Maybe I like worn-out things. At least they're original and not a cookie-cutter leather loafer. Let me guess..." I tap my chin and take in the immaculate shoe on his large foot. I see the meticulous stitching, the honey color, the comfort it no doubt provides with a nice insole. "Fresh from Italy, I presume."

"Man, it's so nice being rich. What's it like being poor?" His eyes glow at me.

He likes this.

He enjoys messing with me.

He smiles.

I smile.

Oh, honey, two can play at this game.

I have nothing to lose anymore, and right now, I'm feeling brave.

I dart my tongue out then bite my bottom lip on purpose.

He blinks and looks away from me.

"Cold and Evil, do you get off on arguing with me?"

"Tulip, you can get me off whenever you want. Wanna meet me under the bleachers later? I don't mind slumming."

"Who told you my middle name?" My breath whooshes out as Mrs. White talks at another table, assigning another movie.

He laughs.

"Did you rape me?" The words come out unplanned, but there they are, and I'm glad because his face goes from bored amusement to shuttering into a mask.

I watch him intently, cataloguing each little change,

searching for the truth in the granite-cut curves of his face. His jaw pops, betraying emotion, but when he looks me straight in the eyes, all I see is an arctic winter in those wolfish depths.

"Well?" I add, my hands clenched, hiding under the desk.

"I don't have to take by force what is offered to me on a daily basis. I've never, *ever* touched a girl unless she begged for it. You aren't even on my radar, Tulip. But hey, the offer's still open for a pity fuck."

Not on his radar—good.

"But you were there."

"Doesn't mean it was me. And I left that party—with my very willing date. You watched me leave. Remember?" His eyes cling to mine, searching for something.

I frown. Why would he bring that up? Such a specific detail.

"You're one of them and I can't believe a word you say," I bite out. "You're all liars."

We're facing each other now, our heads tilted low, our voices hushed, mine angry, his taut and firm.

"We're all liars—sure," he mocks. "I saw you drink Fireball like it was iced tea. I watched a video of you dancing in a circle of at least six guys."

"Huh, I thought it was more. Did you count them? Funny, I didn't see you in that video."

"Because I don't do that shit. And I left. Remember?"

What is up with him and this *remembering*? The whole school knows I don't recall much. I shove it aside.

"Am I too poor for you?" I say. "Poor little old me."

"I don't participate in videos because I have a football career to think about. College recruiters look through social media," he says tonelessly, unflappable control holding strong.

My mouth tightens. I'd give my right boob to see Knox Grayson lose his cool.

"Yeah, everyone knows you're high and mighty. Everyone kisses your ass. Guess what—I don't. I think underneath that exterior is a guy who's got some real problems. Mommy and Daddy not love you enough as a baby? Is that why Dane is still snorting coke or whatever?" I pause, feeling triumphant at the thunderous expression he now wears. "Oh, yeah, I know what it looks like. Grew up with an alcoholic, drug-addicted mom. See, it's bad all over, right? No matter the social class we belong to, when it comes down to it, we're all just humans with the same problems. Mine's dealing with not remembering what happened that night. Yours is...I don't know. You're just a cold sonofabitch."

It was quite a speech and he blinks rapidly, his chest inflating as he flashes a look over my shoulder to glance at Dane. He gazes back at me, eyes hard, but at least there's heat there, dark and deep and angry. "Leave my brother out of this."

Huh. If there's a chink of weakness in Knox, it's his brother. I file that away under the Things That Piss Off Knox dossier.

"All I had that was mine—my body—was taken without my consent, by you or one of your precious teammates. There's nothing else you can do to me, Cold and Evil. Go tell your little brat pack that today. Something's going to trigger my memory and when it does, I'm going to kill him with my bare hands."

"I'll kill him with my bare hands." His eyes flash.

My heart drops and I rear back, confusion making me suck in a breath.

What?

I search for words and end up with, "Why would you say that?"

His face flattens. "And while you're at it, let it all out. Say everything you've obviously been holding back for months. Do it now. Get it over with."

I frown. How has he gotten the upper hand all of a sudden? "Why?"

"Don't you want to? Isn't this your first time back among us in ten months? Don't think I don't see all that rage inside you. Let me have it."

Is this one of his games?

I swallow, caught between my need to lash out at a Shark —something I've dreamed about for almost a year—and my urge to ask him to explain why he'd kill the person who hurt me. Anger wins. "Fine. I hate you and your friends. You ruined me last year, but I won't let you take this year from me or shape the person I'm going to be. If you make my life hell, I'll do the same to you."

His eyes close, his thick dark lashes lowering briefly. "Oh, Tulip. You can't make my life hell."

"I'd like to see you walk in my shoes."

His gaze goes down to my Converse. "No thanks."

"Asshole," I say, my jaw tight.

"Yes."

"Major asshole. Like the biggest dick at this school, and I don't mean size-wise. I mean douchebag of major proportions. I can't believe girls actually want you. You're disgusting."

"Yes."

"And the truth is, you've probably peaked as a quarterback in high school. Someday you're going to be a lonely, middle-aged man with deep-seated commitment issues. You'll be in AA, hooked on porn, crying over your Chinese takeout—"

His hand scrubs his mouth, and at first I think he's pissed; then I realize his shoulders are shaking.

"What's so funny?" I snap.

His eyes spear mine. "You."

I reach out and ruffle his hair. It's silky under my fingers, and I flinch back, feeling branded.

I just *touched* him.

What is wrong with me?

He freezes at the contact and jerks away. "Don't touch me."

I will my pounding heart to slow down.

Mrs. White clears her throat as she approaches our table. "Well, I'm glad to see you two getting along."

I scoff.

"I've got some movie choices for you," she continues. "You'll need to watch it together and work on the essay. Is that going to be a problem?"

"No," Knox says tersely.

I groan inwardly. "I can't *wait* to work with Knox. What do you have for us?"

She smiles, seemingly clueless about the thick tension that's hanging over our desk. "Ah, well, I have two here, either *Star Wars* or *Dirty Dancing*. Which one?"

"*Star Wars*," I say.

"*Dirty Dancing*," he says at the same time, and I gape at him.

"Seriously? You'd pick 'Nobody puts Baby in a corner' over flaming swords and Jedi, and hello, aren't all guys into starships and killing? Are you male? Use the Force, Knox. It must be *Star Wars*."

He gives me a haughty look. "Flaming swords aside, there are aspects to *Dirty Dancing* we can write about. How Baby brings her family together—"

"Pfft," I snort. "What about Luke Skywalker and Princess Leia? Chewie and Han Solo? That's a family for you, not rich people vacationing in the Catskills—"

"—two socioeconomic groups, the vacationers and those employed at Kellerman's—"

"God. You even know the name of the hotel. And now you want to throw out big words like *socioeconomic*. Surprising—I always assumed you were a bit dim."

"You're supposedly the brain. That's your label, mine is jock. Keep up with the big words, Tulip."

"If you call me Tulip one more time—"

"It's a heck of a lot better than what everyone else calls you."

"—I will smack your face."

There's silence as Knox and I stare at each other.

He shakes his head. "You're mouthy."

"Get used to it."

Mrs. White holds her hand up, her eyes bouncing from me to Knox. A little titter comes from her. "I never expected you to be so vehement about your options. Is everything okay?"

Oh, I'm not backing down now. I nod. "Yes."

Knox sighs.

She grins. "Good! I love the, um, enthusiasm. Let me see... Oh, I have it. There's a number in my head and each of you gets to pick between one and ten. Whoever guesses closest to the one in my head gets to choose—"

"One," Knox says, interrupting her while glaring daggers at me.

"Five," I snap.

She gives me a sheepish look. "I picked one. Sorry, Ava, it's Knox's choice, so *Dirty Dancing* it is. I'll leave it up to you to decide on the topic, but I like Knox's idea about societal differences, or perhaps a discussion of how the romance in the movie has managed to capture the hearts of several generations?"

"Societal differences," I call.

"Romantic aspect," Knox says over me.

We glare at each other.

Are you for real? my eyes say.

Oh yeah, his gleam back. *And this is going to be so much fun.*

She laughs. "Whichever you want. Maybe you can come up with something more original. You need to have it watched and notes turned in two weeks from now."

She walks off, and Knox faces the front. "She always picks one, by the way. I beat you." A dark chuckle comes from him.

I bristle. "Romantic aspect over lightsabers? And here I thought you were a dude."

"'Patience you must have, my young Padawan.'"

I stare at him. "Oh, you *jerk*! You just did that just to get at me, didn't you? It wasn't about the movie—it was about you being all *Let's make Ava uncomfortable.*"

He grunts and lets out a long-suffering sigh. "Everything

isn't about you. Patrick Swayze was my mom's favorite actor, and *Ghost* was the one movie she'd watch over and over."

My ears perk up. "Was?"

He clamps his lips tight.

"What?"

"Nothing," he mutters.

I narrow my eyes at him. Oh, it's definitely *something.*

I pick up my pen and twirl it around. "Keep your secrets then. I don't—"

"My mom died when I was twelve." He rubs his hand over his mouth, as if he's surprised the words came out.

I blink rapidly, trying to realign what I thought I knew about the inscrutable Knox Grayson. How did I not know this?

"Happened before you came to Camden."

Okay, so he lost his mom. Don't feel sorry for him, Ava. Fuck that. He's Knox, a Shark, and he doesn't deserve my—

He gives me a tight nod, interrupting my thoughts. "People die. Life is tenuous, and we get no clue as to when it's going to be over. Not that it even matters. No one really cares."

No one really cares.

"Super dark, Knox." I clear my throat. "Back to the paper—"

"Right. I imagine you don't want to spend any time with me that you don't have to. We're just going to pretend to watch *Dirty Dancing* together."

"I can't imagine being alone with you."

He doesn't answer, and I turn to look at him. He's toying with his laptop, rubbing his fingers absently across the silver keyboard, looking at nothing. Suddenly, he frowns.

"Because you're afraid of me? It wasn't *me*." An odd look fills his eyes.

I study his wavy dark brown hair, the silkiness of it. The guy who raped me had dark hair, I think. Maybe I'm wrong, and I can't trust those memories...

I say quietly, "I just don't like you."

"Thank God." He jerks out a piece of paper from his notebook, scribbles a number, and passes it over to me. "Here's my cell. Don't share it, or we'll have a problem. Maybe we can watch on the same night and talk about what topic we want to write about when it's fresh."

Oh.

Oh.

Knox Grayson never gives out his number. I know because every girl since freshman year has tried to get it, to sext him or whatever. I'm not one of those. Rumor is he's warned all his buddies if they share it, they'll be sorry.

I take the scrap of paper, instantly recognizing that the digits aren't the same as the ones in the letter that's been lingering in the back of my mind since I found it. Well, at least my "secret admirer" isn't him.

"No problem. One night this week? Watch around nine and chat at eleven?" I exhale. "The younger kids get the TV after dinner, and I have to wait for them to go to bed. I don't have one in my room. I could watch on my laptop if you want to do earlier, but I prefer the TV."

"Younger kids? I thought you only had one brother."

I flinch. How does he know about Tyler? I barely talked about him in the years I was here.

"I live at Sisters of Charity. I only have one brother—actually he's my half-brother—but there are twenty little ones there and then the older kids."

"Wait? You're still *there*? I thought you'd—"

I give him a glare. "Where else would I be? I turned eighteen this past January, and they're letting me stay for now but it isn't permanent. I asked for a dorm here, but I don't know if that will work out..." My voice trails off and I lapse into silence. I'm sure he doesn't want to hear the details about me coming back to Camden.

He frowns, his brow wrinkling as if he's in deep thought. He gives me a dismissive glance. "I see. Fine. Just text me when you want to watch it. Whatever."

I stare at the number. Texting him? Screw that. If he thinks I want any kind of contact with him, even if it's via a phone, he's deluded.

But, shit, his number!

So many possibilities. Girls' bathroom, announcing it in class, posting it online, the newspaper—hell, flying it on a banner behind a plane. I sigh. A girl can dream...

He's leaned into my space, that stupid ocean cologne drifting around me. "If you write my number in the bathroom, I will make you pay, Tulip."

I smile innocently. "Me? Never."

"Mmmm."

Thank God the bell rings only a few moments later. It felt like the longest hour of my life, and I dash out of there like a greyhound at the races.

5

AVA

After class, I take off for the restrooms. My stomach growls yet it's uneasy at the same time, my nerves tense and ready for anyone who gets close to me. In hindsight, I should have eaten the toast and eggs the nuns set out, but I was wired. Everything hinges on today. If I can make it...

I find the last stall and sit down.

One class down.

Five periods left.

Pulling the locket out from under my shirt, I brush my fingers over it. Cheap and old, I found it on the floor at one of the various shelters Mama and I wandered in and out of. I recall asking around to see if it belonged to anyone, but no one claimed it, and since there wasn't even a picture inside, I finally decided it was meant to be mine. I snap it open and stare down at the tiny picture of Tyler, his big eyes and spikey brown hair. We look nothing alike. "Such a sweet baby," I murmur. "We got this, bozo."

One final breath then I leave and walk down the hall, staying on the right-hand side near the line of lockers, headed toward the headmaster's office. Everyone walks and talks around me. Piper has zipped off to her second class, and I won't see her until lunch.

Sometimes the loneliest place on earth is in the midst of a crowd.

But that's okay. I'm here and that means something.

I enter the office, and it's frantic with students and teachers milling around. First day craziness.

"What is it, doll?" says Mrs. Carmichael, the office secretary. Unsurprisingly, she looks flustered, her faded brown hair up in a tight bun with a pen tucked behind her ear. Little strands stick out everywhere. Slightly plump, she's wearing a flowy blouse with giant pink flowers on it.

I clear my throat. "Headmaster Trask asked me to come in this morning. My name is Ava Harris. I would have come earlier, but I barely made it to my first period."

She blinks, her back straightening, obviously registering my name. Yeah, I'm *her*.

I gaze back at her blankly. *Please don't pity me.*

She nods. "I see. Are you sure he didn't mean the end of the day?" She looks over at the headmaster's shut door. "He's very busy on the first day back."

Someone, a deliveryman, bumps into me as he carries in a large box full of printed pamphlets and places it up on the counter. She signs for them, obviously forgetting about me, and I start to argue and let her know he told me I was to come in the morning, but I decide to let it go. I've had enough confrontations today.

RING!

The bell dings over the intercom, and I watch tardy students through the glass doors, darting around and running to class.

I let out a sigh. My other class is on the opposite side of the building. I turn back to ask for a hall pass, but she's arguing with the deliveryman, telling him the colors are all wrong.

I'm about to leave when I see Knox come out of Mr. Trask's office. Wait a minute—I can't see the headmaster in the morning, but *he* can? Huh. My face reddens, and I clutch my books close to my chest.

"Problems already?" he murmurs as he stops in front of me.

Mrs. Carmichael looks up and calls Knox's name, telling him she'll write him a pass back to class.

My lips compress. "I'm supposed to see Mr. Trask, but it looks like you took up any free time he might have, and now I'm relegated to going to class."

"Oh." He turns to Mrs. Carmichael, who's busy writing him a pass. "Maxine, Ava was supposed to see the headmaster. Will you buzz him?"

Maxine? Seriously?

She cocks her head and moves her gaze from me to him. She looks annoyed, but clearly she's too busy with the pamphlet man to argue any further. She gives us a quick nod.

"I don't need your help, Cold and Evil," I mutter. "Why were you in there anyway? Trying to change your schedule so you don't have to sit with me in class?"

His gaze brushes over me. "Oh, I'm going to enjoy sitting next to you. You're quite fascinating, charity case."

"Why, sitting next to the King of Camden is certain to be the most scintillating experience of my whole life."

"He'll see you now, Ava. Head on in," Mrs. Carmichael says as she gestures to the shut door.

"Later, Tulip," he murmurs, walking past me.

"Stop calling me that!" I snap to his back as he walks out of the office, broad shoulders swaying.

Giving the secretary a nod, I open Mr. Trask's office door.

A short, balding man in his fifties, he wears a genial expression on his face as I stand in the doorway. He smiles carefully. "Ava, there you are. I was waiting for you, come on in. Have a seat. It's wonderful you decided to come back to Camden."

Sitting in a plush, brown leather chair, I nod my head in agreement, but I know there wasn't much choice for me in the matter. Goals—they're what pushed me to walk back into this hellhole.

Another tenuous smile from him as he comes around and sits on his desk, his hands folded in his lap. "As I mentioned on the phone last week, we can easily add your grades from last year to our curriculum here. It even appears you're ahead in calculus. The tutors at Sisters of Charity did a great job with homeschooling."

I smile, but just barely.

The tutors sucked. I actually did everything myself. I researched and found a homeschooling program accepted in Tennessee public schools, read the material myself, and took every test, legitimately and without cheating. A few times I even snuck into local colleges near the group home and sat in the back taking notes. Thankfully those classes were so packed no one seemed to notice.

"You won't be disappointed by your decision to put last year behind you. Camden really is the best place for you."

This is the worst place I could be.

In fact, my original plan was to go back to the public school where I attended middle school, but there's Tyler, and I have to think about his future too.

Mr. Trask pulls out a stack of papers in a folder and opens it up. He's holding my actual permanent record and my fingers itch to snatch it out of his hands, wondering if the keg party is documented there. I'm certain it is. Every football player at the party was reprimanded, suspended for a week while the police conducted their interviews. A fucking week. As for me, I never came back to Camden after that night, spending a few days at Piper's until I went back to the group home.

That was then.

This is now.

He says, "Your GPA will continue to be competitive with the rest of the student body, and you'll be eligible for final class rankings." He places a piece of paper in my hand. "So if you'll just sign here, you will be fully enrolled again. Just like you never left."

"Any word on housing?" When we spoke on the phone last week, he said we'd discuss it today. I didn't expect him to agree, but living on campus would make things easier, especially the terrible morning commute from Nashville. Plus, the nuns aren't responsible for me anymore, and even though they've given me this extra time, they need room for other kids.

"Ah, yes," he says, smiling. "I have very good news. There's an opening in the dorms and it's yours. No charge."

Surprise makes me blink. I came prepared to battle for a free dorm room. "But you weren't even sure the board would agree to pay for my housing. What's changed?"

He nods. "Actually, we have an anonymous donor who's offered to cover the cost."

"Who? I mean, I assume most of the board is angry with me for last year."

He sighs, an uncertain look on his face. "The person wishes to remain anonymous. And, I assure you, the board is *not* angry with you. We want to help you. I have two daughters myself, and I just..." He stops, clearing his throat, obviously pushing aside whatever he was going to say as he looks at me, thinking, choosing his words carefully. "As you know from our conversation earlier, we don't normally allow local residents to utilize the dorms, but since you're a special case, I've overruled that policy and granted the opening to you. You can move in today if you like. Miss Henderson is the dorm mom and she's expecting you. Just show up after school and get settled."

I'm flabbergasted. That's at least ten grand for the whole year!

Who was it? A guilty parent who knows their son hurt me?

Regardless of who it is, having housing here will make life much easier. I'll have a private room where I can study and focus. Sure, I'll miss Tyler, but I can visit him every afternoon, and it's not like we share a room or keep the same hours except for dinnertime anyway. The younger kids sleep on a different wing from the older kids at the group home.

I nod, moving on and focusing. "I mentioned my brother Tyler and his situation last week. He's six and has special needs, and the crowded school he's zoned for in Nashville isn't doing him any favors. They barely pay him any attention." I chew on my lips, recalling an incident last year where he actually left the school and wandered off near the river. It was a frantic four hours until the police found him on the shore tossing rocks into the water. What if he'd fallen in? What if someone had abducted him? It's a terrible part of town, addicts living in abandoned buildings on every corner. I'm used to those places; he's not. "I want him at the Camden elementary campus. I know you have a department devoted solely to helping kids with special needs."

He stands, walks around to his chair, and sits. "Your brother...that's an entirely new scholarship, and our board has already fulfilled our quota for the year. You, on the other hand, were a previous student here, one with incredible SAT scores."

My chest rises. I think about my brother, his small-for-his-age stature and slightly disjointed fingers. Diagnosed with fetal alcohol syndrome at birth, he has some developmental delays and attention issues. He's never going to be everything he can be at the place he's zoned for.

My resolve builds. "With all due respect, Mr. Trask, I'm not coming back unless he's enrolled. One of the nuns has agreed to drive him back and forth every day just like they did for me before I turned sixteen. He needs this, and he's not unruly. He's kind and sweet and smart, and all he needs is a place with good people to care about him. And he's an *orphan*. Our mother abandoned him." I hate using that word, but if it helps, I'll throw it around.

He grimaces, and I continue.

"I've already filled out all the paperwork." I pull it out of my backpack and set it on his desk. I copied it using the printer at Lou's diner. "There has to be a spot for him at the elementary campus. Just one." The thought of seeing Tyler actually get the services he deserves makes my palms sweat. I swallow, thinking fast, my mouth saying things I don't know I can deliver on. "Look, forget the scholarship for him. I...I can pay you back a little at a time. I have some savings and a job. I'm a great waitress. It won't be much, and you can charge me interest or whatever your administration prefers, but I swear, I will pay for his tuition, and then when I get to college, I can get another job, maybe one that pays more, and—"

"Ava." He cuts me off. "I can't give you a loan. To even enroll him with a payment plan, I'd need half of the money. Do you have fifteen thousand dollars?"

My gut clenches. "No."

"My dear..." His voice softens. "All monies for scholarships have already been allocated for this year. It's out of my hands."

I stand up. I didn't walk in here today just to be turned down so quickly. I'm prepared to fight. I look down at the Anaïs Nin quote on my backpack, words I put there with a sharpie. *Life shrinks or expands in proportion to one's courage.*

Never give up, Ava.

"Then ask that donor, or call the administration at the campus to check for sure, because I promise you this: if you don't find Tyler a spot on your roster, you're going to lose me. I can drive down the road to Morganville, and they'll roll out the red carpet. You and I both know my scores are some of the best this school has ever seen. You wouldn't have called me and *asked* me to come back if I wasn't poised to put Camden at the top of the list of best private schools in the state. Do you really want your biggest competition bragging about my scores?"

I'm bluffing about Morganville, who also happens to be our biggest football rival. The only reason I haven't approached them already is they don't have the special needs program Camden does.

"Plus, I came back here. *I came back.* Doesn't that look good for those future students who might be wondering about the *moral* quality of the young men you're educating here? Maybe there's a future football star out there wondering if Camden is the right place for him. Maybe there's a smart girl who can afford Camden, but she goes to Morganville instead because she's heard rumors." I hesitate. I do like him, always have, but... "I get requests for my story from reporters who don't have a thing to do with this town, who aren't afraid of the money here. Would you like to see me on some national morning show? I'd hate to draw unwanted attention back to Camden and perhaps suggest that this school and town didn't do enough for me." My voice cracks. It's a lie. There are no reporters. Nobody gave a shit about what happened to me.

He takes his glasses off and wipes at them slowly, a surprised expression on his lined face. His eyes crinkle as he squints at me. "I don't remember you being quite this...assertive."

"There's a lot that's different about me, Mr. Trask."

He runs his gaze over my hair, giving me a long, searching look and then a sigh and a nod. "I see that, and I'm sorry for it. Deeply."

Just give me what I need.

He smiles briefly. "Let me make some phone calls and get back to you by the end of the day. Will that work?"

Nodding, I move to the door. "He's the only thing I'm living for right now. If he's not near me, this"—I wave my hands around—"is a no-go. I won't sign anything."

He nods. "End of day, I'll let you know."

I walk out of the office and, lo and behold, Mrs. Carmichael has a pass ready.

I saunter out into the hall, feeling proud that Ava 2.0 does indeed have a backbone.

All I have is this one year to set everything right, and if I'm going to be miserable here, at least my brother will get a fresh start.

6

Class with Ava has me extra wired. Sitting next to her was intense, the smell of her hair when she moved, the way her lips puckered when she was pissed at me, and those eyes—don't even get me started. I don't like the heightened emotions she brings out in me, how she has this ability to goad me with just a look.

And when she touched me? Oh, fuck nah. I didn't dig that at all.

But right now it's my brother I'm thinking about. He missed gym class, and I was barely able to force myself to sit still until the bell rang before going to look for him.

I open the door to the workout room inside the field house and there he is, pounding his gloved fists into the professional sparring bag hanging from the ceiling. Sweat drips down his face as he pummels the bouncing apparatus again and again.

Eminem blares from his phone, and I jog over and turn it

off. He ignores me, face red and inscrutable as he continues his workout.

I cross my arms, watching him. "You missed the sprints Coach asked us to do on the field. We went over plays for our opening game and you weren't even there. Gym is still a class. You get a grade for it."

"I'm sure he won't mind me missing one day." He barks out a laugh. "But you...if you missed, there'd be hell to pay."

"We're a team, Dane. I just want you to stay focused. Football helps with your mood swings."

He shrugs, grabs a towel, and wipes his face.

Exasperation makes my voice rise. "You're acting off, almost—"

"Crazy?" His voice trembles around the edges as if he's fighting emotion.

I stiffen and narrow my eyes. "You're not crazy, but I don't think you've dealt with what happened at the bonfire party. I know it brings back all those memories of Mom—"

"Oh and you have? PLEASE. You're just as messed up as I am—you just hide it better. You run around in secret and dig up everyone's past. Tell me, does she know you know everything about her?"

I exhale. "No."

He studies me. "I don't know what you're doing with her, but it's weird. I don't trust it." He brushes past me to head to the showers, but I grab his arm.

"Forget her. I know you're using again, and I don't mean pot and Molly. You're doing the hard stuff—"

"So?" He tilts his head, and in that moment, his vulnerable expression reminds me of Mom's then I'm sucked back into the past and seeing her floating face down in our pool still wearing her nightgown. I swallow thickly, trying to push those images away, but little tendrils of those last memories sneak in until I can see Dane and me coming home from school, calling her name. Usually, she'd be at the piano, pretending to play even though I knew she'd grown to despise it, or she'd be knitting, not anything in particular, just a long, knotty rope of nothing.

The night before, she and Dad had had one of their epic arguments—he wanted her to go back to the mental health facility, had begged her to listen to reason while she screamed at him to just leave her and never come back. The reverberations of that suffering emotion had lingered even when we'd left that morning, us heading to school and Dad off to New York for a business deal.

I rub the scar on my face.

Dane flinches, watching me. "Stop thinking about Mom."

Ignoring that, I forge on, "Look, I can't walk in on you overdosed, you feel me? Not like Mom. You're the only person I care about, and if you leave me, who the hell is going to remind me that I'm a dick and shouldn't be keeping tabs on Ava Harris?"

He looks away from me.

I study his face. "Dane."

"Knox."

"Stop with the attitude."

He heaves out a sigh. "Why? Dad isn't coming back for another week, and don't you think he should be?"

I give him a quizzical look. Dad said he'd be back today.

He smirks. "Suzy sent the text. Guess you haven't checked your phone."

I exhale, dropping his arm. Suzy is our nanny and lives at

our house off and on, keeping an eye on us, cooking dinner and making sure the fridge is stocked and the grounds are taken care of. She's really more personal assistant than nanny now.

A flicker of defeat crosses his face. "I hate him, you know."

"No, you don't. He's our dad." And he's just as screwed up as we are. "If you're doing this to punish him, the only person you're hurting is you. And me." I sigh. "If Liam is encouraging you to do the hard stuff, he isn't your friend, Dane. Don't be stupid when it comes to him."

Dane's been in this strange spiral since the kegger. He was out of control that night, too, high as shit, all over Ava, dancing with her, his hands on her waist—

As if he knows what I'm thinking, he says, "I didn't do *that* to her, brother."

He may be screwed up, but underneath that screwed-up exterior, no is *no*.

He'd never assault a girl.

I know my own brother.

"Does seeing her bother you?" I ask. "Maybe you should talk to someone."

He gives me a look. "I'm not Mom. I'm fine. I have meds."

He's done therapy on and off, but now, I sense more is wrong, and I'm never wrong when it comes to him. And Ava is back.

"What do you remember from that night? Tell me again."

He shoves a hand through his hair. "Not much."

I've caught his little looks at her. I mean, we've all checked her out. It's hard *not* to notice her. She's devastatingly beautiful, although I don't think she knows it. There's no fake there. No expensive perfumes. No makeup except for those lips.

Maybe it's the way she smiles, just a little curve when she's amused, her lips pouty and full.

Dane shrugs. "I thought she was pretty, but she wasn't part of our crowd." A smirk flashes. "Plus, I avoid the nice girls—just like you. She's the one girl who never gave you a second glance. I like that about her for sure. Shit, the way she looked at you during class was the best laugh I've had in months. She hates your guts—"

"Let's not talk about it."

He raises an eyebrow. "What's up with that *she can sit with me* shit? Chance's going to be pissed."

He is. He turned his back to me in the hall after class and marched off.

"She isn't with him."

His eyes flare, and he laughs. "Well, well, well, is a girl finally going to ruin the best bromance at Camden?"

"I don't have a thing for Ava."

"Because you're a loyal sonofabitch."

"I don't want to be near Ava, and it has nothing to do with my best friend."

A sigh of relief comes from him. "Good. She's trouble. About that night...I woke up the next day at Liam's. I drank my ass off, but I would never..." He exhales. "There's no way I'd ever hurt a girl."

It's the same story he's had since day one.

He looks down. "You gonna give me a ride home after practice?"

His matching Mercedes is in the shop from a fender bender last week, driving too fast around a curve and hitting a guardrail, scratching the side. Liam was with him, and part of me wonders if he was high even then.

"You gonna go see Coach and tell him you're sorry you missed today?"

He looks at me over his shoulder, resignation on his face. "Yes. Happy? Right now I need to clean up and get to World History." He looks down at his watch. "I'm late already."

He disappears into the locker room, and I jog over to his backpack, unzipping it and riffling through the contents. There are no drugs, although I'm sure he knows how to hide them.

The question is, is he keeping other secrets from me too?

7

AVA

I'm giddy when the text comes in from Trask that there's a place for Tyler at the elementary campus and he's arranged for me to meet with the headmaster there this afternoon. Apparently one of their scholarship students transferred at the last minute when his parents moved. Do I believe it or did Trask buy my threats? I don't know, and shit, I don't care how it happened, but it did! As I walk down the hall, several students give me wary looks, and I just smile. *Yes, yes, yes!* My baby brother will be one block away from me during the day, and I can maybe even jog over there during lunch and—

No, I can't just walk into the school and watch him. They have rules. He'll be okay, he will, and he'll be getting the best services in the state. I giggle. I can even go to his parent-teacher meetings and soccer games.

I let out a deep breath as I step outside the entrance of Camden.

DAY ONE IS DONE!

LIFE DOES NOT SUCK!

All those good feelings deflate when I see Louise is sitting cock-eyed in the parking lot. Most of the cars have left since I stayed in the library for an hour studying until the crowds had dispersed. Dammit.

I walk up to the Jeep, and the left back tire is decidedly flat. I lean down and inspect it.

Well crap.

I eyeball the spare on the back and let out a sigh as I whip off my blazer and toss it inside along with my backpack.

Five minutes later, I've found the jack and have placed it in the right spot on the axle—according to the dusty manual from my glove box I briefly perused.

An idea hits, the memory of that letter left in my locker. I tug it out of my backpack and reread it again.

If you need ***anything****, I want to be there for you.* Ha! From a Shark. Let me tell you about a bridge I have for sale. Brooklyn Bridge? It will only cost you a little. Right, right.

I have to admit, it makes me curious. Oh, trust me, I don't buy for a second that a Shark might actually be my secret admirer—*utter bullshit*—but color me intrigued.

Showtime.

I type the digits into my phone and send a text.

Shark, got your letter. Who are you? How did you know my locker number?

The reply is immediate, and my hands clutch the phone.

Ava. I can't believe you texted me.

Wonders never cease. You left me your number, dumbass. WHO ARE YOU?

I saw you today and you took my breath away.

I blink rapidly.

LIAR. This is all a joke. A stupid one. Fuck off.

I believe you. About the party.

Not going there.

I fire off another text.

Well, Mr. Shark, I have a flat. I wonder who's responsible? I got new tires this summer. You think this is just a coincidence?

No reply.

I stuff my phone back in my blazer and run my eyes over Louise. Anger makes my fists curl as I inspect the tire. I expected the name-calling, the sneering glances, even Jolena getting in my face, but to damage my property—*oh, good grief, Ava, this cannot be unexpected. You knew when you agreed to this that the people you're dealing with believe they are above the law with their money and status—one of them got away with* rape.

A few minutes later, I'm turning the jack's rotatable clasp counterclockwise and lifting the deflated tire off the ground. It's hot as hell and sweat drips down my face.

"Trouble again, Tulip? It seems to follow you wherever you go," says the deep voice behind me, and I imagine what I must look like to him: butt high in the air, my body straining to turn the jack.

I keep working, never pausing. "Keep moving, QB1. Nothing to see here but a girl who knows how to change a tire. Quite fascinating for you, I'm sure." I blow at a piece of hair that's gotten in my eyes. "In fact, I'm quite unusual in your world, am I right? I'm nothing like those girls under the bleachers." I twist on the jack, still refusing to look at him. "I don't fuck guys under bleachers. I only sleep with guys who care about me, who want me *in spite of* where I come from."

I close my eyes in exasperation, glad he can't see my face.

What is it about him that pushes me to make these remarks?

Please leave. Just go away.

But he doesn't.

"How do you know about the bleachers?"

I heave out a curse word. Me and my big mouth.

He bends down next to me, looking at me, but I refuse to return the favor. I stare at my tire.

"Tulip? Have you...*seen me*? Or just heard rumors? Girls like to talk, but you don't really socialize with our crowd." There's a hint of embarrassment in his words; I expected gloating.

Curiosity makes me finally set the jack handle down and face him. His hair is damp from football practice and sticking up in all directions as if he left quickly without showering. He's standing with his legs apart, his muscled arms crossed, wearing a white vented jersey with the number one on it and tight red football pants.

"Please. Word gets around, Knox. We all know how you like it, but yes, I saw you—twice after a game, and once in the freaking middle of the school day when I went to the field to pick up my poms I'd left."

He frowns. "Three times? Shit." His body tenses. "I think the odds of you catching me three times are quite low."

Uh...

He studies my face, and I feel it getting warm. His eyes widen. "Did you *look* for me?"

"No! Stop it. That's just gross."

And it's also the truth.

After I saw him the first time, I slipped under the bleachers after a game on purpose just to see if he'd be there, and oh boy, was he. He was hot, his head thrown back, still in his uniform, sweat dripping down his face, his lips twisted as he plowed some girl from behind with the grace of a powerful animal, barely leashed and close to veering out of control. Wild. Intense.

He bites his lips, a red blush rising up from his throat to his cheeks. "Fuck."

I gape. "What? I'm shocked you're actually embarrassed. By the way, is it true you only do it from behind?"

He glowers at me as his hands clench, and a fissure of triumph runs through my body. I finally got to him.

"Ugh, you saw me!" His hands tug at his hair.

"Uh-huh."

He blows out a breath. "Look, erase that from your head."

Not likely.

"Just the thought of someone like you...seeing me like that..." He grimaces and scrubs his face. "I'm sorry you saw that."

"Who is *someone like me*?"

"No one. You're no one here."

Huh. Is that right?

I laugh bitterly. "Today when I said you'd peaked in high school and you're going to end up alone and crying and addicted to porn? I forgot to mention you'll probably spend most of your time drunk-dialing skanky ex-girlfriends and hookers. You won't ever play football in college. No one will want you. You suck. You can't even win a state championship, and trust me, this school demands one. The rumor is I really screwed up last year's season. Not sorry."

I expect him to get pissed.

"Actually, you did get in my head pretty good this morning." He sighs. "But if you tell anyone that, I'll call you a liar."

I do a little clap. "Ohhhh, I screwed with the great Knox Grayson. This moment is sweet! Do I get a medal? How about a mention in the yearbook? Oh, how about an honorary sash to wear? I'll have it say *Beat Knox At His Own Game*."

He opens his mouth and then closes it.

"What?" I ask.

"Nothing."

"What?" I snap.

He grimaces. "You really should stay away from me, Tulip. You shouldn't have sat next to me. I don't want to be your friend."

"Huh. You offered, remember? Walk away then. Get on with it, Shark. I didn't ask you to stop and talk to me. Shoo."

He studies me, unmoving. A gust of wind catches his hair, moving it over his scar, and he brushes at it, never dropping those smoky eyes from my face. The silence and tension builds between us, and I...I find that it's more than just disliking him. It's electric, thrumming through my veins.

I shrug it off. "Besides, I'm not afraid to sit next to you. I've done self-defense training recently, and honestly, I *can* hurt you if I want to. Groin area. Throat punch. There's even a special headlock where you pass out."

My words bother him, and he grimaces then looks away from me. "I didn't hurt you that night."

I know. He wasn't even there. He left early with Tawny.

I'll kill him with my bare hands.

But his brother...

He reaches down and rubs his hands across the rubber. "Slow leak?"

I pause and wipe at the sweat on my brow. "You think? Or did someone do it on purpose?"

His thumb presses against a spot on the tire, his eyes studying the wheel as if it's a puzzle. "Puncture, and not a nail. Looks like someone sliced it."

I exhale. I already saw the cut. "Brilliant deduction, Sherlock. It doesn't matter. Besides, I have a spare, and I know how to change a tire."

"Let me do it."

"I don't need you to help me, okay? I can *save* myself. Been doing it all my life."

"I know you can save yourself."

"You don't know anything about me!" I sigh, frustrated. I don't want him here. "Why are you being nice, Knox? You don't want to be my friend!"

His eyes meet mine, searching my face. "Do you need a reason right now—in this heat?"

A bead of sweat slides down my throat. His eyes watch it.

"Fine," I say. "You want to take the spare down from the back? Also, do you happen to have a lug wrench in your car? I do, but mine's all rusted and..."

Before I can finish, he's already jogging over to a black Mercedes-Benz SUV, popping the back, and riffling through it. He holds up a sparkly new wrench and runs back over. I try really hard to not notice how gorgeous he is.

He bends down next to me. "First, let's get the nuts off."

I almost say *That's what she said*, but then I remember who he is—not my friend—and stop.

Bending down with him, I watch as he removes the last nut, slips the tire off, and puts the spare on, the tightly roped muscles of his forearms straining as he lifts and secures it. He glances up, catching my eyes. "Why are you smiling?"

"I'm smirking in a condescending way—big difference. Just enjoying the sight of Cold and Evil doing hard work." I grab the flat tire and attach it to the back of my Jeep. He stands, and I feel the heat of his gaze watching me.

Knox Grayson never paid me much attention in the years I went here, and the truth is, I'm a bit discombobulated by his nearness—in class today, in the office, and right now.

I turn and we're just...staring at each other. More of that stupid tension rises.

A prickle of awareness goes down my spine, as if somehow he knows what I'm thinking.

He's the first to break our concentration. With one step, he's closer to me. Reaching out, he fingers a piece of hair that was in my eyes and puts it behind my ear.

First I freeze.

Then I take a step back. "Don't do that," I snap, frowning.

"You touched me in class. I owed you."

I put my hands on my hips. "I can't figure you out. I keep seeing and talking to you today."

He shoves at his hair. "You interested in me? Get in line. Every single girl here knows what I'm about." His eyes capture mine and he drags a finger down his scar. "They're either repulsed by this or they're fascinated. Which are you?"

I squint at him, waiting for that tiny bit of fear I felt from him last year to come back. It doesn't. "Love 'em and leave 'em, right?"

He shrugs nonchalantly, and my eyes follow the movement of his broad shoulders.

"How'd you get that scar anyway?"

His face tightens, and I see a glimpse of pain before it disappears so quickly I wonder if it was ever really there.

"It's not jagged. A nice, clean cut, almost like a knife. Did you do it?"

"No!" He flushes, glaring at me. "Just shut up about it."

Ah, the pain of that scar still rankles.

One more thing to file away in the Knox Grayson dossier.

"Fine, it's a secret. I have one on my inner thigh from a fork. Got it from the only foster home I stayed at. There was an older girl who didn't want me sleeping in her room. I was ten. See?" I slightly lift up my skirt, showing him the stretched-out mark, which is about the size of my pinkie. "I slept with a rock under my pillow after that."

He moves his gaze up slowly, landing on my face. "Did she ever try it again?"

"No, but I was ready. I would have done whatever it took to keep her away from me."

"Fierce little thing."

I snap my teeth at him and his lips twitch.

"Don't laugh at me unless you want me to go into more excruciating detail about your sad, sad future."

He raises an eyebrow. "Damn. Can't help it. You're—"

Whatever he was about to say is cut off.

"Knox, you look like a mechanic with that wrench in your hand. Nice. Let me snap a pic for posterity," says a voice behind us.

My breath hitches. I flip around and chills dance down my spine. It's Dane who's spoken, and with him are Chance and Liam. Dane takes his phone out of his pocket and takes a picture of us.

Chance has that stricken look on his face again, like this morning.

Liam laughs and I focus on the big footballer. His white hair is still long in the front with those stupid swooping bangs. He smirks at me, meeting my gaze, and I shiver. It's the first time we've come face-to-face all day, and I'm extra glad our schedules don't overlap.

Chance sends an angry look at Knox, his jawline grinding. "Dude, we're going to The Coffee Bean to hang. Aren't you coming?" he asks, his voice accusatory, his attention bouncing from me to Knox.

Chance looks almost...

Acting out of instinct, I flip my hair out of my face, and his eyes follow the movement, a hungry look there.

I straighten my shoulders, adjusting my white shirt, which is noticeably sticking to my skin in the heat. And, guess what—Chance's gaze goes there too, lingering on my chest.

Well, well.

My anger stirs. He has the nerve to look at me as if he wants me, yet he called me a slut? Out of *everyone* here, he should have believed me.

"Yeah, unless you're too busy helping *her*," Liam adds snidely.

Knox gives me a glance then looks back at them. "Nah, I have studying to do. You do too, Dane."

Dane sweeps his eyes over me, a knowing smile on his face. "Got to admit, this moment is priceless though. Knox and Ava. Ava and Knox. How does that sound, Chance? Has quite the ring to it, doesn't it?"

Chance flushes red.

"Shut the fuck up," Knox says sharply.

Dane pulls his hair out of the manbun he has it in and shakes it out, the strands brushing his jersey. He points those eyes that are so much like Knox's at me. "Wanna join us, Ava? I'll buy you whatever you want if you don't have the money."

Oh, what a little prick. My hands fist.

"What the hell, Dane?" Chance says. "Be serious!"

"Yeah, babe," Liam adds. "Maybe we can talk about that video of you dancing. Do you remember that? You've got some sweet moves on you, I'll give you that—"

"That's enough!" Knox roars.

There's silence, and my heart races.

There's an undercurrent of tension between them all, and part of me senses it may not just be about me—but maybe it is? Shit, of course it is. Last year their team sucked and they all blame me.

I lick my lips nervously. Here I am, alone in a school parking lot with four of the football players who were at that party, and as much as I want to be cool, my hands tremble—

"Yo, Ava! You good?"

I start when Wyatt pulls up in a souped-up black Chevelle with a hot pink stripe down the hood, rap music blaring and the motor so loud I'm surprised I didn't hear the vehicle approaching.

We all turn to look at him. He's wearing a Camden baseball hat and a wide grin.

Maybe it's something he sees on my face, because he turns his car off and gets out, sauntering over to us.

He tosses a casual arm around my shoulders as if we've been friends forever. "You doing good, locker neighbor?"

Locka neigbah. He scans his eyes over the group and lingers on the jack I still haven't put away. "You need a ride?"

"I'm good, just had a flat. Someone cut my tire. Knox helped me change it."

Liam laughs, quickly covering it with his hand when Knox scowls.

Wyatt narrows his eyes at Liam then looks at me. "Heard you got into Arlington Dorm. Saw your name on the resident list when I checked in after school. Looks like we'll be living together—well, on different floors. They tend to keep the boys separate from the girls, although you are welcome to drop by my room any time. I make a mean bowl of popcorn."

"Yeah, I haven't had a chance to check in. I still have some errands to run." I keep my eyes on his face because panic flutters, lingering just under the surface.

His arm tightens around me. "I'll help you move in. It's furnished already, but for the love of God, bring your own sheets 'cause theirs are rough as hell."

"Yeah, okay." I bet my sheets would horrify him too. "I have to drive back to Nashville and grab some things then meet someone, so I'll be there later."

"I'm out of here," Chance growls, his shoulders tight with tension as he stalks off toward an Escalade several spots away.

"Yeah, I'm bored already," Liam adds before following him.

Dane makes to follow them, but Knox grabs his jersey and snaps him back. Dane doesn't put up much of a fight and I hear Knox muttering under his breath, words I can't hear. Dane settles for staring at the ground.

Chance and Liam get inside the black Escalade and peel out.

Relief hits me. Two down.

Wyatt's giving me directions to the dorm and tips on parking when Knox's voice cuts in, his tone soft. "Ava, if you're okay, I'll go."

I glance at him, trying to maintain a neutral expression. "I'm fine. Thank you for the help."

He's still holding his wrench, and his face...it's not shuttered this time. In fact, it's layered in emotion as he watches me with Wyatt. "Take care of her at that dorm, will you?" he says to him.

"She's in the best of hands," Wyatt murmurs.

He and Wyatt exchange a long look, then Knox nods and gives me one last glance, his face back to stone.

He and Dane walk over to his car, their heads close as they talk.

Once they've pulled out, I turn to Wyatt, who's now inspecting my new tire. He tells me I'll need to get a new one because the spare sucks. Yeah, I know.

"You know the football players well?"

He shrugs, a *meh* expression on his face. "I play baseball, and jocks tend to hang out. We've been to a few parties together, but I ain't like them, see. I'm no Shark." *Shak.* He breaks out another grin. "Stupid name, right? I mean our mascot is the Dragons. I'm still considered new here, and they don't like outsiders, but when you're me, you don't give a fuck."

I study that eyebrow piercing, the sleeve of tattoos on his forearm, a mix of hummingbirds and roses intermingled. Recognition hits.

"Oh my God! You're Wyatt Carrington! Your dad—your dad's the lead singer of the Snowballs, right? Indie band from

Boston? Started his career as a model and switched to music back in the nineties?" Serious drug problems, lots of rehab...

A slow blush starts up his neck. "Most people don't recognize me until I tell them—"

"No, you look just like him. Geeze. I love their music. How did you end up in Sugarwood?"

"My mom's originally from Nashville. She went here. My parents divorced and I came with her last year when she moved to Franklin, Tennessee. It's about an hour from here, so I was able to get a dorm."

"Ah, I'm sorry about your parents."

He shrugs. "Dude, my dad was a serial cheater—and the drugs? I'm shocked he's still alive. I don't blame her."

"So are you in cultural shock here in the South?"

"I don't miss the cold weather, but the southern accents crack me up." He smirks.

"Have you listened to your accent?" I laugh. "Hey, thanks for being nice to me this morning. I wasn't ready for it. First day jitters."

He gives me a fist bump. "We'll be friends if you tell me you're a Red Sox fan? Yes?"

"Is that the sport with a long stick? I don't know jack about baseball."

"I can live with that. Just don't ever bring up the Yankees and we're golden."

I laugh, then my eyes follow Knox's flashy car as it pulls out onto the highway. I chew on my lips. "Hey, what do you think about Knox Grayson?"

Wyatt follows my gaze then grins wistfully. "I think he's hot. That tight body and those guns on his arms... If only he went that way. Damn shame."

My eyes bug out. "Wait...what?"

He chuckles then gets going with a full-blown laugh, slapping his leg. "Ava, you should see your face. I'm gay. Everyone knows."

I shake my head. "But...you're so..."

"Masculine? Athletic?"

I giggle. "Yeah, okay, sure, all that. I didn't mean to stereotype. My bad." I pause. "Thanks again for stopping."

He strikes a pose, bending his wrist and totally putting on airs. "Ignore those assholes, darling, because we're going to be great friends."

A new friend.

"Also, I can't find you on Instagram, Twitter, Facebook—nothing. Where do you social?"

I roll my eyes. "I deleted everything when I got tagged in a ton of negative comments about the party."

He takes that in, mulls it over. "Fuck that. Forget them."

I smile. "Hey, you got any musical talent like your dad?"

"I play guitar like a madman."

"I sing. Wanna teach me how to play sometime?"

"Oh, yeah, locker neighbor." When he grins, his face is open and full of sincerity, and a warm feeling grows in my chest.

It's not a bad end to the day at all.

But tomorrow will be here soon, and I'll have to start all over again.

8

I twitch in my bed. I'm in that weird half-awake/half-asleep state where it feels like what's happening in your head might be real even though the logical side of you knows nightmares can't actually come to life.

But maybe they can.

Just wake up and it will all be over.

Just wake up, wake up, wake up...

Fresh from school, I dash into the kitchen and Mom is cooking, and heck yeah, I feel good. Man, I've missed seeing her. She bakes the best bread. Makes the sweetest lemonade. She's so pretty, long dark hair and hazel eyes. And when she smiles, it makes you feel like the king of the world.

You're not her favorite, *a voice says, right here in the middle of the kitchen, but I already know that and I brush it away. Doesn't matter. She's my mom.*

I start talking, telling her about school and football and what a kickass year I'm going to have—

Why is she wearing her nightgown?

Why is she wet?

Settling in on the barstool across from her, I lean in close and snag a piece of the bread she's baked.

"Roast?" I ask.

Her lowered head doesn't rise from the cutting board. She keeps making those careful cuts, the blade sharp as it glints under the kitchen lights.

Water drips from her hair onto the counter.

"You're wet. Let me get a towel."

She doesn't take the towel from me when I bring it over.

"We should play piano tonight," I say. "Like we used to."

Nothing.

She isn't right.

She's not.

She doesn't even know I'm here.

Fear and dread mix, clinging to me, clogging up my throat at some barely there tangible truth that I know is right there, but I can't seem to grasp it.

"I've MISSED you," I call out desperately.

Slice. Slice. Slice—

SOMETHING SHAKES me and I hear yelling.

"—Knox! Knox! Stop! Wake up!"

"What?" I mutter groggily.

Dane crouches next to my bed, bent over and hovering.

"Did I call out?" I push up to the pillows.

He stares at me, sticking his hands in his hair. "Dude, you're shouting the house down! I had to wake you up."

"Nightmare." I swallow thickly.

He crosses his arms. "Must have been a doozy." He exhales. "Move over."

"What? Why?" I squint, staring up at him. My head is still on Mom. I saw her...I saw her. I haven't dreamed about her in a long time, and she was still alive to me for just a few seconds.

"Come on, man. I'm sleeping in your big-ass bed with you and when you start that yelling, I'm going to smack your face, so think about that, huh?"

I huff out a laugh. "In my bed?"

"Are you dumb? Wake up and smell the twin brother instincts. YES. I'm not coming in here again, and if I'm here, you won't do it."

"How do you know?"

"Just do." He shrugs, giving up on me moving over, and stalks over to the other side of the bed then flops down.

It's a king-sized bed, so there's room for both of us. Meh, I can't complain. The company might be nice.

Earlier, we came home to an empty house. Suzy had already left for the night and Dane and I had dinner in front of the TV in the den, salmon and grilled asparagus she'd made. We didn't talk much except about homework and practice. I was hiding that I was pissed at Dad for not being here. He was quiet for other reasons. At eleven, I finished loading the dishwasher, turned on the alarms, flicked off the lights, and we crashed, each of us in our respective bedroom. The big house was deathly quiet as we went up the stairs. I wish we'd move to a different house and escape all these memories.

"What was your dream about?" he asks.

"Nothing."

He sighs. "Yeah, right."

The dream—shit, it reminds me that I was never Mom's favorite. You could see it in her eyes when she looked at Dane, the affection and affinity. Maybe she just thought I didn't need as much. Once at the park when we were small, another kid pushed Dane off the ladder to the slide, and he took a tumble and hit his head on a rock. "*Why did you let them hurt him? You're the strong one*!" she yelled at me. I went back to the slide, found that kid, and punched him in the nose.

Anything to win her heart.

"We haven't slept together in a long time," I say bemusedly, pushing those thoughts away and throwing him one of the pillows I keep mostly on my side.

"Yeah." He stares up at the ceiling for a moment. "Knox?"

"Yeah?"

"I've been having bad dreams too. Ever since that kegger."

My chest feels tight, and I roll over and look at him. "You never mentioned it before."

He sighs and rubs his eyes.

"What about?"

He swallows. "I gave Ava shit today, and I shouldn't have, but she messes with my head."

I know.

"What specifically happens in your dreams?"

His jaw tightens. He crosses his arms, which looks funny while he's lying down.

Unease gathers and builds in my gut. "Dane. Just look at me. I'm your brother. No matter what you tell me, that will never change."

He shows me his face and it's tortured, his mouth turned down, his forehead creased. "Last week, I dreamed I was in those woods *with her*."

Apprehension ratchets up higher, but I keep my face blank. "Why would you dream that? You weren't there. You left with Liam."

"I don't know why." His eyes cloud over. "It freaks me out."

"Are you hurting her in your dream?"

He shakes his head. "No, but I'm there, and it's just me and her alone. It's dark and she's on the ground. I'm standing over her and her eyes open and she screams. Then I wake up. I wish Dad had never told us about her police report. Maybe that's it. Or maybe it's not, and I was there—" A long gust comes out of him. "What the fuck is wrong with me?"

"You weren't there. And don't do drugs, asshole."

He sighs, avoiding my gaze again. "Can we turn on the TV? Maybe watch some football or something?"

"Sure." I click on the remote and bring up a game. I have noticed he's been sleeping with his TV on for a while, and I get the feeling he's up a lot more than I realize. "You want a glass of water too? Maybe a blankie or a teddy bear?"

He tries to grin. "Well, if you're getting up, I'll take some water."

I roll my eyes and throw the cover off, pad into the bathroom, and pour two cups of water. I walk back over, giving one to him and keeping one for me.

"Cheers," I say dryly.

"To a good football season. It's your year, man," he adds.

"Mmmm."

He drinks his, sets it on the nightstand, and plops back down on his side. "We can't tell anyone we slept in the same bed. You feel me?"

"This never happened." I lie down next to him.

"But if that dream of mine comes back, or yours...well..."

I turn on my side, pulling the covers up. "You can sleep with me whenever you want, bro."

"It doesn't make me a pussy," he mutters.

I laugh. "I never said it did."

"You're thinking it."

"Sounds to me like you're trying to convince yourself. Go to sleep."

The game playing on the TV casts dark shadows on the wall behind me and I watch them. Still restless from the dream, my head wanders to how badly I want out of this town. Out of this empty, lonely house.

And Dane...wherever I end up, I'll always take care of him, just like Mom wanted.

Ava dances in my mind, the way her shirt clung to those lush curves today—

Flipping over, I punch my pillow and shut those thoughts down.

A few minutes later: "Knox?"

"Yeah?"

"You're all I've got in the world, man."

You're all I've got in the world. Dane-speak for *I love you.*

I reach over and take his hand for a second. "Me too. Now go to sleep."

~

Nobody's happy at six o'clock in the morning, but excitement builds inside me. Early morning practices? Bring it. Football cuts through the emptiness, and shit, I need it.

I want to play in college, but there aren't a lot of scouts beating down my door. Last year we sucked, losing five games straight by the end of the season, our worst record in forty years.

Coach Williams personally questioned all of us about the kegger, but with no proof, the assault was forgotten as the weeks went on. By the time Christmas rolled around, no one talked about her except in whispers.

Is it because our football team is on a shiny gold pedestal?

Is it because most of this town is run by our fathers?

Yeah. All of that.

Dane picks up a ball and we pass it back and forth to warm up.

I feel a bump in my back and turn to see Chance walking up with Liam. He gives me a thumbs-up, and I give him a nod, feeling relieved. Guess he's over seeing me with Ava.

Both of them are holding to-go coffees.

Coach, a tall burly man with bushy eyebrows, finishes making notes on his clipboard about who has shown up. "Knox, take the offense and run sprints then we'll line up for scrimmage. No pads or helmets. Limited contact." He sweeps his eyes over us, including Liam. "Keep it clean today, boys."

Yeah, yesterday, there was some pushing and shoving, mostly between the offense and defense.

The offense gathers around, Dane and Chance on either side of me. Dane is the tight end and Chance is my go-to wide receiver. "You heard him—put your pussy coffees down and let's get to work." Chance rolls his eyes but dashes off to set his cup on the bench. "Ten sprints to the thirty and back, then line up on me. Let's kick some defense ass today, got it?" We all clap.

Under the rising sun, I finish my sprints first with Dane and Chance. We jog up to the fifty-yard line to wait.

Liam and a few of the other defensive players make their way over, and Liam opens his mouth. "What's up with you and Ava yesterday? You two buddies now?"

"You don't know anything about what happened to her tire, do you?" I reply.

He laughs. "If I did, I wouldn't tell. I'm no snitch like Ava is."

"Don't say her name again," I say, cracking my neck. "It doesn't belong here on the field. Brand new year."

"You giving me orders?"

I straighten my shoulders. "I'm the captain. I know what's best for our team."

He nods, and for a second I think he's going to let it drop, but then his jaw pops. "She's back and it brings that shit up again. I didn't appreciate police officers interviewing me like I was a suspect last fall. What if they start doing that again, huh?"

"Your dad's the mayor—I think you're covered." Chance smirks.

"Yeah, I don't want any questions either," someone grumbles, but I don't see who it is.

"—that's what I'm saying," comes from another.

Liam sends whoever said it a chin nod then looks back at me. "You act like you're on *Law & Order* when it comes to her and it's annoying as fuck. First, you came to all of us last year like you suspected *us*. Now you're changing her tire? Bullshit.

If you're hot for her, just bang her like you do every other girl and get back to being our teammate."

My fists curl, and I know I need to focus on building this team back up—without discussing Ava—but I can't stop myself from commenting. "*Something* happened to her, and the person who did it is one of us or a senior from last year," I say, reaching for the pretense of diplomacy by including them. We only had four seniors last year and only two of them showed up at the party. One left early with his girlfriend, and the other guy ended up passed out in the back of another player's truck and was driven home before things really got going.

Some of the guys around me nod in agreement, their faces set.

"We should put it behind us," says a junior from the offense.

But some of them give me hard, heavy-lidded looks. Brandon, another defensive player, is one of them. With carrot-colored hair and brittle dark eyes, he's in line to take Liam's place after he graduates.

He steps forward and nods his head toward Liam. "I'm with him. I don't want any questions either, not from the police and not from you. She lied to cover up cheating on Chance. Who knows who it was, but none of us did anything illegal."

Cheating on Chance? A scoff comes out of me. Shaking my head, I recall a few times when I wanted her to, when I looked at her and—

Glancing at Chance, I see he's no help, not with his eyes on the ground.

I shouldn't react. Nope. I should just stop talking, put this aside, and focus on playing the game.

"I don't even know who you are," Liam grunts. "She's chum. She's Shark bait. She's nothing."

"You brought her up, not me." My voice is soft.

Dane jostles against me. "Dude. Let's play football."

Liam barks out a rough laugh. "That shadow of doubt hangs over all of us, even you. You think I don't see the way some of the teachers look at us? The headmaster?" His face hardens. "Even Jolena looks at me different."

I shrug. "I doubt you need to worry about Ava showing up to anymore of our parties."

Liam locks eyes with me. "If she does, I figure I'm owed one tussle in the woods. If I'm going to be accused of something, I should at least get the chance to actually enjoy it." He grabs his crotch and grins. "She'll scream for more like every other girl."

Everyone on the team freezes, and I...I feel like someone blindsided me with a two-by-four.

My right fist connects with Liam's face. His head snaps back but his surprised eyes never leave mine. Rage colors his face and his punch comes quick and accurate, hitting me in the eye before I can dip down. I can't even feel it. *Oh, hell yeah, bring it.* I've been itching to hit him forever. I think about the first time I saw him and Dane snorting coke at one of Liam's barn parties. We got into a scuffle then, but I didn't hit him nearly enough—

He shoves at my chest, trying to push me away, but I grab his shirt to pull him back and slam my fist into his eye.

"Stop!" Chance jumps between us, but I wrestle out of his grasp and face off with Liam again.

I spit. "Get in line like everyone else and follow the rules *I* set."

"You hit me first! Some captain you are," he calls out, his chest puffing up.

"Stop, please!" Dane begs, clutching my arms as some of the defensive players pull Liam away.

I jerk out of his hold and nod my head at Liam. "And you call him your best friend? Did you not *hear* what he said?"

I'm talking about Mom and what she went through, but they don't know what broke her in the end, and their eyes bounce back and forth between us, watching Dane pale.

"And you," I say, spinning to Chance. "She cared about you," I growl. "And she doesn't lie. She walked back in here because she's better than you...and me." I tug at my jersey and let it pop. "How does it feel to know you turned your back on a girl like *her*? Wake up, Chance."

His mouth gapes. He's stunned. "Knox..."

"Everything okay, boys?" Coach's voice cuts into the tension as he approaches us.

A long exhalation comes from my chest.

I'm losing it, but I can't seem to stop myself from caring. I've kept this anger and resentment bottled up for months, thinking I had control of it, but since she came back...*fuck.*

Coach looks at all of us warily. "No more bullshit. If you want to be a team, you need to start acting like one." He pauses. "If this is about last year, we're past that. Got it?"

I glare at Liam.

"Knox! Do you want a championship this year or not?" Coach touches my arm and focuses a hard glance on my face.

"Yes, sir." I nod, slowly forcing my shoulders to loosen.

I turn steely eyes on Liam, smirking at the swelling I see

under his left eye. Figure I'll have one to match. I lean over to him, keeping my voice low. "I mean it. Say her name again and I'll fucking hurt you."

Anger colors his face and he sneers but can't hold my gaze.

That's right, asshole. Be scared.

9

AVA

Tyler looks up at me with wary blue eyes, and I read the nervousness there. I smile down at him. On the other side is Sister Margaret, holding his other hand.

"W-Will they like me?" he asks as we walk into the elementary campus of Camden and head toward the sign that points to the headmaster's office. Dr. Rivers, a lady I researched online, appears to be well-educated and admired by colleagues and former students here. I met with her yesterday after school, and she's expecting us. I see her down the hall, approaching from her office. I look back down at Tyler. Geeze, he's so small compared to kids his own age. Like many children with FAS, he has small eyes, thin lips, and a small upturned nose. He's holding his backpack with fingers that are disjointed and knotty, not that it holds him back. He's a normal rambunctious kid who loves sports, especially running. His little legs are quick, and he can move like the wind. He does have slight hearing loss and thick wraparound glasses sit perched on his nose, but thankfully he was spared heart or kidney defects.

I lean down until I'm at eye level. "You better believe it. Plus, you're brave."

"Like when Luke and Han take down the Death Star?"

I laugh. "Just like that. They were just like you once, little but strong."

"Will I get a medal like they did? Will people clap and stuff?"

"A gold star for sure, and I'm always cheering for you."

He nods. "Okay, I'll do it."

I sigh. Dang, I'm going to miss seeing him at the group home. "If you want, you can spend the night with me in my dorm and I can bring you to school tomorrow?" Sisters of Charity isn't run by the state of Tennessee, and thankfully there's some leeway in the group home's rules. I'm eighteen and his sister; they've agreed to let me sign him out for little excursions before. I'm not actually sure if he can stay the night with me, but I glance up at Sister Margaret and she nods.

I straighten the collar on his little blazer, which I picked up yesterday. Dr. Rivers stayed late for me, which was nice of her.

He bites on his fingernails. "Maybe later I'll stay over. I-I like to sleep in my own bed. And Axel is there. He might miss me."

I smile. Of course. That's his home, and Axel is his best friend.

"Okay, that's cool. We can go get an ice cream later this afternoon and you can tell me all about your day."

He nods.

"Be good, okay? No darting off from your teachers, bozo. I mean it."

He looks away from me, that look of stubbornness I know he gets from me growing on his face. "Th-They better be nice to me or I'll cut their balls off and stuff them down their throats."

Sister Margaret rolls her eyes.

"You can't say those things here."

"You say them," he replies.

Sister Margaret gives me side-eye.

I hold my hands out. What does she expect? I was shuffled between tents under the bridge, a foster home, shelters, and inner-city apartments.

Tyler looks up at me. "I-I could have said *fucking* balls, so it's not a bad word. Boys have balls. And a dick—"

I hold my hand up. "Nope. Can't say that word either. School is a lot like Mass, okay? We have to be respectful."

The nun shakes her head, but I swear I see her lips twitch.

I ruffle his hair. "Did you know they have a killer art department here? Check out that mural. It was done by students."

He looks to where I'm pointing, an awed expression growing on his face. He adores drawing.

Dr. Rivers has reached us, wearing a smile, and I squeeze his thin shoulders. Tall and attractive, she's dressed in a cream suit, her hair up in a sleek chignon. She's here to greet us, which is noteworthy. I've never even been able to even talk on the phone with any of the administrators at Tyler's old school.

My heart clutches, and hope—that thing that's been so delicate and tenuous with me for months—grows a little stronger as I watch her bend down and greet him then offer to show him to his class.

She stands back up. “Tyler’s going to have a fantastic day, I assure you, and I have your number in case we need you.” She looks at Sister Margaret and nods. “We have the group home’s number as well. Everything’s all set.” She pauses. “Also, congratulations on getting him enrolled. Headmaster Trask pulled quite a few strings to get everything arranged.”

Good.

She smiles. “He’s going to fall in love with his teachers.”

That well of emotion pulls at me again, making my throat tighten. I look around at the artwork, the plush furniture I can see inside the classrooms, the excited faces of teachers as they greet each student. I can’t be his real mom, but I can do this. I can give him a good start. “Thank you.”

She nods and begins to walk with Tyler down the hall.

He sends me a final wave then gets distracted by a little girl who runs up to him, takes his other hand, and leads him off along with Dr. Rivers.

I did the right thing by coming back to Camden. *I did.* He’s going to be okay.

10

AVA

"Holy cow. That's quite a shiner you've got there, Cold and Evil," are the first words out of my mouth when I take my seat next to Knox in class. I barely made it here after dropping Tyler off, but the high school starts half an hour later than the elementary campus, so I had enough time. Even sat in my car for five minutes, waiting until the last second to get out. Still, I'm not late, and Mrs. White isn't even standing at the podium yet.

My seat is a mere few inches from his, and I'm aware of the heat from his leg next to mine.

Knox eases away from me, putting more distance there, giving me a half-shrug as he keeps his gaze on his laptop. He's erecting a force field. A big one.

It makes me want to tear it down, zap it with a ray-gun, peel back the layers, and see what's underneath.

"If you don't want to talk, all you have to say is *Be quiet, Ava* in that deep voice of yours."

Dang, why did I have to say *deep*—like I've noticed what his voice sounds like.

He taps his fingers on the top of his thigh.

I've never seen someone so self-contained. Along with that force field, he's got a few armored tanks set up on the perimeter when it comes to me. Locked down with cannons itching to fire.

Do not engage with Ava, they seem to declare.

It's always been that way with him when it comes to me.

Except for that *one* time...

"Come on, Ava, let's go upstairs to my room." Chance breathes in my ear. His hands are on my ass, palming me as we dance.

Loud music blares from speakers set up around his den. His parents are out of town for Labor Day. It's not a Shark party, like their postgame keggers with only football players and whoever they invite, but more of an all the popular kids from Camden shindig. A few people from Hampton High. Some townies.

"Be mine for real, baby." His voice slurs.

"You're drunk."

"So? Everyone is."

"I'm not." Nerves hit me. Maybe I should be—to fit in. Only, I don't like alcohol and what it does to a person.

People move around us, dancing slow, lost in the deep thump of the vibrating bass. A couple make out on the couch. Liam has Jolena pressed against the wall in an alcove in the foyer, her hands pinned above her head as he kisses her. She hooks a leg around him and tugs him closer. His hands lift her skirt up from behind and I tear my eyes off them.

Chance kisses me as his hands slip under my peasant blouse and brush against my stomach. "Babe, you feel so good. I promise I'll go easy."

I glance around.

Nobody is looking at us.

Except for him.

Knox.

He isn't dancing, but unbidden, my eyes keep going back to him, keeping tabs as he sits on a loveseat in a dark corner, his position separate from the rest of the crowd. His figure is shadowy, but the broad shoulders and muscled arms splayed out along the top of the seat give him away. I know he's there; I feel the menace emanating from him, like a king watching his subjects. There's a pretty girl standing behind him, someone random. I don't know her. She has her hands in his hair, scraping her nails over his scalp then drifting down and massaging his neck and shoulders, the movement of her languid ministrations sensual and slow, sliding from his silky hair to his chest. Another girl sits at his feet and rubs his thighs, her hands caressing. Don't know her either.

With a sly look up at him, she moves to the crotch of his jeans.

My heart races, and it has nothing to do with Chance's fingers caressing my skin. I barely notice.

His voice groans. "Don't you want me, Ava?" He doesn't wait for me to answer, picking me up and sitting with me on the couch, maneuvering me so I straddle him.

I still see Knox.

He won't take his eyes off me.

I watch with fascination as Knox bites his lower lip, digging in deep, so hard I expect to see blood bloom there.

I return his glance, letting him see that no, I haven't forgotten seeing him nearly naked in that locker room, and yes, somehow he's crawled inside me, sitting behind me in class, those long looks he gives me at lunch when I sit next to Chance.

The girl asks him something and I wish I could hear what she says, but I figure it out when she unzips his jeans and her head lowers.

My stomach drops.

"What are you doing?" Chance asks when I jump up off the couch. My chest rises and I put my hand on my flushed cheeks. I lift my eyes to Knox, and he's a statue, body tense, watching me.

"Bathroom," I mumble, slipping away from his hands when he reaches out to grab me.

"Babe—"

"Give me a few minutes," I say firmly then slide farther away from him, jostling between people dancing.

I march past Knox with my hands clenched, my face turned from him so I can't see his expression, so he doesn't know he's in my head instead of Chance.

What is wrong with me?

Thank goodness the bathroom down the hall is empty. I dart inside and stand for a moment and stare at myself in the mirror. I should leave. I should just walk out the front door of this house and go back to the group home, but my car isn't here. I rode with Piper and she's out there having a good time. Last time I saw her, she was making out with a guy from Hampton High.

"I just need a minute," I mutter to myself in the mirror. I shove the shower curtain to the side and step into the pristine clawfoot tub, jerking the curtain back into place. Maybe, just maybe, if I hide here long enough, the party will end, Knox will leave, and Piper and I will go back to her house.

I lean back against the rim of the tub and will my body to relax.

Fat chance of that when the door opens. Dang it—I didn't lock it.

Peeking out around the edge of the curtain, I see Knox leaning against the door, his head thrown back, his breathing heavy. My eyes search for the girls from the den. They aren't here. My lip curls. Well, that blowjob didn't take long.

Peeking, I watch as he scrubs his face and walks to the sink, turns on the cold water, and splashes his face. Once. Twice. Water drips down his cheek to his tan throat, slipping inside his tight black shirt. He looks up at his reflection and grimaces, his fingers trailing down his face. "Ugly, stupid, asshole motherfucker." I hear him grunt. "You can't have her."

Leaning over the sink, he clutches the edge with one hand while he unzips his pants and takes out his shaft. It's long, thick, and hard, like the rest of him. My breath hitches when he strokes himself, groaning, eyelashes fluttering against his chiseled cheeks. My ears tingle at the sounds he makes, the slap of his fist around his length as he works himself. He grabs his mushroom-shaped head and twists it, shuddering and rubbing the drops of white at the tip down his skin. "Hades and Persephone," he mutters, almost angrily, as he shoves his jeans and underwear farther down. Slick, slick, so slick and wet, he thrusts into his hand in a greedy way, a flush starting at his neck and working its way to his face. Every second he leans down and groans stretches out and lingers, every tick of the clock dense and thick with anticipation. I bite my lip before the sound I want to make escapes.

Seeing the head Shark jack off shouldn't mean a thing. It shouldn't!

It's nothing, just nothing.

Yet it's everything.

My pelvis gets warm, desire curling. Holding my breath, my hand plunges into my jeans, rubbing at the soft mound between my legs. My sensitive nipples pebble, as if he's right here with me, touching them. What would his caress feel like? Soft or hard? I remember him under the bleachers. Wild. Hot. Intense.

Wiggling, I move lower, pushing at my jeans. Fire burns inside me when I slip my fingers under my panties and touch soaked skin, skating over my clit. A shuddering groan escapes my lips, and I freeze, coming back to reality when I sense a change in the air, a quiet tension replacing his sounds.

Did he leave? I didn't hear the door open—

The curtain is ripped back and he looms over me, his throat working soundlessly as he rakes his eyes over me and stumbles back, falling on the floor.

"Ava! What..." He hurries up to his knees, his face horrified. "Shit, shit, shit, what are you doing in here!"

Embarrassment flares on my cheeks. I can imagine what I look like lying here in the tub, my hands inside my panties. "Same as you, apparently," I mutter. I stand up shakily and try to maneuver over the rim of the bath, but I forget my pants are at my knees and I end up falling.

He springs then, moving to help me as I simultaneously tug at my clothes to get them back up. He wraps his arms around my waist to steady me, but we end up tumbling down on the tile with me on top. His chest presses against mine, and I'm barely keeping myself from melting, wanting to curl into him. His thick erection is between us, and my body throbs with something I've never had, for a sweet pinnacle, to feel that elusive release, and now—

"You can't be in here with me," he grinds out, his hands on my upper arms. His grip is hard enough to bruise, but I don't care.

I wrench out of his grasp and reach out to his face. He thinks he's ugly? Never.

I lick my lips as my hand falls to my side.

"Chance," his voice scratches out raggedly. He looks shaken and a little wild, and it's the most revealing emotion I've ever seen on his face.

"Why didn't you say something when I came in?" He scrubs his face, scooting farther away from me, his back leaning against the door.

"Does it make me a voyeur to say I was enjoying the show? Most definitely a deviant."

He shudders. "You don't even like me. I frighten you."

"I'm not so sure about that."

He tucks himself back into his underwear, wincing.

I bring my pants up and zip them. My heart thuds painfully, my movements jerky, unsatisfied.

Voices outside the door move him to action and he jumps to a stand with athletic grace, yanking his pants up. He goes back to the sink and splashes more water on his face.

"Get up, Ava. Get the fuck out." He clings to the edge of the counter.

"Why were you staring at me out there?"

He stiffens. "I don't have to answer your questions. Don't you know who I am?"

"Screw you, head Shark. I want to know!"

"Stop yelling."

"Then tell me. What's going on with you?" With us.

I stand up. I'm brave—for now. I admit he makes me nervous, that darkness I sense in him, the opposite of Chance. "Did she suck your cock?"

I'm tormented by the image.

His eyes swirl with emotion as he glares at me in the reflection of the mirror.

"No," is ripped from him.

"You want me."

"No."

"Liar."

Silence reigns as he seethes, fighting something inside himself. He flips around and stalks over to me. "You belong to Chance."

"I belong to myself!"

"Have you fucked him?" His hands clench.

"No!"

"You will. He loves you." A pause as his jaw pops. "And he's my best friend." I eat up the expression on his face, so unused to seeing that vulnerability in his features.

"He hasn't said so. He's never asked me out for a real date, and I've never met his parents. I'm his little secret at school." Oh, he's been sweet, but he has yet to take me to dinner or the movies or ask me to come to the football parties with him. "I don't fit in with your group."

His chest rises.

"Break up with him." His words are flat.

But I know he doesn't mean break up with him so you can be with me, *because if anything, I know that wouldn't be Knox's style. He cares about Chance and he'd never in a million years pick up where his best friend left off. Goes against everything he believes, I think. Loyalty pours out of every bunched-up, tense muscle in his body right now.*

Shame washes over me. Dipping my head, I rub my eyes.

I just...

I just...

His scarred face.

His deep, stormy eyes.

Something twisted and dark that resides in me yearns for him.

And I don't even know when it snuck up on me.

I just know the real me gravitates to broken people. Their secrets. I wonder what mysteries made him like this, what or who gave him this fragmented heart, the fractured sense of how he sees himself with that slash on his face.

"I'm sorry," I mumble, and I guess I'm sorry for not being strong enough to say those words out loud.

"Nothing's happened between us, Ava. Get that sad look off your face."

He misunderstands.

I'm not sad for what I just did. I'm sad because he's out of my reach.

He swallows. "Shit, don't break up with him. I shouldn't have said that. He's good. He'll treat you right." Then, "Just stay away from me," he pushes out, his voice gravelly and rough as he puts his back to me, and I sense him gathering himself, fortifying, building up his force field.

His shoulders heave with a long exhalation.

"Knox?"

He puts his hand on the doorknob. "What?"

"You're not ugly. You're beautiful."

He pauses but opens the door and slams it shut.

Eventually, I come out of that bathroom after I hear slamming doors and cars driving away. I tiptoe out and find Chance passed out on the couch. Even in sleep, he's handsome, his full lips parted as he breathes heavily. Beer bottles litter the coffee tables. A half-smoked joint burns in an ashtray. My gaze goes back to him. I should *break up with him. Can you even call it breaking up when we aren't technically dating? His eyes open and he groggily sits up. "Babe...where did you go?" He gives me a squinty look. "Did I screw up? You look weird."*

I sit next to him. "Are you embarrassed by me?"

"No!"

I nod, forging ahead. If I want this, we need to talk. "You keep pressuring me for sex, but I'm not easy, Chance. I want a guy who's proud to be with me, one who takes me on dates." I wave my hands around at the mess of his house. "And before you say this was a date, you're wrong. I want you to come to the group home, meet my brother, and pick me up."

He recoils then frowns, his forehead scrunching up. "I didn't realize you were...old-fashioned like that. It's just the height of football season and being a Shark, we kind of just do what we want..." He trails off, wincing. "That didn't come out right. I'm sure as shit not talking to any other girls right now, Ava." He reaches over and cups my nape, pulling our faces close. "Hey, don't get any crazy ideas of leaving me, okay? We have a game Friday, but Saturday it's just me and you, feel me? I'll do whatever it takes to make you happy." A lopsided grin curves his lips. "And I'm sorry for pressuring you. You're just so beautiful and I'm horny. Plus, everybody else was getting lucky."

I give him a wan smile. "Yeah."

That Saturday night never came, though.

Because on Friday, I went to the keg party.

WITH A DEEP BREATH, I come back to reality and class. I push those moments with Knox away from me.

Not able to help myself, I look back at Chance, feeling that wave of disappointment and anger that inevitably strikes me when I see him.

As if he knows I was thinking about him, he looks at me.

His hand is clasped tightly with Brooklyn's. Oh, how fast he ran to her.

"How you doing, Brooklyn?" I call out. She's pretty with sleek chestnut hair that curls around her face. Her mouth twists like she's eating a lemon, ignoring me.

She's Jolena's bestie. What did I expect?

Flipping back around, I study Knox's hard profile. "*Pew-pew-pew.* That's me shooting down your troops, you know, those guards you station around yourself so you don't have to talk to me."

"Mmmm."

"He speaks! Or mumbles—I can't tell."

"We're in class," he says dryly.

"Hasn't started yet. You know, I was thinking about Patrick Swayze. *Ghost*, admittedly, is an excellent movie if you like pottery and spirits and crazy mediums. *Point Break* is my personal favorite of his. The surfing, jumping out of planes, adrenaline junkie, and those abs—sign me up. But *Road House*, now that's like top three worst movies ever made. I appreciate his fighting skills, but the storyline—a pacifist slash bouncer? Pfft."

"What are the other movies on your worst list?" He still won't look at me, but he leans a miniscule bit closer, just a hair.

"*Showgirls*. Elizabeth Berkley as a Vegas stripper—no thanks."

"Not a *Saved by the Bell* fan?"

"Nope. And it goes without saying *Saw I*, *II*, *III*, *IV*, *V*, and *VI* all suck."

"What about *Saw VII*?"

My mouth gapes. "They made another one? Say it ain't so."

"So." He smirks and looks down at his laptop.

He's almost there. Just needs a little more pushing...

I tap my pen on the table. "How did you get to be the head Shark? You're a jerk, A-plus on that, but I don't really see you as part of some hierarchy of school society. You're really more of a stoic loner, I think. If you weren't rich, I bet you'd be a gang leader. The Knox Gang. You'd have a cheap shark tattoo on your neck. Real badass."

Come on, Knox. Break. Show me who you really are.

"Good thing I'm rich."

"You still jacking off in bathrooms?"

He starts. "You still fingering yourself in tubs?"

"Not lately."

"Too bad."

"Sometimes I wonder what might have happened if you hadn't left that bathroom. I wonder how things might have been different. If I'd gone to that keg party for *you*, if I'd been with you—"

"Ava, stop. Please."

Whatever infinitesimal inches of ground I gained have vanished. He scoots his chair away from me.

"Something about me really gets under your skin. What is it? I don't think it's the whole *she's a scholarship girl and so not worth my notice* angle. Nope, it's deeper."

He sighs.

But I don't want to stop.

"You asked me about Persephone and Hades once. Remember that? It was one of my favorite myths, Hades falling for the beautiful goddess. He wasn't interested in any of those other she-demons that lurked around his domain. He only wanted her."

"I have no idea what you're talking about."

"It's rather romantic in a god and goddess sort of way. He did kidnap her, I suppose, but he loved her, and kidnapping is really minor compared to what some of those other gods did. She loved him deeply in spite of everyone warning her to stay away. She ate those pomegranate seeds because she knew her mother would never let her live in Hell."

"She only got to live there with him for six months out of the year—then she had to go back to her mother. To me, it sounds like their relationship couldn't have been that solid."

"So you do remember." I let him hear the satisfaction in my voice. "And as far as being solid, absence makes the heart grow fonder and all that. Did you miss me when I was gone?"

My breath hitches as I wait for him to reply, but like the wily devil he is, he avoids my direct question and asks me one instead. He turns and gives me an even better look at his eye, the skin puffy and purple and painful-looking. "I also recall Hades rising up from hell in his black chariot, snatching Persephone, and carting her down to live with dead people. He tricked her into eating those seeds so she'd want to be with him. Is that a sign of a good relationship?"

I shrug. "She was in love with him and she knew it was the only way. Admittedly, he probably scared the bejesus out of her, but she took a chance on her man."

He grunts. "Really? No one wanted them to be together. None of the gods approved. Who'd love the king of the underworld?"

"The right person."

He inhales.

Jolena walks past our table and gives Knox a withering look, and I pause.

That black eye…hmmm.

"Your eye has to hurt. It's like it's sentient, like it might step right off your face and tell a story. If it did, I'd ask it why the hell Knox Grayson lost control the night of Chance's party."

His eyes flare at me.

"Fine. I can tell you're clamming up as usual. Let's discuss the fight you obviously got in. I saw my mom with a couple of shiners, you know. Tyler's dad, Cooper, was a real winner—no job, on drugs, angry. Once, he had her pinned against the wall while he smacked her face. One side. The other. Back and forth. Red welts. Her feet dangled right off the floor, just like in the movies—can you believe it? Vodka bottles rolling—geeze, always with the dang vodka. He looked over his shoulder at me and said, '*Leave or you're next.*' I ran." My chest rises rapidly at my admission.

He leans in. "Where did you go?"

"I didn't come home for three days. Went to my inner-city school, ate lunch, and went to the tents at night. There were always open ones I could crawl in and no one would notice, plus it was spring and the weather was nice."

He scowls. "Shit, Ava. Under the bridge? Anything could have happened to you! Why didn't you go to the police?"

"Rich kid, please. You don't get it. If I went to the cops, they'd call social services and put me in another foster home. No thanks. I'll take the devil I know any day."

A long exhalation comes from him and I see his hands clench. "What happened when you went back?"

Shrugging, I say, "They were fine, all kissy-kissy. She was

pregnant and I was just sticking around for my little brother to arrive anyway." I pause. "Sometimes I wonder if she's still alive."

"What about your dad?" His eyes search my face.

"Ha. He was the lottery winner. He left Mama before I was ever born. Last I heard, he worked on an oil rig in the Gulf."

A brief frown flits over his face, then it softens, his lips parting.

"I don't want you to feel sorry for me, Knox. I have Tyler. He's mine. He's everything." I touch my locket and his eyes follow the movement, his gaze drifting over me until I feel flushed, until surely he can see I'm not thinking about anything but him and how he makes me want to tear off his mask—

I clear my throat. "You really should put some ice on that, or a steak or something. Don't you have a minion who will run to get you whatever you want? Tylenol? Blowjob?"

His lips twitch.

"Did you get in a tussle over a girl? Doesn't seem like your style, to be honest. You keep tight control on your emotions—that is, unless you're under the bleachers." I flash him a grin.

He reddens but gives me an amused smirk.

Piper dashes over, pushing her cute glasses up on her nose, and I give her a surprised look, so caught up in Knox that I realize I'm barely aware of anyone else in class. She gives me a hug, and some of the dread from walking through the entrance today fades away. "Girlfriend, the dorm news is so awesome! Score! You're only five minutes from me now! Party time. We can study together too!" She does a little fist pump in the air. She looks over her shoulder when Dane walks in and takes his seat at their table. "Oh, great. My pompous partner is here. He is so…ugh. Gotta go. I'll come by tonight and we'll celebrate with Mountain Dew and Taco Bell —your favorite, right? I'll bring them. Talk later, 'kay?"

And then she's bouncing away and plopping down in her seat next to him.

He gives me a long look. "Her parents are the ones who took you to the hospital, right?"

How…

He smirks. "Your mouth is open."

I close my lips. "You're so weird. I never thought you ever paid any attention to my comings and goings. Also I never told anyone that. Maybe she did?" I eye him warily.

"No. I asked about you once. She told me to jump off a building and stab myself on the way down."

"Sounds like her—cute but sassy." I look back at Piper. She's glaring at Dane, and I distinctly hear her say, "Just watch the stupid movie already, jockass. Yes, the spider dies. I'm sorry you can't handle it! God, you are such a baby."

Dane just looks at her like she's an alien. I bet he's never even talked to her at Camden, and now he's stuck.

I turn back, laughing a little.

"I'm glad she's your friend," Knox murmurs.

"Even with Piper, I feel so weird here, like I'm on the outside looking in. I'm not the same anymore."

He stills and I tense up.

Gah, why am I blabbing so much? I just can't seem to stop.

"But you…you rule the school," I say. "Girls adore you. Guys are envious. Everyone wants to be next to you, wants to bask in your glory. You're never lonely. Praise be."

"Mmmm."

Oh my God, his noncommittal answers are driving me up the freaking wall!

Mrs. White still hasn't started class yet. I wish she would so I'd shut up.

"So tell me about the shiner," I say.

He lets out a heavy sigh and leans in closer, closer, until I can smell his ocean scent.

"Someone pissed me off."

"Obviously, but who would dare?" I make a pretend gasp and clutch my heart.

He huffs out a laugh. "You keep surprising me, Tulip."

I'm about to comment—with what, I don't know, but I do know I enjoy sparring with him—when Mrs. White dims the lights and begins *The Wizard of Oz.*

"Today we're going to watch an iconic movie, and I want you to take notes on the metaphors and symbolism you see..." I tune her out, having a hard time concentrating, my mind still on Knox.

He passes me a note, his handwriting neat and careful. He didn't use script writing, though, choosing to print the letters. *We still on to watch Dirty Dancing soon?*

I glance up to make sure Mrs. White isn't looking; she's settled in at her desk and looking over a textbook.

Sure. Nine good? Tomorrow? We can use FaceTime if we want to talk while it's playing? Or we can just chat after it's over? I don't care. I slide the note back over to him.

Hmmm...if you don't care, why don't we just watch it together? I think that would be easier than trying to FaceTime. That way we can bounce ideas around for the essay and take notes. More organic. You can come to my house. Suzy will be there if you want a chaperone. She's kind of our nanny/manager.

I read it over twice to make sure I didn't misunderstand him.

Cold and Evil wants to watch it *together*? With his nanny? Good Lord. He still has one? I smirk. And at his house? I assumed we'd watch separately and then figure it out later. That's what we agreed to.

I look around to make sure I'm not in a parallel universe.

Dorothy plays on the screen, but I'm not really watching. I sit for a full five minutes, thinking about my response, and I notice that the longer I pause, tapping my pen on the note, the more antsy he becomes, legs bouncing under the table, his fingers drumming against the desk. Still holding his note, I dart my eyes over at him. He's watching me. Carefully. Intently. Little side glances. Almost grudgingly, as if he really doesn't want to.

He bites down on that lush bottom lip of his, and warm tingles move through my body as my heart picks up. There's a fluttery feeling in my stomach—

No. I pass my response over to him.

Why? he sends back.

You know why. You're one of them. You're THE SHARK.

So? I just fill a role here. People want someone to fear. Am I so terrible? Didn't I help you with your tire?

You did. Thank you. No.

He lets out an exhalation, scribbling his response, then passing it over. *I got into a fight with Liam. That's why I have a black eye. Not a big deal.*

Huh. I guess football players tussle a lot.

I send him a reply.

Does he look worse than you? What was the fight about?

He reads it and shoves a hand through his dark hair.

I wait, almost expectantly, for him to write a reply, but I get nada.

In fact, he ignores me for the rest of class, and when the bell rings, he jumps up and darts away. I watch his broad shoulders maneuver through the crowd, jostling to get out of the classroom. A few guys call out his name and he waves at them. Then I see Tawny. She waltzes in and latches onto his arm, aligning herself with him. She's not a cheerleader, but she's the kind of beautiful that makes your eyes linger while you wonder what kind of genetics created such startling perfection. Luxurious golden brown hair to her waist, a soft oval face, a delicate nose—it's all very pleasing to the eye. Ugh.

He pauses, looks down at her with a frown, and then stares back at me.

I arch my brow.

Now that's the kind of girl who jumps at the chance to come to your house, my eyes say.

I give him a thumbs-up while he studies me. He hesitates then tosses an arm around her shoulders. They pause at the entrance as other students maneuver to walk around them, but Knox doesn't care; he blocks any door he wants.

I see profiles when they turn, talking. His sharp jawline, the glossy hair my fingers touched. Her hand skims his neck. She tilts her face up and stands on her tiptoes. She's asking him something. I know that look in her eyes. She likes him, a lot.

And then...

Surprise ripples over me. I see them at the keg party last year, his hand tucked in the pocket of her jeans as they left the party.

But... Wait, wait, back up.

First I kissed Chance.

My heart pounds and I flinch as the details that were once locked away slide into perfect clarity. Closing my eyes, focusing on concentrating, I let the images creep in. Chance's kiss, long and deep and sweet. My immediate response to the pressure of his lips, delving into his mouth. How badly I wanted our date the next night. He was going to pick me up and take me to dinner. It might seem silly to want something *so simple*, but for a girl like me—one who's never had big things—it's the little things that take up room in my heart: soft rain, starry nights, shy looks, leaves falling, a good movie, Tyler's smile, chocolate cake—and a date with your guy.

I love you, Ava, Chance said in my ear, his hands curling around my waist, holding me like I was porcelain.

He kissed me and said *that* and I didn't even remember! Holy shit. I blink.

I was already trashed, but the words are vivid now, a hot brand in my head. And what was my response? No clue, but I lifted my head from Chance's shoulder and instead of meeting his lips again, I met the gray eyes of Knox Grayson glittering at me. Only two feet away. I could have reached up, stretched out my arms, and touched his unsmiling face. I could have unfurled his clenched fists.

He took a deep breath as our gazes clung.

Chance kissed my neck, and I trembled when I looked at Knox and he let me see...he let me see...a window inside himself. Anguish mingled with want. Longing.

Standing there by the fire, with Tawny by his side, he pressed two fingers to his lips and sent the touch to me. With twenty-twenty vision, without the alcohol clouding me, I saw *him*, saw the slow, regretful way he tore his eyes off of me and Chance.

Then—*just like now*—he tossed an arm around Tawny, escorted her to his car, and opened the door for her. He disappeared. And I…I was left behind.

My eyes find them now at the doorway. They haven't moved.

He bends his head to her—my chest squeezes—getting lower and lower. My breathing intensifies. Unbidden anxiety ratchets down my spine.

I resist the urge to stamp my foot.

Look at me like that *again*, I want to shout.

Someone bumps into me.

Another nudge, this time on my arm. "…Ava…are you listening?"

The male voice penetrates and I start, glancing over.

"What?" I snap at Chance. He's been standing there for a while. My hands, which have been clinging to the edge of the table, loosen their grip, and my back straightens. I toss a look around him. "Where's Brooklyn?"

He flushes. "She left already. Ava…" He stops, his mouth opening and shutting.

"What do you want?" I gather my purse off the back of the chair. I need out of here. I don't want to rehash that night, and I can feel him psyching himself up for something.

"You hurt me," are the words he finally pushes out.

What fresh hell?

"*I hurt you?*"

He tries to hold my eyes but dips his head. "I can't take it anymore. You've only been here two days and I can't…" He trails off.

"Can't what?"

His head rises. He struggles to speak, the words pulled from him. He looks as if he's in some kind of crisis. I almost think he weaves on his feet. "I can't stop thinking about you."

"*Now*?"

He nods.

I blow out a breath. "Really? Where were you when I needed you, huh? You weren't thinking then. You left me at that party to hook up with your current girlfriend." Somehow I keep my voice even, almost calm, but I feel the rage lingering, just waiting to pounce.

Shame—or at least I want to think it's shame—colors his face.

Bitterness whips in the air like a tornado. I know I shouldn't engage with him, but maybe I need closure. We never got that. I got his text and wrote him off.

"Tell me something, how could you tell me *I love you* one minute then leave me at that party the next? A brave person would have believed me. Cowards pussy out, Chance. You *quit me* like I was trash. Even now, I can't believe I let you get so close to my heart..." I bite my lip, shaken by the torrent of words that have come out of me. I did let him close. God. I let myself be vulnerable for him.

He swallows, blue eyes downcast. "I'm sorry—"

I cut him off right there. "Yeah. You are. And the worst thing of all is maybe it was you. *Maybe it was you.*" My voice breaks, just a little, and I snatch it back.

He nods as if he expected that but sucks in a breath. "It wasn't. I'm not capable of that. You know me. I've been thinking—"

"Please don't."

"I can't stop it, Ava." His eyes flick to the doorway, where Knox and Tawny still are. I can see them in my peripheral. "And everything Knox has done and said was right, and I've been wrong. *I am sorry.* You're right about me. I messed up. I should have made you stop drinking, been more protective, or made sure I left with you—"

"But you didn't. Ha."

What has Knox done and said?

His eyes close briefly. "I've never been in that situation. I never cared about a girl like you. I didn't dream someone I knew, a friend of mine, would hurt you—"

"Save your apology!"

"I know! I hate it, okay? I hate it! I can't change how I reacted!" His voice rises, but there's no one here to hear us. The room is empty except for that maddening couple at the doorway. I refuse to look at them, but I can feel them there like a dark shadow.

"I always thought I was a strong person, but I'm not," he adds as he scrubs his face. "Ava, *please.*" His chest rises, expands. "I've...missed you. I've imagined you in the hallway a hundred times. I didn't play one football game without looking at the sidelines and wishing you were there. I've played back that night in my head over and over, but I was drunk too, and I wasn't thinking right. You ran off to dance, and all I saw was you at your first Shark kegger, leaving me for someone better. I didn't do the right thing. I reacted like a sniveling, jealous asshole. I let you down and you got hurt."

Ugly emotion tightens my throat and I kick it down.

He closes his eyes. "Tell me how to make it better."

I scowl at him, really looking at him. The way his sandy hair is full and thick, how my fingers felt brushing through the wet strands after a game. His strong shoulders when he hugged me so tight. All the little notes he'd leave for me in my locker. *You're beautiful* was the first one. *I'll be yours, if you ask* was the second. And then, *I dream of you more often than I should.* Oh, I recall them and that last one got to me. So good. To imagine he wanted me... I imagined us at prom, at college together, me walking down an aisle toward him. Who *was* that girl? I got foolish. I forgot life isn't kittens and rainbows.

"I know it's too late to change anything—"

"Stop. Just stop talking. Don't come near me and I swear to do the same."

"I don't want that."

"I do!"

He flinches, looking like he might say something else, but he dunks his head and brushes past me.

My chest heaves. Big breath in. Long sigh out.

I hear the warning bell and other kids rush in from the hall to take the seats around me. I dash to the door and Knox and Tawny are still there. WTF. Go already!

She has him pressed against the wall, her manicured, red-tipped hands dancing over his chest as she daintily frowns at the bruise on his face.

His eyes cling to me. Knowledge gleams there, of my conversation with Chance. First-row seats to that little show —was it on purpose? Maybe. It feels like Knox always has a reason for everything.

I'm about to pass them when I stop and turn back around. I ignore Tawny and glare at him. "Tomorrow night. Vanderbilt library. I'll meet you on the steps at seven and we can watch the movie together in one of the study rooms. I have an

ID because I used to go last year when I was doing home-school stuff."

"Alright," he says softly, his eyes studying my face, as if looking to see if I'm okay. He moves Tawny away from him, literally pushes her shoulders until she's fuming prettily. She sends me a little glare and whispers in his ear. I definitely hear *bleachers* in her rush of words. He shakes his head at her.

I smirk.

She saunters off and I watch her, but when I turn back, he's got those gray eyes on me.

"Should we eat first?" he asks.

"Please. This is not a date."

"Agreed, but my stomach will growl. It might disturb the other people studying. Plus, I'll be fresh from practice, and I get queasy if I don't get protein."

He is...*ugh*.

My hand goes to my hip. "First I have to drag it out of you to hear what happened to your eye, and then you want to watch this stupid movie together. Now you insist on eating."

"It's just food. Why can't we eat? If you came to my house, Suzy would make us dinner."

Nope. Not going to a Shark's house.

"Meet me at Lou's Diner and we'll drive over from there. The restaurant is on Elm Street in Nashville. Happy?"

He huffs out a laugh. "Just two students watching an iconic romantic movie for a class. It's a plan, Tulip."

"See you, Cold and Evil." I walk out the door.

Why did I do that? is racing through my head as I leave.

I blame it on Chance and his half-assed apology.

Maybe that memory of how Knox looked at me.

Whatever.

I push it aside and pick up my steps as I jog down the hall. Crap. I'm going to be late for English. Mr. Banks is old, though, and it takes him a few minutes to get his roll out. I can sneak in and sit in the back. I dash down the mostly empty corridor to my locker, my steps picking up when I see Brandon Wilkes, one of the football players. All crazy red hair and jacked muscles, he slows as he passes me and sends me a leer. He flips around, sliding black eyes over me as he walks backward. "Get the message, snitch. We don't want you here."

"Asshole," I mutter and keep marching.

It's not until I reach my locker that it makes sense. Scribbled in black marker on my silver locker are the words **LEAVE SLUT**.

My mouth dries. Nausea boils in my stomach. That word. That *fucking* word.

Someone is behind me, and she laughs.

No matter how many times I walk through the doors of Camden, they'll never forget who I am and what happened to me—

Shake it off. No self-pity allowed. Zero.

With fumbling fingers, I open the lock, take out my book, and slam it shut.

When I turn, Jolena is there, eyes sparkling. She holds her hands up. "Don't blow up at me. I didn't do it, but boy do I like it."

The final bell rings. We're late to class.

She doesn't move, smiling still.

I tilt my head toward my locker. "You think that bothers me?" It KILLS ME. Loneliness sucks at me and I clench my fists. "What a joke. At least it's not, oh, I don't know—a violation of my body. Yeah, that is so much worse. Plus, the missing comma is deplorable. Whoever wrote it is an idiot."

"Stay away from the football players, Ava," she calls to my back as I walk away. "And I don't just mean Liam. Knox too. He belongs to us. Don't forget it."

How can I forget?

On trembling legs, I walk to the office and find Mrs. Carmichael. In a toneless voice I stare at her flowered blouse and tell her what's on my locker, and she murmurs words I barely hear. "Oh, no, terrible...kids these day...so sorry for you. I'll get maintenance on it, I'm sure we have something to remove it..." Blah, blah, blah.

She hands me a note to class and I accept it then run to the bathroom, finding the last stall and sitting on the toilet, my legs tucked up so no one can see me. My stomach rolls, thick and heavy, and I shove it down.

I call the elementary campus and ask for Dr. Rivers. Time passes, but I don't care how long it takes until her voice is on the line and I ask to speak to Tyler. She tells me no, they don't pull students from class to talk on the phone. I tell her I need to hear his voice just for one minute, and can't I please, please, please just talk to him, and eventually I say I don't think I can get up and go to class until I hear his voice. There's a long silence until finally, Tyler comes, and I hear him talking to Dr. Rivers, some shuffling, and then his tiny breathy voice on the line, saying hello, and I close my eyes.

"How's your first day, bozo?" My voice isn't right, but at least I have it.

"Balls! It's amazing!" I feel the smile on his face all the way from his school. "We're doing science and I got a partner and we got to lay down on this long paper and outline each other and now we're gonna use yarn to make the blood vessels! Isn't that cool? Isn't it?" He sighs.

"So cool."

He goes on and on and we make a plan for him to come eat tacos with me and Piper tonight, and it's well past the minute I told Dr. Rivers, and then he's gone and she's on the line, asking if I'm okay, and should she call Mr. Trask, and I lie and tell her I'll be fine. I hang up and touch my cheeks to make sure they're dry; they are, thank God, because please, I don't want to cry.

Not here in this godforsaken place.

Walking out of the stall, I look at myself in the mirror. Pale. Too skinny. Dark shadows under my eyes. Black hair. I'd be goth if not for the bright uniform. From my purse, I fish out my red lipstick and slide it on, considering my reflection. I can be strong for Tyler. I can make this shitty road *mine*. Own it. Use it. And someday, someday, I'll have a beautiful road, smooth and easy and perfect.

"So you aren't going to let these assholes get to you, Ava?" I say to the scared girl in the mirror.

"No. Not yet. I'm not quitting. Only cowards quit."

Whipping out a marker, I leave a little message on the wall with hearts around it.

Then I walk out and go to class.

11

I'm nervous when I pull into the parking lot of Lou's. My heart is jumping in my chest at the prospect of seeing her, and it's so wrong. Chance flashes through my head, his broken words to Ava and, *shit*, just the way he stared at her with his heart in his eyes. About time he tried to apologize, but I wasn't surprised she refused him. Considering what happened to her and how he let her down, I'm not sure forgiveness is in the cards.

There's a wall around me, but she's got one up too.

She's the eye of a hurricane, the winds of her pain whipping around her.

I pop my visor down to look in the mirror and straighten my freshly showered hair, tugging on it to soften the right side of my face. *Here goes nothing.* I exit and stop for a moment in front of the glass door, checking my reflection. Jeans and a tight shirt that shows off my arms—check. Cologne she says she hates but really loves—check.

This isn't a date, asshole.

Uh-huh.

So why am I rippling with anxiousness?

My palms are clammy when I open the door to Lou's, which is in a really shitty part of town.

A grizzly-looking man with a beard in a stained white apron sits behind the counter. He gives me a hard once-over. His lips tighten. "She's sitting in the back."

I nod. Okay, so he knows who I am and he doesn't like my puss at all. Fine, fine. Not here for him, and I can't even blame him.

My steps are too damn eager as I walk to the back of the diner and slide into the red booth across from her. I saw her in class today, but we had a pop quiz over *The Wizard of Oz* and there wasn't time for talking. She ate lunch with Wyatt and Piper, clear across the cafeteria from the Shark table. I watched her, pretending I wasn't when Dane asked me why I was distracted.

Wearing frayed cut-off shorts and a faded yellow *Sex Pistols* shirt, she's heartbreakingly beautiful. Her hair swings softly around her shoulders, and I feel a pang for the blonde style she wore last year. I may have had a weakness for her hair. Stupid.

"You're early. Eager to get started?" she murmurs, setting her laptop aside and looking over at me.

Clearing my throat, I check out the interior of the diner. Cracked linoleum on the floor, walls that need another coat of blue paint, old Formica booths, and a dingy metal napkin holder next to those generic squeezable mustard and ketchup containers. A dark hallway at the back leads to a narrow space where I imagine the restrooms are. It's not an ideal place to be alone with her for the first time without anyone from school here, but I'll take it.

I settle in, stretching out my legs. My foot brushes hers under the table and she subtly pulls it back while I mutter an apology. "Yeah. Guess you still beat me here. Did you work a shift?"

"Not today. I saw Tyler earlier. He lives nearby at the group home. How did you know I worked here?"

Oh, Ava. I know so much.

I wave her off.

"How is he doing at Camden Prep?"

Her head cocks. "Dude, how you'd even know he was there?"

I shrug and bite back a smile at her *dude*. She's getting more comfortable with me with each little moment. Is that what I want? Right now, in this moment, fuck yeah.

"Trask emailed the board and asked for a scholarship for him. My dad is on the board. He mentioned it." Several times. That was a strange phone call on Monday when I heard the hesitant tone in Dad's voice as he asked me if Ava was really back. Since he is on the board, he also knew Trask wanted her back, and although he felt uneasy about it, he voted yes to call her and offer the scholarship for her senior year. Like me, he recalls the spiral Dane went into after the kegger last year.

"I take it he's found a good place?"

One of her soft smiles graces her face, and I inhale at the effect it has on my insides. "He freaking loves it so much. Loves the administration, the teachers, the kids—everything."

I finger the menu that's behind the napkin holder. "That's why you came back, right? I figure you marched into Trask's office, bragged about your big brain, maybe tossed in some threats, then asked for him to be a student."

She chews on her bottom lip. "Why would you think that?"

"You've got balls. It's what I would have done. And I can't think of any other reason why you'd come back."

Her lashes flutter for a moment on her cheeks as if what I've said makes her feel pleased.

"Wow, Knox. You've spent a lot of time thinking about my motives. Glad I've been on your mind."

Only for about three years.

"What can I get you?" It's the guy from the counter. He scratches at his beard and gives Ava a tender look then throws me a scowl.

She smiles broadly up at him. "Burger and fries for me, Lou. Hold the mayo. Extra tomato. You know how I like it. Coke."

Bushy brows furrow in my direction. "You?"

"Same. Water to drink." Dammit. I hate tomatoes. What is wrong with me?

He wanders off and yells to a girl in the kitchen who's busy over a grill.

"He doesn't like me."

She laughs. "Ah, poor Knox, doesn't have any friends in the city. I've worked here for three years, and Lou treats me well."

"Good."

She leans in. "I'll tell you a secret: Lou's terrified of the nuns when they drop Tyler off here to eat with me. Calls them female Darth Vaders."

I look back at the burly man and smile. "Really? You should convince one of them to say, 'Lou, I am your father.'"

She cocks her head. "Cute, but actually that line is misquoted. It's not 'Luke, I am your father,' but simply, '*I* am your father.' So many good twists in *Star Wars*, but that line, even after watching it over and over, still sends tingles down my spine. It feels like a lie, like it's just part of his sick mind games, but Darth Vader is speaking the truth and he knows it will wound Luke and cause him to question everything."

My lips twitch. "You really are a movie nerd."

"The best." She toys with her pencil. "My favorite line of Darth Vader's is 'You don't know the power of the dark side. I *must* obey my master.' You can taste the fear in his voice. You see his internal struggle and how, maybe, sometimes, the light still calls to him, yet he can never go back." She laughs. "Hey, stop. You're gaping at me. Okay, fine, I geek out over the franchise, which really means I'm in hell, ranking the movies in my head, considering the debatable cuteness of aliens clearly designed for market reasons only, being tortured by the painfully obvious plot holes that drive me insane. Tyler loves them too. He's just as much of a geek as I am."

I just look at her. Damn. She's so fucking... "I'm amazed by you. Rank them for me."

"You aren't even ready for this conversation. Have you watched them all?"

I shrug. "Not sure if I caught the last couple."

"Who are you?" She gives me a horrified look.

I laugh. "Football takes up most of my time."

She scoffs. "You don't deserve to hear what I think until you've seen every last movie in chronological order, not in the order of release date. Lots of debate about that, but that's the camp I'm in."

I let out a long sigh, and just to annoy her... "We really should have gone with *Star Wars*. You could write us an essay with your eyes closed."

Her color deepens. "Sadly, *you* had to pick the right number! So now it's some stupid romance!"

I laugh.

She watches me, her aquamarine gaze lingering on my face until she clears her throat and looks down at the table. "Are you sad you don't have friends at Lou's?"

"Not at all. I'm on a date."

Her eyes widen. "No you're not, Cold and Evil. This is a school-related activity!"

"You're wearing makeup." She is. Her lashes are long and curled, her cheeks rosy—or maybe she's blushing—and instead of that glittery red lipstick she's been wearing, I see shiny pink lip gloss. Lipstick? Whatever they call it.

My lips twitch at her outrage and she slowly softens, her face brightening until she grins. "A girl can wear makeup and it not mean a thing except she wants to feel pretty. And if I had social media, I'd totally tag you with me just to piss off your buddies."

Sighing, my head goes back to yesterday. "I saw your locker. I'm sorry for it."

I hate how her face gets that faraway look on it and her shoulders hunch over. "It's mostly gone. I came in today and it looks like the staff had scrubbed even more."

Ah... "Chance and I went back into the school after practice yesterday. He scraped the last of it off with a scouring pad. Apparently it was in permanent marker and the janitor had a hard time."

Her shoulders shift, fidgeting.

"It was Chance's idea."

"Whatever. Let's not bring him up."

Lou sets down our food and walks away.

She digs into her fries, popping one in her mouth, and I watch. She points at my plate. "Don't let it get cold."

Right, right—focus on the food, not Ava.

Okay, how am I going to covertly get these tomatoes off?

"So, you know my middle name. What's yours?"

"Knox." I grin. "And before you ask for my first name, I'm not telling. See if you can figure it out."

"Let's see. Maximilian? Eugene?"

I bark out a laugh.

"Megalodon?"

"You think I don't know what that is?" I pop an eyebrow. "I'm not a nerd like *some* people I know"—I smirk—"but I'm smart enough."

"Okay, hotshot, what is it?"

"Extinct species of shark that lived over three million or so years ago. Believed to be related to the Great White. And no, that is not my first name, but you're funny."

"Richard? Dick for short, definitely."

"I have an uncle with that name."

"Fort? Yep, that's it. You're a big stone building that holds all the gold and no one can get inside."

I take a bite of my burger, gag a bit at the tomatoes, chew it down, and wipe my mouth. "Nope. Forget me. Tell me something about you."

Because Ava...shit, I want to know everything.

She thinks, her brow wrinkling a little.

"Tell me about your first kiss," I blurt and then immediately wish I hadn't. Despite my joke earlier about this being a date, it isn't.

She studies me, eyes lingering over my lips. "You first."

I take a sip of water. "Fourth grade. Her name was Cissy Meadows and she was the fastest runner on the playground, even the guys. She challenged me to a race at recess and I beat her. She was so pissed." I laugh at the memory. "She started bawling her eyes out and I felt so bad for her, I laid one on her lips. No tongue. Really just wanted her to stop crying."

"Did she?"

I grin. "She followed me around for the rest of the year begging me to do it again."

She narrows her eyes. "And you did."

"Yeah, lots of times. First girlfriend I guess. By sixth grade, she moved away. Don't know what ever happened to her. Nice girl."

"Ah, the early, charmed love life of Fort Knox Grayson."

I toss a fry at her. "When was yours?"

She mulls it over, and somehow I feel like I've done something wrong. It's just a kiss question, which from me is ironic as hell considering I don't even enjoy kissing on the lips anymore.

"You don't have to tell me."

She shakes her head. "No, it's cool." Looking down at her plate, she says, "I was maybe twelve, right before Tyler was born. I was in my room—we had an apartment then, with Tyler's dad. It was a great room, though it was smaller than my dorm here, and I had posters of Taylor Swift and Katy

Perry on the walls. I fancied myself a future pop star." She inserts an eye roll. "Mama had gotten me this karaoke machine from the Goodwill and I was singing when Cooper came to tell me to shut it off."

My hands clench. "Tyler's dad?"

She nods. "Mama was trashed and had gone to bed earlier. I knew I shouldn't have been up and making noise." Her face pinches. "He was a tall man, burly and mean, but he thought he was handsome. He told me to go to bed and I hopped to it. He pulled the covers up, leaned down, and kissed me on the mouth..." Her voice trails off.

"You don't have to—"

"No, I *want* to tell you. It helps, you know, in an odd way. Makes it real." She sighs. "His breath smelled like cigarettes and liquor. He stuck his tongue in my mouth and his hands... they...I felt them trying to get under the covers."

Revulsion creates goose bumps on my arms. I picture her, small and young and afraid.

She blinks rapidly. "I kneed him in the nuts and screamed my ass off. The walls were thin in that dump, and maybe he was scared Mama would get up or the neighbors would call the police, or maybe he just chickened out. Either way, he left the room. Honestly, living how we did, I was lucky nothing horrible ever happened to me, which is why the keg party is so frustrating. I protected myself all those years only to be helpless hanging out with a bunch of rich kids." She plucks at her napkin. "All in all, it could have been worse with the things Mama did for extra cash. Since the moment she left us, all I've wanted is to dig myself out of where I came from and find my own way. Be independent, go to college, get a real job, take care of Tyler. Big dreams for a twelve-year-old." She grimaces. "Dang, I kind of killed the conversation there. Sorry."

The muscles in my shoulders have tensed, and I roll my head back and forth. Twelve. Fucking twelve years old.

"What happened to him?"

"Cooper? He and Mama left a few days after Tyler was born. Dumped us at the group home. Mama was Catholic, although she never took me to Mass. I owe the nuns for any religion I have. Those two leaving was the best thing that ever happened to us." She waves her hands. "Topic change! I want to know about this rumor that you only have sex from behind." She waggles her eyebrows and my body heats, tightening. "Well?"

"Who wants to look at my face?" I say the words lightly, but underneath...

"You're beautiful," she murmurs. "Hello, Tawny with the red claws—she was all over you yesterday."

"I don't want Tawny." That ship sailed last year.

She shoots me a furtive look while she chews on a fry. "Oh? Who are you banging on the regular this school year, then?"

"No one."

Her eyebrows shoot up. "Truly?"

I pick at my burger. Fucking tomatoes. "Yep."

"But why? You're...you, and everyone wants to be a bleacher girl—or so I've heard."

I push my food away. "Saving myself."

"For marriage? Waiting till you're a middle-aged has-been who peaked in high school?" She chuckles.

"No."

"Ah, I get it. Some lucky girl under the bleachers at the

first game of senior year. Sweet. Good plan. Typical top Shark behavior. Anticipation…then wham bam, thank you ma'am! Drawing it out."

A slow blush crawls up from my neck to my cheeks. I still don't jive with her seeing me. "You gonna come spy on me? Don't even try. This girl doesn't do bleachers."

"Ohhhhhhh, this is good." She leans in over the table, pushing her plate aside. Turquoise eyes glisten with mirth. "Are you…are you a bit of a romantic, Fort Knox?"

I laugh. "What defines a romantic?"

"Secretly loves rom-coms, listens to moody songs about unrequited feelings, writes pretty love letters and leaves them in girls' lockers."

My chest constricts sharply—it feels like I can't breathe.

She impatiently taps her fingers on the table, and I wait a full minute before answering her.

"Now, Tulip, does that sound like me? I'm just a muscled-up football player who might be *a bit dim* with too much money, an elitist attitude, and a long line of girls who can't keep their hands off of me. I mean, can you imagine me writing love letters? I'd just text her." I pause, taking a sip of my drink. "By the way, someone plastered my number in the girls' bathroom this week. *Knox Grayson's real cell number. You're welcome*, is what it said. Little hearts all around it. You wouldn't know anything about that, would you?"

"How terrible. Man, you can't trust anyone these days. Who on earth would do that to you?"

"Ah, Tulip. Don't pretend. I'm going to have to get you back for that."

She blushes, not even denying it. "Did anyone call?"

"Hmmm. Twenty texts last night. A few this afternoon. Guess I'll need a new phone."

Her face explodes in a huge grin as she slaps her hand on the table. "I'm not sorry. Not even a little."

"Minx."

"Guess you aren't *too* pissed at me?"

I arch a brow. I was angry when the texts first started coming in, but it only took a little inquiry in reply to one of them to figure out where it came from, and by then it was obvious who the culprit was. Shit, I can't even be mad at her.

Her eyes flash at me, holding mine. "Back to this girl you're waiting on—does she go to Camden?"

"Mmmm."

She pouts. "That's a noncommittal answer, Fort Knox. Come on, tell me. Your secrets are safe with me."

"You can't be trusted with a phone number!"

She laughs.

Lou places down the tab in the middle of the table, and Ava and I both dive for it at the same time. "This is mine," I say as we both pull on it.

She tugs. "You are not paying. This was my idea!"

I give it a pull. "I totally manipulated you into eating with me. You didn't even want to hang out with me, but I wore you down."

"You did—*asshole*—but I'm paying!"

"No girl pays for me, and I have money—"

"So do I! I work!"

"I know you do! Why are we yelling?" I gasp out.

"I don't know!" She picks up a fry and tosses it in my face, and when I bat it away, she pounces forward, takes the bill, and waves it at Lou, who's watching us with his head cocked.

"I'm paying, Lou! Don't let this rich preppy jerk give you money, you feel me?"

"Yes, ma'am," he rumbles then turns to go back to the front. "Don't take the boy's money. Let me get on that right away."

I shrug, holding my hands up. "I give up. You win. I'll get it next time."

She doesn't say anything to that, just rises and gathers her things. I follow her to the front where she pays our tab, gives Lou and the girl behind the grill a hurried hug, and joins me at the door.

We walk out into the night air. Our arms brush, and for once I don't pull away.

"You wanna ride with me?" I hear myself offering, then regret it. *Shit.*

She turns to look at me, and I get tense, my palms sweating again, that anxious feeling sticking to me. I think about her sitting in my car with me, the close proximity, the way her hair smells, like vanilla, and how close her arm would be to mine—

"I better not," she murmurs. "It would be out of your way to come back over here instead of hitting the interstate to get back to Sugarwood."

"I don't mind."

Why can't I shut up?

Shit, is this me? Shuffling my feet on the gravel, looking at a girl, and wishing...

"I'll meet you there," she finally says, her hands clenching the straps of her backpack.

Does it bother her to imagine being alone in a car with me?

I exhale. “Okay. See you there.”

“Try to keep up with me and Louise,” she calls as she sashays away.

“Louise?” My eyes devour her ass. Shapely. Pert. Perfect. I tear my gaze away.

“My car! Named her after Lou!” She gets in and drives away, and I pull out and follow her.

12

After parking, I turn the corner on the Vanderbilt campus, and she's already waiting for me. Somewhere in the traffic, I lost her car, and I make a note to be sure I follow her out to wherever she's parked.

It's not quite dark yet, so I have a good view, and she hasn't seen me yet. She's sitting on the steps in front of a fountain, her head tilted down as she scrolls on her phone. As if she feels me looking, she glances up and pushes a strand of hair out of her face.

"Dude. Why are you just standing there? Come on!" She waves me over.

I huff out a laugh and jog toward her.

"What's in the backpack? It looks bulky," she asks, eyeing me.

"Laptop and a surprise."

"Ohhhh, what is it?"

Her eyes gleam, and now I'm worried she won't like it.

"Just snacks."

"Caviar? A good merlot? Perhaps some canapés or cucumber sandwiches?"

"Shut up, Tulip. I brought Snickers and Tic Tacs."

"Classy." She grins. "We'll have to be sneaky—no food allowed."

I watch her eyes, feeling a buzz in my blood with all the eye contact between us tonight. Usually, over the years, our eyes have met in those short once-overs where we both look away or the long glances from me to her when she's not looking.

We walk through the open doors of the library and she lets out a little sigh as she takes in the grand foyer, the massive rows of books, the front desk.

I'm watching her—can't help it. I'm in Ava overload. "You love this place."

She nods, almost shyly. "It's a dream to come here. Vandy rarely gives full scholarships, so it's not likely I'll be able to afford it, but it would be amazing. They have a killer pre-med program here." With a deep exhalation, she does a full pirouette and smiles. "Come on, I know where the study rooms are."

"I get it now. You feel comfortable here and at Lou's—that's why you agreed to watching the movie here."

She shrugs, and I follow her up three flights of stairs until we get to a quiet area—though aren't they all? This one has cubby areas and small rooms lining the walls. In the middle are tables with students reading or working on their laptops.

She takes the lead and we circle the area while she peers into various rooms.

"All the bigger rooms are taken, so we'll have to take one of the smaller ones."

"It's just the two of us. It will be like we're in class," I say.

Only we'll be alone.

She clears her throat. "Right. This one, then." She nods at a small space to the right with just enough room for a desk and—

"Dang it. There's only one chair." Her arms cross.

"Wanna sit in my lap?" I say the words, but I don't mean them. It's a joke. Right?

She flushes. "No. You wanna sit on the floor?"

"I don't mind. I can drag a chair in here from somewhere," I offer.

She mulls that over and looks around. Most of the chairs at the tables are taken, and the ones that aren't have books sitting where a person isn't.

"We came all this way, and we aren't just going to give up because we don't have a chair. The small room is fine. I promise to not touch you."

"I know. You never touch me," she murmurs.

A whoosh of air comes out of me, but she isn't paying attention as she walks inside ahead of me.

"It's perfect." I set my laptop on the desk then plop down on the carpeted floor with my back to the wall. "You take the chair. I'll sit behind you."

She bites her lips, her hair dipping down. Her eyes glow when she looks up. "You're so mean."

"Moi? Why?" I ask dryly.

"Because you brought Snickers and what you really want is for me to sit far, far away so you can eat them all."

I pull one out and wave it at her.

She snatches the laptop and places it on my legs as she sits next to me on the floor. "Now bring up the movie." She pauses. "Unless, of course, you're afraid of being close to me?"

My gaze slides over her carefully, trying not to linger on her bare, long legs, the pink color on her toes. "Fort Knox is afraid of nothing."

She snorts. "Don't think I didn't notice how you didn't answer my question." Her legs brush against mine briefly before she scoots over and puts space between us.

"Mmmm." I click play on *Dirty Dancing*. Anything to keep her out of my head.

This watching it together thing was your idea, I remind myself.

Several minutes later, I give her a candy bar and take one for myself.

"Yum, dessert. Thanks." She takes a big bite of hers and smiles.

Shit. Just...*shit*. Have I ever seen her this *close* to me, relaxed and smiling?

"No problem." I look away from her mouth and focus on the movie as Baby tries to dance with Johnny, failing miserably.

Several minutes pass and I pretend to watch, hyperaware of every twitch she makes. Every now and then, her lids lower then pop back open.

"You tired?"

"No."

I smile at her lie.

"Did you know Kellerman's is a real place, but it isn't in the Catskills?" she says quietly as her head leans a little, inches from my shoulder. "I looked it up after you mentioned it in class."

"Where is it?"

Her gaze refocuses as she blinks. "Virginia, and it's called something else—Mountain Lake Resort. It looks like a magical place to spend a summer."

"Where's your favorite place to vacation?"

She smirks. "Never been out of Nashville, but I'd love to see the ocean some day. Sand between my toes kind of thing. I'll go when I'm done with college, take Tyler with me. He would flip. Someday."

I have to look away from her face.

She's too...sweet.

Vulnerable.

I ease my body away from her, just a few inches. I have no right to be this close to her, not after what I did—

"What was your favorite vacation ever?" she murmurs, interrupting my thoughts.

I don't even have to think about it. "When I was little, maybe seven, my parents took us skiing in Colorado. They were getting along then, or at least they still seemed like they cared about each other. Dane and I tore up the bunny slopes. Dad loved it too. Mom liked to stay in the cabin and make us hot chocolates when we got back. The snow was beautiful and white and clean. It felt like only good things could happen in a place like that." I clear my throat. "Honestly, I can't remember a good vacation since then. My dad started working all the time, my mom was diagnosed with bipolar depression, and then everything else happened."

There's a long silence. Johnny and Baby are on the screen, but Ava and I stare at each other.

"*Everything else* just covered a whole lot of stuff you aren't saying," she says softly.

My heart dips. I really don't want to talk about Mom and the final straw that tore her down. It's too close to what happened to Ava. "Tulip, don't... Let's just watch the movie."

At first, I think she's going to press me, but something she sees on my face changes her mind.

"Of course." She turns back to the screen and the moment is gone.

Time passes, and I watch the movie, or do I? The images are there, but she's here, and my muscles are wired, and why did I want to do this and why am I torturing myself with someone I can never have?

I don't want to even be her friend.

So why do I want to know her favorite color?

What's in that locket she clutches?

What makes her happy?

Why does she love tomatoes?

I glance down at the notebook she's been half-heartedly writing in, reading her notes.

Who calls a grown woman Baby?

Awkward, but opinionated. She's the real hero. Courageous. Forces her family to see what she sees.

Johnny is hot. Dude can dance. He's kind. Cares for his friends. Men should be kind. Kisses AMAZING. Dang. He knows how to look at a woman. And dance. Heard he was a ballet dancer in real life.

Romantic aspect: First love. Love in adversity. Love between opposites. Palpable chemistry, that's for damn sure...

And then the pen falls out of her hand, her body sways, just a little, coming closer, and her head bobs forward, then back to the wall, then she's lying on my shoulder. Out cold.

The room is hot. Fucking stifling.

My hands clench.

So close.

So damn close to me.

A broken girl.

A fierce girl.

Just for me.

God, how I want that.

Her body shifts imperceptibly closer to mine until the side of her face presses against my chest. The final scene plays as the staff dance and Johnny catches Baby when she does that fancy jump thing. I barely notice—hell, I'm barely breathing when the credits roll, and I still haven't moved five minutes later, afraid to jostle her, to lose how good she feels, the warmth of her arm against mine, the scent of her hair in my face.

Moving slowly, my hand touches her hair, my finger drifting over the edge of her jaw. So delicate. So soft. Sliding a strand of hair behind her ear, my head goes back to last year when she was in that tub at Chance's and I was...well, doing what I was doing. I was so pissed and angry at myself, at her, watching her dance, *with him*, driving myself nuts imagining them doing more. She was his, and I'm an asshole, but I'd *never* hurt my best friend.

My hand caresses her nape, that delicate skin under her hair—

"What! What did I miss?!" She jerks back, wiping at her face, shuffling away from me.

And she's gone.

My hand falls. I can't look at her, so I stare at the laptop.

"Crap! Did I miss the ending?" She blows out a breath.

Inhaling, I say, "It's over, Tulip."

And I don't mean just the movie. I have to shut down this rollercoaster she's put me on.

A sound of frustration comes from her lips. "Ugh! I was wiped out! First week of school and work and Tyler and *school*..." She pauses as a small bell dings in the room. "And they're closing in fifteen minutes! We didn't even talk about the movie!" She stands up, hands on her hips as she paces as much as she can in the room. "What now?" She checks her phone. "It's almost ten and the entrance at the dorms will be locked—"

I finally move when my legs feel steady, standing up next to her. "Come on, I'll walk you to your car. Don't worry about the notes. We'll figure it out in class."

She frowns, gathering her backpack. "We can sit on the steps outside the library, on the fountain where there's plenty of light, and go over—"

"No."

"Why not? I'm not sleepy anymore. I can call Wyatt, and he'll open a side door for me—"

"No."

She pauses, tilting her face up, looking at mine. Granite. I'm stone. Have to be.

Her shoulders rise. "I see."

I stuff my laptop in my backpack and gather up our trash from the snacks.

She watches me. "Are you pissed because I fell asleep?"

"I just need to go, charity case."

Her lips thin. "We could have done this over the freaking phone."

But she's talking to my back because I'm already walking out the door and holding it open for her.

Our eyes meet. Hers are a stormy sea. Mine are...shit, they're cold, I hope.

She takes a little breath, straightens her shoulders, and slides past me. I inhale, just one more time, just a hint of vanilla.

"I have to go...check on Dane." Which is true. He sent me several texts already, asking where I am. He's home alone, and I haven't responded, and that isn't like me.

She doesn't reply and I follow her, keeping a step between us as we go down the three flights of stairs, moving past other students on their way out. She walks with her shoulders rolled back, confident, like she belongs here—nothing like Camden where she alternates between forced viciousness and that vulnerable bend in her frame.

She smiles at someone who catches her eye, a guy, and he turns around backward to watch her ass. Giving him a withering glance, I continue on, catching up to her until we're side by side.

We exit, past the steps, past the trickling fountain, all the way out to the parking lot, to her car. Neither of us speak.

She opens her door, throws her backpack in the passenger side, and starts to get in then stops and pivots to face me.

Her chest rises. "What is wrong with you? You wanted to do this. You wanted us to watch it together. Why are you such a dick—" Her eyes widen and she reaches out a hand and touches my chest. Confusion clouds her face. "Knox, why... why are you shaking?"

Her palm flattens to my heart, and I wonder if she can feel how fast it's beating.

My mouth dries. I blink. I might pass out.

We just stare at each other, and the night is warm, and her hand is hot, electric sparks firing from her to me. I think if you tell yourself something enough, over and over again, just maybe you can make it come true. I can't have her. I can't have *this*. I can't, I can't, I can't, I can't.

I'll settle for me. For Dane. For football.

Your life is so fucked up, a dark voice insists, laughing mirthlessly.

If only you'd staked a claim before Chance.

If only...

I jerk away from her and she gapes at me, shaking her head in confusion.

"Knox?"

I look away from her and stare at my feet. Familiar shame and guilt ride me hard, slugging at my heart, ripping it apart.

I left her.

I fucking left her because I was upset because she kissed her *boyfriend*.

How messed up is that?

I want her.

I fucking do.

But you can't take a beautiful, soft flower and crush it under your cleats, not when she's halfway to broken already.

"Tulip..." I push out, and I don't even know what I'm going to say, but she ignores me, because I've stood here like an idiot for too long.

She's in her car and "You Need to Calm Down" blares from her speakers. Wearing a frown, she pulls out, and me... I'm just standing there, watching her taillights.

13

AVA

"…And then Dane said, 'But why does Charlotte have to die!' I can't believe we got through the movie at my house. He sniffled at the end even after I said at least Wilbur got her eggs and that means there'll be little baby spiders for him to take care of, and he just glared at me. I swear, I think those drugs have addled his brain." She stuffs a burrito in her mouth as we eat lunch on Friday then wipes her lips and lets out a groan. "Okay, okay, I wore my Bambi shirt when I knew he was coming over, you know, just to make him uncomfortable. Was that mean? He never said anything, so I guess it was okay." Another groan. "I mean, come on, what guy is so ridiculously soft about animals?"

"I don't care how he feels. Asshole Shark," I mutter.

"I saw Knox turned your paper in early today. How was it?" She gives me a careful look, and I'm sure it was apparent in class that Knox and I were barely speaking. Gone are the snide comments. Gone are the tentative glances. Since the movie night, he's a different person. We had this fun camaraderie at Lou's, and then it all went wrong when I fell asleep. Did I say something in my sleep? Nah. He's just...

Out of your depth.

Playing games.

I glare at my Diet Coke. "He didn't even ask me to help write it, just wrote it himself, and on top of that, he switched our romance theme for feminism without asking when he was the one who liked the romantic aspect. Jerk. Big stupid jerk. Should have been *Star Wars* from the get-go."

"At least you didn't have to do it," Wyatt says with a grin.

The thing is, part of me was looking forward to hashing out our ideas and working together. He gave me a copy of it today when I walked into History of Film, and when I said, "Dude, what the hell?" he only gave me grunts and nods. Caveman!

I read his essay, huffing, while he sat next to me, tense and wired.

"Maybe he really is pissed I wrote his cell number on the stall in the bathroom. Dammit, I should have written it at Lou's. Missed opportunity."

Wyatt's eyes flare. "You're the one who blabbed his super-secret phone number?"

"Weak moment." I grin.

He puts his fist up and we bump. "Sneaky. Remind me to never tell you my secrets."

"Meh, he really didn't care that much," I say. I haven't told them about us at Lou's or Vandy. Part of me wants to just pretend it never happened, because hello, he has.

Inevitably, my eyes scan over to the Shark table. He's there, sitting next to Tawny. She keeps chatting up at him, batting those lashes. He barely notices her, typical, and focuses on his phone. Dane sits on the other side of him, pushing food around on his plate, his eyes at half-mast. In class, he was the same, sluggish and off. Chance sits across from them, Brooklyn plastered to his side. I don't see Liam and Jolena. Come to think of it, I haven't seen them at the Shark table since the fight earlier this week.

I glance back to Wyatt and Piper. "So, Knox has a black eye and Liam does too. I'm assuming the fight was at practice, but what's the word on the street? Anyone know what it was about?"

"No clue. I've been buried in homework and trying to keep my grades up there with a certain someone," Piper says.

"Me." I laugh.

She giggles.

Wyatt cocks his head. "I may have heard it was over you."

I drop my burrito. "What?"

"Seems like Liam was badmouthing you and Knox shut him up."

My mouth drops. "*Me?*"

"You," he repeats.

"But why?"

He shrugs. "I can't even begin to understand how he thinks. He keeps shit close."

No joke.

Wyatt dips his fry in ketchup and tosses it in his mouth. "Why are you staring at him?"

"I'm not!"

He laughs, glancing down at one of the hummingbird tattoos on his forearms. He gives it a little brush, his face thoughtful. "I saw that your locker was scrubbed pretty good.

Heard it was done after practice by a couple of football players."

"Chance and Knox," I mutter as I push my burger away from me. The words were mostly gone by the end of the day it happened, but I was able to see a few faint outlines, the E in leave, the L in slut.

It was Chance's idea, Knox said.

My eyes linger on Chance, and he glances up and stares right back. Brooklyn tugs on his arm and he finally drops his gaze.

Piper follows my gaze. "Jockass! I hope he rots! Saying that *you hurt him*. What a dick." She shakes her head. "Geeze, he was all over you last year—"

"Let it go," I grumble. We've hashed this out in my dorm room, and I'm sick of thinking about it. I blow out a breath. The truth is, I'm exhausted. Last night, I had dinner with Tyler at the group home, worked a shift at the diner, then came home and tried to do homework. Between Knox and this hellhole, my nerves are stretched thin, and there's dread and unease nipping at my heels. The flat tire and locker incident won't be the end of it. Something else will happen.

The bell rings and we gather up our trash. Piper and Wyatt head off, and I dash to the restroom. I'm walking down the hall when my phone vibrates with a text, and I pull it out of my blazer pocket.

Hey. I've been thinking about you. How's your day?

Well, well, I'd almost forgotten about my admirer. A small part of me—a silly part—briefly entertained the idea that it was Knox. He did come to change my tire from out of the blue.

But I asked him at Lou's in a roundabout way if it was

him, and while he didn't say no, he seemed cool about it. So, not him.

I stop in the hall and lean against the wall.

What do you want? I type.

Students rush past me, but I'm oblivious as I wait for his response.

You.

Could this person be Chance? He said some revealing things in that apology, and he did leave me little notes in my locker last year...

Is this Chance? If it is, you can go fuck yourself sideways. And I hope you pull a groin muscle and break your penis.

Ouch. That sounds painful.

Yet...he doesn't answer my question.

I watch the dots on my phone, my heart beating faster than it should.

I read something for my Contemporary Poetry class and it made me think of you.

I rack my brain for who's in that particular class, one of the senior favorites. I didn't take it because my focus is math and science. History of Film is my only elective.

Yeah? Send me the poem.

I expect him to send me a name and title, but instead a longer text comes in, the lines typed carefully.

I yearn for her,
To ease the monsters in my head.

My hard heart wants the glass heart in her.

Obviously, I am out of my mind.

It's good, short and succinct.

Nice, SA. I happen to like poetry.

SA? He sends.

Secret admirer, duh.

"Slut," a male voice mutters as he jostles past me in the hall and keeps moving. I don't even try to see who it was. It's the second time today. Pushing down the singe of pain those words cause in me, I look back down at my phone.

What am I doing texting with someone who could be an enemy?

Besides, it's my free period and I want to check out the new auditorium upstairs. They started construction last year, and I left before it was finished. Maybe I can think there. Catch my breath. Think about my goals and hope they can sustain me. As long as I pop by to see the librarian who's in charge of my period and tell her I have some teachers to check in with, she'll give me a pass to roam a little.

I have to go, I type out.

What class?

Screw that. I stuff my phone back inside my blazer and book it to the library.

After getting my pass, I head to the stairwell that leads to the fourth floor where one of the inside entrances to the new auditorium is. My footsteps are soft as I take the second flight. I'm adjusting my backpack when I hear the first-floor door open and someone comes into the quiet stairwell. A guy's voice is speaking, and I pause at the familiar cadence I hear, the slow, burly drawl.

Another voice, soft and cajoling and female, hits my ears.

I strain to hear their conversation, getting frustrated when they lower their voices. They don't seem to be actually moving up the stairs, so I take a few steps back and hunker down next to the concrete barrier, working up the nerve to peep around it. The key to good eavesdropping is not getting caught.

Rising up slowly, I take in Liam and Jolena. With his back to me, he's leaned down toward her small frame, and she's taking a step back from him, crossing her arms over her chest.

Oh, drama.

Not able to hear them, I settle back on my heels and maneuver down one more flight, trying to be a ninja.

Jolena's voice reaches me. "Brooklyn said you were flirting with that Brandy girl in your English class."

He scoffs. "Come on, I asked her for a pen. A *pen*. Brooklyn is stirring up trouble."

"Is she? What about the girl this summer? The one who kept texting you?"

His voice lowers. "I explained that already. Don't make me repeat it."

She lets out a frustrated noise.

"Ah, baby..." he murmurs.

She says something with intensity, her voice low and garbled.

A long pause, then, "Don't preach to me, Jo. Knox will get over it, or if he doesn't, I don't care. He hit me—over her. Don't you take his side because you screwed him once. Yeah, you think I don't think about that every time I see him?"

She mumbles something. It sounds like *I love you.*

Liam tilts her chin up. "I know, baby. I love you too."

Gag.

"He thinks he runs this place, but I'm the star around here, and we never would have won the games we did if it wasn't for my defense."

It rankles that I can't see his expression, and I wish I could see his face, see *his* black eye.

She puts her hand on her hip, and I start when I hear my name.

His voice tightens. "Can I help it that she was all over me that night? You know how girls are with me. I always tell them no, baby. Always. You're my number one. I left that party with Dane and we crashed at my house. I never touched her. I had my wingman with me, all night."

Huh. She can't get past the video, and I don't even remember dancing with him!

My eyes shut as dark thoughts seep in. No matter how many times I tell myself it wasn't my fault, bitterness rears up and I recall that I did dance with football players. I drank a lot of alcohol, some of it mine, some of it someone else's. I DID. I own that.

But for someone to use me...no, no, no.

They kiss. Full-on tongue. Gross.

No way am I staying for a porno.

I inch away to leave, and a clatter sounds as my phone falls out of my pocket and crashes onto the concrete floor next to me. The make-out noises stop and I cringe, trying to back away while snatching up my phone. I hear the stairwell door bursting open where they are. Relief washes over me.

Still in stealth mode, I risk another peek and see Jolena still there, her shoulders hunched as she pulls a compact out of her purse to fix her lipstick. Her hands shake as she sucks in a deep breath and pats at her auburn hair.

I frown, having a little epiphany as I crouch down. Where's her pride? Her self-love? She reminds me of Mama, accepting excuses when someone treats her horribly, pretending he isn't doing her wrong. Money and a pretty face and her queen bee status sure haven't gotten her much. She left me at that party and I seethe whenever I think about it, but part of me, I realize, pities her.

Forgetting her, I take off again, opening the doors to the third floor. Utter silence meets me until I turn the corner and run smack dab into a broad chest covered by a white button-down shirt, one that smells like pine.

I look up into gray eyes, taking in the manbun and handsome angular jaw.

"Watch where you're going, sweetheart," Dane says. "You never know who's up here."

The hall is empty, and he's too close to me, our chests almost touching. It's the first time I've been alone with him with no one around, and I push him away from me, harder than I meant to, making him stumble.

He straightens, tosses his head back, and laughs, running his eyes over my hair and face. "I see why he's drawn to you."

My teeth clench. "Who?"

"You know who."

"Just stay away from me," I call out, my voice more shrill than I intend.

His eyes narrow. "Don't hurt him, Ava. Don't mess with my brother."

What? "You're crazy."

He lets out a gruff sound. "You don't know the shit he's

been through. He acts like it doesn't bother him, holds it in so tight I'm afraid he's going to crack someday, but he's got a heart. He does, and if you even think for a minute you're gonna possibly ruin his last chance at playing football—"

I shake my head. "What on earth are you talking about? How can I hurt your brother? He's the one playing hot and cold with me!"

He clamps his mouth shut. "Nothing. Forget I said anything."

"Are you in some delusional world where you think I have power over him?"

He taps his hand against his leg, those flinty, dilated eyes on my face.

"You're high. Back off and leave me alone." I whip around to go in the opposite direction—

"Ava!" There's a desperate quality to his voice that forces me to turn around and answer.

My fists curl. "What?"

His face is weird, drawn up and twisted, strangely vulnerable.

"What is it? Say it!"

He closes his eyes briefly as if he's waiting for me to disappear, but I hold steady, feeling as if I can't move. He's got something to say.

"Knox went to every single football player's house after you went to the police. He raked them over the coals, even the seniors who are gone now. He pissed off the team. We lost games because he pointed his fingers hard at every guy who danced with you, including *me*."

Confusion pummels me. Why? Why would he feel responsible for me?

Forget that.

My chest rises. "Was it you?" I snap out. "Apparently I was all over you and I have no memory of it. Don't think I missed anything." I eye him up and down and scoff. I'm brave right now, so brave, because he...he looks as if he's in some kind of internal war with himself.

He swallows and looks away from me, his throat bobbing. "I'm not...like ...that. You aren't the only one who doesn't remember much from that night."

I'm walking away when his voice reaches me, that tinge of anguish back. "Ava, wait."

I ignore him, keeping my back to him as I hold my arm up and flip him off.

His next words make me freeze. "Knox hired a private investigator to look into that night. Nobody knows but me and our dad, but he followed up with him for three months, trying to get to the bottom of what happened, and I don't even know why he cares except that he..." He trails off and I turn around.

"Why would he care so much?"

He shakes his head.

"Why?" I yell, putting steel in my voice.

He flinches. "Shit. Our mom was assaulted. Like you."

The air is sucked out of the hallway and I gasp, my hands holding my chest. I study Dane's face. "I didn't know."

"Hardly anyone does." He stares at a point over my shoulder and clenches his fist, seeming to try to gather himself. He does a bad job of it because his hands shake as he stuffs them in his pants. "She was a pianist for the Nashville Symphony. She came out a side door at night after a concert to get to her car and two guys...they...they..." He takes a shuddering breath. "They broke her arm. Cracked ribs. She was in the hospital for a few days…" He gasps out, "They raped her and left her in an alley."

Horror claws at my throat at those images, making me sick. I take deep breaths, trying to align this new information in my head and process what it means. "Dane…I'm sorry."

He doesn't really hear me, I think, or he doesn't acknowledge it. He continues, the words sounding as if they're being wrenched from him by force. "My dad kept most of it out of the papers, but that fear on her face when it got dark, when she'd double then triple-check all the doors in the house, when she'd sit and just look off into space…I saw that. Knox saw that. Once, in the middle of the night, she drove to where it happened and wandered around the streets in her nightgown and bare feet. She was never the same. My dad isn't the same." He closes his eyes and sighs heavily. "Fuck all of it."

Then he's edging past me, kicking open the door to the stairwell and disappearing.

Trying to wrap my head around the new information, I don't even realize I've stepped into the dark auditorium, blinking to adjust to the change from the bright lights of the hallway.

Their mom was raped. Like me.

I can't—I can't think about it right now.

My eyes sweep over the cavernous space, taking in the plush new seats, the wide stage with deep black curtains on either side. Written up above in old-style Greek letters is *Camden Prep*. I focus on the stage, lingering on the spotlight equipment poised in the rafters, just waiting to bathe someone in light.

I settle down in one of the chairs and lay my head back,

staring up at the heavy gold chandeliers that hang from the ceiling while I mull everything over. I don't know how long I sit there before the adrenaline rush finally eases and exhaustion comes roaring back.

My lids feel heavy...

Strong arms carry me, tucking me inside a car. He murmurs something as he buckles my seat belt. Hands cup my cheeks and stare down at me, his gaze searching mine, a questioning look on his face. "Ava—"

The sound of a piano playing jolts me awake. Beautiful and flowing, the notes are a familiar tune, Demi Lovato's "Skyscraper", a song about a girl people think is made of paper but who is tough with her sharp lines; she's a high-rise with broken windows but still standing, and no one can tear her down.

The player is skilled and intent, catching the low notes with the faster higher ones, the music executed with precision yet layered with emotion. Someone knows how to play. I ease up and stare toward the stage, at the black baby grand front and center.

I suck in a breath, feeling rocked. His head is tilted low, his fingers moving delicately and swiftly over the white and black keys. He's dressed in that vented white practice jersey, his football pants on, ready for practice.

Not thinking much about what I'm going to say, I stand up and walk toward him.

He's oblivious to me, the intensity of the notes he plays consuming him.

Who *is* Knox Grayson?

He ends the song and throws his head back, eyes closed as he drinks in those final notes, his lips slightly parted.

Clarity tiptoes in my head, my dream merging with the truth.

"You found me at the party." My voice is low but enough to pop his eyes open.

He jerks up from the piano stool. "What are you doing here?"

"You're playing my song."

"It's not your song."

"It is!" I call out, my own confusion combined with what Dane told me pricking at me. "I sang it at the party and you were thinking about me when you played it so don't pretend with me. You found me, put me in your car, and took me to Piper's." Placing my hands on the stage, I heave myself up and sit on the wooden floor, glaring at him. I'm not sure if I'm ready to rip his head off or hug him.

He just stares at me, emotion working his face, fists clenched, until he slowly shuts it down, composing himself with deep breaths. His gaze rips away from me. "How do you know I took you to Piper's? I didn't... You never contacted me or asked me."

I cross my legs and tug at my skirt. "I just remembered it. It's weird, the more time I spend at this place, the more the memories come."

He buries his hands in his hair. "Ava..."

I swallow, looking away from his chiseled, beautiful

features. It hurts how much he's ignored me for the past two days, and now this.

"I'm glad you found me, okay, but you didn't take me to the hospital. Maybe if you had, they might have found something in my system besides alcohol. I can't be sure, but my gut says someone *did* do something to my drink. Maybe then everyone would *believe me*."

He walks over and sits down next to me, keeping just enough distance between us so that he doesn't touch me. Ha. I'm sick of that, for sure.

His face is troubled. "Ava...please believe me...I didn't know you'd been assaulted. I saw you at the party earlier in the night, and I assumed you'd had too much when I found you."

"Why did you come back?" I ask sharply.

"Dane." He bends his head for a moment. "He doesn't know when to stop, and I keep tabs on him. After I took Tawny home, I went back to look for him, but I found you. *Just you.*" He whispers out the last part. Grimness flashes over his face. "I didn't know...how bad it was for you. It never entered my head that—"

"Didn't you see that..." I stop, mentally pushing myself. "I didn't even have underwear on!"

He shakes his head and says gravely, "I was just shocked to see you. I didn't look there. I saw you on the ground and assumed you were trashed. I didn't know where you lived—"

"So you took me to Piper's and rang the doorbell."

He swallows. "Right. I thought you'd sleep it off. Then, the next day I heard you'd gone to the hospital." His face hardens. "I had no idea. You looked okay to me. Sick maybe, definitely drunk. As soon as I knew the truth, I went to the police and told them how I found you and took you to Piper's. I felt terrible. If I had known—"

I shake my head. "The police never told me that! Why wouldn't they?"

He gets a pained expression on his face. "The police here know who signs their paychecks, Ava. It's a small community run by rich men. Liam's dad is the mayor, my dad owns half the town, and you...you don't matter to them, not when it comes to protecting the people here." He stares down at his hands. "I'm sorry."

The detective's words come roaring back. *"Miss Harris, is it possible you consented to sex? Your behavior at the party was, well, indicative of..."*

I breathe. Big inhalation. Long exhalation.

"The police questioned me for hours," he continues. "They had a timeline for everyone who was there and who they left with, but because I'd left early, I couldn't help with those alibis. If it's any consolation, they looked at me harder than anyone. I looked suspicious because I picked you up. Then my dad showed up and the cops let me go."

A harsh laugh comes out of me. "I'm no one in this town, but the rest of you...ha. I'm no one. Just a nobody girl." He doesn't respond, and I push on. "Dane said the team suffered. He said you questioned everyone personally and hired a P.I. for me."

He starts, and I study him intently, trying to catalogue every expression he gives me. He's such a brick wall, and like always, I want to knock it down. "He told me about your mother. I'm sorry about what happened to her. Is that why you hired a private investigator? Guilt for not taking me to the hospital?"

He whitens, his shoulders tensing. "Shit."

"You don't like to talk about what happened to her, and I get it. It's not pleasant, I imagine, seeing someone unravel and there isn't a damn thing you can do about it."

"She had a lot of issues before she was assaulted, Ava."

I inhale. "I hate it when you call me Ava instead of Tulip, you know. You're putting distance between us. Even now, when I know you aren't the big bad Shark you want me to think you are." I huff out a breath.

He grows quiet. Then, "Can you forgive me for not taking you to the hospital? For not—" He stops, his top teeth biting down hard on his bottom lip.

"What?"

His lashes flutter against his cheeks.

"Just say it. Please." I don't know why I'm begging him, but he's so close, so close to telling me what I sense is just right there.

"For not staying, okay? I should have stayed, but I left because..."

"You saw me kissing Chance."

He closes his eyes. "If I'd stayed, maybe—"

That moment plays back in my head, when Chance said he loved me and Knox was standing right there with Tawny. The anguish on his face...

Was it real?

I shake myself, pushing that away for now.

"It wasn't your fault, and I never want you to feel guilty for something you had no control over."

"But...I didn't even do the right thing when I found you! It drives me crazy!"

I'll kill him with my bare hands.

Moments tick by.

"I'm starting to think no one really knows you. You hire a private investigator, you fight with Liam over me..." I murmur, shaking my head.

Tentatively and carefully, he reaches out and touches my hand. "Don't you know me, Tulip?"

My body tingles at the use of my middle name combined with his hand, and dang, it's such a simple thing, but...

"You've told me more than the cops ever did."

My frustration ebbs away, leaving bitterness and regret, yet in the end, I can't blame anything on Knox. I went to that party. I let my guard down. I own that.

"Thank you for taking me to Piper's. You might have saved my life. I seriously entertained the idea of a coyote getting me," I add, trying for levity, but he doesn't laugh. "Anyway, I could have choked on my own vomit out there in the woods."

His jaw tightens.

I sigh.

"I'm *not* mad at you." I stand up.

He stands, gray eyes holding mine.

"But I can tell you can't make up your mind about something when it comes to me. You're holding back."

He crosses his arms. "Trust me, that's a good thing."

"Is it?" I cock my head. "Tell me, what else have you done for me lately? Someone paid for my housing, and you were the one who came out of Trask's office before I went in —after I'd just told you I wasn't in the dorms. Was that you?"

He drops his eyes and paces around the stage.

"Knox?"

He waves me off and plops down on the piano seat. "I

blamed myself for not staying at the party and making sure nothing happened to you."

"Uh-huh. We've established that point. You're not answering my question."

He nods. "At the same time, I got all this information about you from the P.I.—how you grew up, how your mom left you with a baby, how you beat the odds and managed to get a scholarship to Camden. You're a bright star in this shitty place. You're not like anyone I've ever met."

"Was it you?"

He stands and marches over to me, staring down at me with those hot eyes. "I know underneath that tough-girl exterior, you'd do anything for the people you love. Do you know how rare that is? People may say they *care* and *love*, but from what I've seen, they only look out for themselves. You, though, you feel so intensely. You love so hard you came back to Camden for your brother—"

"Is there anything about me you don't know? When I was spilling my guts to you in class and at Lou's, did you already know those things?"

"I knew about your mom. I knew she left you, and I knew you lived on the streets sometimes. I knew Trask had asked you back and you requested to live in the dorms, but—"

He stops and swallows, his brow furrowed. He turns back to me, meeting my gaze, holding it steady. Still he doesn't speak. I see that mask slipping back onto his face.

"Knox? Don't you pussy out on me. This is the most honest conversation we've had, and I want to hear it all."

I move closer, and part of me knows it throws him off, makes him uneasy. The smell of him, like summer and ocean waves, surrounds me.

My eyes trace the hard lines of his jaw, the long, strong nose, the way his dark hair falls around his face.

When he speaks, the words come reluctantly. "You've always fascinated me, okay? Since day one, since the moment you waltzed through those doors with your long blonde hair and eyes full of all that hope. Everyone else comes here and they already have everything, but you had nothing—nothing except your power. You barely looked at any of us, especially me, and I knew then you were untouchable, knew you deserved better than any guy at Camden." He pauses. "Then Chance...you gave him a shot."

He thinks I have *power*?

I'm *untouchable*?

A small laugh comes from me, some of that confidence I've lost along the way reemerging. The king of Camden sees me...he sees *me* as someone I never have.

He touches my hair, just barely. "You walked in Monday with all your hair cut off and a different color and, fuck, I was sad."

My heart thuds. "Really?"

"Mmmm. When I sat behind you in class, I used to touch it with my pencil, and you never even noticed. You smell like vanilla, do you know that?"

I'm afraid to say anything, to stop him.

"Every day I'd get a little braver and *barely* touch my pencil to your shoulder, your arm. I was afraid to want you, then hurt you—"

The auditorium door creaks open and we hear two voices —teacher voices.

"We're not supposed to be in here," I hiss.

He grabs my hand and pulls me behind the black

curtain. Somehow I end up in front of him, his chest to my back with the heavy curtains inches from my face. I feel the hard muscles of his body, the brush of his hips at the small of my back. His hands land on my shoulders then fall. I inhale.

The air around us crackles. He's right there. Against me.

I can't breathe, and it isn't a bad thing. It's intoxicating.

"Is there a back exit?" I whisper.

There's a small slit in the fabric and he reaches around me, his bicep teasing my cheek as he peeks through. "Don't worry. It's Maxine and the janitor, Carl." His voice is ragged and gravelly.

He played with my hair—

"How are you on a first-name basis with the staff here?" Am I really trying to have a conversation with him when all I want is...

We hear smacking sounds.

My eyes flare. "What are they doing out there?"

His hand lands on my shoulder after parting the curtain again. His fingers toy with my hair, and my body clenches, sparks igniting and giving me goose bumps.

"Making out." He growls as if speaking the words is torture. His hand slides to my nape, barely a touch.

"No way," I whisper, trying to gain control and pretend his body isn't plastered to mine, every single inch of delicious muscle.

"Look for yourself," he says, his lips brushing against the skin of my ear. He moves the curtain so I can see, leaving a small sliver of a gap so he doesn't have to hold it.

Sure enough, Maxine and Carl are in an embrace near one of the seats on the far right toward the front of the stage.

He's a small man, a bit rotund, but he knows his stuff, his hands on her boobs. *Go Carl.*

I can't even think straight, but somehow I say, "Her bun is down and he's got some amazing mutton chops. Dang, now he's unbuttoning her shirt."

"Hmmm, they look like they're enjoying it," Knox says, his right hand moving to my hip like it's a homing beacon.

I watch Carl and Maxine with envy, hearing her breathy little gasps when he cups her breast. He moves his lips down, takes a nipple in his mouth, and sucks.

My mind is dirty, so dirty, because I'm picturing Knox doing that to me.

"Do you like watching them?" he murmurs.

"Maybe." I melt into him, feeling more of him, his cock that's most certainly hard. My head eases back and rests on his shoulder.

"Tulip, fuck, what are you doing to me?" he mutters, his hand tightening, his other one grasping my other hip.

"I'm not doing anything," I gasp out.

"You're killing me," he rumbles in my ear. His tongue licks at the top and bites down, and I moan.

We still when Maxine's head comes up and she looks around the auditorium, squinting in the darkness as if she knows we're watching.

"Now you've done it. We're gonna get caught," he whispers.

"You're the one who bit my ear," I murmur breathlessly, excited and scared, and...

"Did you like it, Tulip?"

"Yes." I close my eyes. I can't see his face, and I wish I could.

The bell rings, and neither of us moves. Carl and Maxine do though, straightening their clothes and murmuring to each other.

"We have to get out of here," I say after a while when neither of us has spoken. "I have a class."

"I can skip. It's just gym."

"You can't miss football."

"I will." His nose presses into my hair, and my breath hitches. He's being so careful with his little touches, but I sense the coil of tension buzzing inside him.

I just...

I'm afraid if I turn around, this spell will be broken.

"Truth or dare, Knox?" I whisper after Maxine and Carl exit the auditorium.

His hands slide up my arms and land on my shoulders, kneading the muscles there. "You want to play games, Tulip?"

"Yes."

He tilts my head to the side and kisses my neck with the softest touch, and I'm languid in his arms. "Dare."

It's quiet in here, so quiet.

"You were supposed to say truth," I mutter.

He laughs quietly against my skin.

"Fine. Let me turn around then. That's your dare."

He grows still, his hands tightening. "Why?"

"Rules of the game. Let go and let me face you."

"I changed my mind. Truth it is."

"Did you pay for my housing?" I ask huskily.

A long pause, then, "Yes."

God, he's so... Why have I never seen his...*kind nature*? How could I have been so blind?

I yank myself out of his grip and flip around to stare at him.

"Tulip...shit...you ask for too much from me." He shifts us so we aren't pressed so tightly together, yet he leans his forehead against mine.

I count his lashes, the dark curls thick and lush like a girl's. I trace the line of his granite jaw. My eyes linger on the scar on his face.

"Truth or dare, Knox."

"Isn't it my turn?" he pushes out, his gaze wary.

My chest is tight, an ache there. "No. This is my game."

"Truth, then."

"What's between us?" My voice shakes. "Since last year, there's been this connection and I can't explain it."

His eyes close briefly. "I know how it feels to walk into a room and feel as if no one really knows you. So do you."

I stare up at him, running my eyes over his broad shoulders, that powerful chest that's *so still* right now.

"Truth or dare, again, and you can't say truth this time. My rules," I say.

"This isn't a very fair game."

"Just do it my way this one time, and I'll owe you one."

He inhales sharply as if he knows what's coming. His hands cup my face. "You are pushing all my buttons right now, do you know that? I'm barely keeping my hands off you, Tulip, and once I let go—"

"Truth or dare, Cold and Evil. You pick, and you better choose the right one, damn you."

"Dare."

"Kiss me." I run my finger over that slice through his upper lip.

He shudders, his eyes lowering, pupils dilating. "I don't kiss on the mouth, but you're looking at me like...like..." His voice grows huskier as he takes a step closer until finally my chest is against his. I sigh into the hardness of the power I feel underneath me, the friction of his jersey against my button-down.

"Do you want this fucked-up mouth on you, Tulip?"

"Yes," I whisper, heat firing through my body at the *frankness* of him. At this moment, I want his fucked-up mouth all over me. "I'd like to know if...if it's still good for me."

He stares down at me, the air thickening between us. "You're treading on thin ice..." But his actions don't align with his words. He's sliding his hand into my hair and palming my scalp. His breathing intensifies when his lips hover over mine. "Tulip—"

Before I chicken out—or he does—I arch my neck and press my mouth to his, giving his scar my attention first, pressing small, lingering kisses to that indentation before parting my lips and sliding them across his in delicate strokes.

Seconds pass as I kiss him and he just stands there, until finally, he groans and wraps his hands around my nape, angling my head to get deeper. He murmurs my name, his lips hesitant then changing as I nip at him, tugging on the bottom one. His strong arms tighten around me, taking control of us, his tongue tangling with mine, caressing, our breaths mingling. His fingers scrape across my scalp as if he wants to get closer, to inhale me.

The heat of his mouth, the urgency of it sends waves of fire to my lower body, and I kiss him harder. Desire thrums through me, and it feels like I'm discovering a secret within him, kicking at his hidden layers, searching for the real Knox.

"Tulip," he groans when we stop to breathe.

"Don't stop, please." It feels too good. Kissing him is like I've spent a day in the sunshine, and when night comes, the stars will only shine for me.

"I want to kiss you, I want to..." His mouth takes mine again, hungrily, with a ferocity that makes me want to crawl inside him for more, *so much more*.

"Am I doing it right?" He presses his open mouth to my neck and sucks on the tender skin, his teeth dragging.

"God, yes." My hands slide up to rub his shoulders, tugging at his shirt, wishing it would magically disappear. I ease under his jersey and explore him, his six-pack, the rippling muscles of his chest.

"You're shaking," I say, recalling how he trembled outside Vandy.

"I'm scared."

"Am I the first girl you've kissed in a long time, like really kissed?"

He nods. "But that isn't why I'm scared. I've always wanted to kiss you, Tulip."

He comes back to my lips and takes them again, his tongue declaring dominance and ownership. Kissing him is like freefalling into a hot fire, and maybe I should be afraid of this, but I crave the way his chest burns against mine, the way it ignites every atom inside me. He tastes like spearmint and sex and everything I want—

He breaks us apart, his eyes gunmetal hot, his sensuous, wicked mouth swollen.

"Fuck." His chest heaves. "You're too much. You taste so

good—" He takes my mouth again, his hands everywhere, in my hair, on my neck, grazing over my pebbled nipples before landing on my hips. "Tell me to stop, please, Tulip, tell me, tell me..."

My skin throbs and I kiss him back with intensity. "Can't."

"Tulip," he whispers, moving us until I'm against the wall and he's hovering in front of me, his lips back on mine. "You... drive...me...insane," he gasps out in between kisses. My hands cup his ass, and my pelvis swivels against his, aching for that tent in his pants. He mutters a curse and lifts me up so my legs can curl around him. I lock them around his waist as he dips his head and places his lips on the rise of my breasts. His teeth tug at the erect nipple underneath, sucking and biting through my thin shirt and bra.

"You're so hard to stay away from," he murmurs, coming back to my lips and taking them again.

Sighing in his mouth, I rub against him while sweet friction eats at me, pulsing through my body. I've been scared before this, worried part of me would never want a guy again. The nuns made me attend a few therapy sessions after that night, and I recall the doctor telling me to expect anxiety when I had a sexual relationship, but right now, all I feel is need and want and desire and hunger—for him.

"Am I going too fast, Tulip? Am I?" he says raggedly as his hand slides under my skirt and traces the waistband of my panties.

"I dare you," I say.

"Tulip," he groans and slips his hand inside, brushing his fingers through my wetness with feather-light strokes while I shudder. He tugs on my hair, arching my neck back as he stares down at me, desire swirling in his eyes. "I want to hear you come. I want my name on your lips when you do, so bad, so fucking bad..." His breath hitches while his finger dips inside me and moves in and out.

"Never...I never have..."

"You will," he growls as his thumb finds the upper part of my mound, teasing me with a hesitant touch, making me breathless as I arch to get more, just more. With his face flushed, he takes deep gulps of air, his eyes heavy and low. We're moving fast, so fast, as he gets into a rhythm, working his fingers, circling and dancing and touching and—

Tingles skate over my spine, pressure building and building, until I'm gasping and clutching his shoulders.

"So sweet, so sweet," he says in my ear, and the scent of his cologne, sunshine and sea, the feel of his quivering chest under my hands—all those sensations sharpen to a laser focus until I explode into a million shards of lightning, my body clenching around him as I call out his name, writhing against his hand.

I float down, lazily and softly, as he kisses me.

Dimly, I'm aware of more sounds around us, other than our breathing. Voices grow louder, students filling up the auditorium.

Knox tenses next to me, trying to get his breathing under control. "Fuck. There's a class coming in."

I let out a shaky breath. "Chorus probably."

He lets me slide down from him and I realize my clothes are barely even out of place, top still buttoned up, my skirt draping over my thighs. There's a damp spot on my shirt, but I can put my blazer over it.

I glance up at him, taking in the bulge in his pants, the

tight expression on his face. A tendril of unease washes over me. "What's wrong?"

He licks his lips, tearing his gaze off of me. "We can't do this."

My chest squeezes. "Why?"

He takes a step away from me, avoiding my eyes. "Stop asking me questions I can't answer."

Some of those old insecurities come crawling right back, slicing through me and going straight to my head. I remind myself of his coldness for the past two days.

"Am I not good enough? Not up to your standards? Afraid of what your friends might say? Not bleacher-worthy?" I don't mean that last part, because I don't want to be that girl, but he's distancing himself. Again.

And if there's one shred of anything I have left after that night in the woods, it's my pride. Hell, if anything, *I* should be the one pushing the Shark away.

I've opened myself up and he's the one retreating?

Can't also means *no*, and he's said it very clearly.

He closes his eyes briefly and looks as if he might say something, but he doesn't, and sometimes when people don't speak, they say *everything*, don't they?

Maybe he doesn't really think of me...like that.

Maybe...

Shit.

PITY. He feels sorry for me.

Because of his mom. Because he didn't take me to the hospital.

Red flames on my cheeks as I gather myself together mentally, trying to separate my body from how hot we felt together.

And he's still just standing there, his expression uncertain.

"Ah, I see how it is," I mutter under my breath.

"Do you?" he says, and then the rest of his words come at me in an angry rush. "You want to pretend I haven't wanted you? Go ahead, tell yourself those lies. But the truth is, you don't know who hurt you that night. You're still reeling from the aftershocks and I'm not good for you—" He stops abruptly. "Forget that. We have to get out of here before we get caught. There's a side exit to the right that leads outside and goes around to the library. You take that and I'll walk through the auditorium—"

He's dismissing me. Us.

"Don't tell me how I feel about that night! Maybe it was your brother who hurt me."

He looks stricken. "No, no, Tulip. It wasn't."

All that seething anger rushes back and fills me up, wiping away everything we just talked about. My fists curl. If there's one thing I do know, it's that Knox will protect him until the end—and me? I'm just collateral damage.

I glare at him and he stares back, reading my face. "Tulip, don't leave pissed. I didn't mean for this to happen. We can just forget about it—"

Forget? Ha!

I cross my arms. "Too late for that. You just ruined what could have been—nothing, just nothing! *You* take the exit and I'll walk through the auditorium, Cold and Evil."

"Please. Don't—"

Ignoring him, I whip around and fumble through the curtains until I'm in the small stairwell that leads to the aisles.

Halfway running, I dash through the students filling the seats. I find my backpack near the rear, grab it, and run for the double doors. I don't stop, my breathing torn and weak as I stumble into the stairwell and make it all the way down to the first floor.

Forget him, dammit. Forget him forever.

14

I'm jogging down our quiet street on Saturday morning when I see Dad's white BMW glide up to our wrought iron gates at the end of our road. His finger pushes in the code and his car moves down the lane to our three-story, Spanish-style mansion. About damn time. Sweat drips off me, and my muscles feel like lead after getting up early and running, but I pick up my pace. Normally, I'd sleep in a few hours on Saturday, saving my run for the gym later, but I woke up early, my head replaying Ava and me in the auditorium on Friday.

Ava with her lips on me.

Ava walking away from me.

She says she doesn't blame me for what happened, but it doesn't change the fact that deep down, part of me knows I can't be involved with her.

There's too much going on with me.

Dad looks up from the kitchen counter where he's making coffee. "Hey! I thought you were asleep still. Morning run?"

He half-smiles, but there's appreciation in his tone that I'm keeping my endurance up for football. He played quarterback for Camden back in his day, and him watching Dane and me play has been the only stabilizing aspect of our relationship.

Wearing a suit, even on a Saturday, he's tall, about six four, with dark brown hair. In his early forties, he's going gray a little at his temples, but that doesn't stop women from falling all over him. Maybe he dates while he's in New York, but somehow I doubt there's ever been a serious girlfriend. In the years since Mom passed, he's never once mentioned a woman.

Sometimes I'm afraid I'm going to end up just like him, pushing everything down and locking it away. We barely saw him this summer except for a short vacation at our beach house on Kiawah Island where he spent the majority of his time on his laptop and phone while Dane and I roamed nearby Charleston.

"Couldn't sleep," I say before walking to the fridge, grabbing a Gatorade, and chugging it down.

He pours his coffee in a mug and takes a long sip.

I settle in on one of the barstools at the white granite island in the middle of the kitchen. "It's good to see you." I can't keep the sarcasm out of my voice and he hears it, a grimace crossing his face.

"I missed your first week back at Camden. How was it?" He does a double take when he searches my face. "Your eye has purple under it. Fighting already?"

My lips tighten. I've been known to use my fists, especially in middle school when everything went down with Mom. Most of the time, I save it for my opponents on the football field. I've learned to control my temper, but this week, well... "Shitty. You need to be here more. Dane's not right."

Sighing, he takes a seat. "He seemed fine this summer. Isn't he taking his meds? Should we call his therapist and get him more sessions?"

"Maybe. I can't exactly watch over him every day. He's using again, more than usual. I know he's been high at school, and he didn't come home last night."

He starts. "Suzy—"

I frown. "She's mostly here during the day, and *she* isn't his parent. I'm the one trying to keep up with him. And don't freak out. He texted me that he was at Liam's."

He loosens his tie and gives me a sweeping look, a scowl on his face as he takes my words in. "So, Ava Harris is back. I saw where the bank cut a check to Camden for housing. I assume it was for her since Trask mentioned she'd requested it?"

I press my lips together.

"You're still spending your money on her? On a girl you barely know?" He inhales.

"I don't barely know her. She sits next to me in class."

He starts, frowning heavily as he gives me a hard look, as if trying to figure me out. He never liked me hiring the P.I. back in November, but Dane and I both have access to our own money that Mama left to us. I insisted and insisted and threw in his face that it was my money and I could do whatever I wanted with it. That was a strained few days after we got back from the U2 concert after our police interviews and I told him what I was doing. He told me I was ridiculous, his face angry. He looked like he wanted to tussle with me, but that's never been his style. I told him I didn't give a shit what he thought. He wasn't the one at that party. He wasn't the one who *left*. Eventually, he came around to the idea because he thought it might help clear Dane and me if the police pressed us harder. They didn't.

"I did pay for it."

"Why?" His eyes search my face. "You can't change what happened, and you had nothing to do with it."

"I'm not trying to make up for what happened to her," I say tightly. "Nothing can do that."

But...

I want her to be happy.

And being with me won't do that. The fact that she even wanted to kiss me blows my mind.

Changing directions, I say, "Dane keeps dreaming he was there in the woods with her."

Dad pales and his mug clatters on the countertop. "What the hell?"

A long exhalation comes from me.

"Guilt?" he whispers.

I stare at him, refusing to answer that niggling question. "Regardless of the reason, don't you think you need to stay home for a while?"

He nods, brushing my words away. "How are you? Football good? You hear from any scouts?"

Jesus. I wish he'd wake up and see what's going on. "Season starts in one week. Home game. I'd like to see you there."

"I wouldn't miss it, son. I'm just...overwhelmed at work."

Dane picks that moment to show up, stumbling into the kitchen from the same outside entrance I used. I hear the roar of Liam's car as he pulls out.

"Dad! Hey! You came home!" He smirks as he leans against the counter. His jeans and gold Dragons shirt are rumpled. There's a joint tucked behind his ear.

Dane's flat eyes find mine, and I shrug. *This is on you, dude. You knew Dad was arriving today.*

"Late night?" Dad says tightly, eyeing him, lingering on his ear.

"I tried to tell you," I murmur as I walk past Dad to grab milk for some cereal.

Dane sighs. "I'm standing right here, bro."

"I wanted you to hear it, asshole," I say. "Did you enjoy your night?" I pull out the rolled joint. I really don't care about the pot. I've done my own dabbling on and off, but I dislike the lack of control.

He snatches it back. "Practically legal."

"Not in Tennessee," Dad mutters as he takes it from Dane. He rakes his gaze over his son, no doubt seeing the bloodshot eyes. "What did you do last night?"

He shrugs, shifting his eyes from me to Dad. "Liam had a shindig at his place."

I bark out a laugh. A party I wasn't invited to, not that I give a shit. "Who was there?"

Dane straightens, giving me a glare. "Most of the defensive guys, some girls from Hampton High. Very low-key."

Yeah, I bet. I've been to Liam's parties. He lives on a ten acre estate in the boonies and his parents give him free rein to do whatever he wants out at the barn.

Dane eyes the kitchen stairwell that leads upstairs to the second floor. "I just want to crash."

I look expectantly at Dad, hoping he'll do something.

"Your curfew is midnight on weekends," he says to Dane

as he rubs his jaw. I think I see helplessness in his eyes. "Pull an all-nighter again, and you're grounded. Your car is still in the shop, but once it gets out, you won't get it back until I say so, got it? And I'll take that phone away. Football season is here and you need to focus."

"Didn't know you cared so much," he mutters.

A few moments tick by, the tension in the room ramping up.

Dad lets out a long sigh. "I do care, Dane. I'm going to take some time off. I just need to handle a few more meetings in New York—"

"Yeah, yeah, sure," Dane says, grabbing a water bottle from the fridge. "Heard it all before."

Anger blooms red on Dad's face, his fists tightening. "I'm going to make an appointment with Dr. Forest for you."

Dane slams down his water. "Fuck that. I'm not going to therapy."

"You will," Dad says. "I'm still your parent—"

"You don't have a clue what I do!" Dane cries out. "I hate this empty fucking house and I hate you." Those last words whimper off, his voice cracking in anger. He's perilously close to tears, and his fists clench even as he eyes the stairwell again.

Dad closes his eyes.

"Head on up," I say softly to Dane. "Sleep. I'll get us takeout for lunch later. We can all sit and talk."

He shuffles off, but before he gets to the steps, he stops and looks back. "Dad, I don't...I don't hate you. I'm just tired."

"I know, son. We'll talk later."

He nods and goes up the stairs.

As soon as he's out of earshot, I turn back to my father.

He slumps. "He's just like Vivie, all the ups and downs."

"It's worse now, and if you can't see it, you're choosing not to."

Frustration hounds me. Jesus. I want to be a man, but I'm just a kid, only seventeen, and I don't know how to fix *this*—my dad, my brother, our spiraling relationship.

He picks his coffee up. Worry lines his face. "I'll work on this, okay? I promise."

Later, after I've gone out and picked up lunch, I head up the stairs to check on Dane. I don't see him in his bedroom or his bath, so I head to mine, and that's where I find him. Huddled under my covers, clutching a pillow to his chest. The blinds are up and I ease them shut then put the TV on mute, letting it play. For some reason, I bring up a blog on my phone about how to watch the Star Wars movies in chronological order of events, and I click on *A Phantom Menace*. I wince. That's the one with Jar Jar Binks, and I've seen it, but this time, it will be with fresh eyes, and I'll think about Ava and her enthusiasm, her lips on mine—

Shit.

I bring the movie up on the TV, and soon I'm sucked right back into my childhood when I watched it with Dane and Dad.

With a sigh, I sit down on the side of the bed with him next to me. Even while sleeping, it's clear by his drawn expression and the paleness of his skin that he isn't really resting.

He's going to be okay, I tell myself as I watch the movie.

He will. He's all I have, and I'll make sure of it, no matter what.

15

AVA

"Welcome back to the hellhole, Louise," I murmur as I get out of my car and pat her. Another week has slowly passed by and it's the start of a new one, but I'm still freaking here, digging my heels in.

Today is week three, and I'm going to get through it. I AM.

With a sigh, I jog through the parking lot toward the entrance. My hair is up in a high ponytail and swishes against my back. It's scorching hot today, and I whip off my blazer and drape it over my arms before heading in. My shoulders shift inside my snug shirt, moving around to loosen the seams. It's not a good fit for me, and I guess I've filled out more since last year. I could put in a request for a new uniform since all scholarship students are allowed three new ones each year, but there hasn't been time.

Several Sharks, maybe seven or eight—Knox, Dane, Chance, and Liam included—lean against the wall in the foyer when I open the door. Girls encircle them.

"Slut," comes from a low male voice in their group as I pass, and the girls giggle, the sound grating and clawing, but I keep walking.

Tyler, I remind myself. He's the endgame.

A low thump comes from behind me and I turn around to see that Knox has shoved Brandon against the wall, pinning him with one hand, the other at his neck, knotted in his collar. Their backpacks lie scattered on the marble tile. Knox's face is flushed and Dane pulls at his arm, trying to talk him down.

As I stand rooted to the spot—*dammit, why am I standing here watching them?*—Chance's gaze sweeps over the hallway, probably checking for teachers, and stops on me.

He freezes, his nostrils flaring as he studies me, taking in my face.

I flip him off. Childish. Don't care. Screw them all.

"Ignore them. Testosterone-addled morons," Wyatt murmurs next to me and tosses an arm over my shoulder, and I lean into him, needing reassurance.

"Do you have any clue how much I adore you? If you weren't gay, I'd kiss you," I say on a long sigh, taking my gaze off the Sharks.

He brushes a hand over his gelled hair then taps me on the nose. "I'm irresistible to all sexes. I could pretend I've had a sudden change of heart, tell everyone your beauty turned me straight and all I want is you. Would you like that, locker neighbor?"

"You're only offering to make me feel better. And don't you have a teensy little crush on your teammate Jagger?" He mentioned it grudgingly at lunch one day when I asked how baseball was going.

A grunt and a *thud* sound come from where the Sharks are, and Wyatt stares over at them. "Don't look, but Knox just slammed his fist right into Brandon's face. And again. Shit."

I flinch, and of course I look. There's a circle around their group, and it's impossible to see what's going on.

"Chin up, love. Don't let them see you even care about their petty squabbles."

I groan. "It's about me. Someone called me a slut when I walked in." I turn my face away from them. "Is… Do you see Knox? Is he okay?"

"Oh, it's breaking up. Mmmm, his fine ass is good, nary a scratch, but he's pissed as hell. Brandon is bleeding like a stuck pig and holding his nose." He laughs. "Oh, and here comes Trask, so they're all scurrying like rats. Time to adios! Let's scram."

He pissed off the team, Dane said.

I shove down the ache that blooms in my heart for Knox—even if he has been ignoring me in class, only speaking when we have to and barely looking at me.

As we head to our lockers, someone catches Wyatt's gaze and he turns red. Craning my neck, I see Jagger. Lean and muscular with buzzed hair and an easy grin, I don't know him well, but he seems nice. He isn't part of the popular inner circle, so there's that.

I poke Wyatt in the arm, trying to forget the scuffle. "Did you have a good weekend? Hang out with the baseball guys?"

He smiles.

"Any progress?"

His eyes linger on his crush. "Nope. He's not out of the closet, obviously, or I'd be all over that, but I get this feeling from him when he looks at me, ya know? We went to this pizza place Saturday, kind of a teambuilding thing, and he sat next to me. He smells so good..." He lets his voice trail off and sighs wistfully.

Leaning against my locker, I settle in next to him as we both watch Jagger talk to a girl who lives in the room across from me at Arlington Dorm. Her name is Camilla, a cute senior from California. With short, pixie-style blonde hair and delicate features, she has a soft, quiet, reassuring air about her. I've attempted a few conversations with her, but she just frowns and rushes back into her room. I get it. Besides Wyatt and Piper, no one wants to be my friend.

"Is he seeing Camilla?" I ask. I can't recall ever hearing they were a thing, but then, I'm not in the know anymore.

Wyatt shakes his head. "He doesn't date anyone." The first bell rings. "Come on, let's head to the assembly in the gym."

I start. "No class?" I battle down the disappointment of not getting to sit next to Knox for an hour. I've said I'm going to forget him, and I totally should, of course, because that's what a normal person should do...

So why do I feel this deep emptiness inside when I think about our conversation in the auditorium?

Why is he *still* fighting his teammates over me?

"Yeah, they announced it Friday at the end of the day. A few college recruiters will be in the gym, mostly Ivy Leagues like Harvard, Yale, yada, yada. You've really been spacey lately. I didn't see you around much this weekend."

I frown. I'm not surprised I missed the announcements. I'm usually anxious to get out of here at the end of the day.

"Worked two shifts at Lou's and hung out with Tyler." The group home sponsored a garage sale this weekend, and I helped out with that too.

A voice comes over the speakers telling us to go to the gym, and we head that way. Along the way, a group of Sharks jostle around us, and Wyatt takes my hand in his, giving it a squeeze. "You good?"

"Yeah."

Half an hour later, I'd made the rounds with a few of the local state universities who've set up tables, grabbing brochures and talking. Several of them are promising, and likely where I'll end up. I avoid the Vandy table, but I can't keep myself from gazing at it longingly. Blowing out my breath, I look around the room. Piper's deep in conversation with someone from UT, and Wyatt mentioned he was going to check out the baseball rep from one of the colleges. Jagger's next to him, and I don't have the heart to bother them.

The bell for our next class rings, and it seems as if the assembly may go on for a while. I decide to head out and see if we'll have class in second period. Walking out the gym doors, I exit down the steps into the blaring sunlight and take in the campus, the sprawling, elegant buildings and lush landscaping. Such a pretty place. "Too bad every single day is a freaking nightmare," I mutter under my breath as I take the last step on the stairs—

Something hard whacks me in the back of the head from behind, solid and forceful, shoving me forward. I teeter, grasping for the handrail, but miss it. I yelp as my body falls, my legs folding as I careen down, knees landing on the concrete to keep my face from hitting first.

"Cunt," a male voice says from behind me, and before I can twist around from my prone position or catch my breath, he puts his foot on my back, pressing me back down. "That's where you belong, bitch, at my feet—and don't you forget it." His voice is low and growly and tense, laced with anger.

"Stop!" I yell, and the pressure disappears from my back.

He mumbles a curse and runs.

I cover my head and whimper as darkness tugs at me, and I'm in the woods again, those dark trees rubbing their ghostly fingers together, hard sticks and cold leaves under me, and I can't move, can't move, can't move, and he's on top of me, and I can't breathe, can't see his face, can't stop him, can't talk, can't do anything and I want to make him stop, please, please, please, please—

"Ava! What the hell?"

Someone bends down to me, firm hands touching my arm and trying to turn me over. I shove them off, slapping at his fingers as I gasp for air. My stomach jumps and I let out a long wail. Shuddering, I suck in a breath and try to hold myself together.

You aren't in the woods. You aren't.

Don't cry, Ava. Not here. You haven't yet, and you never will!

I swallow down the emotions and roll over to my back, biting back pain that ricochets through my head.

"I'm...fine," I finally push out.

"No, your knees are bloody. What happened? Did you fall?"

I blink up at Dane and flinch away from him, scooting to the side, but I only end up scratching my elbows more on the ground as white-hot pricks tingle up my arms.

"Someone hit me on the back of my head—" My voice hitches as I scramble farther from him and manage to get in a sitting position, rocking back and forth as I wrap my arms around myself. Deep breaths rush out of me. I dip my head to my chest. Inhale. Exhale.

"Who was it?" he barks out. "Tell me and I'll find him!"

"For all I know, it was you," I whisper.

"Oh, Ava." He bends down and sits in front of me, staying a few feet away as if he knows any little thing will set me off. A long sigh comes from him. "I was in the restroom in the main building and just came out to hit the assembly then heard you yelling." His gaze skates over me with a frown, and he reaches out. "Come on, let me see your head."

"No!" I hit him on the arm with my fist.

He takes the first hit without even a twitch, but he catches my fist in his palm when I go for his throat.

"Ava, come on, sweetheart, just let me help you."

"Leave me alone," I manage to say, but that anxiety is rushing back, and my head spins, dizziness slamming into me as I try to stand up. Black dots dance in front of my face. I sway on my feet and his arms come around me and lift me up; I wiggle to get away. *Ugh!* I don't want his help.

"Look, you're upset. I'm taking you to the nurse's office," he says, his face tight with suppressed emotion. "You can tell them what happened and it'll be alright. Things will be okay, I promise, I promise, I promise. Just take one day at a damn time. That's what I do."

Maybe it's the tinge of despair in his voice that makes me stop squirming, or maybe it's the careful way he holds me; either way, I ease up. I need a minute and it's obvious he isn't going to cart me away to some hidden place as he makes his way to the double doors of the main building.

"Hang on a sec. I need to..." I feel him adjusting me as he pushes the handicap button to open the entrance. My head rests against his arm, and he smells like fresh pine and spice. Looking up, I stare up at him, recalling our confrontation on the third floor last week, him telling me about his mom, how broken his words were. His face is more haggard than it was several days ago, cheeks hollow, the skin under his eyes bluish. His nose is red and swollen...

"Move out of the way, peons," he says sharply as he stalks down the hall, and I hear the rumble of the underclassmen as they go to second period.

Someone jostles into my feet, and I wince as they mumble an apology and scoot away hurriedly.

"Don't touch her, assholes!" he yells, sending a scathing look to whoever it was.

He's halfway to the office when I tug on his sleeve.

He looks down at me, brow wrinkling. "Better?"

No. My head throbs and my knees buzz like bee stings from the cuts. "Wipe your nose before we go in. You've got some, um, white powder—"

He lifts me closer to his face as he leans his head over and uses his sleeve to wipe his nose. "Caught by the charity case. Don't tell Knox, 'kay? Our secret?" He gives me a pleading look then shuts his eyes briefly. "Ava, I'm a dick, okay, a giant fucking asshole, but you know I didn't hit you out there. And I'm sorry I gave you grief your first day here. It wasn't about you—it was about me." He chews on his bottom lip hard, like Knox does, and he looks so much like his brother.

I sigh. "Just let me down, okay? I can walk."

His arms tighten around me. "You had a panic attack then

almost passed out. You tried to beat me up, pathetic attempt that it was. Plus, Knox would want me to take care of you."

I grunt. "I used to think you two weren't anything alike, but you're both stubborn."

He arches a brow. "I'm the charming one. He's the heavy."

"Good heavens!" Mrs. Carmichael exclaims as Dane saunters into the office with me like he does it every day. "What happened?" She leads the way to the hallway to the left that connects to the nurse's station.

"Someone jumped her outside the gym. Hit her on the head," Dane mutters darkly. He eases me down and she promptly makes me sit on a cot then proceeds to hammer me with questions while yelling for the nurse. I haltingly explain what happened. She frowns and dashes off, mumbling about an incident report.

A nurse comes over with a penlight and checks my eyes, tells me I don't have a concussion, just a small lump on my head. Dane lingers, taking a seat in the corner to watch me.

A few minutes later, Mrs. Carmichael is back and hands me a folder. "Just fill these out when you can, and the headmaster will probably want to see you later." She looks over at Dane. "You need to get back to class."

He gives her a wide grin, eyes a little spacey. "Ah, Maxine, come on, I'm the hero here—let me make sure she's okay."

She puts her hands on her hips.

He grins. "Just let me hang out for five minutes, cool?"

She huffs but seems to decide to ignore him and look at me. "Dear, is there someone I can call to check you out?"

I huff out a laugh. Someone to call?

"I'm eighteen. I can check myself out."

"Of course. Sorry. I thought you might want to go to the clinic in town," she offers.

I don't need those bills, and I've had worse. "I just need some Band-Aids for the cuts on my knees." I flash my elbows where my shirt is torn and grimace. "These too, I guess."

The nurse is already swabbing them with alcohol and heading to a set of white drawers to pull out bandages.

Mrs. Carmichael frowns and gives me a nod then looks at the nurse. "Fine. Just rest here until you feel like going to class."

Eventually, the nurse leaves me and I stretch out on the cot, a long exhalation leaving my chest. My socks were torn in the fall, and I glare down at them. I really need more uniforms.

"Why are you still here?" I say to Dane as he taps on his phone. "I'm fine now. No one's going to bother me back here."

He glances up at me. "Do you really want me to leave?"

No.

"Suit yourself," I mutter and flip over, yanking on the thin covers the nurse left. Facing the wall, I close my eyes and allow myself to crack, just a little, biting my lip and holding back the tears that haven't stopped wanting to come out. Now that it's quiet, the event replays in my head, leftover adrenaline and anger rushing through my veins at how helpless I was. *Again*.

Somehow I fall asleep, my body slowly relaxing to the everyday sounds of Mrs. Carmichael talking on the phone in the next room and the noise of teachers walking down the corridor to their break room. Later, I wake to voices speaking in hushed tones several feet away.

I ease over and see Dane and Knox, their heads close, and I hear my name.

"Whoever it was, they whacked her good," Dane mutters. "She was on the fucking ground, brother. Somebody hurt her *here* right under our noses—"

"You're awake," Knox says, striding over to me. "You okay?"

I sit up, gripping the edge of the cot and wincing at the brief bite of pain from moving so fast. "Fresh as a daisy."

"Liar," he mutters and rubs his hand over the back of my head, barely ghosting over the lump there. I freeze, wanting to arch into him, hating that I enjoy the attention from him. "Still hurting?" He bends down to me, and it almost seems as if he might touch my face, but he doesn't, letting his hand fall.

"The nurse gave me Aleve and Band-Aids. I'm ready for battle, Cold and Evil."

"Not an answer," he says softly.

Dane watches us, a wary look on his face.

Knox glances over at him. "He's been here for a few hours. I was in Trask's office and didn't know what happened until Dane texted me."

A long sigh leaves me. "Did you get in trouble for fighting?"

His lips tighten, a dark expression on his face. "No. He's going to let Coach take care of it. I'll be running sprints tonight after practice. Brandon won't be calling you names anymore."

I frown. "I don't want you fighting my battles. Don't do it again."

He sighs. "Can't seem to stop, Tulip. Now, who do I need to take down for this?"

His voice is cool and calm, but I hear the steel underneath.

"I didn't see his face. He hit me, not with his fist, I think. It was too solid and big, maybe a textbook, then he put his foot on my back, called me a few names." I swallow down the fear. That *voice*. It was the guy from the woods.

"Motherfucker."

"Yep." I push to stand and take a big breath. "What period is it?"

"Lunch. Where are you going?" he says as I walk around the room, spying my backpack that someone must have dropped off. Grabbing my blazer that's lying on top, I slip it on, wincing but glad it hides the holes in my shirt. I lean down and swing my backpack up and over my shoulder. My fingers linger over my locket for a moment and my spine straightens.

"Ava?" Knox has moved and is standing next to me. "Maybe you should head to the dorms and rest. If you want me to drive you, I'm sure Maxine will—"

No.

He doesn't want to kiss me.

We can't do this, he said.

"I'm fine." I brush past him, walk over to Dane, and stare up at him. A faint smile tugs at my lips. "Next time, I'll hit you harder, asshole."

He smirks. "Yeah, yeah. Maybe I need to teach you how to hit, sweetheart."

"Meh, I was holding back," I say. My efforts to fight him were half-hearted. Even as upset as I was, I recognized that it *wasn't* Dane's voice who said those words to me.

He scrubs his face and gives me a little grimace as if to

remind me—*Remember what you saw on my nose? Can you just forget that?*

I send him a shrug. *Maybe.*

He rolls his eyes.

I think back to those words he said while carrying me: *Things will be okay, I promise, I promise, I promise.*

Yeah, someday it fucking will be okay. Not today, but soon. The guy from the woods lashed out at me, which means he's getting careless, and if he's getting careless, he's scared…

"Don't tell me you're actually going back to class?" Knox says as he crosses his arms.

"Why wouldn't I? Just another day here."

He exhales. "Ava, come on, let me take you home."

Home? I don't really have one.

Ava? I want him to call me Tulip, dammit.

"I agree," Dane adds. "You're pale."

Huffing out a laugh, I throw him an *Are you serious?* glance. Has he looked in the mirror lately?

Dane laughs and shakes his head as if he reads my mind.

"Ava, I don't think you should go to class. You need to rest." Knox again. His jaw pops and he reaches out and takes my hand, his thumb brushing over the top of my hand.

And there it is, just a tiny touch from him and electric tingles dance up my arms and over my body. I look down at our hands.

He's worried.

He keeps fighting my battles when he clearly has his own.

His gray eyes cling to mine. "Please."

My body clenches at the mere sound of his voice. I want *him* so much, yet it's so much more than simple lust or desire;

it's deeper and stronger and crazy and how have I let him scale my fortress?

He wants me, *and he fights it*.

I don't want to think about the whys of it.

I lick my dry lips, and it takes everything inside me to pull my hand out of his grasp.

This is my journey, not his.

I walk out of the nurse's station and head to lunch.

16

AVA

Love dies.

Then you're at the end of my kaleidoscope,
Broken, bright shiny pieces.

Obviously, you can't love me.
And neither should I.

The text from SA comes in on Wednesday night as I sit on my bed, my laptop and textbooks scattered across my quilt. Earlier, I had a quick dinner with Tyler at the group home, and now I'm at the dorm and bored, my homework looming.

Ava? You there?

I stare down at my phone. It's been several days since I heard from him, and I can't stop the curl of excitement in my chest.

Another poem? Wow, you're really into this class. Same

author? I ask.

Yep.

Funny. I googled that last one you sent, and it never came up anywhere. The internet is a pretty amazing tool. Wanna tell me who wrote it?

He doesn't respond for several moments, so I open a bag of Doritos and chomp down on a few. I'm grinning around my munches, imagining SA squirming. I can't help but think about Knox, holding his phone somewhere, typing. Maybe he's at home. Maybe he's in his car and had to pull over because he can't stop thinking about me.

I scrunch up my face. I wish.

I was too embarrassed to admit I wrote them.

Oh, it's getting good now.

Yeah, the jock who writes poetry. For me, I assume? I send.

YOU.

They're pretty nice.

I scroll up, read the poem again and type, **So you've never been in love? You said it dies.**

My parents didn't even want to be in the same room as each other. He loved her one day and she loved him, then they both changed.

SA is a bit of a pessimist.

Another text comes in. **I care for my brother. He's all I care about. Who have you been in love with?**

I sit up straighter in bed. Knox cares for his brother.

Ava, tell me—who have you loved?

Gah, we're getting personal, and part of me can't resist it. It's a place to pretend we might just have something special, and I want to trust SA; I do. His poetry is revealing...

I loved a boy once. He moved to Texas for college.

Do you still see him? Email him? Text him?

SA is poking a little hard.

Another text comes in. **Never mind. I don't want to talk about him. I don't want to think about you with him.** Then, **What was his name?**

I laugh out loud.

Luka.

Luka with his shaggy brown hair and cigarette burns on his arms. We started off as friends, but nights were lonely at the group home and soon we were sneaking into each other's room, talking about our hopes and dreams. I loved his crooked smile and shy glances. I don't know that our emotions were the kind of love that's forever, but he was my friend, and I trusted him. We fumbled through sex, and while it was never the way I've read about in books, it was enough.

My eyes widen at the next text.

I only want you.

My fingers clutch the phone as I type out a response.

Is that what this is then? A way to woo the girl you can't have?

No response.

WHY did you leave that letter if you aren't going to tell me who you really are?

A hard, rapid series of knocks sounds on my door, making me yelp. It's past eight and visiting hours ended a while ago. In fact, the hallway's been eerily quiet tonight, an almost expectant air in the stillness. I frown and type.

Hey, someone's at my door. Weird, right, this late?

He doesn't reply right away, and I feel antsy about the knock. I set my phone down and look at my black booty shorts and camisole—not exactly how I want to greet someone.

"Who's there?" I call out, but all I get is a whole lot of silence.

I look through the peephole, but no one's there. Anxiety drifts over me, giving me goose bumps. I've been more cautious since the hit at school, especially since no one knows who it was. According to Trask, there aren't any cameras in that part of the gym. Of course not.

I bend down to my hands and knees to see if I can see feet or a shadow, but it's only the bright white lights of the hallway. I consider calling the resident assistant but quickly dismiss the idea. It's just a knock, right? I could text Wyatt, but he said earlier he was headed out to grab dinner with some guys from the baseball team. I think he'd come up to my floor if I asked, even though visiting hours are over.

Still...

There's *no one* there. Someone probably just knocked on the wrong door, realized it, and moved on. Maybe it was for Camilla.

Yet, I can't stop myself from pacing the floor, feeling that anxious pit in my stomach expand. I stop in front of the door and soon it's not just a door; it's the woods at night.

Another knock then "Ava!" The voice is male and low and instantly recognizable.

I fling the door open, relief washing over me.

"Knox! What are you doing here?"

My eyes run over him. He's still in football practice clothes, his hair damp and pushed back off his face. I swallow at his roped forearms and tanned skin, the sculpted muscles beneath his pants.

I cock my hip against the doorframe.

"Got done with practice, was just around the corner. Thought I'd come over and check on you, see how your head is. Plus, you might need me."

Need him?

"Someone knocked on my door a few minutes ago—it wasn't you?"

"Nope, but I can guess who." He looks down the quiet hall, studying the closed doors. He even walks to the end of the corridor, opens the stairwell door, and checks it out. I notice he's carrying a duffle bag. Weird.

"Who would you guess? Also, what's up with the duffle? You planning on sleeping over?"

"May I come in? I can explain." He leans against the edge of my doorway, and he's wearing a cocky grin. It's so different from how he is in class that I feel disarmed.

I cross my arms. "Why the heck is King Shark standing at my door asking to come in?"

He smirks. "Trust me, Tulip, you're going to need me." He holds up the duffle bag. "I have supplies."

I arch a brow. "Color me intrigued." I do a sweeping motion. "Please, come in."

He waltzes inside, running his eyes over my small room, taking in the twin bed against the wall and the small dresser that come standard with the rooms in the dorm.

"You need to decorate," he says, looking around.

I scoff. "Yeah, my neighbor Camilla has these cute twinkle lights up around her bed. I haven't had time." Or the money to burn. "Trust me, this is plush compared to my room at the home."

He turns to face me. "A girl like you deserves pretty things."

I frown, shoving that comment away, something I've learned to do well with him. "What's in the duffle? A cute lamp? Some posters?"

He gives the room one last look. "No time to waste with small talk. These need to be filled stat, and I suggest changing out of that white shirt and putting on pants."

What?

He opens the duffle and pulls out a bag of multi-colored balloons.

"Are we going to have a party? I'll call Wyatt and Piper." I'm joking. I'm not in the party mood.

He darts a look at me. "Prank night at Arlington. Wyatt didn't tell you?"

I shrug. He's spotty in the dorm, plus he's on a different floor.

"It's an annual thing, and I heard this afternoon that it might be tonight. Seems it's a secret until it happens then all hell breaks loose." He pauses. "Hijinks are about to ensue, and if someone knocked on your door, that might have been code for *Get ready.* Unless you want to hide under your bed and hope for the best..."

I rear back. "I was born ready, and I have heard of prank night. Even the staff gets involved, right? Or at least they let it slide as long as we clean up? Guess it slipped my mind since I've never lived in the dorms until now." I eye him. "Thank you for paying for my room. I don't think I ever said that the day in the auditorium." Because things got a little hot and heavy. "I'm going to pay you back someday."

He pauses in his handoff of a wad of balloons. "You don't

have to. Here, you take these and start filling them."

"Bossy Shark," I murmur as he drops half the balloons in my outstretched hands then rushes into my tiny bathroom.

I follow, and he's in the small shower with the cold water on, his hands filling up a pink balloon.

"Take the sink. Don't fill them too much—we don't want them to burst." He grins widely, and I blink, gaping at the football player in my shower.

"You're like, really into this, aren't you?"

"Less talking, more filling, Tulip. I came to help you and we're gonna kick ass together, you feel me?" He flicks water in my direction. "Get to work."

I like this side of him. "You participate every year?"

"Nope. This is for you."

This is for you.

I let that settle and file in his dossier to savor when he's gone.

A few minutes later, we've collected a pile of about fifty balloons, and he's placing them back in his duffle with careful hands. I've got damp splotches on my camisole and his shirt is soaked and sticking to him, catching spray from the faucet.

"How many do we need?" I ask.

"All of them. This isn't a night you want to be shorthanded." His eyes drift over me, starting at my legs, lingering on my chest before coming up to my face. "Babe, as much as I like seeing you in booty shorts, you need to change. I'm talking sweatpants and a long-sleeved shirt. Tennis shoes might be a good idea so you don't slip."

I gape again. "How bad is this going to get?"

Another wide grin.

I shake my head. "You are crazy. Fine, fine, let me change." I march over to my dresser, pull out a pair of leggings, and pull them on over my shorts. When I turn around, he's watching me, eyes low and heavy. "This work?"

He clears his throat. "Anything works on you."

There's a clatter out in the hall as if something metal has hit the floor.

I yelp, nearly jumping off the floor. "Is that the start? What was that noise?"

He walks over to me slowly, puts a finger to my lips. "Don't be jumpy. I won't let anyone hurt you. We got this, babe."

My heart flies. Holy shit, he's touched my lips! I feel a sudden rush of heat, and I must be crazy because my mouth opens and I nip at his finger. "Don't call me *babe*, Shark. I'm the least *babe* girl there is in the whole world." And Chance called me that.

He lowers his hand slowly. "Don't call me Shark and we have a deal."

"Fine."

"I'm not giving up *Tulip*. I like it very much."

"Didn't say you had to."

His gaze lands on my mouth. "Good."

The moment is broken when another clatter comes from the hallway.

He walks back to the door.

"What's the signal?" I say, secretly hoping he shushes me again.

"We'll know it when we hear—"

HONK!

A blaring air horn slices through the silence, loud and irritating. "Oh shit!" I yell, adrenaline pumping.

He grabs the duffle and puts a few balloons in my hand. “Follow me,” he says, and then he inches the door open.

We enter the hall, and he’s crouched down to make himself a smaller target. I instinctively follow close behind.

“Use me as a shield, got it?”

I nod, feeling the heat coming off his back, tracing my eyes over his broad shoulders—

Ugh. I’m about to get into a water war, and all I can think about is a guy.

The hallway is as quiet as a church on Sunday.

“I’m starting to think the prank is you making me think there’s something going on.” I peek over him to get a better look around and see a cluster of girls several feet away.

A huge water balloon bursts on my chest, and I sputter.

“Booyah! Nailed one!” calls a female voice as a group of underclassman girls run toward us from the end of the hall, flinging balloons.

“Hit ’em!” calls Knox, and I return fire, hitting the floor instead of the gaggle of girls. Dang. How did I miss all of them?

“Your aim sucks,” he groans, and I glare at him.

“I’m just warming up. Give me a minute—”

Another one hits me on the cheek, water drenching my face and sliding down my throat.

“You know, we could just hide in my room,” I call out as I lob another one and it bounces off the wall. One of the girls picks it up and throws it back at us, hitting Knox square on the head. I bite my lip to stop the giggle.

He was looking at me, caught unaware, and well, it’s funny. He wipes water off of him. “We could hide in your room if you want.”

I shiver. There was...a little bit of heat in his voice.

I pick at a piece of purple balloon stuck to his face. "No, I think I like seeing you getting clobbered with water balloons by a bunch of girls—"

One flies past us, splattering on the floor. "True. We can't let these whiny underclassmen beat us."

I pick up another one, and just when they're about twenty feet away, I sail it across and it splats on Camilla's pretty blonde head. She just darted out of her room wearing a bemused expression and got in the way. I grimace, wishing I'd hit someone else. She's not *exactly* rude to me, just withdrawn.

Knox nails two of the girls, which slows them down, but there are only two of us and several of them, including a group of guys who've suddenly shown up.

We run down the hall to see another group approaching from the opposite direction, throwing balloons at us and at the group behind us. Shit, stuck in the middle. Apparently, it's a free-for-all.

"In here!" Knox yells, yanking open the door to a maintenance closet near the stairwell.

We dive in and shut the door, hearing balloons burst outside.

He glances down at my water-soaked camisole.

"I told you to change. Your nipples are hard."

I elbow him. "Eyes on my face, football player."

He stares at me. Frowns.

"What?" I ask.

"How are your knees and elbows?"

"Good." They are better, nice and scabbed over and itchy, but they don't hurt.

He exhales and gets a grim look on his face.

I sigh. "Knox...don't. I'll be okay."

I don't want to dwell on it, and I don't want him losing friends over me either.

There's a long silence as we stare at each other.

He scrubs his face and looks away from me. "I'm sorry about the auditorium—"

Someone out in the hall screams and giggles, cutting him off. "Let's just have fun, okay?" My chest twinges and I rub it before dropping my hands.

"What's wrong?"

I look away from him. "Nothing."

"Who's in your locket?" he asks softly. I glance back at him and pop it open, and he leans in to study it. "Tyler?"

I nod. "He's all I have."

He tucks a strand of hair over my ear. "Yeah, I get it. It's Dane for me."

"Catch them!" someone exclaims from the hallway.

"I'm allergic!" another girl yells.

"What the hell—" Knox says just as a white and black furry arm reaches under the door, claws extended as it pats around the floor.

"Holy cats! That is a cat, right?" I ask. "What on earth is going on out there?" Ludicrous statement, considering the mayhem.

He opens the door, and a small striped feline darts into the closet, gives us a scathing hiss, and then hides behind a mop bucket.

We lean past the door and peek out. People—and cats—are dashing everywhere.

I frown. "Why involve innocent animals? Geeze."

Another water balloon hits me in the side of the head as we venture out. "Dammit!" I yell at whoever threw it, but they're already running away.

"Ava! Knox! Follow me!" shouts a familiar voice. It's Wyatt as he runs past, arms full of balloons.

We dodge people as we catch up with him, taking the stairwell. Girls and guys with water guns chase after us while Knox throws balloons at them, beating them back until they shut the door. *Nice job, QB1.*

We rush down to Wyatt's floor and enter the hall, where I come to a halt, slipping a little on the water. Holy white hell. There are no cats, but a white powder coats the wet floor and walls. Flour?

The lights suddenly go out and I scream.

A tall frame pulls me close. "I got you," Knox says. "Get on my back."

I climb him like a monkey, wrapping my arms around his shoulders and my legs around his waist. Well, at least I'm not thinking about the dark anymore. He runs down the hall, and I don't even know how he can see except for the few windows at the end that allow a little bit of moonlight in.

"Where are we going?" I press my face into his neck, hoping he's not aware that I'm totally smelling him.

"Wyatt's. I figure he went to his room. I know the way."

He fumbles around, opens a door, and darts inside, setting me down on my feet.

Sure enough, Wyatt is in the middle of the room, holding flashlights. He tosses one to Knox, who catches it. He laughs, looking at us before focusing on Knox. "Knox, didn't know you did prank night."

"Came as Ava's backup. Didn't think she'd like being surprised."

"Yeah, it would have been nice if you'd told me." I glare at Wyatt, and he grins and waggles his eyebrows.

"What's the fun in that?"

"A friend would have, jerk," I grumble.

He snorts. "I meant to but time got away from me at our baseball dinner."

Uh-huh. *Jagger.*

The lights blink back on, and suddenly a Bluetooth speaker in Wyatt's room explodes with a familiar tune by Rick Astley. It blares out in the hall as well.

"*Never gonna give you up, never gonna let you down, never gonna run around and desert you...*"

"Someone hacked all the speakers," Knox says, shaking his head, his face incredulous. "This thing gets nuttier every year."

"Seriously, is the entire building being rick-rolled?" I exclaim. "I'M IN HELL!" Wyatt and Knox start laughing, and I join them, saying, "It's fun, okay, it is, but this song...it's driving me bonkers."

"Let's get back out there," Knox says with relish as he grabs a handful of balloons. He's way too pumped for this, but I'm feeling it too—as long as he's with me.

"One, two, three..." he yells and pulls the door open then we rush out.

HONK!

The air horn blares again, and everyone in the hall freezes, wails of disappointment coming from every direction.

I look around. "What's going on?"

"Prank night is over. I repeat, prank night is over," is the announcement that comes over the loud speakers. It's a female voice, probably Miss Henderson, the dorm mom. "Please grab a mop, broom, or stray cat and put the building back together. If everyone will return to their own floor, we'll get this place back in shape. If you *don't* return Arlington Hall to pristine condition, this will be the last prank night allowed and all underclassmen will blame you forever. And please, oh please, will whoever hacked everyone's speakers turn off Rick Astley? I can't even think with that on."

"Dammit!" Wyatt says. "That wasn't nearly long enough."

We laugh, saying goodbye as we head back up the stairwell to my floor. Sure enough, Miss Henderson is standing there, her hair everywhere, out of its usual little bun. Even her shirt and jogging pants are soaked. She tilts her head toward a cage. "Put the cats in here. In the future, please don't bring small animals." Her voice is stern. "They could have been hurt, and I do not approve. In fact, I plan on writing up those involved. If you know who's responsible, please let me know." She picks up one of the smaller cats and rubs its head, giving us all side-eye. A few of the girls giggle and she glares at them. "I believe I counted six. I want them all rounded up and safe."

"My bet is on the freshman girls. Amateurs," Knox murmurs as he looks at the group who was laughing. A couple call out his name and give him little finger waves as they check him out.

"Hey, Knox," a pretty brunette says, giving him flirty eyes. "You should have been on our team."

Another one shouts, "Wanna come help us clean up, Knox?"

They stare at me and a few whisper behind their hands,

and even though most of them are younger than me, I figure everyone knows who I am.

I give them death glares.

Camilla steps forward, blocking them from my view. "I'll take care of the cats, Miss Henderson. If they don't belong to anyone, I'll make sure they find a good home. I work at a humane shelter."

Nice person.

I open the closet where we hid to grab a mop. Something darts toward the door then changes its mind and heads back inside, huddling in the corner.

"It's our little friend," says Knox from behind me. He was collecting pieces of balloons and stuffing them into a trash bag Miss Henderson gave him.

I pick it up, but she claws at me and tries to jump down.

"Easy now," Knox says, taking the cat from me.

She hides her face in the bend of his muscled arm.

I scoff. "Seriously? Why would she go to you but not me?" I pet her and realize the fluffy fur is hiding skin and bones. "She's so tiny. Are you going to take her to the cage?"

He glances down at the cat now lying on her back in his arms and kneading her little paws into him. "Maybe he wants to come home with me."

"She. It's a she. See, no balls."

He smirks. "Okay, maybe *she* wants to come home with me."

"I see—you dig cats. Let me add that to the list of things in my file about Knox Grayson."

"You're making a list?"

"Big thick dossier. Plays piano, likes cats, hates kissing."

His jaw drops. "Hey, that is not true—"

Camilla stops in front of us. "Those stupid freshman girls. You wanna hand her over?"

Knox shifts, fidgeting. "What's going to happen to her?"

"I heard some of the girls saying they picked up the cats from a dumpster near an alley downtown. Pretty sure they don't belong to anyone. I imagine she'll get adopted at the shelter. She's little and cute."

He mulls that over, lifts her up, and stares into her black and gray striped face. "I'm going to give her to Dane, and her name shall be Astley."

"I think that means he's keeping her," I murmur to Camilla.

She nods, looking pleased. "I'd get her checked out at the vet, though. She'll need meds and all that."

Knox says he will, and after the rest of the cats are accounted for and the hallway is sparkling clean, he follows me back to my room. Miss Henderson has left our area, probably to check on the other floors, so she doesn't see him sneak in.

"I really needed prank night," I murmur as he sits on my lone wooden chair with Astley, softly rubbing her fur.

The big football player is holding a kitten, and my fingers itch to take a picture.

"I have some soda. Do you want a Coke or something?"

He takes in the textbooks and laptop on my bed. A conflicted look crosses his face. "It's late. We have school tomorrow."

I fiddle with the Mountain Dew I've pulled out of the fridge. "Ah. Dangerous to drink a soda on a school night. Noted."

He shrugs.

I clear my throat. "I have a few cans of tuna. Let me get some for your new baby."

He rolls his eyes. "Can you get some water too? She might be thirsty."

I huff out a laugh, grab the tuna, and open it, setting it on the floor near the bathroom. Before I can get her some water in a mug from my desk, she's already got her face in the can, eating delicately.

"She's kind of prissy," I murmur, watching as she leans down and swishes her tail.

"She's perfect."

"You think Dane will like her?"

He looks up at me. "Yeah. She'll be good for him."

I plop down on my bed, moving the books and my laptop then adjusting my pillows at the top so I can be propped up.

We don't talk, and he seems on edge, alternately watching Astley and checking his phone.

He's antsy, like a tiger in a cage who wants out but isn't sure how to escape.

It's awkward. No, scratch that—it's weird AND awkward.

"Why are you smiling?" he says gruffly, startling me.

"You look terribly uncomfortable, and it makes me happy."

"You like me uncomfortable?"

"Immensely! I love it when you aren't sure what to say or do."

"Like now?"

"Plus, you came to help out with prank night, and now you have a new pet. Fort Knox is breaking apart and getting soft, little by little."

He grins then. "So I'm not usually like this?"

"Like, fun and lovable?"

He blinks at those words, his lips parting, and he starts to say something but stops.

"Go on, say it," I say. "As one guy told me the first day of class, *just get it all out*."

He takes a deep breath, stands, and walks over to the bed, making my heart skip a beat. "Truth or dare, Tulip, and you can't say dare."

Oh.

The tension tightens in the room as tendrils of excitement flash through my nerve endings.

I bite my bottom lip, anticipation rising. "Payback, I assume?"

"You bet."

Shit. I can't read him right now, not that that's unusual, but his eyes are low and heavy.

"Okay, I'll play. Truth."

"Were you in love with Chance last year?"

"I thought I was. I wasn't."

His gaze glitters at me as if he's trying to decide if I'm telling the truth. "Hmmm."

"My turn—"

"Nope," he says. "You had three times in the auditorium, remember? Truth or dare?"

I stand up and face him, nervous with my heart pounding in my ears. "What do you want me to pick?"

"Lady's choice." His chest rises rapidly as his eyes linger on my mouth.

"Truth, again."

"Last year, did you want me as much as I wanted you?" His words are husky.

I shiver. "Yes."

"Fuck..." A long sigh comes from him and he scrubs his face.

"Don't wimp out now, Cold and Evil. Ask the next one so I can get my turn."

A low grunt comes from him as if he's not sure it's a good idea for us to continue this game, but he sucks in a breath and finally says, "Truth or dare, Tulip?"

"Dare." Dare, dare, dare, baby. I don't know what's going to happen, but...

The electricity in the air cranks up, the hair on my arms rising as he breathes deeply, his face open, so open and full of heat, and I don't know what I'm doing here, but I'm in the moment, and he's so close and...

"Kiss me," he growls.

I take the two steps necessary to press my chest against his. Slowly sliding my hands up, I shudder at the feel of him, the silky quality of his practice jersey, the way his muscles spasm against me as I caress his collarbone, the hollows of his face. My fingers trace his eyebrows, marveling, amazed by how indescribably gorgeous his features are. And he wants me. I can see it by how still he is, the tense way he holds himself, as if he doesn't want to startle me.

My hands tangle in the hair around his neck. He puts his hands around my waist and tugs me closer, until we're one. I slide my tongue over his parted lips and he gasps, and I don't think I will ever get tired of the little truth that he kisses me, kisses *me*, when he doesn't anyone else. Moaning, I nip at his bottom lip and pull with my teeth, and his hands clench around me, his tongue darting out and caressing mine. He groans my name and deepens our kiss, his lips hard and insistent, his hands now pressing on my ass. A tornado twists inside me, desire ripping and tearing at the very heart of me.

Will every kiss by him always be like this?

When I pull away, I stroke my hand over his cheek and stare up at him. "You kiss like it's your last."

His lashes flutter as he licks at my finger, sucking it into his mouth, making me breathless, the sensation sending waves of heat to my lower body.

Hang on there, body, there's still a game to play.

"Truth or dare, Knox?"

"Which one do you want?" he asks, eyes glowing

"Truth."

"Ask."

"How did you get your scar?"

I just need him to tell me, to open up when I know he hasn't to anyone else except probably Dane.

He sways on his feet. "God, Ava..."

I cup his face. "Scars serve as medals of honor, and the strongest hearts have the most. I like your scars. Share them with me."

He takes a breath and his words slay me. "My mother sliced my face open."

I force the shock to not show on my face. It's not what I thought he'd say. I entertained the idea that maybe he did it to himself even though he denied it the day he helped change my tire. I blink, reorienting my thoughts. "Why?"

He moves to my bed and sits down, and I follow him, curling my legs up. His throat bobs, emotion stark on his face. "She went through these fugue episodes, more after the attack. I woke up one day and she was straddling me, a kitchen knife in her hands.

She lashed out...she didn't know who I was." He stumbles over the next words. "She told me I was ugly after it happened, but she didn't know what she was saying, so please don't think badly of her. I don't. I'll love her always...she was my mom."

I bite my lip at the pain in his voice.

"She killed herself a month later."

Tears prick at me as those images flicker in my mind, and I shove them down, pick up one of his fisted hands, and press it to my lips. I kiss each knuckle, unfurling his fingers until they're no longer clenched.

"I know I'm not ugly, but sometimes, sometimes, it gets in my head a little, and I...just...I don't know...can't stop thinking about it. I mean, if my own mom hurt me, then what the fuck is wrong with me? Then I remind myself that she had serious issues, but shit, the scar bugs me. I see it everyday in the mirror, and it's a reminder that maybe I didn't help her enough, that I should have seen how bad off she was that day we left her to go to school and she...she ended it." He sucks in a breath. "It just...made me push people away. I didn't want anyone to know what happened and I didn't want to ever fucking kiss a girl again."

"I'm sorry it happened, Knox." God, what else can I say? He's been through so much more than I ever realized.

He nods, sighing. "Dane has similar mental issues, I think."

I wince.

"What?" he asks.

"He was doing coke the day I was hit outside the gym." I describe how I saw the powder on his nose. "I kinda sorta said I wouldn't tell you, not really out loud, but with my eyes, and now I'm a snitch again and we haven't really been talking—"

He squeezes my hand. "Thanks for letting me know. Now, can you truth or dare me again? Because I really feel like this conversation took a nosedive."

I turn to face him on the bed. "Okay, truth or dare?"

"You sound so serious," he murmurs.

I pop him on the arm lightly. "I am! It's the only way to get you to talk to me."

"Ah, Tulip, I always want to talk to you..." He trails off. "Truth."

"Are you SA?"

He pops an eyebrow. "SA?"

I dart my eyes at him. "Don't play innocent. You wrote me that letter and you've been texting me these poems, and if it isn't you then I'm in deep shit cause I think SA is nice and I may really want to kiss him—"

"Yes."

Warmth washes over me.

"You're smiling," he murmurs.

"Mmmm, I guessed it, so many clues there...how you showed up to help with my car, the mention of your brother..." I let my words drift off, thinking back to that letter. "Whose cell number do you use?"

"One of Dane's burner phones I took a while back." He grimaces. "I really tried hard to not be stalkerish."

"Did you have anything to do with Tyler getting his scholarship?"

His lips quirk. "That was all you, Tulip. Vicious girl. I bet you made Trask wet his pants when you waltzed in there and laid down the law."

I blush and scoot closer to him until our legs are touching. "Truth or dare?"

His chest rises and he rakes a hand through his hair. "Shit. Truth?"

"*Why* did you come tonight?"

He lets out a frustrated growl, all male. Hot eyes drift over me. "I want you so bad I can't think straight."

Oh, sweet Jesus. There it is. Somebody give the man a gold star.

"Because you're slumming?"

"No!"

"Because you plan to use me for some evil plan?"

"No!"

"Because you feel sorry for me?"

"No!"

"Because you just can't help it?"

"Yes!"

His hand tilts my face to his and I drink him in, the scar that slices down his cheek, those eyes that burn —*for me.*

I play with the V-neck of his jersey, wondering what he looks like with his shirt off.

"What makes me so special?"

He cocks an eyebrow. "Does that even need a response? Don't you see how incredible you are? How fucking hot and sweet and strong? And what happened to you at the party—figuring that out doesn't stop, you feel me? It's not over for me. I *will* find him, and when I do, I'm going to make him wish he'd never been born—"

"Shhh." I refuse to let what happened that night ruin *this* moment. "One more time. Truth or dare?"

His eyes lower to half-mast. "I believe you are out of turns."

"Pretend I'm not," I say softly. "And you best say dare."

"You're quite the master player. Dare."

My heart flutters and my hands are clammy. I know what I want to ask for...

"Take your shirt off. And the pants while you're at it, right down to your underwear."

He gulps air. "Ava, wait a minute now..."

There he goes, holding back and wanting to protect me, but doesn't he see how I feel? He gets a weird look on his face. "Were you like this with Chance?"

"And by *like this*, what do you mean?" My hand reaches out and brushes the hair from his face, and he grabs it, pressing a hot kiss to my palm.

I like that feral gleam in his eye. Jealousy.

"Badass. Mouthy. Sexy as fuck." His hands cup my cheeks and he leans in, hovering over my lips. He changes direction, his nose running up my neck. He nips me on my throat then sucks hard, and I gasp.

"Chance doesn't know this side of me," I say breathlessly. "Only you."

He tugs on my hair. "Thank God. He never could have handled you, Tulip."

"You haven't completed your dare."

Our eyes cling for a long moment, and then he murmurs. "Technically, it was *my* turn. Truth or dare?"

"Dare," I whisper.

"*You* take my clothes off." He swallows thickly and stands up from the bed, his chest rising rapidly.

Standing up, I lift his shirt, grazing my hand over his

upper chest then dropping the jersey to the floor. He toes his shoes and socks off, kicking them aside while I work on his slick pants, pushing them down until he's in his tight black underwear.

My heart clutches. He's beautiful, all hard muscles and broad shoulders and tanned skin, his legs thick and powerful.

He bites his lip. "Tulip, please...please...I'm dying to..."

"What?"

His lashes flutter. "Fucking devour you like I've imagined a million times."

"Please do."

He pounces then, like the tiger he is, his arms closing around me and pulling me in for a hard kiss, holding nothing back, his tongue dueling with mine, sucking and nipping. He's ferocious with his mouth, his hands clutching my shoulders so tight, as if he's hanging on to me.

"Get...this off," I mumble, and my camisole is pulled up, by him and me together. His fingers unsnap my bra until my skin is bare, and he groans as my flesh presses against his.

"Tulip...so sweet," he whispers, his mouth closing around a nipple, and I clutch his head as blazing flame burns over my body, my legs scissoring with need. His teeth graze over one peak then the other, and I shiver. It's never been like this, never this intense, never this hot feeling on my body, the way I burn.

He pushes at my tights, grunting when he sees the booty shorts underneath, his fingers stalling out. "Are you sure, Tulip? Are you? Because I want you, but I don't want to scare you or make you feel like you have to be physical with me. We can cuddle. We can crawl up in your bed and watch those goofy *Star Wars* movies while I play with your hair."

"I am," I rush out, helping him slip the shorts off. I want something good. I want to not worry about a dark night in the woods, I want to replace it with beautiful things. With him.

And I know he's a Shark and I'm not, but he's *kind*, and I trust him, I do. He's proven himself to me in so many ways.

He looks at me, his irises dark with desire as they rove over my body. "So beautiful."

He sweeps me up in his arms, making me laugh.

"What's so funny?" he muses.

"You're just so…strong. I like it."

"Good." He lies down next to me on the bed, his lips on mine. We take up the whole mattress, but I don't even notice. I melt into him, basking in this need and want he's kept on a leash.

My back arches up when he kisses down my body, hands tracing over my face, my breasts, his mouth moving from one nipple to another, teasing me and sucking. He dips his tongue in my belly button, tasting my hip bones with a soft bite.

My core tightens, and my eyes roll back in my head at the friction, at the feel of his powerful body against my soft one.

"Tulip, I want to…" He presses little kisses to my stomach, his tongue flicking at my waistline as he toys with my panties.

Something makes him stop and I rise up. He's staring at my underwear, and all at once I'm embarrassed. They aren't special: white cotton, standard issue from the group home with my initials on the inside. "What's wrong?"

"Nothing. I'm just…nervous. May I?"

The big bad Shark is nervous? It only makes me want him more.

I nod and he slides them off, easing them down my legs.

His fingers skim over my wet folds and I throw a pillow

over my face. In the auditorium, we were so rushed, but this is slower and he's right there...

"Don't be shy now, Tulip. You're so brave. Unless...unless you want me to stop?"

I whip the pillow off my face and throw it on the floor. "If you stop, I will kill you with a lightsaber. I have one in the closet. You wanna talk about a dark side? I've got one."

"I've watched a few of them because of you," he murmurs as his fingers dance over me, skimming over my mound, never quite hard enough, not nearly enough until he eases a finger inside me and I moan.

"Uhhhhhh, good." I can't breathe.

"Is this okay?" he rasps, and I nod, trying to move so I can touch him too, but he holds me back, so I wait and fall into bliss, my hips rising up against his fingers.

My breaths come in erratic pants and when I look at him, he's intent on me.

"More?"

"You're torturing me." I don't know why he's even asking. I am his right now.

"How about more torture?"

"Lightsaber, remember? Don't stop."

He laughs and pulls me to the edge of the bed, gets on the floor on his knees, leans down, and holds my legs apart. Part of me feels vulnerable and nervous. I've never done this, never, and it's with him and that means something special—

His head dips and my fingers grip the quilt on my bed, clawing at it when his slick tongue brushes lightly over my center, lingering on my bundle of nerves. He groans. "Tulip, you taste so good, like, like destiny..." He leans closer, his nose trailing up my inner thigh. "I want to consume you, eat you up so fast, but I'm trying to go slow..." Another long, slow lick up my center, and I shudder.

"Knox, Knox, that, that..." My chest heaves. "Ohhhhh... don't stop!"

Cupping my bottom, he settles in and teases me, never quite enough pressure, his touch light and excruciatingly slow, swirling his tongue, wicked, so wicked as he draws intricate patterns on my clit, stoking the fire inside me hotter until I'm burning...

My body tightens, tension building at my spine.

His finger curls inside me, rubbing and stroking, and I can feel his breath on my skin, his tongue as he sucks—

Lights burst behind my shut lids. The universe becomes just him and me as sensations ripples across my skin.

"Knox!" I writhe underneath him, shameless as I press harder into him.

I'm boneless when he moves up and touches my face.

"You like?" He grins.

"That...that...when can we do it again?"

He throws his head back and laughs, satisfaction evident on the planes of his face.

And nothing matters. To see him laugh, to put joy there... being with him is so easy, and we laugh together, and I just... gah...I'm so close to falling—

"What are you doing to me," he says when I reach up and kiss him hard and long, sucking on his tongue with a fast rhythm, imagining him fucking me to the same beat.

Without our mouths parting, I use my hands to push down his underwear. He's thick and hard and long, his crown veiny and wet. I stare at him, getting a good look, nerves kicking in at how big he is even as my core clenches in anticipation. Wrapping my fingers around him, I stroke from his base to the tip, my thumb skating over the silky skin.

He groans, hovering over me. "Tulip, please..."

"Please what?"

"Harder."

Increasing my pace, I pump him with long, firm strokes while he kisses me.

He gasps for air, his chest shuddering. "Condom. Do you—"

Before he can finish, I jump off the bed and dash to my chest of drawers. They're two years old, but they're there, thank you, in the top under my underwear. I grab one and whip around and he's already up and behind me. With hands that tremble, he takes the package from me and rips it open with his teeth, his gaze never leaving my face. He slides it on and picks me up. My legs lock around his hips. Somehow we're back on my bed and he's on top of me.

Slowly, he rises above me and teases my entrance. His face is flushed and small beads of sweat dot his brow.

"So good..." I exhale. "Don't hold back, Knox, please..."

His hands clench around my waist as he strokes in all the way, stretching me, the fullness tight. He stops and holds me, clutching me.

"What's wrong?"

"I...haven't been with anyone in a while," he growls.

I smile, remembering our conversation at Lou's. He was waiting on me.

"Are you going to come too soon?" I tease.

He huffs, slides back out, and enters me again, swiveling his hips, getting a new angle that makes me shiver. "No. I'm going to fuck you till you see stars, Tulip."

"Always wanted to see the universe up close."

He huffs out a laugh.

He owns me then, taking control, moving my hips up, his strokes hard and solid, each slide precise and sure, my wetness coating him, the sounds of us, our bodies slapping together, our heavy breaths are all I can think about.

Leaning over me, he hitches one of my legs over his shoulder and gains momentum, his voice in my ear, dark and husky. "I want to know everything about you. What you eat, except for tomatoes, God, I hate those, what you dream about, what songs you listen to, what makes you laugh, what makes you happy, how you feel when I fuck you. I want you breathing for me. I want you begging me for more of this. I want you kissing me, just me. I want you, Tulip, you, you, you, you..."

His finger circles my clit in tandem as he takes me, and I writhe underneath him. He does it so well, so good until I can't breathe, until I'm thrashing as I clutch his ass and dig my nails in. "Tulip..." he grunts. "I'm close. Come with me."

He moves faster, faster, his cock thickening even more and I call out his name, undulating under him. He cups my face and goes over with me, his breath hard and unsteady as he kisses me with our eyes open. Emotion claws at my heart as my body pulses around him in the aftershocks.

I want you kissing me, just me.

God. His words.

I'm falling so hard, dancing near the edge of the vastness that's him.

And I know there's barely any trust left in me for guys, but for him...

I want this. Whatever it is.

17

Coiled and tense, I'm waiting for her in the parking lot. Okay, what's the etiquette for seeing a girl after you've had sex with her? I mean, I know what happens after the usual girls, but she's...*her*.

Her Jeep parks a few spaces over from mine and I jog over. She gets out of the car, bends over to grab her backpack, and turns to face me.

My heart skips. Fucking skips.

Last night.

Well.

It's all I can think about and I'm ignoring those voices in my head, the ones that tell me to tread carefully, to go slow.

I just...

Want her.

I shove down niggling warnings that prick at me, reminding me that I have other commitments. Football. Dane.

One day at a time.

That's what I've been telling myself since I walked out of her dorm last night.

For now, she's here and I'm here and I refuse to go one more day with this need for her unmet.

She slings her backpack up and over her shoulder. There's a hesitant look in her eyes.

"Sleep well?" I ask, fidgeting as we take off for the entrance of Camden.

A slow blush rises up her cheeks. Her head dips, a vulnerable expression flitting over her face. "Yeah. You?"

My head goes back to last night, when I had her under me, all the things I told her, about my mom, admitting I was SA. I didn't leave her dorm until nearly midnight, and walking away from her in that bed was hard.

She smiles, her lips curving up, lush and pink. "Hello. Earth to Knox."

"Great."

I slept like crap. Once I got home—with a mewling cat in my arms—Dad was sitting in the kitchen, demanding to know where I'd been. I paused, getting Astley settled with some sandwich meat from the fridge and a water bowl as I contemplated my answer. Truth is best.

"I was with Ava. I'm with her," I told him finally. Damn, it felt good to get it off my chest, to finally tell him I want her, I want her next to me, I want her so fucking bad that no one even matters—

With his wide eyes searching my face, he interrupted my thoughts. "Knox, son, that girl is trouble for your brother. He can't get over what happened to her, and just maybe, there's a reason—"

"You don't get to tell me who I see," I snapped back and then stomped up the stairs.

"Your brother still isn't home," he called at my back, and I stopped in my tracks.

I came back in the kitchen and we sat on the barstools. After a few texts, I figured out he was at Liam's. Dad and I both went to bed exhausted.

I finally got to sleep, then Dane woke me up around three, crawling in on the other side of my bed, eyes hollow and empty. I watched him get under the covers and turn over to face the wall, his shoulders shuddering.

Was he crying?

Why didn't he spend the night at Liam's?

When six o'clock rolled around, I couldn't sleep, so I got up and ran for two miles, then came back, showered, and let Suzy fix me breakfast while Dad got ready for an early flight to New York. I went through the motions automatically, my head on Ava. Wondering if she was eating something. Wondering if her lips were as swollen as mine.

I come back to the present when she nudges me.

"How are we going to do this?" she asks as we get to the front doors.

I don't have to ask what she means. I see the tension on her face as I open the door, and she glides through, her finger plucking nervously at her skirt. I take it and clasp it in mine. She's not sure what we are, and neither am I, yet here we are.

She bites her lip, eyes darting around at the students in the foyer.

"They'll fall in line." Or I'll eviscerate them.

I don't see any of the other guys. Dane said he'd ride with

Liam this morning, and they're going to be late considering Dane was barely awake when I left.

Eyes are on us as we walk to her locker. Brandon walks past us, his mouth swollen and cracked from where I hit him. His steps falter when he sees me next to her, and I feel her stiffen.

I smile/snarl—whatever you want to call what my lips do.

With a huff, he pales and moves on.

Ava fidgets. "Knox, I-I don't want your team to—"

"Please, trust me. Just keep walking to your locker," I tell her.

She nods and when we get there, she undoes her lock, grabbing her textbooks. She turns around, and I tilt her face up, kissing her long and deep. Her backpack falls to the floor, her arms curling up around my neck. Jesus. God. Krishna. *Whatever.* I want to drown in her. I want to eat her slowly then fast—

"Get a room, locker neighbor." It's Wyatt and his laconic accent that pulls us apart. He's smirking. "Prank night must have ended well." His eyes focus on me. "If you hurt her, I'll make you regret it, Shark."

"What's going on?" Piper says, sliding up next to us. Her eyes widen when she takes in my hand around Ava's hip. "Um, did I miss something? Was there a comet last night that altered everyone's brain? No? Maybe someone had a lobotomy? Still no? Huh. Then someone please tell me why a Shark is looking at Ava like she's a slice of pie?"

"Just Knox making a statement," Ava murmurs and glances at me. "Try to rein it in for class, 'kay? I don't want to be sitting in Mr. Trask's office explaining the PDA."

Piper frowns then turns to Ava. "Don't we hate him?"

"Apparently not," Wyatt drawls, tossing an arm around Piper. "They were making out like gangbusters before you walked up. Putting on quite a show."

"We weren't making out," Ava says.

"Pretty much," I say.

She rolls her eyes. "Let's go to class."

Chance walks down the hall, Brooklyn next to him, and I pause. Nothing like ripping the bandage off right now.

"You go on to class. I've got something to do."

She looks past me, following my gaze, and gives me a nod as she and Piper take off, their heads tilted together. I can only imagine what Piper's asking.

I walk over to Chance, who hasn't seen me yet.

"Hey," I say to him, nerves kicking in. How am I going to do this? *Oh, by the way, last year when you were seeing Ava, I wanted her, and now I've had her and don't think I'll ever let her go?*

I glance at Brooklyn. "Can you give us a moment?"

"What's up?" Chance says as she heads to class. "You ready for the game tomorrow? Anxious? I heard a scout from Auburn is coming."

So did I. I've kept thoughts of it locked away and will focus on it when I need to.

I study him. "I'm with Ava."

He pauses, and a long sigh comes from him. "With her?"

"She's mine."

Shoving a hand through his hair, he glares at me as his nose flares. "You're my best friend. You know I still care about her, and when you want a girl, you just take her and then it's over. Is that what you're telling me? You want to screw my ex?" His face tightens. "Or have you already?"

Not answering that.

His hands tighten around his books.

"Are you angry?" I expect him to be, but I don't want to lose him...

"Yes." His teeth clench. "How do I know you didn't hurt her at the kegger?"

"How do I know it wasn't you?" I reply sharply. Part of me knows he's not like that, and that's what I've been telling myself for months, but...

His fists clench. "Because I loved her, and it pisses me off for you to even think that!"

I exhale, trying to shake off the anger I feel toward him. "You had your opportunity, Chance. You have Brooklyn. Ava is mine."

He shakes his head, a knowing glint in his eye. "No, she isn't. You may think so, but that girl is *nobody's*. She belongs to herself. She's different from everyone else here. You can't own her like your dad owns this town—"

"Do you know how she grew up? She used to live under a bridge. Her mom was an addict and dumped Ava with a newborn baby. Tyler's like her kid. Do you know *her*? Really?"

His eyes narrow.

"You deserted her when she needed you." I've never said those words aloud to him, but boy have I thought it.

He closes his eyes, some of the heat leaving his voice. "I made a mistake, and I think about it every day."

"What are you two girls gossiping about?" It's Liam, weaseling his way over to us. We've barely spoken except for football, and I give him a surprised glance. "Is it about Knox showing up at prank night? All those underclassman girls went nuts with pics of you on social, man. *Knox is so hot. Knox is at Arlington. Knox is holding a cat.*"

Chance blows out a breath and looks away from me.

Liam frowns. "You two having a little tiff? Things not well on the offense, Knox?" He smirks. "Let me guess—Ava. Jesus, I'm sick of her."

"Shut up, Liam," Chance snaps. "Just stay out of it."

I realize my twin isn't with Liam. "Where's Dane?"

He shrugs. "Went to pick him up, blew the horn and texted him. I got nada. Guess he's not coming. He was wasted last night when I dropped him off."

"Yeah? Where were you guys?" I ask.

Liam curls his lip. "Had a little get-together in my barn, some girls from Hampton High dropped by, sweet as hell—"

Jolena approaches and he shuts up, giving us a sweeping look. *No blabbing*, his gaze says. Whatever.

"When you went to pick him up this morning, was my dad's car there? White BMW? He usually parks under the portico outside the front door." He was supposed to leave for New York today for a meeting, but he hadn't left by the time I did.

"No."

"Suzy's black Camry?"

He gives me an annoyed glance. "Didn't see it, but I'm not his babysitter. He's probably just skipping."

My throat dries. When I left, Suzy was taking care of Astley and making an appointment for her to go to the vet. Had she left already?

"I even got out and knocked on the door," Liam continues. "He's sleeping in and will show up."

My lips tighten. He doesn't have a car! I guess Suzy could

bring him later, but...

Ignoring them, I open the Finders App on my phone, and sure enough, Dane is home. I think about him shuddering when he crawled in my bed last night—

Jolena lets out a startled gasp as she looks at her phone. She shoves it in my face. "Did you go to prank night with *Ava*?"

I look at the picture of me holding the cat. Ava is next to me, a little smile on her face. Damn, she's beautiful.

Liam leans in and then looks at me, eyes gleaming. "Ah, didn't see that one. You hitting that finally?" He smirks at Chance. "Sorry, man. What Knox wants, Knox eventually gets."

Jolena shakes her head, her eyes hard. "What is going on? How did I miss this?"

"Catch up, Jo. He's with her," Chance says, his face tight. "I'm going to class."

He stalks off, heading to History of Film, where I should be going.

"Let's get out of here," Liam says to Jolena, throwing his arm around her as they leave.

I think for half a second, debating going to class and seeing Ava or checking on my brother.

I whip around, head for the exit, and run for my car.

"Dane!" I call out as I walk into the kitchen, but no one's there.

I check the den. The TV is on ESPN, but no Dane.

I jog out the French doors to the pool, my heart pounding.

I've caught him out here before, a flat look on his face behind his sunglasses as he sat in a lounge chair. The place is eerily quiet except for the line of waterfalls along the pool wall that cascade down. Running, I scan the perimeter, the pool house, the cabana, the outdoor kitchen.

Twisting around, I dash back inside. "Dane!" I bellow.

Nothing.

I take the kitchen staircase three at a time and run to my room. He's not there.

I step back into the hall and head to his bedroom. The door is shut and I swallow, closing my eyes, visions of Mom face down in our pool pulsing in my head.

"Dane?"

His bed is empty and his room is a total wreck, clothes on the floor, fast food drinks on the nightstand, his prescription bottles strewn about.

The sound of the shower comes from his bathroom and I call out his name before I step inside. The white, wall-to-wall marble-tiled bathroom is almost as big as his bedroom. Steam rises, clouding the mirrors.

My heart lurches when I see him huddled nude on the floor of the walk-in shower.

His knees are pulled up to his chest, water falling over him. I fling the door open and relief makes me weak. Panting, I crouch to the floor at the edge of the shower, water droplets hitting my face and clothes.

"Dane? Hey, man, I'm here," I whisper as I reach over and turn off the water.

He doesn't reply, just rocks back and forth.

Fear and dread snake over me as I glance around the room, my gaze landing and freezing on a package of razor blades on the sink. Adrenaline seizes me and my eyes dart back to him, but I don't see any cuts or blood.

"Dane? Come on, man. It's me."

He moans, his head still lowered.

Shit, shit, shit. I rub my face. I can't *make* him do the right things, and emotion, dark and thick, slides over me.

I don't know how to fix him.

I wish I were better at this, but I'm just...

Just a fucking kid!

I barely know anything.

Since he won't talk, I do, my voice gentle, ignoring the razor blades for now. "I was worried when you didn't come to school."

Several seconds pass.

"Let me get you a towel." My legs feel weak as I push myself to stand and open the cabinet, grabbing a white one.

When I turn, he's watching me, eyes empty.

Give me strength. Please, God, I don't know if you're real or if you're listening, but this is my brother and he's messed up, and he's all I have, and...and I don't know the right things to say and if I lose him—

I get in the shower with him and sit next to him and throw the towel over his shoulders. I'm not sure how long we stay there, my arms tight around him until he finally starts to cry. Long, earthshattering sobs. I'm terrified, but I don't let go.

"I'm here, I'm here," I say softly.

"I want to die," he says in a ragged voice into my chest. His fists pound into my arms, and I take it. "I can't do this shitty life anymore. I'm so tired of being lost and going on and pretending I'm okay when I'm not, and I know it and you know it, and I'm not strong, I'm not. I'm weak and I can't shake things off like you do and carry on like she didn't die and leave us and leave us and leave us and, fuck, I miss her so much..."

Helplessness eviscerates me. Tears clog my throat until they're falling with his. I lift his face and press our foreheads together. "Dane, please, brother, please, you can't leave me here. She's gone, she is, but I'm here for you."

He looks up at me, his face twisted. "Maybe you'd be better off without me. I keep bringing you down and you keep worrying and worrying..." He shudders, his voice halting and etched in pain. "You're going to hate me."

"Never."

Several moments pass as he weeps, and I keep my arms around his wet body. I feel the tension in him, as if...

I push the hair out of his face. "Come on, talk to me. Tell me what brought this on."

A long exhalation comes from him as he leans his head back against the shower wall. In a toneless voice, he says, "I remember...what happened to Ava."

I flinch, revulsion crawling over my skin. "Are you saying it was you? Because no way—"

"Might as well have been," he says bitterly. "It was Liam. And I knew it this whole time."

I can't breathe. Anger and rage coil inside me, itching to get out. Liam. Liam. Liam. I'm going to pound my fists into his face. I'm going to rip him apart, and then I'm going to do it all over again—

He grabs my hand and clenches it until it hurts. "I know you want to run out of here and kill him, but you have to hear all of this. You have to hear my part."

"I'm not leaving you," I tell him brokenly, my shoulders

hunching.

He gulps air. "Liam, last night, he...he had a small group at his barn, some of the players, and he was hot after some girl from Hampton High. We were drinking and he pointed toward the Hampton girl and said, 'Tonight I get a trophy from her.'"

"What does that mean?"

He closes his eyes. "It just sounded like something I've heard before, like it knocked something loose in my memory." He scrubs his face. "It kept niggling at me. Then it hit me. I recall being at the bonfire and watching him slip off into the woods. He set his drink down on a stump, said, '*Trophy time*,' and followed Ava."

His words sink in, and my hands clench. Different scenarios fly through my head—

"It's my fault too. I was there. I was THERE. And I've known for ten months."

"You just now remembered," I tell him.

"Maybe there's other stuff I don't recall." He pauses, his hands wringing. "Last night, he wanted to do some coke, and I didn't, and he kept asking me why and when I said I was tired, he just got this hard look on his face, like he *knew* I remembered something. I could tell he regretted saying the trophy thing." He takes a breath. "So before he brought me home, he asked me if I remembered that I roofied Ava's drink at the kegger, and I said no, I didn't give her anything to drink, and he just laughed and gave me that aw-shucks routine and said, 'I saw you giving her drinks but I won't tell anyone.'" Anguish glazes his face as he looks at me. "I wouldn't do that, would I? Not after what happened to Mom..."

"No, you wouldn't," I assure him, and he just stares at me.

"I'm your brother. That's what you're supposed to say because you love me, but what if I did?"

"You didn't!" My gut fucking knows it! "Look at how the idea of it wrecks you! You didn't!"

He flinches and I exhale and ease him up by his arms, helping him stand.

I make him sit on the toilet as I lean over the sink, turn on the water, and splash my face. After drying my face, I pick up the razors and face him. "Dane, you can't quit on me, okay? I'm going to get you help, and you've got to stop with the drugs, and..." I stop, swallowing.

What does he need? He needs me and Dad. We need to circle the wagons and get him straight.

He dips his head. "This is what's been eating at me, and for months my brain has been telling me I knew something. I don't want to be part of that, to hurt a person like Ava." He bites his lip, trying to fight the tears, but they're back, coursing down his face. "I'm sorry, God, I'm so sorry. I know you care about her, and what have I done?"

I watch him and wrestle with my emotions about Ava, knowing I have to be strong for him. "Come on, let's get you dressed." I dash into his room, grab him some joggers and a T-shirt from his chest of drawers, and press them into his hands. Inside, I'm seething with suppressed rage over Liam, but somehow I manage to keep it from spilling over. Liam's been at the center of Dane's issues for months. Oh, I'm not stupid, I know my brother has problems, but Liam, *that motherfucker, I'm going to kill—*

"I can't go to school," Dane murmurs.

"I know." I'm just glad he's putting his pants on. I don't want to think about the broken boy in the shower.

"How does peppermint tea sound? We can talk. Are you high right now?"

Isn't that what old people do, coffee and tea until everything's okay?

He shakes his head, and when I meet his eyes, they still have that vacant look, but his pupils are normal.

After I change into some sweats and a shirt that isn't wet, we walk downstairs to the kitchen, and I put the kettle on, wishing Dad were here. He's on a plane and won't land until noon. We're going to need his help. None of this can go wrong if we want to keep Dane safe from himself while also making sure Liam gets what he deserves.

I send Dad a text, not really saying what's up but letting him know it's an emergency and to call me when he gets service. *Don't need to leave a trail*, runs through my head, because I'm paranoid as shit. There's no real proof it was Liam, and if we run and accuse him now, more than likely, he'll point his finger at Dane and say it was him who drugged her. Hell, he could even say it was Dane who followed her into the woods. All kinds of different possibilities run through my head as I make our tea, dunking the herbal bag.

Dane sits at the marble island and sips his until there's color in his face once again. He eyes me. "What are you thinking? Do I need to go to Ava—"

I hold my hand up. The last thing Dane needs is to be around Ava. He's teetering on the edge and his guilt is palpable, a tangible thing.

"Liam's at school and we aren't. That's what I'm thinking." I take a sip, looking at him over the rim of my cup. "We need proof." Or maybe I just need to see it for myself, to confirm everything Dane has said, because while I trust that he didn't hurt Ava, his head isn't on quite straight right now, and I need to see for myself what Liam did to her. My hands tighten.

He nods, watching my fists. "If you beat him up, you'll be arrested. They're somebody in this town, Knox. His dad is the fucking mayor. We need to wait for Dad before we go to the cops."

Frustration gnaws at me. "But if he was talking about trophies, I'd like to see them."

Dane starts. "How? I don't even know where he keeps them."

"Where do you keep your drugs? The good stuff?"

"Bedroom. High up in the closet inside a box under a bunch of sweaters."

I nod, making a note to go find them later and dump them. "Then, we're going to get into his bedroom. That's where his secrets are. His parents are working. He has a maid and a chef, right?"

He nods, a nervous look on his face. "What are you thinking?"

I'm not thinking straight at all. I'm operating on instinct.

"We knock on the door, tell them you left your phone in Liam's room, which makes perfect sense—you were there last night, and it's legit if Liam asks because he tried to text you this morning and couldn't get you." I pause. "Plus, if we find his...whatever he keeps, and by now, I'm thinking underwear..." I pause. "I need to see it, Dane."

Dane gives me a long look. "You're in love with her."

I don't respond for several moments. "I tried to stay away from her." *For you.*

He sighs and stares down at his tea. "Just...just don't let Dad put me at Lakeside, okay? Mom hated that place."

Lakeside is a private facility where Mom stayed on and off.

"Maybe you need to stay for a week or so—"

"No. I don't want to not see you! I'll go back to therapy and that's it." He swallows. "I'll go today if you'll go with me. I need you, Knox."

I exhale and nod, knowing I'll probably need to convince Dad of it, and then make us a quick breakfast of scrambled eggs and toast as we talk more, letting him settle. I watch him closely, feeling better as his color brightens and he eats everything on his plate.

After I've called Suzy to check in and let her know we're home today so she won't be surprised if she sees us, I look at him. I don't want to push him to do too much, but...

"You really want to sneak into Liam's?" he asks.

I nod. "If you don't want to, I'll do it."

He exhales. "I want to. Maybe it might jog a memory if I hurt her. I mean..." His lashes flutter. "What if it was...both of us?"

"It fucking wasn't," I say firmly as I grab my keys.

AN HOUR LATER, the deed is done, and we leave Liam's and get in my car. I drive to the end of their lane before I have to stop and let Dane vomit. It went pretty much like I thought it would, me smiling at the waitstaff while Dane nodded and went along with me, then we went to Liam's bedroom on the second floor. We shut the door, locked it, and divided the room. He took the closet and I headed for the chest of drawers. I was close to giving up when I lifted his mattress. There, in an Adidas bag, I dumped out panties and thongs, some plain, some frilly. A white pair stood out. ATH was written on the back waistband. Ava Tulip Harris. She put her initials there, the same kind she wore last night.

We stood there and waffled on what to do with them. If Liam got suspicious, he might move them. If we took them, it would be messing with evidence. In the end, I used Dane's burner to take pictures of them, making sure to get Liam's bedroom in the photo. I don't even know if it makes sense to take the pictures, but I'm worried he'll ditch the underwear.

And now here we are.

Dane wipes his mouth. Puts his seat belt back on. "Do you...do you think they'll prosecute me too? I deserve it for not remembering."

My hands tighten around the wheel as I pull out. I don't know if he'll be an accomplice, but either way, this is about to be very ugly.

"In the end, it will probably come down to his word against yours about the woods and what you saw. You were trashed, but those underwear are damning." I mull it over and decide I just don't know enough. "He's going to say it was you. He already dropped a hint when he said you roofied her."

He nods, looking out the window.

A text comes in and I check my phone: a message from Dad saying he's catching the next flight back and will be here in a few hours. I let Dane know.

He leans back against the headrest. "Thank you for coming home. I don't know what I'd do without you," he says as he looks out the window.

He's asleep before I even reach our house.

18

AVA

"Here comes Darth Vader and Tyler. They're getting out of the nun-mobile," Lou says as I walk by with a platter of two burgers and fries for a two-top. Moving fast, I set down the couple's food then bus another table on the way back.

"It's a van. A regular van," I tell Lou.

He grimaces. "They should paint a habit on the hood. Or a starship."

"You're a weirdo," I call out to him, watching as Sister Margaret and Tyler make their way to the front door of the diner.

He throws his arms up. "I'm a nonpracticing Catholic. She's a nun. It feels like she *knows* I don't go to Mass. Don't they have God on speed dial? She probably knows I'm divorced too," he mutters.

I bite my lip.

Rosemary, the cook, calls out from behind the grill in the

kitchen. "You also drink and cuss like a sailor and take the Lord's name in vain—"

"Be quiet! She's about to come in!" Lou shouts back. He lingers behind the register, one eye on the door. He snaps his fingers. "Oh, I almost forgot—a lady brought this by today when I opened up. I think it's a tip." He hands me a note. "She said to be sure you got it."

I tuck it in my apron to look at later.

My thoughts go to Knox. He texted me earlier today and told me he was sorry he had to leave school, but Dane wasn't feeling well, and he'd text me later tonight when I got off work.

Tyler comes in and rushes over to me, and I give him a tight hug.

"How was school? Did you learn anything cool?"

He grins. "They showed me new ways to remember stuff, like I know all the letters. Just say one—I know it."

"T."

"Yes, that's one. Say another."

"Y."

"Yep!"

"L."

"Know it!"

"E."

"Yeah."

"R!"

He squints. "Balls. Did you spell my name?"

"Don't say balls, and yes I did!" I ruffle his hair. "Do you know what order all the letters go in?"

He adjusts his glasses.

"It's a song, bozo. You used to sing it."

He tugs at his shirt. "A, B, C, D..." He goes all the way to T before getting a little confused, but he eventually finishes with Z.

I swing him up and he squeals. Lou and a couple of customers clap.

Sister Margaret smiles. "He regaled the entire wing of boys this afternoon."

I feel myself glowing from the inside out.

On my dinner break, I place an order for us and we take a table in the back. I've just gotten the first French fry in my mouth when in walk Wyatt and Piper. I texted them earlier to see if they had dinner plans.

Piper bounces over and gives Tyler a squeeze. "Give me a hug, big boy!"

They order food at the counter and take a seat with us. Sister Margaret murmurs that she has emails to catch up with on her phone and wanders off to the front. Lou's eyes widen as she approaches, then he scurries off to the back.

"Why are you smiling so much?" Wyatt says dryly, flexing one of his muscles again so Tyler can watch the hummingbirds on his bicep flutter.

"No one called me names today, I'm seeing Tyler, and Lou is terrified of nuns. It's been a great day."

"Sooooo, Knox," comes from Piper. "Is this serious?"

I have no clue. "It's a one day at a time kind of thing."

"And it's really true that he paid for your housing? Isn't that kind of weird? I mean, do you feel like you owe him?" I confessed in film class today about Knox being my donor.

"Not in *favors*, if you get my drift, but I'll pay him back. I've gotten almost three thousand in tips saved this year," I say.

Piper looks around at the dingy diner. "Girl, you're gonna have to wait a lot more tables to get to ten grand."

True, but I can do it. It will just take some time.

"He wrote you that secret admirer letter, so I'm not so sure he wants you to pay him back," Wyatt says with an eye waggle. "He's rich—let him take care of you."

Let him take care of me? Um, no.

Piper scowls. "I don't know about him. He's *the* Shark, and he was mean to you last year. Remember that time he scared you in the locker room after the game?"

Hmmm, I remember, though maybe I wasn't actually that scared.

She continues. "I mean, you're not very experienced, and everyone says he's this bad boy who only has sex from—" She throws a hand over her mouth and looks at Tyler, who's humming his ABCs. "Crap," she whispers. "Little ears. I'll rein it in."

Wyatt laughs, sipping on a Coke. "So, Ava, does he only do it that way?"

A slow blush steals up my cheeks when I think back to last night. "I plead the fifth."

Piper rolls her eyes. "Well, enough about the Shark. I have news! It's incredible! It's..." She pauses, takes a drink, and holds up her index finger in a *wait a minute* motion.

"What is it, bozo?" Tyler asks, and I snicker and elbow him.

"Piper likes to drag things out for maximum effect. Give her a drumroll."

Tyler beats his hands on the table, and Wyatt and I pick it up.

Piper lets her straw go. Purses her lips. "Well, you know

how bad I want to go to Vandy, but we don't have the money, and since most of the scholarships are only half of admission, I wrote a letter to my uncle in Seattle who went there and became a doctor. Never got married and is filthy rich. You met him at Christmas once, Ava."

She has a ton of relatives and I've met several at holiday functions.

She titters. "I asked him very prettily if he would consider making up the difference on a scholarship and he said…YES!"

My lips part. Visions of Vandy dance in my head and jealousy rises up for half a second before I battle it back. Piper deserves the best.

"Whoa," I say, totaling up a year in my head. Tuition is roughly $48,000; room and board is $18,000; books and miscellaneous is $1500; other random expenses are $2500. A year at Vandy is over $100,000, so half of that would be $50,000. She has a nice uncle.

"Nice," murmurs Wyatt.

"Where are you thinking of going?" Piper says to me.

"Community college, then a state school, probably. I haven't gotten all my applications straight. But Vandy—I'm so happy for you. Congrats, Piper." I stuff a fry in and swallow it down. *Don't be sad, don't be.* I smile at her.

"What about you, Wyatt?" Piper beams.

He cocks his head. "Somewhere in Nashville so I can be close to my mom. Maybe Vandy. I haven't worked it out yet. I'd like to play baseball somewhere."

My heart dips as I think of Piper and Wyatt going off to big-time schools without me.

Tyler leans in over the table toward Wyatt. "Did those tattoos hurt?"

"Yes," he replies solemnly. "I don't recommend it for a six-year-old."

"Balls."

Wyatt snorts. "Ava mentioned you're an artist?"

"I draw," Tyler deadpans.

"Yeah? Well, I've been thinking about getting a new one, a dragon for our school mascot. Can you draw that?" Wyatt gives him a steely look, and I smile seeing Tyler's spine grow straighter.

"He's throwing down a challenge, Tyler," I whisper out of the side of my mouth.

Tyler sets down his burger, wipes his hands on his pants, and gives Wyatt a long look. I think I see myself in his eyes. Determination.

"I can draw you the bestest dragon you have ever seen. What colors do you want?"

"Kickass," I murmur. "You should see this kid—freaking amazing."

Wyatt grins at Tyler. "Red and gold. You draw it and I'll see if I like it."

"Deal!" They shake on it.

"Carrot cake!" Lou calls out as he approaches our table with a platter. "It's gonna go bad tomorrow so somebody's gotta eat it!" He pauses at the looks on our faces. "That's a joke. It's good for at least two more days."

Tyler says he doesn't want any carrots on his cake, so Wyatt takes his piece. I laugh as I see Lou box up the rest and hand it over to Sister Margaret to take back to the other Darth Vaders or whoever else might want it.

After everyone leaves, I'm watching their taillights when Lou eases up next to me. "You've done good, Ava. He's happy. You've got friends. You're gonna be okay, right?"

"Yes." I sigh. Lou knows everything since I had to take a few weeks off after the keg party, and while he isn't the type to give hugs, he pats me carefully on the back.

It's ten by the time I pull up at the dorm, park, and get out, thankful for the good streetlights in the area as I fast-walk to the front entrance.

"Ava," comes a male voice on my right, and I nearly jump into the bushes.

"Knox! What in the blue hell! You nearly scared me out of my shoes—"

He's leaning back against his car before he straightens and jogs over to me. "I wasn't thinking. Sorry. I texted you I'd be here, but you must have been driving."

Wearing low-slung jeans and a tight Dragons shirt, he towers over me. Dark hair frames his face.

"You look good," he says gruffly, running his eyes over my frayed shorts and Lizzo shirt.

I laugh, knowing I probably smell like grease from the diner. My smile subsides when I take in his expression. "What's up?"

He seems to gather himself and smiles. "Just missed you."

A blush steals up my face, recalling us naked in my bed. Was it just last night? It seems a million miles away. "I missed you too. How's Dane?"

He takes a deep breath. "He's messed up. When I got home this morning, he...he was at the lowest I've ever seen him. He wanted to die, and I-I didn't know what to do."

Oh, Knox... "I'm so sorry! Is he okay? Is there anything I can do?"

He flinches and looks away from me, scanning the parking lot. "No. My dad's home with him—" He stops when several underclassmen rush out the front doors and call out to him. He gives them a half-hearted wave.

"Do you want to come upstairs and talk? I can sneak you in the side entrance—"

He shuffles his feet on the concrete, still not meeting my eyes. "Nah, I need to go home. Dad, Dane, and I...we're still going over some things and talking. We've needed to for a long time. Maybe...maybe it was a good thing that Dane cracked. Sometimes you have to hit rock bottom before you can crawl back up." He sighs and rakes a hand through his hair.

"True. Maybe his breakdown can be a breakthrough."

His gaze is firmly focused on a point over my shoulder and when I look back, there's nothing there. Why is he avoiding my eyes?

"Do you regret last night?" I blurt.

"No, but..." He exhales and sticks his hands in his jeans. "Ava, I really want this thing we have, but maybe we're moving too fast."

Moving too fast?

After last night?

My chest feels tight. "Is this...a brushoff?"

He closes his eyes. "Please, don't ever think that. I just need a minute to breathe." He scrubs his face. "Dane needs me, and there's a lot going on right now."

A minute to breathe?

Is he...is he trying to destroy my heart?

Those walls are stacking up around him, those armored tanks pointed right at me.

And he's calling me Ava.

Please, no, don't do that, Knox. I can't handle you hurting me, not after what we've shared...

I study the lines of his face, his granite expression, and it reminds me of the way he shut down after the library. "What are you *not* telling me, Knox?"

I think I see fear flicker on his face before he turns it off. "Nothing. I'll be spotty at school tomorrow. Dane's got therapy and I'm coming in late so Dad and I can go with him." He pauses. "Our first game is tomorrow, and I want you to come, but I understand if you don't."

"I won't be there."

"Don't blame you," he says quietly, sighing.

"I hope Dane's okay." I know I'm saying all the right words, but I feel lost, wondering what's really going on in his head.

Several moments pass as neither of us speaks.

I sigh and say, "I should head inside—"

"I didn't want to go to sleep tonight without seeing you again."

I give him a half-smile. "You've seen me. I'm tired and I still have homework waiting on me." I pause. "I'm here if you need me, if you decide you want to talk about Dane."

I turn to leave and he grabs my hand. "Ava..."

My control snaps. "Don't call me that, okay? It just means you're pushing me away, and I hate it."

He exhales heavily. "Tulip...please. It's been a hell of a day."

I close my eyes.

His brother needs him, Ava. They're close. Get yourself together.

It's just...

I take a big breath. "You've had a tough day, but you coming here and telling me you *need a minute* right after last night—it hurts. If it's about Dane, I get it, but if you're not telling me everything, I'm not sure who you are."

He pulls me to him and wraps his strong arms around me. "You know me, Tulip. You do."

I press my head against his chest, listening to his heart beat as he runs his fingers through my hair. He tilts my face up and kisses me softly. "Don't be mad at me, please," he whispers. "Just give me some time."

I nod, battling that uneasy feeling rolling around inside my gut. He isn't telling me everything, but I don't ask the questions that are on the tip of my tongue.

I'm taking a chance on him, because this is the guy who wrote me a beautiful letter, and that's enough—for now.

19

I watch her walk into her dorm, waiting until she's safe before releasing a deep breath from my chest.

Shit.

Shit.

Fuck.

Dad and our lawyers, Chance's dad included, don't want me to tell her anything until we're ready. They showed up at our house today around three and after hearing Dane's story, they advised us to keep up with the everyday norm until Dane is ready to face the police interviews that will inevitably come. Soon, soon. And in the meantime, I have to be around Liam and pretend I don't want to smash my fist into his motherfucking face. I see his trophies again, scattered out on his bed. Those need to stay exactly where they are for now, and if I have to be cordial, I'll grit my teeth and play along even though I don't agree with everything. Dad's worried about Dane, and while I am too, I have a sick feeling in my gut for not rushing to Ava and telling her everything.

Even so, I'm not sure how she'll react. What if she blames Dane? What if it taints everything we have with each other? Plus, there's this niggling thought that maybe I rushed her into sex last night when I shouldn't have—

My phone pings with a text as I get in the car.

Did you see her?

Dad.

Yes. Leaving now.

Everything okay?

In other words, *Did you tell her?*

Fine. Be home after I stop at Chance's, I tap out sharply. **I'm telling him everything. His dad already knows and we need him to know what's going on.**

Okay.

As I start the car, Ava's words come back to haunt me: *If you're not telling me everything, I'm not sure who you are...*

My hands grip the steering wheel as I make the turn to get to Chance's house. My gut is screaming for me to turn around and go up to her room and—

And what?

WHAT?

Tell her Dane will likely be implicated by Liam once it all goes down?

No, no, hell no. He's my brother, and I could have lost him today for Christ's sake. I can fix this before she thinks Dane might be part of it. I can. I'm going to make sure Liam gets what he deserves, even if it means sacrificing—*shit, what the fuck am I doing?*

She barely trusts you already floats through my head, and my chest twinges.

I pull off on the side of the road, my chest heaving, and I

hadn't even realized how tightly I've been holding myself today with the stress of Dane, sneaking into Liam's bedroom, getting Dad home, taking my brother to his first session this afternoon, watching my father run around and call three lawyers and get them over to the house.

Just turn around and go back.

I throw my head back against the headrest and let out a roar as I shake the wheel. *I can't.* I can't betray my own brother. Because no matter how confused Dane is, I know, I know, I *know* he had nothing to do with what Liam did, and she'll understand that.

Composing myself, I pull back onto the road, and a few minutes later, I turn into Chance's driveway and get out.

I knock, and he opens the door. "You look like shit," is his greeting. Then, his shoulders slump. "Look, about today, if you really care about her then—"

"We need to talk."

He shrugs his shoulders, a resigned look on his face. "You and Ava, I heard you loud and clear—"

"Dane knows what happened that night. I need you. I really need you for the shit that's about to go down."

Chance starts, his eyes widening as he searches my face. He opens the door fully. "Come in. We can talk upstairs."

20

AVA

After I leave Knox, I walk into the dorm, and the security guard, an older man in a uniform, checks my ID. "Miss Harris?"

"The one and only. My room is 312."

"Someone dropped off something for you," he says then turns and grabs a vase of flowers on the desk behind him.

I gawk.

He sets them on the counter. Creamy white roses and fernlike greenery hang over the sides of the container. These aren't just regular roses; they're fully bloomed and lush, the velvety petals begging to be touched.

A little smile comes from him. "There's a card."

Staring down at the blooms, I take them and head to the elevator, wondering who they're from. Knox?

I could take the stairs, but my legs ache. I really need better shoes when I work. Someday. When I get enough money tucked away, I'll buy some things for myself. Maybe some of those twinkle lights for my room.

Fingering the folded note, I exit the elevator and head to my door, but I'm too curious to wait until I get inside to read the card. I open it.

Ava,

I didn't plan on sending these, but when I saw them, they looked like they belonged in your hands. This time last year, we were together. You were the best thing I ever held, and I MESSED UP. I own it. I'm guilty of hurting you with my words, guilty of leaving you alone at a party when I should have taken care of you. I'm sorry over and over a million times. It's okay if you never forgive me, just know I will never forget you, the first girl I ever loved.

Chance

I flip the card against my finger.

"Oh, those are gorgeous."

It's Camilla, coming down the hall with a load of laundry in her hands, wearing Star Wars pajama pants and a Camden shirt.

See? We should be friends.

I attempt a smile. "Yeah, they're pretty. Um, sorry about hitting you with the water balloon last night. I was aiming for those rabid freshman girls."

She smiles shyly. "Ah, don't worry about it. Did Knox send those?"

Ugh. No. "Chance."

She makes a murmuring noise. "I heard about his big apology in class."

"Word travels fast."

"It is high school and we thrive on gossip, and you being back is the craziest thing to happen since I've been here. You going to forgive him?"

An unforgiving heart is like rat poison to the one who holds it. One of the nuns told me that once and it's always stuck with me, mostly when I think about my mom. Forgiving Chance? I glance back down at the flowers. I don't think...what do I think? It definitely wasn't Chance's voice I heard when the person hit me in the back of the head, no, not his...

I let out a sigh. Everything is so muddled right now.

Her next words catch me by surprise. "I've always believed you."

I don't have to ask what she means.

Her face scrunches up. "I hung out with the Sharks freshman year. I'd just moved here from California, and no one warned me what dicks they can be."

I'm instantly at attention. "You dated one of them?"

She stares down at her laundry, toying with the edges of the basket. "Ha. You could say that."

Goose bumps rise on my arms at her quiet tone. "Do you want to talk about it?"

She starts, frowning. "God, no. Don't mind me." She pauses. "How's Astley?"

I tell her she's fine as far as I know, then, "It wasn't Knox, was it?"

She opens her door and looks back at me. "It was nothing. I don't ever think about them anymore. Good night." And then she's shutting her door.

She "dated" a Shark. Looks like Camilla needs her own dossier.

Later, I shower, put on a camisole and shorts, and crawl into bed. The flowers sit on my desk, their scent heavy and sweet.

My gaze falls to my apron on the floor, and I groan, getting up to move it to the hook on the back of the door.

Then I remember the tip that was left for me and pull it out of the pocket, open the envelope. It isn't a tip.

Ava,

Surprise! I'm back in Nashville and I want to see you so bad. One of the guys under the bridge told me you work at this diner. Meet me there tomorrow after school. Please. I'll come by every afternoon until I see you.

Mom

My hands shake and I fall back on my bed, numb. *What the hell?*

Two messages, both unwanted, on the same day. Crap. I tear the note into shreds and toss it in the trash.

What the heck does she want?

Tyler?

No way. *She left us.*

Like hell I'll meet her. I fire off a text to Lou and let him know what's going on, and he replies and tells me to take a few days off and lay low.

My phone pings with a text, and I snatch it up.

I can't breathe, beautiful girl.

Give me a minute.

To catch up with you.

Wait for me.

It's SA/Knox, and his words make me whimper. I clutch the phone, itching to reply, but in the end I set it down.

21

AVA

"Residents of Arlington Dorm! It's football time at Camden Prep! Tonight's game is against our biggest rival, Morganville Academy! Come on out and watch the game! Go Dragons!" Miss Henderson announces over the intercom on Friday afternoon. I hear her taking a deep breath. "Get to the stadium and scream your tits off!"

I burst out laughing.

Piper clamps a hand over her mouth. "Did she really just say that?"

"Balls, as Tyler would say. She did," Wyatt murmurs from the desk where he's checking out Tyler's dragon drawing, which I picked up today when I saw him briefly at the group home.

"Football is king here," I say.

"I'm glad you decided to go to the game, girl. You're a badass, and you're gonna show those assholes they can't keep you down!" Piper calls out as she watches me rummage through my closet. She looks cute with her strawberry blonde hair pulled into schoolgirl pigtails and wearing a gray sweatshirt with a huge Camden dragon on the front. She even has a bright red C sticker on her cheek that clashes with her pink glasses.

"Yep." Part of me dreads going, wondering how I'll feel, but the other side wants to see Knox play, wants to see his face.

He came in late today and was waiting for me by my locker after lunch. He looked harried, and with his last text on my mind, I softened more.

Last period, the players and cheerleaders led a pep rally in the gym, and I watched him laugh and joke with Chance and some of the other players. He caught my eyes up in the stands and sent me a kiss on his fingers. After school when he walked me to my car, he mentioned the game, and I told him I'd think about it. Then, he kissed me, and all sane thoughts flew right out of my head...

Piper joins me at the closet when I pull out a pair of skinny jeans and a Camden Prep crop top. With the other hand, I hold up a denim sundress. "Which one?" I shake the two hangers at her. "Strappy flats with the dress or Converse with the jeans?"

Piper wrinkles her nose. "Hmmm—"

"Just wear what you always wear," Wyatt says. "You're pretty in anything."

I grin. "First, I love you. And second, you're right. Don't want to overdo it. It's just a game. Jeans and shirt for the win."

Later, I feel the buzz of excitement in the air as we walk toward the stadium. I notice a familiar tall man at the bottom of the bleachers, watching the crowd. We're several feet apart when our eyes connect. Wearing slacks and a button-down shirt, he looks as if he just came from work. A red Camden hat is on his head, the mahogany hair longer than standard for a businessman, the curls silky and dark brown. His expression seems anxious as he stares at me.

I elbow Piper. "Hey, isn't that Knox and Dane's dad?" I've seen pictures of him before in our school directory because he's a board member.

She follows the direction of my nod. "Oh, yeah, that's him. Good-looking for an old dude, right?"

"Mmmm."

"Heads-up—Queen Bee and bitches arriving in three... two...one," Wyatt mutters, and I look up to see a group of cheerleaders headed our way wearing cheer outfits, matching makeup, ponytails, and hair bows.

"Library is the other way, charity case," Jolena snips out when she sees me. "No one wants you here."

Great. Here we go.

I stop in front of her and hold my hand above her head. "I thought you had to be at least this tall to ride one of these football players, Jolena. But don't worry, I won't snitch on you."

She startles and smacks my hand away then stalks off.

Wyatt laughs. "I bet Queen Bee will use that line on some other girl next week."

"Nah, she's too short," I say. Then, "Dang, I can't believe I wanted to be one of them."

Piper pats my back. "Stick with us, girl."

We reach Knox's dad, and there's no mistaking the resemblance up close. Same chiseled jawline, same patrician nose, those broad shoulders.

I don't think he recognizes me, but then he steps in front of me, smiles faintly, and sticks out his hand. "Ava Harris, right? I'm Dane and Knox's dad."

I nod and clasp it in mine, swallowing down nervousness. "Mr. Grayson. Nice to meet you. These are my friends, Piper and Wyatt."

He shakes their hands as well. "Call me Vance, please." He looks at me. "It must be hard for you to come to a game. I'm glad you did. Would you like to sit with me?"

My eyes flare and I glance at Piper and Wyatt, but both of them have moved away, chatting with some other students. I see Jagger and Camilla in their midst. Yikes, I'm alone with a parental.

"I thought I'd sit with my friends," I say rather lamely.

"I'd like to get to know you a bit, if you don't mind." He shifts his feet, fidgeting, and he's so obviously uncomfortable...

I sigh. "Sure. Just let me tell my friends." I dash over to Piper and tell her I'll find them later then head back to Mr. Grayson.

He nods. "Let's find some seats then—the stadium is filling up fast. Morganville brings a big crowd as well."

We make our way to the top and talk about mundane things as the players come out on the field: the weather—*it's hot*—and the expectations of the team this year—*high*. He points out a man wearing an Auburn hat a few rows over and tells me he's a scout here to watch.

"This is Knox's year for a championship," he says with a proud smile.

I take it all in, nodding and smiling in the right places. He sits very still and rather tense, just like Knox, and good grief, why does he want to talk to me?

The first quarter starts and moves slowly, neither side scoring. I'm glad to see Dane playing, but it's Knox who keeps my attention, the confident way he walks on the field, the way he handles the ball—until he throws an interception, a pass that Chance misses.

His dad groans as Morganville runs the ball back for a touchdown.

A timeout is called by the Dragons.

He watches them jog off to talk to their coach in the huddle. "Knox thinks highly of you," he murmurs.

Okaaaay. Let's do this.

There's a long pause as the band plays a song just a few sections away.

"And I want you to know I'm sorry for what happened to you. Knox mentioned he told you about my wife."

Oh.

He pauses as if I might say something, but I don't.

A long exhalation comes from him. "Dane is dealing with some mental things right now, and I'm sure you already know he's been using drugs."

"Yes."

He shoots me a wry smile. "When he was a baby, you should have seen the way he emulated Knox, trying to keep up with him, to swing as high, to climb the tree. And when he fell, Knox was the one who picked him up. My boys are like night and day." His gaze lingers on Dane. "I haven't been the best dad, especially lately, and it's taken a pile of shit to get me back on track, but I want to do right by them. I want them to have everything." He sighs. "That's what a good parent does, right?"

"I wouldn't know."

He gives me a glance.

"Don't feel sorry for me," I say quietly. "I'm going to be awesome someday."

Something dawns on his face. "Ah, so that's it." He lets out small laugh, but it doesn't sound cheerful. "You have fire in you, Ava. He's told me about how you grew up, your mom, your brother." His gray eyes, so much like Knox's, trace over my face. "It takes a phoenix to rise from the ashes. I guess he thinks you are one." He doesn't necessarily sound displeased about it, yet his voice is resigned.

"I see. Is there a reason you wanted to talk to me?" Let's cut to the chase, buddy.

He grimaces. "Don't be wary of me, please."

"Mmmm." I see why Knox loves to use noncommittal responses.

"Let me ask you something. Do you ever wonder what it would be like to just start over, without all the events of last year hanging over you, to meet new people, to move on?"

I stare at him, meeting his gaze directly.

"I did start over. I came back. Full circle."

He nods. "I heard what that cheerleader said to you. Does that happen a lot?"

My lips tighten as my gaze lands on Jolena on the field. "Yes."

He nods as if expecting the answer. "I mean this with all due respect, but Knox isn't ready for you. He's still got a whole football season to get through, plus Dane."

Well. There it is.

I scowl at him, a retort on my lips—

"Just let me finish, please," he continues, a pained but determined look on his face. "You're young. He's young. You have your whole lives ahead of you. College, careers. I didn't meet my wife Vivie until I was twenty-three, and I knew right away she was everything. Have you ever considered how good it might be if you met Knox on a level playing field, when he isn't swamped and you have a firm grasp on what you want to do with your life?"

"You misunderstand, Mr. Grayson. I *do* know what I want," I reply. "I'm going to med school. I'm going to take care of *my* brother."

"I've heard." He sighs, hesitating before he speaks again. "Unfortunately, Dane doesn't need to be around you right now—which is not your fault. It's *his*." He takes his hat off and rakes a hand through his hair. "And you'll...you'll see that later."

See *what* later?

I push that aside for now. "I remind Dane of his mom." It's apparent every time he looks at me.

"Yes, there's that, and Knox is torn between you and his brother." He pauses, as if to let his words carry weight.

I frown, trying to understand what he's not saying. My chest rises in agitation. "Is this a talk where you try to convince me to break up with Knox?"

Not that I'm sure we're a couple yet...

A ghost of a smile flits over his face. "I'm not sure I could convince you of anything. You seem to hold yourself well. I just want my boys to be happy, and Knox isn't happy."

My heart picks up, his words pricking at me, reminding me of Knox from the past two days: quiet, unsure, exhausted.

"Just…think about a fresh start, a new beginning somewhere that doesn't have someone writing on your locker or hitting you in the back of the head. Would you like that?"

I smile, but there's no mirth in it. "What do you have in mind? You've obviously given this some thought."

He closes his eyes. "Please, don't be upset. I only say these things because I love him. Is that so terrible?"

From out of nowhere, a rush of emotion tugs at my throat and I blink rapidly. No, it doesn't make him terrible at all. It's heartbreakingly beautiful.

I just…never had a parent looking out for me.

"I know you're very smart," he continues. "Mr. Trask speaks highly of your academic abilities."

"Yes."

He takes a breath. "I'd like to propose that you leave Camden behind and find a new school."

"Run away from all these elitist assholes? Pffft."

He lets out another small laugh. "So much fire…"

I just sit there quietly, remaining still.

"I have connections at NYU, my alma mater," he murmurs a few moments later. "I can get you in easily with your scores. I'd also be willing to help you financially."

"I find New York very cold." I stare straight ahead. My hands start to shake and I tuck them at my sides. Who the heck does he think he is? Paying me off to leave here?

"I also know about your brother. I imagine you might want to take him with you. I can help you, get him in at a school near the university—"

My chest heaves. "I don't want your money or your scholarship."

He smiles wanly. "Not surprised. Do you think you love Knox?"

Do I love him? Is the sky blue? Is the night dark? God, I'm so there with him, teetering on the edge of his world, wanting everything with him.

"You haven't been with him for that long, Ava, and distance might tell you if you're unsure. You're complete opposites. You come from different worlds."

"Hades and Persephone were happy." There's a hitch in my voice, because...because he *is* making good sense, and my only defense stems from Greek mythology. Pathetic. We've only been "together" since prank night, and while we do have a history from last year, we never acted on it because of Chance, then the kegger, and I...*dammit*, why am I doubting everything now?

Another wan smile from him. "Just let him breathe. Let yourself breathe. Come back when the timing is right."

I shake my head. He sounds so damn reasonable—just like Knox did last night.

"I only want what's best for what's left of my family." There's a catch in his voice, and as much as I want to dislike him, I see the desperation on his face, the love for his kids...

I finally stand. "I think I'll finish the game with my friends, Mr. Grayson."

His eyes are damp. "I'm sorry if I said things that hurt you."

"You're just...taking care of your sons," I say grudgingly.

He looks back out to the field, and I realize we've missed most of the second quarter.

I take the first step on the bleacher then he calls my name, follows me, and presses a card in my hand. "Here's my cell. If you change your mind or just want to talk, call me."

I flinch as a thought enters my head. Is Knox on board with this idea of me leaving Camden? I glance back out on the field and see he's on the bench, watching us.

Walking away, I stick the card in my pocket and start to head toward Piper and Wyatt, but then I detour and head to the bottom of the bleachers, over to the gate where I can see the players.

Do you ever wonder what it would be like to just start over, without all the events of last year hanging over you, to meet new people, to move on?

No, Knox would never want that. Right?

Later, I'm next to the fence with Camilla, our eyes on the field as the minutes tick down on the clock. We're three points behind and the home crowd cheers loudly.

Knox takes the field and lines up, his jersey covered in green and brown stains from being tackled on a couple of big runs, and he has a slight limp, but I smile at his focus.

"Hike!" comes from the field and he takes the snap then runs a quarterback sneak to the left side, straight into the end zone, putting us ahead.

Our entire sideline jumps up and down as the band plays our fight song over and over.

The other team gets the ball, but our defense stops them on three quick plays as everyone watches the clock tick to zero. Students, cheerleaders, and band members run onto the field. Nothing like beating your number one rival.

I stand still, knowing I wouldn't feel comfortable out there, but my eyes search the crowd for Knox.

He emerges out of the throng, holding his helmet and

looking up into the stands until he's engulfed by people giving him hugs and smacks on the back. He shakes them off after a bit and steps away, scanning the stadium. For me, I think.

I wave and call his name, and his eyes find mine. He pushes his way over to me, ignoring the press of cheerleaders and students.

I walk down the edge of the field as he approaches. With his helmet off, his hair is wet with sweat, and he runs his hand through it. He has black face paint under his eyes, and combined with that scar, it's intimidating and sexy as hell.

"Nice game, Cold and Evil." My words are light.

He stretches a hand across the fence and weaves his fingers into mine. "I didn't think you'd come. I'm glad you did." He reaches across with his other hand and pulls the back of my head toward his. The kiss is salty and I can feel the heat radiating from his skin as his body tries to cool him down after his exertion on the field. Our mouths part and I lean my forehead against his.

"You kicked ass."

He grins. "I saw you with my dad. What did he say?"

"Not much. I left him to get a closer look."

"Did you like him?" I hear uncertainty in his voice, and relief flows through me. Knox can't possibly know about the things his dad said to me, because he didn't even know I'd come tonight.

"He's your dad and a lot like you—what do you think?" I didn't dislike him, though I wasn't a fan of his message. Besides what he had to say, I thought he was a nice guy.

He's about to speak when another voice breaks in.

"My house, out at the barn. Keg. Ten o'clock. See you

there," Liam calls out as he runs over to Knox. His expression cools when he sees me and he shoots Knox an assessing, hard look. "You coming, QB1? We have a lot to celebrate. Some of the Morganville cheerleaders are stopping by."

Knox looks at Liam, and I can't see Knox's face, but I sense the tension coming off him in waves. Even so, his words are smooth as silk. "Yeah. Dane and Chance are with me. See you there."

Liam gives him a broad smile. "That's what I'm talking about. See you there."

"You're going?" I say when Liam walks off, my voice incredulous. I mean, we didn't make any plans today, but the keg party? Seriously?

He rubs his face, smearing the paint. "Don't freak out. Monday I can explain everything."

Confusion hits. Monday? "What's happening then—"

"Give me tonight, Tulip. I'm not going because I want to, but because I need things to look normal. I'll text you, okay?"

Look normal?

Does he mean for football, to keep the peace between the players over me?

Knox lives and breathes football, and I can't change that. I shouldn't want to, but—

"Awesome game, Knox!" Wyatt and Piper call out, interrupting my thoughts.

He accepts their praise then gives me a lingering, soft glance until his face tightens. "Later, Tulip."

And then he's dashing off to the locker room.

I feel winded as Wyatt and I walk back to the dorm. Piper has already left with her parents.

"He's going to the kegger?" he asks when I tell him what's going on, anger coloring his voice.

"That's what he said."

He scowls. "Asshole. Are you okay?"

"Not really." My head is jumbled up, working through Knox's comments and thinking about Mr. Grayson's.

I'm young. He's young.

Anger stirs inside me too, imagining Knox at the kegger with other girls—

Ugh.

Just stop.

I trust him, right?

He paid for my housing. He hit Liam over me. He wants to protect me.

And what is it costing him, to go against his team?

I shove down my misgivings as we reach the dorm.

A woman calls over from across the parking lot. She takes off in a jog over to us.

"Ava! Oh my God. Wait a second!"

"Mom?" I gasp out, still halfway thinking about Knox.

I shove that aside and rub my eyes. Six freaking years and here she is, wearing faded leggings and a shirt with a stain on it. Her hair is long and stringy, the brown strands lank.

Wyatt grunts, and I realize I've clamped on to his arm.

"Ava?" he whispers. "Do I need to call security?"

My mouth dries. "No, not yet."

She's reached us and comes to a halt, drinking in my face. She smiles widely, but all I can see are the bruises on her arms.

"Ava, sweetheart, it is you," she says breathlessly, holding her hands up in a prayer motion against her lips.

I swallow. "What are you doing here?"

She takes Wyatt in, and I see the moment she knows he's got money: his shoes, his designer jeans, the beautiful tattoos. "Hi." She glances back at me. "You have nice friends, Ava. I'm so glad."

This isn't happening.

I look up at Wyatt. "Can you give me a moment?"

"No. You haven't let go of me, and there's a reason for that."

"Wyatt, please." My throat tightens and I beg him with my eyes. *Please.* I don't want him to see her, to know the details of where I come from. I told Knox, but that was different. She wasn't here in person then!

He lets out a sigh, frowning. "Fine. I'll be inside." He points his fingers at his eyes then at mine. "Watching you."

"What are you doing here?" I ask my mother once he's out of earshot.

"I wanted to see you, of course."

I clench my fists, taking that in. "Well, here I am. I'm surprised you recognized me."

"Your hair is different and you're taller, but there's no mistaking that pretty little face." She rushes over closer and hugs me, and I hug her back automatically. She cups my face. "You sure are gorgeous, baby girl. Just like your mama when I was your age."

I tug out of her grip. "Why are you here all of a sudden?"

She licks her lips and looks out at the parking lot. Following the direction, I see an old beat-up Toyota sedan and a man sitting in the driver's seat.

"Is that Cooper?" I snap.

She waves me off. "Ha, no. He left a while ago. That's

Keith. He's my man. We've been together for a few years. I don't know where Cooper ended up, maybe still in California."

I point at the bruises on her arm. "Good one, huh?"

She frowns. "No need to judge me. How's Tyler?" Her eyes seem to light up.

Pure terror washes over me. "He's fine."

"How bad is he? Does he hurt?"

She's talking about his FAS diagnosis. When he was born, there was so much up in the air as far as how well he'd do the older he got, and Mama missed all the tests he went through, the medical exams.

But, I lie. Hell yeah I do, because if she's here for him, to use him somehow, I can't... "Constant medical care. Nearly blind."

Please forgive me, Tyler. You are amazing.

"I'd love to see him." She rubs her arms. "Is he still at Sisters of Charity? Are they taking good care of him?"

I suck in a breath. Not going to answer that. "Technically, he isn't yours anymore. When you leave a newborn, the state of Tennessee considers that as you *giving up* your rights." It's called the Safe Haven Law and while I don't know all the specifics, I do know that it enabled her to leave him without breaking the child abandonment laws. She walked away and that was it. We were left in the hands of the nuns.

She gets a faraway look on her face and sighs. "I did the best I could for him. The nuns are good." She toys with the edge of her stained shirt. "I drove past there, you know, and saw a kid getting out of that van they drive. He had these thick glasses on and..." She bites her lip. "He looked like Cooper. Was that him?"

"There are twenty little kids there. How do I know? And he looks nothing like Cooper."

She shrugs, letting it go. "You didn't come to the diner again. Why not?"

"How did you know where I go to school?"

"I followed your Instagram last year. You deleted it though. How are you, baby? This is a fancy place, all these pretty buildings, and look at you and that hot guy. Is he your boyfriend? He looks rich."

"He's a kid. He doesn't have money, Mama."

"But I bet his family does. Good for you. That's what you need, a rich guy."

"Mama, stop."

The guy in the car opens his door and gets out, leaning against it as he lights up a cigarette. He's skinny, like Mama, with slouchy clothing and tattoos on his neck and face, and they aren't nice ones like Wyatt's. He sends us a long look, and I feel him checking me out as he blows smoke in the air.

I focus back on her. "What do you want?"

She laughs, her eyes wide as she looks me up and down. "Come on, let's be sweet. I've missed you and it killed me to leave you, but if I hadn't, Cooper would have worked his way to you, and he might not have just hit you, you see. And Tyler…poor defenseless baby. I miss having kids." She pauses. "I saw that kid, and it was him, and he didn't look terrible to me. You lie, Ava."

"What do you want?" I yell, my patience stretched thin, my nerves on edge.

She stiffens, looking petulant. "Aren't you happy to see me?"

I exhale as the past tugs at me a little. "I'm glad you're

okay. I haven't heard from you since you left. I thought...I thought you might be dead."

She laughs. "I'm not."

I blow out a breath. "Mama, what do you want?"

Her lips turn down. "Money."

Now, the reality behind her note and visit are crystal clear, and I swallow down the hurt it causes me even though I expected it. "I see."

"But if I can't get any, maybe I'll call one of those family lawyers, see what it might take to get Tyler back—unless you can help me? What do you say? I bet you have some money saved from waiting tables, or maybe your boyfriend has some cash? Just a little would do me a lot of good, baby girl."

My eyes flare. She's probably still using. I don't smell any alcohol on her, but that doesn't mean she isn't high, and it's dark out here...ugh.

I don't believe she'll call anyone. She doesn't want Tyler; she just wants the money, and she'll only wear me down, lingering around the diner and school, and geeze, she's my mom, she's my *mom*, and I haven't laid eyes on her in so long...

She was a terrible mother, so bad, but she's *still* the person who brought me into this world, and I can feel that tiny, fragile bond right now, twisting in my heart. I feel like a little kid all over again, wondering if she's okay, if she'll hug me, if she'll be home when I get back from school.

My shoulders slump. "I'll give you everything I have."

She smiles broadly.

"But I never want to see you again."

A long sigh comes from her. "Ah, Ava, you're mean. Guess you get it honest."

Yeah.

She sends a thumbs-up to the man in the parking lot and I cringe. "We just need to get to Memphis, you know, and we ran out of money a while back, and it will give us a good start. We all need fresh starts, don't we? Thank you, baby girl."

"Yeah." Feeling queasy, I tell her to stay put and dash inside the dorm and up to my room. I lift up my mattress and count out my three thousand dollars. The money doesn't really matter right now. I can always work more.

"You are not going back out there without me," Wyatt states when I come back to the lobby.

"Okay." I exhale.

With Wyatt next to me—*thank you God for sending me a friend like him*—I walk back outside and press it into her hands.

"I'll call the cops the next time," I say, running my eyes back over the man who's still watching us. "He looks like he might have warrants out. Wouldn't want him to go to jail, or you to go for harassment."

Her mouth quirks up. "Just like me, you're hard and ready to fight." She laughs harshly. "Don't blame you a bit."

"What the fuck just happened?" Wyatt says as we watch their taillights leave a few minutes later.

My chest hitches, feeling lost, like I want to chase her car down, even with that scary man inside, and beg her to stay and just be a mom and be like Knox's dad, but, no, *no*—those thoughts are foolish and she chose her path a long time ago.

I swallow down the past. "I was blackmailed by my mom."

"Dude. You have some weird shit going on."

"Oh, Wyatt. You have no idea."

He cocks his head and mulls something over. "Did you

know you were mumbling the whole way back from the stadium?"

"What was I saying?"

We approach the doors.

"'I'm too young. He's too young.' I think you meant you and Knox, of course." He rolls his eyes. "But I want you to know—that look on your face when your mom left... You aren't young, Ava. You're ancient. And Knox? He's there too."

I don't know what to say about that.

He tosses an arm around me as we walk back into the lobby. "So, it's Friday night and it's just you and me. What do you want to do?"

I shake my head. "I'm just...lost."

He exhales, holding me tighter. "Let's get in my car and just drive. How does that sound? We'll roll the windows down, let the night air in, and blare some rap music. You can tell me what a hot dude I am and that Jagger is going to fall in love with me."

I can't help the grin on my face, and I reach up and kiss his cheek. "I love you. Marry me?"

"Same. I insist we register at Pottery Barn. Sheets and towels and candles. Would you mind if Jagger marries me too? Three-way?"

I laugh. "No, you'd never pay any attention to me. Come on, let's go for that drive."

22

AVA

I wake up with a scream, my body shaking as I wrestle myself out of a nightmare about ghostly trees and coyotes circling me as I lie in the woods. Gulping in air, I try to orient myself in the darkened room and control my rapid breathing. The attack from last week sneaks in.

That's where you belong, bitch, at my feet—and don't you forget it.

I close my eyes, my hands clenching the quilt.

Something so familiar about... But it's gone.

Forget the dream. Get some sleep.

With a glance at my phone, I see it's seven in the morning, way too soon to get up considering Wyatt and I didn't get home until midnight. I toss over and beat at my pillow, trying to get comfortable, but an hour later, it's pointless, my head is still replaying last night.

Why is Knox pushing me away little by little?

Why did his dad offer to send me to New York and take care of Tyler? He's never even met me before, yet he'd be willing to fork over thousands of dollars just to get me out of Camden? It doesn't make sense. Obviously, he wants Knox to focus on football and his brother and not me, but—

I pause.

Why *does* Dane dislike being around me? I can accept that part of it is because of what happened to his mom, but something doesn't feel right, and a sense of foreboding creeps over me, heavy and thick, crawling down my spine.

I get out of bed, take a quick shower, and throw on some shorts and a Cranberries shirt. After making my bed and going over some homework, I'm still antsy and frustrated. At ten, I call Wyatt, and we make a plan to meet at a coffee shop in town.

We've just settled in at a table next to the window when a black Mercedes SUV drives past the shop and parks across the street. Taking a sip of my coffee, I watch as Knox, Dane, and his dad exit the vehicle and walk toward the police station.

"What are they doing?" Wyatt murmurs, following my gaze. "Trouble with the Graysons on a Saturday?"

"No clue," I reply, frowning.

The three of them stop at the entrance where three other well-dressed men are waiting. One of them is clearly Chance's dad, a slick-looking older man with sandy hair and a trim frame. Although I've never met him, I used to follow Chance's social posts when we were together, plus I've seen him at school a few times to drop off or pick up his son. He's a lawyer. *A lawyer.*

My eyes land on a policeman who's walking down the sidewalk toward them, and I suck in a breath, recognizing his face as the man who interviewed me last fall.

"What's going on?" Wyatt calls out as I jump up, almost knocking over my coffee. He takes a napkin and dabs at the small spill that sloshed on the table.

"I don't know." I breathe quickly as my heart pounds. "But whatever it is, it's... Something feels off." I stop, grabbing my purse and dashing for the door.

By the time I push through the exit, they've disappeared into the precinct.

"Ava?" It's Wyatt and he's followed me.

What...what the *hell* is going on?

Why are they meeting with the police, armed with lawyers?

"...do you want to go back inside and wait for Knox?" he's saying, and I realize he's been talking to me for a while.

"I'm going in there to find them," I push out, my chest rising and falling quickly, so quickly.

He hesitates for a moment then nods. "Ride or die."

We cross the street, enter the station, and walk up to the front desk. The place is mostly quiet, a few officers milling around, and I search their faces, not seeing the one who just walked in. Knox and Dane and Mr. Grayson are nowhere in sight.

The lady at the desk gives me a small smile and checks out Wyatt's tattoos. She's older with gray hair and little glasses. "May I help you?"

I lick my lips. "My name is Ava Harris." I pause, taking a breath. "May I see one of the detectives who worked on my case last fall?"

If she remembers me, she doesn't show it, and I suppose she sees tons of people coming through here. She sits down at her computer and gives me an expectant look. "Detective's name?"

Panic brushes at me. God, I can't even recall. I haven't wanted to think about him and those hours spent here, and I...

"He just walked in with the Grayson family," I say.

She nods. "Bryant Thomas. He's busy. Would you like to give me your number and I'll have him call you?" She reaches over and hands me a form. "Just fill this out with the specifics of the case, and he'll get back to you."

The paper shakes in my hand. Would he? Would he *really* call me? He never has before. They dismissed me. They never even told me Knox drove me to Piper's! They forgot about me as soon as I walked out!

"Ava?" Wyatt asks as he leads me over to some chairs in a waiting area. "Want me to fill it out for you?"

No, no, no, it isn't even about the detective at this point; it's about Knox meeting with him, that entourage of lawyers.

Fumbling in my purse, I pull out my phone and fire off a text to Knox.

I know where you are, Shark. I saw you walk in.

It takes him three minutes to walk out from a hallway to the right. Standing with my fists clenched, I watch as he jogs over to me in jeans and a Camden shirt. I dismiss how...beautiful he is.

I don't know him, I don't, and he isn't who I thought he was, because if he—if he's known what happened, how could he do this, how could he *not* tell me, how could he—

"Ava," he starts, his face white. "What—"

"Stop. Don't. Time to breathe? Really?"

His chest expands and he looks around the room before

coming back to me. "I can explain—"

"No. You tell me right now what's going on with you and your dad and your brother meeting with lawyers at a police station on a Saturday with the detective who interviewed me, and don't lie to me. This can't just be a coincidence!" My voice rises and a few people send us glances, but I don't care, not now, not in this place with all those memories in my head.

I recall Knox's words to me after the game. How his dad looked at me so warily.

"You and your brother and your dad—did you really think I wouldn't figure it out? You wanted to tell me on Monday? *Monday*," I sneer. "How could you?"

He tries to take my hand, but I snatch it away.

"Please," he says, his voice colored with dread. "Please, listen to me." He looks around the room. "Let's go somewhere and talk—"

"Dane remembers something! That's what all this is, am I right? You and him and the lawyers? I'm not stupid, Knox! He knows, and he told you, and you need *time to breathe* right after we have...a moment together that I thought meant something. So no, I'm not going anywhere with you!"

The lady from the desk appears next to us, her eyes darting from me to Knox. "Is everything good here?"

No, no it's not.

"We're leaving," Wyatt murmurs to the woman then steers me to the exit. "Sorry if it got a little loud."

We step outside and Knox follows us, stopping me with a hand on my arm. "Ava, please—"

I whip around. "I'm no one to you. No one."

Knox scrubs his face. "Please let me talk."

"More telling me to *slow down*? I knew something was off

with you!"

The silence stretches around us, thick with tension.

"Talk to him," Wyatt tells me softly. "I'm not leaving." He wanders off to sit on a bench a few feet away.

I rub my hands over my arms, feeling chilled in the sun as I try to hold myself together. I want to be strong, I want to prepare myself, I want to walk away from him with this anger hot in my chest, but...I have to know. "Tell me why you're here!"

He grimaces. "When I went home Thursday morning, Dane told me he remembered seeing Liam follow you into the woods."

My eyes shut as revulsion inches over me, bit by bit, images from the party flashing one by one, that horrible carnival ride. I'm in those woods again and he's on top of me, holding me down, and I can't breathe, I can't move, I can't scream—

I wrench myself to the present.

"Liam?" I gasp out, shuddering as it clicks. "*His voice*...I recognized it in the stairwell when he talked to Jolena, and outside the gym that day—" My stomach jerks. "He was angry, and I didn't...connect the dots, but he hit me."

Knox's eyes flare, and I bend over and clutch myself, bile rising.

He tries to hold me, but I push him away. "No!"

I lean against the wall of the police station, and I'm not even aware of how I got there. Knox is next to me and Wyatt has moved as well, his arms around my waist as I cling to him.

"Is he going to be arrested?" I gasp.

Knox closes his eyes. "I don't know. It's been hard, Ava.

Dane only remembers certain things."

"What does that mean?" Wyatt snaps, clearly on my side while Knox paces up and down the sidewalk.

He stops in front of me, his face torn. "Liam told Dane that Dane roofied your drink—"

"*What?*"

"—but he only said that because he's suspicious that Dane's remembering. He didn't, Ava. He didn't. I know my brother..." He trails off, his hands knotted.

"Spit it out, Knox. This is about me!" I thump my chest, holding myself together with fragile strings.

He gathers himself. "We got inside Liam's bedroom and found his trophies."

"Trophies?" Wyatt mutters. "That sonofabitch."

Knox's face grows hard. "A bag of...underwear. I saw yours. We've been trying to act like nothing is up so he doesn't destroy them. That's why I went to the party last night, plus I thought maybe he might get sloppy and do something or say something. Chance and Dane and I...we all went." He tenses. "I want to hurt him for you, but we're trying to do this right and get Dane's story straightened out, see if there's enough for a search warrant."

Trophies. I want to vomit.

Wait...

"Chance knows?" I ask.

He nods.

"But you didn't tell *me*. Damn you."

He groans, rubbing his face. "I wanted to talk to my dad before I did anything. I'm not... I didn't know how to handle it. Dane, he was so fucked up, and I tried to do the right thing, but..."

"Dane comes first," I say.

"It's not like that," he says quietly. "We just thought it would be prudent to wait and tell you what was going on when we were sure we had enough."

"You're preparing Dane's defense in case he needs one." My hands tremble.

"I have to take care of Dane, Ava. Liam's family has big money around here. Every step my dad has made is carefully calculated." He gives me a pained look. "Dad will get you a good lawyer—"

"Stop." I shake my head, emotions all over the place, rage mixed with helplessness over Liam, anger at Knox, and anger at myself. I trusted him, and he—he pushed me away for his *family*.

I picture Mama's taillights fading away in the distance. In the end, I'm the only one looking out for *me*, and I've known this for a long time. Most of the time I can shove all that down and pretend it doesn't hurt to be left behind by the people who are supposed to love you.

But right now, my chest aches, and I can't think straight with all this information.

"Dane would never hurt you," Knox says. "You don't know him like I do, but I know he's innocent. I have to prove that, for him, for you, for *us*—" He stops abruptly and reaches out, taking my arms as Wyatt eases back, giving us space. "Tulip, please don't be angry with me for not telling you."

I stare up at him. "Why can't I be angry? I point-blank asked you what was wrong—"

"I love you," he says, his gray eyes clinging to mine. "Can't you *see* that?"

I suck in a breath.

"I don't know when, maybe last year, watching you with Chance, then it grew when I hired that P.I. and I got wrapped up in you and how fierce you are, Tulip, so beautiful and so much strength that I don't...shit, I don't know how you do it here at this place when I can't even stand it. I see who you are and it terrifies me and I tried to stay away, but I didn't, even when I swore I would, and now I've hurt you, but you have to take a good long look at me, a fucking long look and see what I'm made of, what makes me tick, and it's about you."

His words rip me apart.

He cups my cheeks, and I search his face.

Knox isn't ready for you, his dad said.

I'm tired, so tired, my body weak as I come down from the adrenaline rush I got when I walked into the station.

And I just...

Need to think.

He swallows thickly. "Tulip—"

"Go back inside, please," I manage to push out. "Dane needs you." I know my mind is scattered, but one thing I'm sure of is that his family is his first commitment, not me, and I don't blame him. He and I have obstacles in front of us. His walls, mine, Dane's connection to what happened.

But...

I love you.

I lock down those words he said to me, shutting them inside that chest and wrapping a heavy chain around it.

"Don't leave. Not like this," he whispers, as if reading my thoughts. "Don't walk away. Things will work out. Don't, please. You belong with me, you do—"

I sigh. "Please, just...leave me be."

I pull back and walk away from him.

23

AVA

I'm sitting at the stone picnic tables outside the dorm that afternoon when a sleek gray Porsche parks in the lot and a guy gets out. I watch as he scans the entrance and heads toward the door, then he slides his gaze over to me and stops. He sticks his hands in his jeans, walks over, and sits down next to me.

This is the closest we've been since I came back and Chance still smells the same, a hint of leather and male spice. It brings back memories.

We don't speak for a few minutes, each of us not looking at the other, just watching some guys tossing a Frisbee on the commons.

A long sigh comes from him. "I fucked up my apology in History of Film when I said you hurt me. I really suck."

"You do," I say, still not looking at him. I flick my eyes back at the parking lot. "Your dad gave your car back?" I shrug as he starts, not expecting me to know. "Piper told me he grounded you from it." I whistle. "That's a long time to not have that sweet ride."

In my peripheral, I see his nod. "He's been pissed with me for months. I deserved it." He pauses, his fingers rubbing at a crevice on the stone table. "Knox said he saw you today at the police station. He said he told you I know everything now."

I sigh, not wanting to go there. "I got your flowers."

He huffs. "Did you toss them?"

"Not yet."

He smiles. "You should. I was at the market for my mom, and as soon as I saw them, I thought of you. We had some good times, didn't we?"

I think about those sweet notes in my locker, the hugs and kisses after games. "Yes."

"I still love you, you know. Can't get you out of my head."

"You will."

"Maybe." Then, "Why did you come back, Ava? Knox said it was for Tyler, and I hate that I never met him. Shit, I did so many things wrong."

Why did I come back to this fucking place...*why did I come back?*

I look up and move my gaze over the campus, lingering on the main building with its ivy-covered turrets in the distance. I hate this place, hate it so much it makes me queasy every morning when I walk through those doors, when I see the faces of those people who didn't believe me, who called me snitch and slut and—

Clarity tiptoes in, softly and quietly, and my bent spine straightens. I've been telling myself I was sacrificing myself for Tyler, to get him into a good school, and while part of that is very, very true, I just as well could have gone to Morganville and taken my chances. Even though their services aren't as good, it would have been better than his inner-city school. No, the truth is, I haven't wanted to look too hard at that gnawing, ugly, *other* reason I've pushed myself to walk into this place for the past few weeks.

I exhale. "I came back for vengeance, to show all of you that nothing in this goddamn world will ever hold me back from finding out who hurt me. I'm Ava Tulip Harris and no one hurts me, but this place, *this place*, I had to come back and show you all that I'm worth more than what someone did to me in the woods." I close my eyes. "And now I know who he is."

"They'll get him, or Knox and I will," he murmurs, taking my hand and lacing our fingers together. "What will you do now?"

I look at him then, studying that handsome face, his piercing blue eyes. "I hate everything about this place. It makes me sick to walk in those doors everyday—even with Knox next to me." It's not an answer, but he nods.

"Do you hate me? Even Knox?"

My throat pricks with emotion. Never Knox.

I wish, I wish he'd told me, but I get it, even as leftover anger still bubbles.

He breaks our eye contact and looks off into the distance. "I'm here if you need anything. I know you don't want that—"

"I forgive you, Chance." I squeeze his hand.

His eyes glisten as they come back to me. "Shit. Thank you."

Turning, I lean in closer. "Go and be sweet and especially kind to the next girl you love." I huff out a laugh. "Even if it's Brooklyn."

"Ava, fuck, I don't even know what to say..." He wraps his arms around me and holds me tight, and we just do that for a long time.

On Monday, I walk into Camden and look around at the portraits hanging around us, all those graduates, and sigh.

Knox, Dane, and Chance lean against the wall near the entrance.

It feels so much like that first day, only this time, there's no dread in me. I've packed up everything that's happened over the past year. Pretty soon, I won't have to shove down thoughts and memories about this place.

Knox meets me, jogging over. His eyes search mine, shadows under his. "Hey."

"Hey."

"Liam was arrested this morning. I texted you." He looks down then back up at me. "You didn't reply."

I nod, not responding to that.

The police called me on Sunday afternoon and asked me to come. They asked the same questions, and I told them about recognizing Liam's voice outside the gym, but I couldn't tell if it even mattered since I didn't see him.

I look away from Knox's stare.

"Everyone knows," he says.

"Good."

He takes my hand and threads our fingers together. His thumb brushes over my hand softly. "We've got this, okay?"

Chance walks up from behind Knox and stands shoulder to shoulder with him.

I nod a hello and look past them, seeing Dane. He won't meet my eyes, but then he straightens and moves toward me, his gait jerky.

Knox sees him and tenses, a surprised look on his face. "Dane—"

He stops next to his brother, slides his hands into his pockets, and exhales. "Ava."

I study his haggard features, the slouch in his shoulders. "Dane," I say solemnly.

The air crackles around us, Knox breathing hard, his hand gripping mine.

"I'd never do anything to you. Ever. Even if I was trashed." He holds my gaze.

I nod, feeling glad, so relieved he came up to me. "You're a Shark and a big pain in the ass, but you're a hero, like your twin, even if you may not see it sometimes. You let me hit you then carried me to the office and sat with me for hours," I remind him. "I don't buy anything Liam might say about you. It was him. His voice. Everything."

I watch as the relief washes over him. His eyes water and he bites his bottom lip. "Ava, shit, I don't deserve any kindness from you, but thank you for being you."

Piper rushes up, sees them, and bursts through. "Oh my God," she pants as if she's been running. "It's all over the local news! Liam, that bastard! I just passed Jolena in the hall and she's wailing and even Camilla is crying and I don't know why! It's crazy." She stops, pushing her glasses up, frowning at my flat face. I'm keeping it together—for now. "Wait, why don't you look surprised? You already knew?"

"Yeah." I nod.

Students mill around us, most of them staring, all of them whispering.

Same shit—well, maybe different shit, but still, it feels the same.

"Let's go to class," Knox says. "I won't leave your side. They might call you out of class, I don't know. Dad can be here in ten minutes. He's got someone for you, a lawyer from Nashville. She's high profile and deals with sexual assault cases—"

"I have to see Mr. Trask right now. Later?"

He frowns then nods. "Alright, let's go—"

"No, I can do it." I give his hand a squeeze and let it go. "I'll be okay."

I head to the office, and Knox is with me every step. "I'm just going to hang out while you talk to him," he murmurs when we get to the entrance, and I tell him he should go on to class.

He looks at me, a determined look on his face. "Not leaving you."

We walk inside the office. "I have an appointment to see the headmaster. I called earlier this morning," I tell Mrs. Carmichael.

She looks up from the papers she's shuffling. "Ava! Goodness, I saw the news. I'm so sorry, dear. Take a seat and I'll buzz him."

I nod and sit on the loveseat. Knox sits with me.

"You're not going in there with me, you know," I murmur.

He takes my hand again, and for a moment, I sigh and lean into him, just a little.

"Tulip, are you still angry with me? That I didn't tell you?"

Angry? I was, definitely, but now...

How on earth can I be? Dane is his family.

"It's hard to stay pissed at you," I say. "It's going to be okay."

"Then why do I feel like something is still wrong?" he mutters.

I rest my head on his shoulder for a second. God, he smells like the ocean and the sun. I'm going to miss him. I'm going to cry for months. I'm going to weep and weep and weep—

"Ava?" Mr. Trask appears in his doorway, his face somber. "I'm ready."

I stand and walk into his office.

"I'll be waiting right here," Knox says.

Twenty minutes later, I've laid everything out for the headmaster, that I know it was Liam who attacked me outside the gym, and of course, he already knows about the arrest. He quickly agrees to keep Tyler's scholarship as long as I want, assuring me that the board members would be happy to. I'm not sure if he's afraid I'll sue the school since Liam's been arrested, or perhaps he just actually cares. He agrees to refund Knox most of the money for my housing.

I accept it all and leave his office.

Knox stands up, searching my face. "Good?"

Relief feels immense after worrying about how Trask would react to me leaving. "Better than I thought, actually."

He exhales. "Was it about Liam? He'll be expelled, even if he gets off on bail, which I can't imagine the judge allowing since his family is wealthy. Let's go to class."

We make our way down the silent hall, and everyone's in first period by now. Mrs. White is probably talking about one of her iconic movies.

I stop at my locker and stare at it, thinking back to that first day and my letter from Knox. Sitting next to him in class. Him changing my tire. Playing my song on the piano. Prank night.

I work the combination, opening it and clearing out the items inside, placing them in my backpack. Photographs of me and Piper I taped up. Notebooks. Pencils. A highlighter.

Knox has grown stiff as he stands behind me, and now he moves closer, his hands on my shoulders, his chest against my back. I feel him dip his head into my hair. "Don't do it, Tulip. Don't leave me. *Don't*—" His voice catches and he turns me around, his eyes gleaming. "Stay with me. I'm giving you my heart. I'm giving you everything."

I whimper. "Knox, I can't."

"Why?" he says in a ragged voice, shoving his hands in my hair and palming my scalp.

I shake my head at him, looking for words. How do I tell him about the hours I spent yesterday, debating and thinking about the future, Knox's and mine? How do I explain that I don't think I can force myself to walk in that entrance one more day?

Even if he is here.

I need my own space to grow and live and forget about this town, and I need to let *him* go so he can do the same.

"Didn't you come back for justice? Come on, Tulip."

I smile because deep down, he always knew how my head works.

I dip my head to his chest and breathe. "I did. You helped me, but that process is done. I can't tell you how lucky I am to have known you, to see you again, to touch you. To make love to you—" My resolve cracks and a tear falls—the first one since I came here—and I hastily swipe it away, but I can't stop them. They come and come, until my arms go around his shoulders and his shirt is wet.

He tips my face up and presses his forehead against mine. "You're leaving me? For real?" His voice hitches at the question, and I close my eyes, forcing myself to finish this.

I trace the outline of his lips. "I came back for Tyler, but really, part of me came back for me, too, to figure out who hurt me, and we did. I didn't plan on you and you didn't plan on me, and you have a future here, and I…I don't. This place holds nothing special except you and Wyatt and Piper."

He clutches my hips. "Shhh, I don't accept this, you hear me? You're just upset, and I can't even imagine how emotional you must feel with everything hitting you like this." He sucks in air. "Don't fuck me up, please. You can't go because I won't get over you. I won't ever find someone like you. I won't ever kiss a girl like you. *I love you.*" He sighs. "Fuck, don't you love me? I think you do, but you never said, and I'm standing here and you're packing up your shit and leaving me—"

Brokenly, I say, "I love you, so much that I'd do anything, even if it means saying goodbye. You need some room to breathe, like you said. You said that for a reason, whether it was about your brother or just something deep down that you know is right. Your brother needs you *now*. You have a whole season of football and a team to take to state. You have big goals and I do too, but I can't pursue them here anymore even though you're the most worthy, kind, wonderful, beautiful person I've ever met. I have to go, I have to, I have to…" My shoulders shake as more tears fall. "Don't make it hard on me, please. Just, someday in the future, find me. Just find me and come up to me and tell me you still love me and want me and can't live without me in your arms—"

He closes his eyes and a tear falls. "Stop, stop, just stop this—"

"Knox, please, let me go..." My face tilts up and he takes my mouth hungrily, his tongue desperate and hot, taking all I have to give him.

THREE HOURS LATER, I'm composed, my face dry as I sit at a restaurant in Sugarwood when Mr. Grayson walks in and comes over to my table. His suit is expensive, but his face looks tired.

"I'm glad you called, Ava," he says with a slight smile as he takes the seat across from me.

He sees I have a coffee and orders the same. He asks if I've had lunch, and I tell him I'm not hungry. He says he isn't either.

He takes a sip of his coffee and gives me a long look. "Have you changed your mind about my offer?"

I pluck at the napkin on the table. "While I've given your words some thought, I have to decline."

He watches me. "I see. How was school today? You aren't there."

I exhale. "I've unenrolled. I'll be getting my GED, and I was wondering if you could help me get into Vandy and get their best scholarship. I don't want your money, just your assistance, and the rest I can borrow on student loans. I'm sure you have connections in Nashville."

"Indeed I do. What about your brother?"

"I have that settled, but I would like some help in applying as his guardian. You know good lawyers. I've had some trouble with my mom showing up recently."

"Is that why you're leaving?"

"No, no, she doesn't really want him, but if I can eliminate any possibility of her having the chance, I'd like to."

"I see," he murmurs. "Have you talked to Knox? He was pretty upset after he saw you on Saturday."

I nod. "I can't promise you I won't ever see Knox again. I love him, but I will stay away for as long as I can. I keep thinking about what you said, about us meeting some other time, and that's all that's keeping me going, Mr. Grayson." I look up at him, letting him see how I'm barely keeping myself together.

Emotion works his face as he reaches across the table and holds my hand. "Let me do all these things for you, Ava."

24

AVA

After retrieving my things from Arlington Dorm, I move into a closet-sized apartment Lou threw together for me over the diner. There's a small bed, a tiny desk, and a bathroom that only has enough room for me to stand sideways, but it's mine and rent-free.

In late October, I dye my hair blonde. Though the color isn't quite the same, more bleached out than honey-colored, I start to look like me, even if my eyes are sad. On Halloween, I dress up as a nun and work the morning and lunch shift at Lou's. He gives me side-eye and calls me Darth Vader but laughs. Tyler is Captain America, and after my shift, I take him trick-or-treating in Piper's neighborhood. Even though I'm in Sugarwood, I don't allow my thoughts to dwell on Knox or Camden. I have new goals, a new focus. I promised I'd let him go for both of us, and I'm trying. God, I'm trying so hard.

I take my GED and pass with high scores. My application to Vandy is rushed through and approved and lo and behold, by December a full scholarship is awarded to me, a special compensation for students with high SAT scores who live in the inner city. Mr. Grayson had to have pulled some heavy freaking strings.

I wave the letter I printed off from my email in Lou's office. "I got it, Lou! It's mine! January! I'll be a freshman!"

He beams and sweeps me up in a full twirl while Rosemary tsks from behind the counter, where she's thrown down an order for me to take out.

He even waggles his eyebrows at Sister Margaret, who's been loitering in the foyer on her phone.

"Our Ava did it!" he tells her, and dang if he doesn't give her a hug too. She's stiff as a board and bats at him lightly.

"Balls. Lou is hugging Sister Margaret," Tyler declares as he draws at a table.

A couple weeks after Thanksgiving, Piper tells me the Dragons didn't win a state championship, but they came in second, and considering how awful their last season was and the fact that they lost one of their best players in Liam this year, she says the entire school is thrilled.

At the end of December, nearly four months after I left Camden, word comes from the DA that Liam accepted a plea deal instead of going to trial. His "trophies" were confiscated at his house, along with videos of the party no one had seen, specifically of him videoing me and murmuring he was going to get lucky. They also found a stash of cocaine and Rohypnol, a common date rape drug. His fingerprints were on the bottle, not Dane's.

Piper told me she heard through the gossip mill that Liam did indeed say it was Dane, that he planned everything and helped him—just like Knox said he would. I lay awake at night and hope Dane's doing okay, hope he's recovering. I picture Knox by his side every step of the way, going to therapy with him, right there supporting him at school.

In addition to Dane's recollection and testimony, Camilla came forward and told the police that Liam sexually assaulted her at his house freshman year. She couldn't remember all the details, possibly drugged. Then a girl from another school stepped up. *The Tennessean*, the biggest paper in the state, ran a whole story detailing what happened to me and his arrest. Instead of risking the possibility of more years locked up, his lawyers encouraged him to take the guilty plea for my assault. He did and was sentenced to fifteen to twenty years, which my victim advocate said was rather steep considering he was a minor when the crime occurred. It's not enough—never—but he's gone for now, and that settles me.

By the time January rolls around, it's truly a new year, and my beginning.

25

AVA

A year and nine months later

I'm late. So late. "No more crack-of-dawn classes," I grumble under my breath as I jog between students, moving like a ninja with my backpack, my coffee, and my laptop. But, I know I'm lying. Early classes are the best. It gives me time to start the day, study, and check in with Tyler after he's done with school at Camden.

"Sorry," I mutter to a pretty coed who gives me side-eye when I accidentally bump into her. My hand protectively covers the coffee I grabbed from the cafeteria this morning.

"Ava!" Piper catches up with me on the sidewalk. She's cute today in her mini skirt and crocheted top, her strawberry blonde hair up in a ponytail. She walked with me from our dorm to this side of campus since she has a class near me, but her short legs can't keep up. I'm raring to go. Something new and fresh is in the air, an expectant feeling lingering with possibilities. Tingles dance over my skin. Goose bumps—in late August!—cover my arms. "Girl. Will you slow down?" she huffs.

"I'm late. It's the first day of this sociology class my advisor wanted me to take. At least it's a break from my normal." My normal this semester is organic chemistry, biochemistry, a genetics class, and two labs. I'm frantic just thinking about it. My advisor warned me that this year would be insane, and boy was she right. I've got the MCAT to study for, plus an application for med school on the horizon. Today begins my sixth semester here, counting the summers.

She blows at her bangs, her shorter legs pumping. It makes me laugh that I can out fast-walk her when she's constantly moving. "You're going to Hess Hall, right? I'm headed to my curriculum class." She's working on a teaching degree.

I nod then Wyatt waves at us and jogs over, catching several girls' eyes with his tattoos and his usual sardonic grin, not that he notices. He ended up coming to Vandy to be close to his mom. Jagger pops up next to him and my smile widens. "Guys!"

Hugs are given all around. We haven't seen them much with the craziness of the new semester.

I tell them I have to dash, wishing I could talk more, but the clock is ticking.

"I'll see you at work," Piper calls, referring to Blue's Bar. I'm the bartender and she's a server. I gave up Lou's when I came to Vandy, although I still pop in and eat with Tyler sometimes. "Later," she says, taking the fork in the sidewalk.

"See you at work!" I look over my shoulder at them to wave bye and slam right into a hard muscular body.

Whump!

His book goes flying, right smack into a girl next to him, then lands on the ground. She yelps when the textbook hits her cheek. She drops her purse, and the contents roll over the sidewalk. Students dodge them, most of them unconcerned as they head to class. My coffee spills straight down my shirt and I wince at the hot liquid.

Geeze. Way to start the semester. "I'm so sorry, guys. I was in a hurry and wasn't looking. My fault," I mumble as I hurriedly brush off my crop top. My boobs will smell like hazelnut all dang day. Obviously, I don't have time to go home. At least my skinny jeans appear unscathed. I bend down and grab my cup, feeling devastated that the coffee is gone. It was the only thing keeping me going. The book I knocked down catches my eye, hung on the corner of the sidewalk, the pages opened, the spine ominously cracked. I close my eyes. *Textbook—expensive.*

I let out an exasperated breath.

"No worries. It's okay."

Nice voice. Deep. Growly. I raise my head up and look at the person I tried to tackle.

A breath whooshes out of me.

I push my sunglasses up on my head to hold my hair back.

HOLY HOT GUY.

He's tall, several inches over six feet, broad shoulders in a tight gold Vandy shirt, low-slung jeans that are molded to him, and black Converse. Dark mahogany hair—longer than what's normally found on guys who catch my eye—is chin-length with soft waves, framing his face.

My heart jumps off a cliff and does a swan dive right into stormy waters. My hands get clammy, and I close my eyes and open them again quickly, wondering if he'll disappear.

Nope. Drop-dead gorgeous is still in front of me.

"My cheek hurts," whines the girl next to him.

Ah. I blink and check her out. Pretty, someone I could see him with. Long, shiny, light brown hair, big green eyes, and a curvy figure.

She gives me a glare and stoops back down to pick up her lipstick.

"It's the first day. I get kinda nuts. Sorry." I grab her wallet and push it into her hand.

"You should slow down," she mutters.

I look back at Hot Guy. He's staring at me.

I bite my lip.

Then get nervous.

Butterflies flutter in my stomach, and that hasn't happened since...well, since high school.

The girl stands back up and asks him if he's ready to go.

He hasn't budged, nor does he reply to her.

I smile on the inside because he didn't offer to help her pick up her stuff either.

"Are you okay?" he asks me.

Am I?

Oh, yeah. Totally. Completely.

On impulse, I know what I have to do. I stick my hand out. "Hi. I'm Ava, sometimes Tulip if you know me well. I apologize for the book. I hope it's okay."

A long moment stretches, and I'm not sure he's going to say anything, and good grief, how stupid would I feel then—

He takes my hand slowly, almost as if he's afraid I'm going to turn and run. "My first name is Lee."

Lee. I savor it, testing it out in my head. It fits. Strong. Silent. Sexy as fuck.

His eyes are gray, his face chiseled and cut with lean cheekbones and a blade for a nose. There's dark scruff on his jawline and he rubs at it. Not once does he take his gaze off mine.

Someone brushes past me, but I hardly notice.

Is the sun brighter? Are birds singing in the trees?

My legs feel weird, like I'm not really standing there. I swallow the lump in my throat.

The universe just...shifted.

"Lee." Stupid me. I say it again.

His full, wicked lips twitch. "Yeah. And you're Ava, AKA Tulip."

"Hey, are you ready? We're late," the girl says from behind him.

"Your girlfriend is calling you," I murmur. "Better go."

"Not my girlfriend."

"Is that right?" I realize I've taken two steps toward him. If I reached out, I could touch his well-defined chest. "She's pretty."

"Hmmm. I prefer blondes." His gaze sweeps over my long hair, and dang, I admit I preen a little and toss it over my shoulder. It is glorious, long and wavy and brilliant in the sunlight. No more dark or bleached hair for me. I'm glad I wore it down today.

"She insisted on walking with me. My cousin actually."

The girl in question rolls her eyes, says she's ready and if he isn't then he can find his own damn class by himself.

"Go on," he replies without glancing at her. "I'll manage."

I stare at him and he stands perfectly still, as if he's afraid to move, while I...well, I'm the idiot girl who spends a full minute—*when I'm late!*—taking in every single inch of him. He's tan like he's been outdoors a lot. His eyes are crinkled at the corners from squinting at the sun. His hands are strong-looking, his fingers long and lean.

"Do I pass inspection?" he murmurs.

"Yeah." I pick up his book and hand it to him, our fingers brushing.

His sensuous lips part, his chest rising, and he looks as if he might say—

Someone hits my shoulder to get around me, and I apologize. Dang. We're standing here in the middle of heavy foot traffic.

Someone calls my name, a girl from the pre-med program, and I start then send her a wave, secretly hoping she doesn't walk over. I come back to his face watching mine as an unsure expression flashes briefly.

"See you around," he finally murmurs before turning and walking toward the buildings at the end of the sidewalk.

I watch him until his body grows smaller and the heads of other students overtake his. With a sigh, I gaze around at the world. *Wow.* The sky is incredibly blue, the grass is greener, the trees lush and full of vibrant color as they sway in the late summer breeze.

I laugh.

I just met a guy.

I just met a guy.

By the time I exit the restroom, where I did my best to dab the coffee off my shirt and walk into class, the lecture hall is packed. I prefer to sit up front, especially if I need to stay awake, but I'm out of luck, and it doesn't bother me one bit because I'm floating on air. I hitch my backpack up and find a seat in the last row at the top. At least it's the aisle and the exit is behind me in case I need to dash out quickly for my next class.

"This professor is supposed to be awesome," says the guy next to me.

"Oh?"

"Sociology of Men and Women." He winks at me, and I read the gleam of interest there.

He's cute with black glasses, a designer shirt, and super white teeth. Rich guy. Lots of money at Vandy, yet where people come from and what they have doesn't annoy me anymore. We're all here to learn, and I fit in *just fine*.

Even in my shabby Converse, pink now instead of black.

He leans over closer. "You wanna study together for this class sometime?"

I shake my head. "Um, I'm seeing someone," I tell him, being blunt. Might as well let him know. My heart is taken.

His smile falters a bit. "Oh. Cool. Sure, yeah. Me too."

I look up at the professor who's walked into the room, and my eyes land on a gold shirt near the front. I sit up straighter. I have to angle my head and peer past a coed with some giant hair—

But, oh, I see him.

My first name is Lee.

My lips curve.

The professor introduces himself and breaks down the coursework, and I take notes on my laptop without looking, watching Hot Guy.

Did he see me walk in?

The professor begins talking, and before long I'm sucked

in, especially when he throws out the term *mating rituals.* I grin, thanking my advisor in my head.

LATER, I'm halfway into my shift at Blue's when Carla, a graduate student and my manager, walks over to the bar and points at me. "Your turn to take the mic."

"I sang one already!"

"You know the drill, missy."

I groan, set down my bar cloth, and make my way to the small raised stage inside Blue's Bar.

"Part of the job, Ava," she calls. "Only way to get those other people up to sing is if you do."

"They just need to be drunk. You should do a dollar beer night."

She huffs. "As if. Now, go sing your tits off."

I'm thrown back to Camden when Miss Henderson said something similar over the intercom before the first football game. The memory doesn't prick like it used to, and I laugh.

"She just likes hearing you sing," Piper says as she brings back a tray of beer and wine glasses. "And you know you like it too." She gives me a questioning look, and I shrug. She's right. I didn't sing for a long time, but once I started working here a year ago, it just seemed natural to hop on the stage and belt one out. There's a piano, but I can't play it. I can strum a guitar, though, thanks to Wyatt.

I've gotten through two songs when a big group comes in. Girls and guys, they're wearing Vandy colors. Blue's Bar is a block from campus, and most of our clientele are coeds.

Carla signals for one more and I nod.

Dipping my head, I sit on the stool and strum the first few bars of "Mercy" by Shawn Mendes. Humming, I start the lyrics, melancholy verses about a guy who needs the girl he loves to show mercy for his heart, to take their love slow. He's prepared to sacrifice it all, but he needs to take some time.

The crowd gets quieter, and I sing the melody, giving it all I have.

A piano begins to play.

Pulling myself from the lyrics, I look over, and Hot Guy has gotten on stage. He's playing, his fingers stroking the keys in time to my words.

Ah, we meet again. A shiver ripples over my skin.

Red colors my cheeks when he pops an eyebrow at me. I realize I've stopped singing.

Well? Aren't you going to finish? his eyes ask.

Why? my face says.

He shrugs effortlessly as his fingers pause over the keys. "I like how you sing," he says softly.

Good enough. I look back at the crowd and sing the rest.

The song ends to a smattering of claps, hardly enthusiastic.

"Ava! I need you! Get over here!" Carla waves her hands at the line of people at the bar.

Right.

I turn back to my piano player, but he's already gone, headed back to that group of students who came in earlier.

With a sigh, I straighten my hot pink Blue's Bar tank and head to the bar, sliding in, taking orders, cracking beer bottle tops, and mixing drinks.

"Beer, please," a deep voice says. "Guinness in a bottle if you have it."

I was bent over, cleaning the ice chest during a lull, but I rise up and prop my elbows on the dark wooden bar. He's sitting on a stool in front of me.

"Lee," I say breathlessly. "Nice piano skills."

He dips his head, a sheepish smile quirking his lips. "Meh. I can keep up."

"They liked it." I wave around at the bar. It's gotten packed in here. All the tables are full and there's a line at the end of the bar for orders. Piper is out there somewhere, harried and full of energy, taking food and drink orders, scurrying back and forth to the kitchen.

He shifts, his tightly roped arms resting on the bar as if he's settling in. I watch as he rakes a hand through his hair, and my fingers itch to test the silkiness of the texture.

"It's my first time in Blue's. Nice place." His lips twitch. "You gonna keep staring or get me that beer?"

"You got an ID?"

He pulls out a leather wallet and pops out his driver's license.

"Hey, what's so funny?" He leans in and looks at it with me, and Jesus, the smell of the ocean floats around him.

"First, you look pissed in this pic. Second, what did you do to your hair? Too much gel. Third, you aren't 21."

"I will be someday. Would you rather see my fake?" he says wryly.

I shrug. Everyone's got one, and Carla isn't looking.

He hands it over and I study it, give it back, and hand him his Guinness, twisting the top off and setting it on a napkin. He can't seem to stop watching my movements, and my stomach gets those butterflies again.

"How old are you?" he asks.

"Twenty this past January."

"Ah. How did you celebrate?"

I roll my eyes. "Working. I'm not much of a party girl."

His gaze slides over my bare arms. Studies my bicep. "Nice tattoo."

"Phoenix." I turn to the side and let him see the orange creature rising up into the sky, red flames in its trail. I got it the summer after I left Camden. Every prick on my skin was a reminder of how far I came to where I am now. I lifted myself from the ashes and started anew. "My brother drew it. You got any?"

"None you can see."

Someone next to him orders a glass of Chablis, a pretty girl with a sorority shirt on, and I pour it for her. I get another order from the person behind her, and Sorority Girl turns to Lee, starts a conversation. He answers in monosyllables until she slides away, looking disappointed.

"You get that a lot I bet." I'm back and staring at him. I can't stop. My eyes linger on his lips. A long breath escapes me.

He tips the beer up. Takes a long swig. "Nah. I'm saving myself for someone. Have been for a while."

"Really?"

"Mmmm." He peels at the paper on his beer.

"You trying out being a monk?"

"Just waiting for a girl."

My hands shake and I stick them in the pockets of my jeans. I clear my throat. "I haven't seen you on campus before. Did you transfer in? What year are you?"

He smiles. "My first year here, actually. I took a gap year after high school to travel with my brother and Dad then took some online classes and worked a few jobs, mostly construction for my dad's company. Wanted to save up some money—for a girl."

I sigh, swallowing. "Ah, travel. Where did you go?"

"The beach at first. We have a house on Kiawah Island in South Carolina."

I picture a sprawling mansion on the coast, waves lapping at the shore. "That sounds nice. Where else?"

"We left there and ended up in Alaska for fishing, then went to Italy. Lived in a villa for a few months, climbed some mountains, saw Pompeii—amazing by the way. My brother..." He chuckles. "He cried like a baby over those ruins, all the people and animals killed in an instant by volcanic ash." He gives me a hesitant look. "He's got a soft heart."

"Bad way to go for sure. Where else did you go?" I'm leaning over closer to him, fascinated.

He laughs, his eyes glinting.

I shrug. "What? I've always wanted to travel. The beach sounds amazing to me. I bet you saw a lot of those."

"Someday you will too..." He pops a maddening eyebrow. I want to lick it.

"Yeah. When I'm done with Vandy. Then medical school, then residency, then...who knows."

He nods. "We spent a few months in Greece. Gorgeous water and beaches. My brother met a girl on the Amalfi Coast, fell in love, and she came back with him."

Warmth fills me. "Ah. Is he happy?"

"He is." He pauses. "Did you know there's a small Greek island devoted to taking care of cats?"

"No shit."

"Shit. Just a bunch of felines roaming over a tiny deserted island. There's a caretaker and everything."

"You like cats?"

"My brother does. He's got one I gave him."

I smile. "What's your major?"

"Don't laugh. Business with a minor in poetry."

I laugh.

"I said don't laugh! I don't even know why it's funny, but everyone laughs like poetry is dumb."

"I wasn't laughing because of that. I'm laughing because... it suits you."

A few of the guys in the back yell when the TV behind the bar replays a Vandy football game from last year. I guess they're getting ready for the new season. Our first game is in two weeks. I run my gaze over the guys he came in with. They're all in football shirts.

Lee wears one too.

"You play football for Vandy?"

He nods. "I walked on this summer. Quarterback. Came in and tried out. Got a spot. Third string, but, hey..." He laughs and spreads his hands. "Some guys peak in high school. Looks like I did okay."

God. I love how he laughs. It's the color of the sun, soft and warm and golden.

I think I must say it aloud, because he blushes.

Then spears me with gunmetal eyes. "You okay with guys who play football?"

"Totally. What's not to like? I know a few of those guys. Dated a football player in high school. Okay, two." I grimace.

"Ah, young love. My competition, by the glint in your eyes."

Someone asks for a Bud Light and I grab one, take the money, and slide it down the bar.

I make my way back to him.

He hasn't moved an inch.

"So third string? You strike me as pretty competitive. Does that sting?"

He shrugs. "I used to think playing was all I needed, even wanted a scholarship from a big school." A faraway look grows in his eyes. "What I really needed was my family. I've learned to be patient. Everything arrives when it's supposed to."

"Vandy isn't a big football college, but it is SEC Division I. You can work your way up to first string."

"Maybe. What time do you get off?" he asks.

I push my hair over my shoulder, and he inhales sharply.

"Doors get locked at midnight. I'm closing, which means I have to clean the kitchen and the tables." I sigh. "Won't finish up till one. I saw you in my sociology class."

"Saw you too. Wanna sit with me next time?"

My body vibrates, buzzing. I try to speak, but—

"Am I moving too fast?" he asks.

"No."

"You got a phone number?"

I scribble it on a napkin and pass it over to him.

He tucks it in his pocket. "Do you like to eat? Like on a date?"

Do I like to eat? I laugh. *Oh, Lee. You're doing everything so right.* "I haven't had a date in, like...dang, never."

"No way. You're gorgeous." His eyes linger on my face, touching on my lips then skating down to my low-cut tank, lingering on my locket.

I lean in and whisper. "True. A guy has never paid for my food on a date. Guess I'm waiting for the right one to walk in."

"Damn." He takes a swig of his beer. "Can't say I'm sad about it. Has he walked in yet?"

"Ava! Stop flirting and help me with these sorority girls!" Carla yells from the end of the bar where she's drowning in Deltas.

"You have to go."

"Mmmm," I say, not moving, reluctant to leave.

He smiles. "You best go."

"My legs don't seem to work. Carla can manage." She yells at me again, and I blow out a breath. "Geeze. Can't she handle those drunk girls by herself?"

"You work. I'm not going anywhere." He stands up from the stool and strides back to his friends, and I sigh, watching him go, my heart jumping fast. He avoids the girls that flock to him, veering to the right and talking to one of the other players. He sees me looking and tips his beer at me.

I see promise in his eyes.

I see...

Me.

Later after we've closed, Piper lets out a long sigh and heads to the door. "Girl, I wish I had the stamina to wait another hour for you, but Wyatt's outside with a ride. I'm dead tired."

"I got it." I'm used to the long hours. "Get some sleep."

She pauses at the door and turns back. "Hey, I saw you talking to someone at the bar earlier. This place was wall to wall with people, and I didn't get a good look at him. Potential date? I mean, I know you tell everyone you're taken, but don't you think it's time to go out with one of these guys who keep asking you out?" She grins. "Oh crap, you're blushing. What did he say?"

I shrug, keeping my secrets. "Nothing."

She leaves and I get to work cleaning up while Carla counts the register receipts in the manager's office. The other waitresses leave. A little before one, I've gotten the place straight and lock up the back.

Carla and I walk out together to the parking lot across the street.

"Someone's waiting at your car," she tells me, indicating the tall man who's leaning against his Mercedes parked next to Louise.

I nod, barely breathing. "It's okay. I know him."

"He's fucking hot," she murmurs then makes her way to her sedan and drives off.

I stand there for a minute, just looking at him. Then, I take a deep breath and walk over, humming.

He's here.

He's waiting.

He's been waiting.

We both have.

Like time hasn't passed, I stop when we stand chest to chest. I reach out and touch his face first, brushing over that scar on his cheek, tracing it down to his upper lip.

He bites my finger.

I jump and laugh.

He grins.

"Thought you were just gonna call me," I say, my shoes absently toying with a piece of gravel on the concrete.

"Wanted to see you before I went to sleep. You tired? I'm sure we can find an all-night place open if you're hungry."

My body tingles with heat. "Not tired. Or hungry." I've never felt so alive.

His hand tucks a piece of my hair over my ear. "When I saw you this morning, I didn't want to rush you—"

"Rush me."

A long exhalation comes from his chest. He swallows. "Come home with me."

"Where's home?"

"Apartment nearby. I moved in this weekend."

"Alright."

He moves around his car and opens the passenger door, and I slide into the sleek leather interior.

He gets in, starts the engine, and pulls out onto the road. There's not much traffic this late, but a few cars pass us, their headlights lighting up his features.

"You're staring," he says on a small laugh, darting his gaze at me then looking back at the road.

Oh, I see the promise in those beautiful eyes of his. The seriousness. The heat. I see *him*. He's the kind of guy who doesn't love often, but once he does, it's with everything he has.

"Can't help it." My throat is thick with a sharp, visceral, primal need to hold him. It's been so long, so fucking long, and now he's here, and I can't breathe or think or—

As if he knows, he reaches over and takes my hand. "Hang on, Tulip. Almost there."

He whips the car into a nice apartment complex near campus, jumps out, and comes around to my side of the car to open the door for me.

"Fuck yes," he groans when I jump up in his arms and lock my legs around his waist.

"Inside," I murmur into his neck, inhaling his scent.

He runs with me, up two flights of stairs and down the hall to a door. Fumbling around, he works the key into the lock and kicks it open.

Briefly, I see a dim room with boxes everywhere, most of them unpacked, his textbooks sitting on a desk, the TV on ESPN on mute. With me in his arms, he falls to a sitting position on a leather couch and I straddle him, my hands running over his face, touching him, fingering his hair, tracing his face, his shoulders.

He holds my eyes and lets me map out his features. He does the same, his lips pressing a hot kiss to my palm, his fingers dancing over the pulse on my wrist. His hand trembles over my heart for several long moments, his breathing rapid as he strokes up to my collarbone then around my neck, tangling in my hair. He buries his face in it and says my name, the tone layered with anguish and reverence, blended beautifully.

My legs tighten around his waist.

I can't let go of him. My breath hitches when he cups my face. I'm underwater and I need him, I need him like air.

"Kiss me," I beg. "Kiss me. God, please, kiss me and forgive me for leaving you, because if you don't—"

He takes my mouth hungrily, a man starved. Our lips cling, ravaging the other, licking and sucking and nipping.

He tugs my shirt off while I rip at his, yanking it over his head.

My bra is blue and lacy and he strokes his fingers over the fabric, cupping me. I groan at the light touch. Longing and craving, pent up and banked for so long, dance and scream along my nerve endings.

"Tulip, all mine, all mine," he says, his voice low as he dips his head and sucks my erect nipple through the lace.

I stare at his chest, my mouth drying at his sculpted muscles, the six-pack, the deep V that leads down to his jeans. I see his tulip bouquet tattoo, the script letters at the top of the pink blooms. My eyes blur. Emotion lifts me and destroys me at the same time as I trace my fingers over the words.

Tulip. Waiting for you. Always.

He gasps for air. "Tulip, damn you, damn you. Don't ever leave me, don't. Stay here and be mine. I did what you wanted. I let you go, I let you find yourself, and I found me too. I did, I did, but I can't do it without you again. I can't look at another beach or mountain or country while wondering where you are or who you're seeing and if you still love me..." His voice breaks as he grabs my face. "Tell me you still love me."

My heart cracks then stitches itself back together. "Lee Knox Grayson, I love you till the end of time. I never stopped. I never gave up. You're my destiny. I'm yours. The universe fucking *owes* me, you feel me?"

He shudders. "I never stopped watching out for you, Tulip. I've known where you've been since day one."

"I didn't doubt it for a moment. You love me. *You love me.*"

"We needed a new beginning and I wanted to give it to you. Maybe you met someone. Maybe you...didn't want me anymore. Maybe you walked away and never thought of me again."

"Never." My lips brush over his.

"I want you so fucking bad, and I know I just showed up—"

"Take me, please, I'm yours."

He groans and kisses me, our hands pulling and fumbling as we manage to get our pants off, our shoes. And then he has me back in his arms and I'm staring down at him, drinking him in. I clutch his head, writhing against his skin, feeling the ridge of him through my panties.

"Shhhh, I got you," he murmurs, kissing my throat, his teeth nipping at me.

I pull his face to mine and kiss him, hard and deep, searching his mouth, sucking on his tongue like I want to devour him. Fast and hard and fast and hard and fast and hard...

I shove his underwear down and even in the dim light, I can see he's long and thick and firm.

"Tulip, I've pictured you in my mind, in my dreams like this, so many long nights without you and nothing is right without you, not beaches or mountains or the sky because I need you, need you, need you. You're the only one who knows me, who sees me the way I am inside." He exhales, moving his hips up against my hand.

Without preamble, he slips his fingers under my lace panties and slides one inside my wetness, and I arch up and ride his hand, rubbing him where I need him. My lips and tongue nibble at his chest, my hands roving over his skin, savoring, wanting him so much as I commit his smell, his taste to my memory.

"Condom," I say in between kisses.

He grunts. "I don't have any."

"You idiot."

He takes my chin. "You're the last girl I was with. Didn't need condoms."

"Same. You're the only guy I want." Pausing for a moment, I say, "It's a safe time of the month for me."

I shove my hands in his silky hair and dig my fingers into his scalp as he eases me up. I'm standing in front of him, his eyes hot as he slowly takes off my panties. I'm a quivering mess, need and hope like birds rushing to the sky. So long, so long...

He bites his bottom lip and takes me in, and I do a twirl while he smiles then pulls me back to him and places me on his lap, my legs around the outside of his thighs. Staring into my eyes, he pumps inside me like silk-covered steel and we cry out then still against each other, our chests heaving.

"Tulip, Tulip, so good, so good, you, you, you, you," he mumbles and slides all the way out then back in, his shoulders quivering. "Sweet, so fucking sweet."

"Knox..." I moan and writhe against him.

He takes me, his hands on my hips, his cock swiveling inside me, his eyes never leaving mine.

My hands cling to him, hanging on as he changes his angle, rotating inside me, the top of him brushing against my clit. He's rough and fast and good, so fucking good as he pushes in and out. His hands burn my skin where he clutches me. His eyes blaze.

He tells me, "You are mine," and when his fingers go between us and flick over my clit with delicious intent, I beg him mindlessly, lost in him, to never let me go, to hold me like this, to belong to him, to be part of his world. I come, my core spasming around him as I scream his name.

"Tulip, Tulip," he calls and goes over the cliff with me, his eyes wild, and oh, oh, I love him so much it hurts.

He breathes into my neck and clutches me tight, rocking me as I hang on to him.

We stay like that for a long time, our hands clinging to the other as he strokes my back and murmurs in my ear how beautiful and fierce I am.

We make love again, slower this time, with me laid back on the couch while he strokes inside me, running his hands over my face, down my throat, to the rapid pulse that beats in my neck. He puts his lips there and owns me, my cries, my gasps, my everything.

Later, he gives me a roomy shirt of his while he changes into loose pajama pants.

"Want to see my place?" he asks gruffly, his eyes on my face, never off me for long. There's a hopeful look about him.

I nod and he gives me a tour. The apartment is big: three bedrooms, three bathrooms, and a kitchen bigger than my dorm room.

"There's room for Tyler here," he tells me.

I nod.

"And I've been researching schools close to Vandy. There are a few he might like—if you want to move in, that is?" He looks uncertain. "I have money from my mom and I've been working for my dad to save up more. I want to take care of you and Tyler the right way."

Oh, Knox.

He pauses. "I know you're independent as hell, but I need you with me, Tulip. I let you walk away. I could have chased after you and begged you to come back, but I stuffed everything down and carried on for my family, to get our shit straight, and we did. But there's no more going slow with me. No more distance. No more time to breathe. It's our time. Us."

My chin trembles with the effort of not crying. "Dane needed you so much, and I did too, but I had to get out of there and carry on and put it behind me."

He strokes my hair. "I get it. Dad told me about how he helped you. He was honest from the get-go the day you left, and I'm happy he helped you with Vandy. I know about you getting guardianship too. Tyler might not want to leave the only place he's ever known, but he's part of you and if he's amendable, I want him with us—"

God. His *kindness* overwhelms me.

Tears slide down my face as I kiss him. "I can move in tomorrow. We'll figure out what Tyler wants."

He wipes my face, and when the sun comes up in our bedroom, we're still awake, lying side by side, touching each other. My leg is thrown over his hip as he eases inside me, one hand on my bottom, one wrapped around my hair. His lips drink from mine, worshipping me.

"The sun's coming up," I whisper.

"Dear Ava, today is the beginning of anything you want," he says in my ear.

I clutch his shoulders. "You. Always you."

EPILOGUE 1

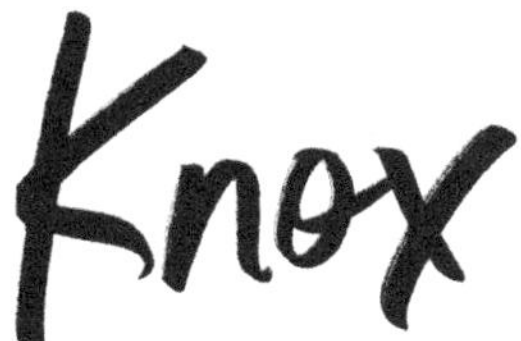

The stadium explodes with applause, blaring music, and flashing lights. Several Vandy teammates slap me on the back.

"Killer throw for that last touchdown, man!" yells James, my go-to wide receiver. "Citrus Bowl Champs! I can't believe it! Best season we've had in years!"

"Kickass season," says Marlon, the quarterback coach, as he gives me a handshake then changes his mind and throws in an affectionate man-hug.

Whipping my helmet off, I murmur a response as the fans rush the field.

My eyes aren't on them though. I'm looking for the

blonde who sat front and center on the fifty-yard line. I did my damn best to keep my head off her during this last game, but she's always there, floating in and out of my thoughts. Her heart-shaped face, those big aquamarine eyes. Her secret smile that's just for me when I kiss my fingers on the field and send them out into the air for her to see.

She jump-tackles me and I sweep her up to my chest. Rightness settles in my bones. *Tulip.*

She buries her face in my neck. "Not bad for a third-string quarterback."

"Mmmm. Good thing I worked my way up to first string. Only took me until my senior year."

She throws her head back and laughs. "Looks like you didn't peak in high school after all. I wonder what's next?"

I kiss her long and hard, oblivious to the camera flashes and media surrounding us. Except for those away games she couldn't make, we haven't spent a night apart since I showed up at Blue's Bar. She moved from her dorm into my place and we never looked back. She's the girl I wanted the moment she walked in the doors at Camden, and I know we're young on the outside, but inside, the heart knows when it sees its forever.

"Anything we want." I press my lips to her palm, my gaze lingering on the two-carat engagement ring on her finger. I asked her to marry me the Christmas after we reunited. Well, technically, I asked Tyler first and he said, "Balls yes. Just do it already. You're already living in sin, and I really wish you'd put up some concrete walls around your bedroom. I'm too young to hear that shit."

The kid in question comes barreling out of nowhere and

clings to my leg. "That was the best game I have ever seen! I want to be a tattoo artist and a footballer," he exclaims.

"We'll need to practice more," I tell him as I ruffle his hair. He moved in with us permanently after we got engaged, and even though Ava worried about his transition from Camden to a local private school near the university, he adapted fast.

One of the reporters has weaseled her way through the crush and reaches me. She sticks a mic in my face. "Knox, you led your team through a stellar season with eleven wins and two loses in the SEC, unheard of for the Commodores. How does it feel to win the Citrus Bowl?"

Tyler squints up at her. "He's got my sister by his side. She's the badass. She's in medical school. He's feeling pretty lucky right now, alright." His head nods with confidence.

That's right, straight from a kid.

He's such a good, bright person, and I see Ava in him every day, that chin that tilts up, determination and grit as he pushes himself. It hasn't been easy, adapting to each other, but he's mine. My heart dips when he smiles. My hands tuck him in at night alongside Ava. The image makes me smile. I'm not your typical college football player who's living the high life with frat parties and girls. No thanks.

"Guess he said it all," I murmur to the reporter.

"Any hopes for the NFL draft? There's talk of you being a first-round pick," she says.

"I'm passing on the NFL. I've got other dreams," I tell her.

Ava just shrugs with a smile. Once upon a time, I pictured myself playing professionally, but everything realigned during the year I took off, and I realized I wanted a regular life working with my dad. The older I get—ha!—the more I yearn for stability and her. It's not a sacrifice to leave the game. I came here. I played. Hell, I won, but my true love is building a foundation, a legacy for my family—plus, *shit* football hurts and takes up too much time. Even now, my hip is killing me. I want a long, long life, unfettered, unchained from commitments I lack the motivation for now.

Dad and Dane jog over and slide in next to us, pride clear on my father's face as he slaps me on the back with a big hug. "Congratulations, son. I'm so proud of you." He gaze encompasses Ava and Tyler and I know besides football, he means them as well. We spend a lot of time with him and Dane, and damn, Dad's face the first time Tyler asked if he should call him Grandpa—priceless. Tyler meant it as kind of a joke, I think, because he's got a sharp wit, but Dad's expression... floored. Then he told Tyler to call him whatever he wanted.

There's a closeness between Ava and Dad that still surprises me when I see them huddled over a stove cooking or talking about Sith Lords and Yoda, and gah, who knew he was such a nerd about a galaxy far, far away. But then, I didn't really know that about him because with my mom, Dad suffered too, distancing himself and locking things away. Now, though, things have changed. That year I spent with him and Dane—I don't regret one moment of it. We took a broken family and learned to heal.

Dane picks me up, no easy feat, and attempts to twirl me around, but he can barely lift me.

"Bro, you have zero upper-body strength," I murmur.

"Because I'm a serious college student." He waggles clear, focused eyes. He's been clean for years, attending NYU. Dad sees him a lot, flying between New York and Nashville.

"This is my future grandfather and uncle. Knox is going to

be my dad," Tyler tells the reporter, who gives him a wide look, laughs, and then bends down to him.

"Is that right? Tell me more."

I guess she's going for the personal interest angle here.

Tyler lets out a long-suffering sigh. "It's a really, *really* long story—and I should know it because my future dad likes to tell it, but it started with a love letter he put in my sister's locker..."

I smile. Technically, it started the moment my eyes met hers freshman year in high school, but I let him begin his way.

Ava meets my gaze, bites her lip, and clasps my hand.

Tyler puts his small hand in my other one.

Dane takes Ava's free hand, and Dad takes Tyler's.

We're a family.

EPILOGUE 2

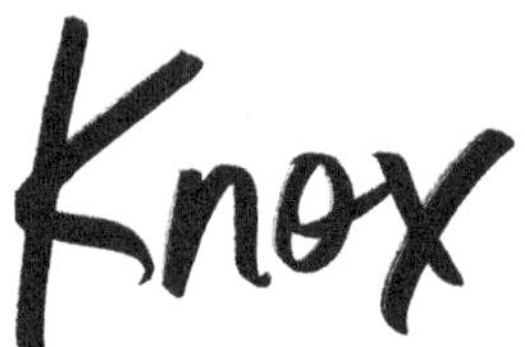

The sun is high in the sky as a breeze blows in from the Atlantic. Palm trees rustle in the wind. A sailboat drifts by on the horizon. I take it all in, leaning my elbows on the railing as I inhale the smell of the beach and crashing waves. I soak it up then turn around to check the burgers on the grill.

Lou lounges on a chair and lets out a long whistle. "Damn, I could retire here. What kind of square footage is this place?"

"A gabillion," Wyatt murmurs. "You should see my bedroom—plush, man, and it's just a guestroom. I love how Ava's decorated. Girl's got great taste."

I smile unabashedly. Yeah, she does. I loved watching her pore over magazines and meet with designers after we bought it last year.

Lou sees my expression and laughs. "God, you two."

Dane hands Lou a beer. "Six thousand square feet. Five bedrooms, five baths. Jacuzzi tubs, stainless steel everything, and five hundred feet of beachfront. Primo property and a mile from our family beach house." He leans in and stares at the burgers. "Knox had to get one bigger than Dad's. Showoff."

That is not true and my eyebrow tells him so.

Since I graduated four years ago and took over some of Dad's investments in the Nashville area, I've worked my way up from a desk job to executive vice president, and it has little to do with impressing my father. It's about me and Ava.

"The one next door is for sale," I tell him slyly. "Maybe your fiancée would like it?"

Ari, the girl in question, lights up and turns to Dane. "Oh, yes, let's go check it out tomorrow!"

Dane rolls his eyes. "Great. We aren't even married yet and here you are, putting the pressure on."

"He's just a happy sonofabitch and wants us all to be," Wyatt says, settling in on a chair next to Jagger and handing him a beer. The two of them have been inseparable since Vandy days. Ava has already told them our beach house is theirs if they want to get married here. She and I were married at my dad's place down the road right after I graduated.

Piper sticks her head out the French doors. "Okay, okay, Knox, I know you're busy with the guys and all, but do you have a moment?" She gives me a wide-eyed look. "Ava—"

I toss the spatula on the countertop and dash inside.

"Why don't you run that fast when I need something?" I hear Ari ask Dane.

I walk into an empty kitchen. Piper points down the hall to the master bedroom, and I head there.

Ava sits on the big bed, a crying baby on each leg. Leland Knox and Persephone Tulip are officially two years old this weekend. My eyes search her. She looks okay, maybe a little scattered, and her hair needs brushing, but hey, when you've got two toddlers—

"Ugh, I told Piper I was fine, told her they cry in tandem all the time. Doesn't matter who's mad or happy, the other wants to be part of it." She huffs out a laugh when Leland burps, his face un-wrinkling at the relief then focusing on me. His pudgy hands reach for me. "Dada!"

Ava shakes her head as I take him in my arms. "I thought the walk on the beach might have worn them out, but nope, not a single eye shut. You might as well get ready—"

"My dada!" Persephone cries until I pick her up too, managing to bounce them on my hips.

"They're sleepy and here we are trying to have a birthday party." Ava stands next to me, her fingers curling under their chins as she hums a song. "Beautiful babies."

Leland reaches back for her, like he usually does, and I know he only picked me to rescue him from sleeping. Ava's an incredible mom, soft and easy and patient, everything she always wanted from her own. Having a baby was part of the plan; twins, not so much, and while it's slowed her down some during her medical training, she'll be completely done soon and wants to work in research.

Leland wipes his nose. "Nap bad," he tells his mom sternly as he pulls on her hair.

"Tyler!" Persephone chimes in.

"Domestic bliss?" Tyler says on a laugh as he comes in the open door. My dad is with him. They left earlier for a movie while the rest of us chilled out this morning.

Persephone wiggles her fingers for Tyler, and he takes her and settles her on his hip.

"Guess what, little P? Grandpa let me drive today!" he says.

I start and sputter as I glance at Dad. "You let him drive? He's not even fifteen yet!"

Dad looks a little pale, and I stop and chuckle. I recall well him teaching Dane and me to drive, featuring lots of yelling and cursing every time we braked too hard.

Dad blows out a breath. "He asked and I thought, Why not? Not sure my car will ever be the same—"

Tyler coos at the baby on his hip. "He's not telling you about the pedestrian I nearly mowed down—"

Ava's eyes flare.

Dad exhales. "They have bike lanes here and she was very pretty, and I saw exactly where your eyes were—"

"She wasn't. I just got distracted—" Tyler huffs.

"Did he cuss at you?" Dane says, walking in and immediately swiping Leland from Ava. My son smiles, giggling at his uncle's long hair.

"Pretty," he gurgles then spits up on Dane's shirt.

He blanches, his eyes widening. "Gross! Gah, I hate the smell of milk." But he doesn't let him go, even when Wyatt and Piper come in, each of them holding out their hands and vying for his attention.

Lou pops his head in. "Food's up!"

Ava laughs, and I guess it's because Lou has taken over the grill for me.

Persephone wiggles her way down from Tyler and throws a look around at Leland, still content in Dane's arms.

"Leeeeeeee, eat! No nap!" she wails out in a demanding voice, and then he's straining to get to her—as a good brother should—and does his duck walk in his diaper to where she's waiting at the door. He hangs on to her shirt, muttering, then dashes ahead, laughing as she tries to catch him.

"P, P, P, I win!"

"No!" she cries and runs faster, and dang, they can't even really run that fast, but we all watch, entranced.

It's such a simple thing, really, seeing them and thinking how lucky I am, and the emotion wraps around me, amazement that I hold happiness in my hands, the knowledge that family is everything.

Everyone files into the kitchen, and I turn to Ava, finding her eyes as misty as mine.

She jumps at me and I clutch her close. It's the little things. God, the little things.

I kiss her long and slow, my tongue tangling with hers, and she melts into me.

Our lines got a little blurry along the way, through broken hearts and time lost, but in the end, we made a full, complete, beautiful circle.

Dear Reader,

Thank you for reading Dear Ava. I hope you enjoyed

Knox and Ava's story as much as I loved writing it. It was one of the most emotional books I've ever written. If you want lighter, check out the short excerpt from my last romantic comedy I Hate You (yep, it really is a romantic comedy), or just head straight to the Amazon store to get the entire full-length standalone novel. It is currently FREE in Kindle Unlimited!

HONEST, heartfelt reviews are like gold to authors, and I read each and every one. If you have a few moments, please consider leaving a review for Dear Ava.

IF YOU'VE BEEN the victim of a sexual assault, please speak with someone who is trained to help. You can call the National Sexual Assault Hotline at 800.656.HOPE (4673) or chat online at **online.rainn.org.**

KEEP READING ALL THE BOOKS.

Love,

Ilsa Madden-Mills

P.S. PLEASE JOIN my FB readers group, Unicorn Girls, to get the latest scoop as well as talk about books, wine, and Netflix:

https://www.facebook.com/groups/ilsasunicorngirls/

Sign up below for my newsletter to receive a FREE Briarwood Academy novella ($2.99 value) plus get insider info and exclusive giveaways!

http://www.ilsamaddenmills.com/contact

BIBLIOGRAPHY AND SOURCES

Bibliography and Sources

Ehrlich, Susan. *Representing Rape: Language and Sexual Consent.* Oxford: Routledge, 2003.

Harding, Kate. *Asking For It: The Alarming Rise of Rape Culture—and What We Can Do About It.* Boston: Perseus Book Group, 2015.

Mulla, Samenna. *The Violence of Care: Rape Victims, Forensic Nurses, and Sexual Assault Intervention.* New York: New York University Press, 2014.

Schwartzman, Nancy. *Roll Red Roll.* Sunset Park Pictures and Multitude Films, 2018.

Todd, Paula. *Extreme Mean: Trolls, Bullies, and Predators Online.* Toronto: Signal, 2014.

EXCERPT - I HATE YOU

Chapter 1
Charisma

There are worse things than seeing your ex for the first time since he dumped you: root canal, hairy wolf spider on your pillow, watching your dad kiss your sixth grade teacher.

I shudder at those thoughts as I whip my car into the parking lot of Cadillac's, a local bar and hangout spot. A long exhalation leaves my chest as I turn off the ignition.

Welcome back to Magnolia, Mississippi, and Waylon University, folks. It's time to face the music, which is the guy who broke up with me in front of all my friends at my own freaking eighties-themed sorority homecoming party last October. I'd worn a sleek fedora and carried a kickass whip a la sexy Indiana Jones style, and he'd been in yellow parachute pants and a ladies-sized small tank top that clung to every muscle on his chest. We were totally fine—until it all went to hell.

That was almost three months ago, and I haven't seen him since.

But tonight—*tonight*, I'm going to see him face to face, because I have to prove to myself that I'm over him. I'm not leaving until my eyes meet his and—

Dang, I don't know what will happen after that.

My bottom lip hurts where I've chewed on it during the drive from the house to here. Maybe he's not inside. I picture him laid up in his dorm room surrounded by jersey chasers. They're probably rubbing him down with hot oil right now, caressing those bulky, tight muscles on his back, most definitely the wiry, roped ones on his forearms—

Stop. Forget the wide receiver.

Clenching the steering wheel, I scan the parking lot for his black truck and don't see it, but the place is packed for a Wednesday night in January. Everyone is back from the holiday break filled with new optimism for grades, social status, and what the future holds. My future? In six months I'll be out of Magnolia and living a whole new life, one that doesn't involve smoking-hot football players with rock-hard abs who tell you you're beautiful but in the end are just big fat liars.

My eyes land on the door of the bar as a group of students spill out of the entrance. They stumble around laughing and talking, and my heart twinges. That used to be me. I used to be the life of the party—but look at me now, the girl who's basically been in social hiding since Blaze ended things.

New semester, new you, I mutter. I'm not going to be the

pathetic creature I was a few months ago. No more Wallflower Charisma! Party Girl is back! It's going to be awesome!

"*Car door is open,*" states the snobby car voice lady who lives inside my older model Nissan Maxima, and I realize I've been sitting here with one leg in and one out, my mind running. I smirk at the technology that was put into these cars in the early 90s—not at the fact that they were able to crack the code on how to record some British woman's voice and play it, but how they decided this groundbreaking technology should be used to alert the driver to the most obvious things.

"Washer fluid is low."

"Parking brake is on."

If Lady Maxima—my nickname for said un-insightful voice—really wanted to help, she would come up with some better alerts.

"Don't chase down the ice cream truck. It's embarrassing and you're lactose intolerant anyway."

"Don't screw that football player. He will only break your heart."

With a nervousness that makes me annoyed, I take one last look in the rearview mirror to check my hair and makeup. My long, dark hair is braided in two loose plaits, the soft pink streaks peeking out here and there. Makeup is smoky eyes and carefully filled-in brows. Lipstick is dark pink. In a perfect world, I imagine my style gives me a sassy femme fatale look, but the reality is I'm just a short nerd girl with pink in her hair.

I get out of the car and stop at the heavy wooden entrance. Dread, thick and heavy, stirs around in my stomach as I contemplate how I'm going to react when I see him. No doubt he'll be with Dani, the willowy Barbie doll creature he picked up with after me. I swallow down queasiness as a chilly gust of wind blows, pushing me closer to the door.

F him.

You may not be the most beautiful girl in the room, but that's not why people dig you. Show them you're back and better than ever.

The bustling sounds of the bar fill my head as I enter, people laughing and Pat Benatar's "Hit Me With Your Best Shot" on the jukebox. *Fitting.* With tables on one side and pool tables and an arcade on the other, the place is decorated like an old-fashioned diner with black and white floors and red stools at the bar. Vintage cars on neon signs blink on the walls.

Playing cool and acting as blasé as possible, I take off my coat and drape it over my arm. Tiny beads of sweat form on my face, and I chalk it up to the stares of everyone in the place. They aren't looking at me, per se, but they are watching the door, waiting for the football team to arrive. With a deep breath, I inhale the greasy, yummy smell of fried food. My stomach growls, and I tell it to chill out. There'll be no messy cheesy fries with loads of ketchup and ranch on the side tonight. My black mohair sweater dress is too pretty...and this is business.

"There she is! Ladies and gentlemen, I give you a person we haven't seen in these parts in ages. The elusive Charisma Rossi! Give her a hand, y'all!" The announcement comes from Margo, the cardigan-wearing, champagne-drinking president of my sorority.

Color floods my cheeks. "Stop that. Attention is what I don't need right now." I scan the room with lowered eyes.

She straightens the headband on her shiny, straight blonde hair and gives me a pointed look. "He isn't here, Charm," she says, her Southern accent sweet as iced tea. "But he will be."

"Who isn't here?"

"Don't play dumb. You're too smart for it. Nice outfit, by the way. Bold with the red stilettos—makes quite a statement." She arches an elegant yet somehow condescending brow as she hooks her arm in mine and tugs me toward the front of the bar. Normally, I wouldn't be so acquiescent to her telling me what to do, but she's taller than me, and I use her as a shield, hunkering down next to her as we walk.

She stops at a big table right out in the open with a clear view of the arcade and pool tables.

Great, just great—right in the middle for everyone to see.

I sigh. "What time did you arrive to score a front-row seat?"

"Chi-Os get the best. I aim to please."

Margo is a Type A tornado on her way to Yale Law. We're nothing alike, but we manage...mostly. She thinks I'm a little wild, and I think she has a stick up her ass. I like her anyway.

My eyes scour the bar again, and I straighten my shoulders. Be carefree. Be nonchalant. BE THE OLD YOU. Right. Only, there's a pinch on my right big toe from my three-inch heels, and I end up standing on one foot like a flamingo to ease the pain. To make matters worse, both arms itch, and I glare at the fluffy fabric on my sleeves. It was a big mistake to wear this, yet I know where my head was when I picked out the figure-hugging dress. I wanted to look hot. I wanted him to see me, take a good, long, second look, and wish he still had me.

"You're scratching yourself. A lot." Margo squints at me.

"Dude, I'm fine."

But I'm not. My skin, from the top of the neckline to the hem, feels like a million ants have invaded. *Mohair, why you killing me?* I'm mid-scratch, trying to be discreet as I reach a spot on my neck, when a group of rambunctious partiers pushes past me to get to the pool tables. I stumble in the process, and someone's cold beer spills down the front of my once awesome but now terrible dress.

Crap.

Double crap.

Well, shit.

I stare down at my wet chest and let out a wail. At least the coldness makes the itchiness feel a tiny bit better.

The guy in question utters a half-mumbled apology and takes off for the pool tables.

"How rude. By the way, I can see your nipples," Margo says as she takes a sip from her champagne flute.

"Perfect—a flamingo with erect nipples," I mutter.

He isn't even here yet and this night already sucks.

END EXCERPT

If you want to continue to read, head to the Amazon store to get the entire full-length standalone novel I Hate You. It is currently FREE in Kindle Unlimited! You can also checkout all of my other books on the *Also by* page.

ALSO BY ILSA MADDEN-MILLS

All books are standalone stories with brand new couples and are currently FREE in Kindle Unlimited.

Very Bad Things

Very Wicked Beginnings

Very Wicked Things

Very Twisted Things

Bad Wicked Twisted: A Briarwood Academy Box Set

Dirty English

Filthy English

Spider

British Bad Boys: Box Set

Fake Fiancée

I Dare You

I Bet You

I Hate You

Boyfriend Bargain

The Last Guy (w/Tia Louise)

The Right Stud (w/Tia Louise)

ABOUT THE AUTHOR

Wall Street Journal, *New York Times*, and *USA Today* bestselling author Ilsa Madden-Mills writes about strong heroines and sexy alpha males that sometimes you just want to slap. A former high school English teacher and elementary librarian, she adores all things *Pride and Prejudice*; Mr. Darcy is her ultimate hero. She loves unicorns, frothy coffee beverages, vampire books, and any book featuring sword-wielding females.

*Please join her FB readers group, Unicorn Girls, to get the latest scoop as well as talk about books, wine, and Netflix:

https://www.facebook.com/groups/ilsasunicorngirls/

You can also find Ilsa at these places:

Website:
http://www.ilsamaddenmills.com
News Letter:
http://www.ilsamaddenmills.com/contact
Book + Main:
https://bookandmainbites.com/ilsamaddenmills

Made in the USA
Coppell, TX
19 August 2023